CLARITY

#1 DIAMONDS OF THE FIRST WATER SERIES

BY

SYDNEY JANE BAILY

WOLF PUBLISHING

Clarity by Sydney Jane Baily

Published by WOLF Publishing UG

Copyright © 2022 Sydney Jane Baily
Text by Sydney Jane Baily
Edited by Chris Hall
Cover Art by Victoria Cooper
Paperback ISBN: 978-3-98536-051-2
Hard Cover ISBN: 978-3-98536-052-9
Ebook ISBN: 978-3-98536-050-5

WOLF Publishing - This is us:

Two sisters, two personalities.. But only one big love!

Diving into a world of dreams..
  ...Romance, heartfelt emotions, lovable and witty characters, some humor, and some mystery! Because we want it all! Historical Romance at its best!

Visit our website to learn all about us, our authors and books!

Sign up to our mailing list to receive first hand information on new releases, freebies and promotions as well as exclusive giveaways and sneak-peeks!

WWW.WOLF-PUBLISHING.COM

Also by Sydney Jane Baily

Diamonds of the First Water

Four sparkling sisters and their dash-fire brother dazzle the London social Season. Enjoy the excitement of Mayfair's ballrooms and the luxury of country house parties in this romantic new series with mischief, misunderstandings, and mayhem. And of course passion!

#1 Clarity

#2 Purity

#3 Adam

More to follow!

Introduction to

DIAMONDS OF THE FIRST WATER

Once upon a time, an Irish family by the name of O'Diamáin emigrated to England from the north of Ireland, from County Doire to be specific. You may know the area as Derry or even Londonderry if you are thinking of it after King James I granted the city a royal charter.

Felim O'Diamáin, who was the youngest son, sailed across the Irish Sea to make his fortune, bringing his pretty wife and two young children with him. As the story goes, they stopped over on the Isle of Man for a perfectly peaceful night before landing at Ravenglass the next day and traipsing through the Lake District.

Another version swears they took the shorter but far more dangerous route north across the sea to Portpatrick, finding themselves in the southernmost part of Scotland. From there, if they indeed came that way, they headed east toward Gretna Green. Not for any quick anvil marriage, mind you, but to traverse the border to England.

No one knows for sure the veracity of either tale, nor particularly cares. Once they arrived in England, Felim did very well for himself, as did his descendants.

At some point during the twelve-year reign of George I, another O'Diamáin by the name of Liam was made an earl for his devoted service to the Crown. During those years in the early eighteenth century, King George also created a few dukes, at least one marquess, some barons, a single viscount, and other earls. But we're not interested in any of them, although some may have helped to quell the riots that ensued when Hanoverian George outmaneuvered any pesky residual Stuarts hoping to claim the English throne.

Nevertheless, our interest lies with Liam. With his new earldom came much wealth and land, specifically in Derbyshire. And naturally, a title. However, George I, being of Germanic descent, didn't find the Celtic name of O'Diamáin tripped easily off his tongue. Neither did he master Gaelic or Manx, for that matter. In any case, with a little persuasion and an extra thousand acres, Liam became William, Earl Diamond, as his male descendants have been known ever since.

Over the years, the earls have enlarged the original house to be an impressive manor, always named Oak Grove Hall, which is the translation of their long-ago home of County *Doire*.

Generations later, while inheriting the earldom and all its assets, Geoffrey, Lord Diamond and his beloved wife, Caroline, have wealth of a different nature as well—five healthy children: Clarity, Purity, Adam, Radiance, and Brilliance. They are known as Diamonds of the First Water, at least by their parents.

This is Clarity's story...

CLARITY

Prologue

1834, Oak Grove Hall, Derby

"You cannot be serious," said a dark-haired young lass of eight. "No one will believe such a lark."

Her companion, a boy of twelve with a shock of tawny-colored tousled hair and more good looks than sense, merely laughed.

"They will believe it when they see it," he asserted, his green eyes flashing with merriment. He continued to tug the satin dress onto the fastest hunting dog in the spacious Diamond kennel.

By the time he'd succeeded in getting its front legs through the armholes, the gown was trampled, soiled, torn, and muddy. It also belonged to the visiting baroness, Lady Aston.

Once he'd secured the dress with a rope around the dog's middle, the youth sent the *canine queen*, as he called it, running with a swat to its rump.

"Home," he called after it, pointing to the large manor house. The dog was no longer looking at him but running helter-skelter, following the mouth-watering scent of recently cooked chicken pie, a platter of which had been carefully carried outside and was currently being served.

Of course, the well-dressed dog didn't know twenty guests were enjoying an early evening outdoor meal on the other side of the house since the weather was extraordinarily mild. But the young lass and the youth knew. They also had a particular dislike for the dress's owner as she was crabby, sour, and had ruined their fun since her arrival a week earlier. She also happened to be the boy's aunt.

Partners in mischief, they stared at one another, her blue eyes wide, his grin growing. And then they heard the screams and the ruckus. It continued. However, when the sounds grew louder and angrier, she bit her lip and began to look afraid. His expression became more of a sickly grimace than an amused one.

"I don't hear any laughter," she pointed out, climbing down from the fence upon which she'd been perched and looking uncertainly toward her parents' country home.

"Alexander!" roared his father's voice.

"Clarity!" called her father.

More voices joined in, crying out their names in a none-too-pleased tone.

She swallowed and looked at him. He shrugged.

Joining hands, they ran as fast as they could in the other direction.

Chapter One

1846, London

Clarity leaned back on the cream-colored velvet chaise lounge and examined the toes of her blue slippers at the other end.

"Of course I recall Alex. It has *not* been a lifetime," she contradicted her sister, Purity, who looked as much like her as to be a twin in height and coloring. Both had the dark hair and blue eyes of their father and their Irish ancestors.

In other regards such as their innate dispositions, the sisters were very different, with Clarity being the more whimsical of the two despite being older. In fact, she was the eldest of all the five Diamond children.

"It's only been... let me think. Gracious! I believe it's been a decade since last we saw him. Longer, actually. I wonder why." At first, she'd missed him terribly but gradually let him slip from her thoughts.

"He was always such good fun," she added.

"Perhaps that is why," Purity said. "Too much fun and too much trouble. Although I remember little of him as you were his companion,

I recall hearing our parents and his parents complain about what mischief he was up to."

Clarity smiled at her own memory of what an amusing playmate he'd been. She'd been in awe of the boy who was older than herself and clever as Tommy-tit. Their mothers were great friends, and their families were often together at the Diamond country estate in Derby.

In truth, Alex was in her memories from the first she could recall, maybe at age three or four. Sadly, by the time she was nine, he had vanished.

Regardless, Purity was correct about the mischief.

"It wasn't solely him," Clarity said. "I believe I helped in most of his wicked capers."

Her fond musings stopped as she remembered what had happened to her childhood friend's parents.

"I suppose there was no reason for him to come after the coach accident."

Purity shook her head solemnly. "I guess you're right. Poor Alex, having to live with that stuffy aunt. Even I recall her, and I was quite young when I last saw that dour woman."

Suddenly, Purity's eyes widened. "Oh my! The last time I recollect seeing him and his parents at Oak Grove was when he dressed up one of the dogs in his aunt's gown."

Clarity nodded, and she couldn't help smiling again. They'd gone without supper after they'd finally returned to the house. However, her mother was so relieved to see them, she had snuck them each a mug of broth and some hot buttered bread. His parents also weren't too angry by the time she and Alex reappeared.

Only his aunt had been livid, wanting Alex to be thrashed with a cane, and Lady Aston had remained furious until she left along with Alex and his parents.

Clarity had never seen any of them again.

Now, according to the newspapers, the Viscount Hollidge would be at the first event of the new social season, following the opening of Parliament the month before. Since January was wretchedly cold, the first ball was occurring in February, which was hardly any more pleasant.

"Maybe he'll stop by before the ball," she mused, thinking how lovely it would be to see her old friend in the private setting of their townhouse rather than the noisy hustle of a cavernous room at Devonshire House.

Would he recognize her? She'd been chubby in her youth, enjoying too many cakes and sticky buns.

Purity frowned. "I doubt he'll suddenly stop by for tea and crumpets, as if it's been a fortnight instead of twelve years."

Clarity laughed. "You are probably correct, but we could ask Mother to send him an invitation." She picked up the book she'd been perusing on paper folding, always hoping the secret of creating beautiful works of art from creasing, crimping, and bending paper would come clear to her. Thus far, she had failed to make anything other than a square.

"Or we could simply wait until the ball," Purity said. "He might be a toad now or a swell. Either way, it would be dreadful to have to take tea with him, unable to escape."

Clarity doubted Alex could ever be other than his amusing self, yet her sister was probably correct about waiting. After all, everyone knew the residence of the Diamond family on the exclusive west end of Piccadilly. If he wanted to visit, he could come calling any day during visiting hours, just as her suitors did.

Still, she could be secretly excited to see her old friend without any harm done.

When Clarity saw him in person a few days later, she wished she had seen him previously in order to be prepared. For while she knew him by his face, she barely recognized him by his nature, and when she understood the man he had become, she wasn't at all pleased.

───※───

Alex was a fish out of water from the moment he entered Devonshire House through its recently renovated entrance hall and up the crystal staircase. In the gilded ballroom, people were dancing, chatting sociably, and laughing. It made his skin feel a size too tight. Worse, it made him think a sturdy birch cane was ready to come *thwacking* down upon his flesh should he so much as crack a smile.

Sighing, Alex tried to release the tension in his shoulders with a gentle rolling motion. Standing up straighter, he surveyed the room from the vantage point of his impressive height.

How to begin? he wondered.

And then he saw her, a gorgeous, dark-haired vision in lavender. Not a namby-pamby version of the hue either, but a rich, deep color like the flowers in full bloom. The woman herself seemed in bloom, too, the way she was laughing and gesturing with her hands, the blush of color on her cheeks. Even from a distance, he could see the merriment upon her face.

Unthinkingly, he moved in her direction, beginning to notice a few people stopping to look at him with undisguised, blatant stares before fans went up to hide whispers.

Lord Hollidge had finally entered society.

Ignoring them, Alex continued around the edge of the dance floor toward her. When he was a mere few yards away, he took in the small group of which she was a part.

She conversed with two other people, a young man and a more subdued young lady who greatly resembled her in looks. With them were two people he abruptly recognized. With a jolt, he realized they were the Earl and Countess of Diamond, if memory of his youth served him correctly.

Then the younger people must be their children. Despite their similarity in looks, he had no trouble discerning which female was Clarity and which was Purity, for his old childhood friend had to be the exuberant one.

Before he took another step, Adam Diamond, the only male child and the heir, caught sight of him. Plainly, the young man had no recollection of Alex since Diamond had been in leading strings when last Alex had seen the family.

"I think we have someone who wishes to claim a dance," Adam said.

The rest of the family looked Alex's way, and he was captivated again by the lavender-clad female whose sparkling eyes flickered over him. Her mouth opened slightly, and then she was the first to speak.

"Alex!" she exclaimed, breaking all boundaries of propriety by closing the last few steps and peering into his face. "It *is* you, isn't it?"

He feared she was about to embrace him publicly. Therefore, he took her gloved hand and bowed over it.

"It is I," he agreed, "Lord Hollidge."

Apparently, that tickled her funny bone. She grinned widely, her pretty lips parting slightly to show white teeth. She also displayed her attractive dimples.

"*Lord* Hollidge," she mimicked. "I'm sorry, but to me that will always be your father."

Alex startled. Not two minutes in mixed company, and he was already reminded of the man whose death he'd caused and with whom it would be better if he could change places. His throat clogged, and he swallowed.

Her smile died. "Are you well? Oh dear. I shouldn't have mentioned your parents. I'm sorry. Since it has been over a decade, I didn't think —" she interrupted herself, looking ruffled and glancing at her parents.

Alex had a feeling she often acted or spoke without thinking. He dropped her hand and turned to the countess and the earl.

Lady Diamond gave him a smile as warm as her daughter's. She held out her hand to him, which he took.

"I am glad you came, my lord," she said. "It has been far too long since we've seen you."

He bowed over her hand and released it. His mother had adored this woman as her best friend. Thus, Lady Diamond was another person injured because of him and his careless actions. Another reason he deserved the night-terrors that had plagued him both at Eton and at Oxford, terrible dreams of carriages and helplessness and death.

Wishing he had stayed on the other side of the room, he continued with a bow to Lord Diamond. Surprising him, the earl expressed great affability by sticking out his hand to shake Alex's. It was an unexpectedly warm gesture.

Following suit, the heir to the Diamond earldom also shook his hand and introduced himself. Then the earl introduced his eldest daughter.

"Undoubtedly you recall Clarity, though she might have been in pigtails at the time. Not to mention she was a plump little thing."

"Father," the glorious creature in lavender groaned, rolling her eyes. "I agree I might have been chubby, but I am sure I was not in braids when last I saw Al—Lord Hollidge."

Then her glance caught his. "Was I?"

"I don't believe so," he said, feeling tongue-tied and vaguely recalling the hair of the little girl who'd been his playmate. It had usually been in a snarled mess if memory served him. He knew his mother was always reminding him to comb his own.

At that moment, he nearly lifted his hand to smooth his hair but stopped himself, knowing his valet had combed it perfectly.

In any case, most of what he recalled about Clarity, besides her dimpled round cheeks, was her willingness to get into trouble with him. They had been a bad influence upon one another, although he had been older; hence, the blame rested on him.

"It's a pleasure to see you," she added.

Alex realized he was supposed to have said that, but this was as new to him as flying.

"And you," he said. Then, because looking at her was like staring at the sun, he glanced away to the other young lady who shook her head, appearing quite exasperated.

"Father should have introduced her properly."

The earl chuckled. "And our next oldest daughter, *Lady* Purity," Lord Diamond continued, this time with decorum.

Without nearly the same eagerness, this dark-haired young woman offered her hand, which Alex held briefly while bowing over it, this time muttering a timely, "My pleasure."

Thank goodness all the greetings were finished. He didn't know what had possessed him to walk over to this group except for the certainty he knew them.

Now he could wander off into obscurity again. The last thing he wanted to do was—

"Find him a place on your cards, girls," Lady Diamond advised.

To his dismay, both daughters looked at the cards dangling from their wrists like tacky price tags in a milliner's shop window.

"Is there a dance you are particularly fond of performing?" Lady Clarity asked.

"No," he said abruptly. Dancing was not something he did. Ever. However, he had taken the trouble to learn, which didn't help stave off the dread of actually stepping onto the dance floor.

"Then I shall choose for you," Lady Clarity continued.

Producing a pencil from some mysterious hiding place, she wrote his name onto her card.

"Please return for the ninth dance," she informed him.

He nodded. "As you wish." Alex could not manage any genuine enthusiasm. While holding a woman in his arms was not a hardship, twirling her around the polished floor without bumping into others or stepping on her toes was going to be a nerve-wracking chore.

She didn't look offended but was a little curious at his demeanor. Then Lady Purity offered him the fourth dance before he took his leave of the family.

Alex intended to do his duty as a single man at a ball and dance, no matter his wish to go home or to his club and drink brandy. Not wanting to be a wall-prop, awkward and unsocial, he sought out any chums from school, pleased to find a few.

Bachelors like himself, they were in better spirits than he, actually looking forward to the evening, so Alex endeavored to copy them.

"In the card room," one swell advised, "there's brandy instead of the insipid lemonade."

"I thought most were drinking champagne," Alex said.

The man shrugged. "Same. Watered down champagne or full-strength lemonade. Give me brandy, any day."

"Never mind that, Brennon," said another man whom Alex vaguely recollected from university. "Not all of us have a lovely lady on the end of our fishing line, as you do. If we're stuck in the card room with the married men drinking brandy, then we won't be able to enjoy the ladies. And that's what most of us are here for. Right, Hollidge?"

Hating to admit it, for it sounded extraordinarily calculated, that was precisely why Alex had ventured out from his luxurious townhouse. It was time. He had an estate and multiple households to run, and he needed a capable, organized, and helpful wife. Then he needed children, or at least one male child.

While it had been practical and satisfying to have a long-time mistress, he had let her go without regret. She'd been discreet, with the good sense not to produce any by-blows he would have been compelled by his sense of honor to claim and support. And while he had never become emotionally entangled, she'd made it possible for him to avoid rushing to snag a wife. Nor had he waited too long. The time was perfect.

Glancing over at the Diamond girls, he instantly dismissed the eldest. Lady Clarity had an air of frivolity and disregard for decorum. She smiled too much, always displaying her dimples, and called him by his first name. They wouldn't suit one another at all. Lady Purity, on the other hand, had demanded a measure of propriety, at least when it came to introductions.

He looked forward to their dance and to exchanging a few private words to determine whether they might suit one another.

Chapter Two

"Like dancing with a stick," Purity declared when Clarity asked how it went. "A stiff, humorless, dried-up stick." By the time Clarity's dance partner returned her to their table, Alex had already dropped off her sister and disappeared.

She wrinkled her nose. "He did appear a little wooden," Clarity agreed, "but I thought he was a little anxious in front of all of us. What did you talk about?"

Purity shook her head. "You would not believe it, but he asked me questions as if he were considering me for a life's mate."

"You are joking!" Not that there was anything wrong with Purity, who would make someone a perfectly wonderful wife, but Clarity knew her sister was all wrong for Alex. He had a mischievous heart and a fun spirit. At least, he had when they were children. Purity, on the other hand, could be somewhat too proper and would never engage in frivolous frolics.

Yet if even her sister thought Alex an old stick, he must have changed indeed. Besides, one didn't decide upon a wife over the first dance.

"Sadly, I am not joking," Purity said. "Before we had made it through the line once, Lord Hollidge asked if I was already spoken for or in an arrangement with anyone else. He asked if I was good enough at mathematics to do household accounts. Before we parted, he even asked if I had ever arranged or hosted a dinner party!"

Clarity frowned. Those did seem the questions of a man hunting for a wife, which *was* the main purpose of these assemblies, she supposed. But one normally spoke of the weather and the quality of the musicians. The gentleman asked to be allowed to come calling the following morning for anything more personal. *How strange!*

She couldn't help wondering if he would be so practical with her. After all, they had a history, and while they knew little of each other now, she had been surprised how warm her feelings had been upon seeing him. More than that, her insides had fluttered pleasantly when they'd spoken, albeit briefly, and when he held her hand.

His face was familiar yet greatly changed. Good looking as a youth, Alex was absolutely dash-fire handsome as a man. She could hardly wait for her turn to dance with him. She doubted Alex had realized why she'd chosen the particular dance, but as he approached, Purity made it clear she knew.

"Here comes your next partner *and* your dining companion. I wish you good luck with him."

Putting her hand in Alex's outstretched one, Clarity let him lead her to the floor for a waltz. Again, there was that flutter when he placed his hand upon her back and stood facing her, awaiting the music.

And then they danced. Perhaps it was the nature of the spirited waltz that caused his silence, but she was most disappointed when he did not ask her questions of a similar nature to those he'd asked Purity. Moreover, when they made eye contact, his expression was absolutely neutral. There was nothing in his visage to remind her of his wicked grin right before he nicked a freshly baked pie from the cooling shelf or tied his mother's bonnet to the cart horse, not caring about the punishment.

In fact, his doting parents had hardly ever reprimanded him with anything more than a stern talking-to.

And while his hands upon her made her feel pleasingly warm, he seemed distracted and distant. When the old-fashioned Rutscher waltz came to a close, he took her arm and began toward the table, appearing eager to be rid of her.

Could that be possible? She was certain she'd done nothing to offend him.

However, her parents had already left the table and were on their way downstairs to the dining rooms.

Just as Alex's steps faltered at seeing the empty table, his head swiveling about at the mass exodus from the ballroom, Clarity put her other hand on him to make him look down at her.

"It's time for the meal, and you are to take me in and sit with me." Maybe without the vigor of the dance, he would talk to her in the old, familiar way.

"I see," Alex said, looking less than thrilled.

She hoped it was because he'd been caught unawares and not because he was forced to dine with her.

"Of course. How stupid of me. The dance before supper," he muttered, as if it was something he'd memorized.

"You have chosen a good start to your social debut," Clarity remarked as they spun about and followed the other guests toward the staircase.

"Have I?" he asked.

"Yes," Clarity assured him. "The food provided by Hart is above average."

"Hart?"

"The Duke of Devonshire. He still prefers to be known by Marquess of Hartington, perhaps because he likes the short moniker of Hart. Devonshire is such a mouthful. In any case, as Lord Lieutenant of Derbyshire, the duke is on close terms with my father. He's come to Oak Grove more than once. I believe you and your parents were there for one of his visits. Sadly, he is growing quite deaf."

When Alex said nothing to any of her prattle, she went back to her original point.

"At some balls, one receives nothing but white, floury soup."

"Does one?" he asked.

Internally, Clarity wanted to give him a poke in the ribs. If she could get only two words out of Alex at a time, this was going to be an exhausting supper.

"Yes, truly." She had to come up with something to get him talking. "Are you residing in the same Grosvenor Square home as when you were a boy?" Well done, she praised herself, having managed to ask him without mentioning his parents.

"I am."

Two words again! "It appeared vacant a long while. I wonder it was never sold," she said, "since it must be a little musty."

Clarity felt him startle under her fingertips resting on his forearm. Yet, since she hadn't asked him a question, he said nothing.

This was ridiculous!

"Is it?" she asked with steely determination.

"Is it what?" he asked.

Ha! Three words out of him.

"Is it musty?" she clarified. "I remember the sweet scent of flowers wafted throughout your home except that time we went into the attic looking for treasure. Why we thought any of the trunks might belong to pirates, I cannot imagine."

She chuckled, recalling the Hollidge housekeeper's ruddy face when she caught them with every trunk open, and their contents, mostly old clothing and linens, strewn about the dusty floor.

"When we were in London, my mother ordered flowers brought weekly to fill the vases," he said quietly. "I had somehow forgotten that."

Oh dear! Clarity had dredged up something painful, she feared. Yet when she glanced up at him as he drew out a chair for her at one of the massive dining tables, he looked not cross, but thoughtful.

"I wondered what was missing but hadn't placed it," Alex added.

"Easy enough to remedy," she said, earning a nod from him.

Then he surprised her by saying, "Our house was never entirely vacant, nor did I ever consider selling it. My aunt always lived there, even while I was away at school or living in Belfinch or traveling round the holdings. I guess she closed most of it off and thus, it might have looked dark from the outside..."

He trailed off as if that much talking was a chore.

"I loved your Belfinch Hall," she admitted, deciding not to think of his old aunt residing in the spacious four-story home on Grosvenor Square, shuffling around in the darkness. "Suffolk is lovely countryside, and the Tudor chestnut paneling in the dining room was warm and welcoming."

He stared down at her, maybe amazed that she could remember such a detail. Then he nodded again.

When all the ladies were seated, the gentlemen followed suit. Everyone removed their gloves, the ladies also closing their fans if still open, before all such accessories were placed upon their laps and covered by a clean, white napkin.

Alex did the same, but stiffly, still managing to seem like a beast of the forest brought indoors by mistake.

"For someone who has not been out much in society, at least not in London," she said as the servers poured wine, "your dancing was rather good."

Finally, he offered the smallest smile she'd ever seen, barely the tiniest raising of one side of his mouth.

"Not perfect, by your standards," he said. "Merely *good*, and even that marked with a qualifier."

Her cheeks warmed, but she was glad he hadn't taken offense.

"No, certainly not perfect," she agreed. "If you had been, then the rest of us who attend these assemblies regularly might as well hang up our slippers."

"I had lessons," he disclosed.

"We all did," she said, "at one time or another." Hers finished when she was fourteen.

"Recently," he added. "Last month, to be precise."

Digesting this tidbit, she blinked.

"I see." Now, she was giving short answers, but the notion of Alex standing before a dancing master at his age... why, he must be about twenty-five... seemed improbable. And then it simply was funny.

Unable to stifle the little bubble of amusement from becoming laughter, she clapped her hand over her mouth as it burst forth.

A few around them ceased speaking while turning to look at her. As for Alex, his expression had darkened as if he were actually irritated.

Dropping her gaze to her lap, Clarity managed to conquer her merriment with thoughts of having lost one of her favorite earrings that night. She added in the recollection of how their housekeeper's songbird had died, keeling over in its cage the day before.

Well and truly somber, she lifted her glance back to her dinner partner. He was fuming.

"You have embarrassed both of us," he hissed.

Eyes widening, she had no response for a long moment. Instead, she reached out for her glass of wine, taking a sip purely for something to do while awaiting the first course. Miserably, she wished the meal was nothing more than thick white pottage and a slice of bread so she could get away from him sooner.

He might look like her old friend, but he was behaving, as Purity said, like an utter stick.

Glancing around, she saw Purity at the other end of the table of singles, with Adam across from her, chatting with a pretty young lady. Their parents were at another table.

Alex is alone with no family, Clarity reminded herself. She must do better to make him feel comfortable.

"I am sorry I laughed when you told me about your lessons. It tickled me, but it shows great dedication on your part, and I did not mean to offer insult."

After a brief hesitation, he said, "Thank you."

Releasing a sigh, she hoped they could get off on a better footing.

"Tell me what you have been doing," she prompted, priding herself on the broad question.

"Doing?" he repeated, before sipping his wine and looking down at the small bowl of soup placed before him, a brown creamy pottage with slivers of vegetables.

"With your life," she clarified. "You haven't been to London, or we would have run into each other."

"Not necessarily," he said.

She wondered if that was the entire answer. Instead of hurrying him, she waited.

"It's true I was away from Town for years at boarding school and then at university. I have returned to London occasionally when my aunt requested my presence but didn't see any reason to go to a ball. Now I am back for the foreseeable future. My aunt has made room for me."

Clarity blinked, realizing that was his idea of a jest—that his aunt was giving him space in his own house. In the next instant, she considered the older lady's sour-face and the fit she had when her dress was draped over a dog. Mostly, Clarity recalled how Alex hadn't liked the joyless woman who was vastly different from his own mother's sweet and fun-loving temperament. Finally, the awful truth dawned on her.

"Are you saying you live with Lady Aston?"

"Yes, of course. My father's sister is the only close family I have. Although I suppose, correctly, she is the one who lives with me, but one wouldn't know it by her demeanor in running my household as her own. I suppose it's because she's had run of the place for a long time."

Clarity nodded, absently slurping her soup while imagining it to be a bleak home indeed.

When she glanced at him again, he was staring disapprovingly. Quickly, she stopped wool-gathering, straightened her shoulders, and set down her spoon.

"Why have you never visited us, either when we were in Town or at Oak Grove?" She also wanted to know why he had never extended an invitation to her family, but supposed that would put him on the spot, which was impolite. If his aunt was in charge, then she had her answer.

"I haven't had the need to go into society until now, so I didn't," he told her. "As for calling upon you, I believe that would have implied I was courting either you or Lady Purity, which would have been premature, incorrect, and presumptuous. As for showing up at your country home, that is not done."

That is not done. The words echoed in her mind. *Where had her old friend Alex gone?*

He was certainly not seated beside her. But later, despite enjoying a dance with Lord Brennon, who'd been attentive at a ball before the Season began and tonight had paid her every kind of compliment, including asking to call upon her during the week, it was Alex who remained in her thoughts when she closed her eyes to sleep.

Chapter Three

Not expecting his aunt to still be awake, Alex was surprised when she'd greeted him at the top of the stairs and invited him into her sitting room for tea.

"I'll have brandy," he told their butler, despite noticing how the man was already pouring him a cup of tea without asking. For an irritating second, Mr. Berard looked to Alex's aunt for permission, then recalling who his employer was, he nodded and went for the brandy.

"Tell me how you fared tonight. Did you find a wife?" Aunt Elizabeth questioned him.

Alex wasn't the least taken aback by her interest. They both knew it was the sole reason he had attended. Briefly, he told her about a few of the ladies with whom he'd danced.

Some were suitable, some even attractive. One had a hair coming out of her nostril, and he'd been unable to stop looking at it, but he didn't mention that to Aunt Elizabeth. She would disapprove of his silly fixation on something that could be easily plucked and remedied.

He was disappointed in himself for even noticing it and for the slight tickle of amusement that had feathered through him. *How asinine!*

When he mentioned the Diamonds, his aunt perked up.

"An earl's daughter would be a good match. And you already have a prior association with the family. Your mother held Lady Diamond in great esteem, as you may recall."

Aunt Elizabeth spoke as if she hadn't shrieked in anger in the presence of Lord and Lady Diamond and demanded that all the children be whipped on more than one occasion.

He remembered only too well how she'd chastised his father for allowing him to befriend the eldest of the children.

"I thought you would be against any such alliance," Alex said.

"Whyever would you think that?" his aunt asked, bemused. "Preposterous! You were all children, misbehaving, disobedient brutes, but you have changed for the better and turned out as well as can be expected. I must assume the Diamond girls have also matured."

Clarity's beaming smile came to mind when she had rushed forward and called him Alex in front of everyone. Moreover, her intrusive questions with which she'd peppered him throughout the meal had nearly given him indigestion. She'd even laughed loudly at his dancing lessons. He doubted whether his aunt would consider her to have changed.

"Lady Purity was demure, reserved, polite," he said. "You would undoubtedly approve."

"What of the eldest? I believe you cannot court the younger when the eldest is as yet unmarried. And they look as alike as two peas in a pod, or they did last time I saw them. Thus, it can be no matter to you which sister."

She was wrong. Once he'd paid attention, they looked nothing alike. Purity was all polished, smooth, and cool in manner and looks, while Clarity was... wildly alluring with an engaging and open manner. The former was preferable to the latter, as far as he was concerned, unless he wanted his home to be a circus with Clarity as the ringmaster.

Perhaps that was a harsh judgment, but she'd slurped her soup and stabbed at a roasted carrot with such vehemence it shot off her plate, causing her to laugh with her mouth uncovered. When they'd risen from the table, she'd carelessly let one of her gloves drop to the floor, and after he'd picked it up and handed it to her, he realized she had a dab of custard on her upper lip.

Desire—strong and potent—had surged through him. He'd nearly reached out and wiped it off with his thumb before recollecting where he was. Instead, he'd handed her a napkin and explained the situation.

It hadn't bothered her at all to dab at her mouth while standing next to the table. He had a feeling it wouldn't have been beyond her to reach over and take another forkful of food or pick up her wine glass for a last sip.

No, she hadn't matured at all, except from a scruffy, fubsy girl to a radiant woman with perfect curves.

"I would prefer to court Lady Purity," he insisted.

To that end, he sent around his calling card the following morning, requesting to visit the day after if acceptable. There was no rush, and he wasn't the type to behave impetuously.

"I guess Hollidge saw something he liked," Lord Diamond remarked over dinner when Clarity's mother mentioned the card brought by the viscount's footman earlier that day. They'd sent an affirmative reply.

"I have to confess," Lady Diamond said, "I am bewildered he is my friend's son. If he didn't have the same look that he had as a youth, I would declare him an impostor. So stern and lacking all mirth."

Clarity remained silent on the matter, continuing to fold a piece of paper she'd brought to the table with her into what she hoped would be a dragon. She refused to judge her old friend based on the interaction at a ball, an unnatural event at the best of times. And Alex seemed never to have attended one before.

"May we all meet him?" asked Radiance who, along with her sister Brilliance, had been far too young the last time Alex had been at Oak Grove to remember him at all.

"Of course," said their mother. "Let's inflict the entire brood upon the young man."

Adam laughed the loudest. "I cannot imagine going to my future intended's house for a little *tête-à-tête* and being faced with the lot of you."

"Future intended?" repeated Purity. "That's a little premature, isn't it?"

Their father and mother glanced at one another before the beautiful red-headed Caroline Diamond raised an eyebrow.

Clarity set down the folded abomination that looked more like a lump of coal than a dragon. Along with her siblings, she turned her gaze to her loving parents.

"Is there something you're not telling us?" she asked.

Her mother's porcelain cheeks turned ruddy, as they were apt to do with the slightest emotion.

Her father, whose dark hair and blue eyes had been handed down to four of his five children, picked up his wine glass, sipped, and sent his own gaze to his wife to respond.

The countess shrugged. "I had an agreement with my dearest friend, may she rest in peace. Only a verbal one, you understand."

"What kind of agreement, Mother?" asked Purity, already pursing her lips with disapproval.

Clarity nearly laughed at her sister's expression, like a prudish headmistress.

"Feeling like sisters ourselves," her mother continued, "Lady Hollidge and I had a fervent desire to unite our families. Therefore, when Alexander and Clarity got on well together—"

"Me?" Clarity yelped. "You arranged for me to marry Alex?"

Purity unexpectedly laughed. "Our Clarity married to that stick in the mud?"

That didn't sit well. "Sister, please don't call him that. I imagine last night was a trial for him, not to know anyone and to jump into such an intricately orchestrated event at his age."

"You don't have to marry him," her mother countered. "It was a whimsical wish his mother and I had, nothing in writing. Besides, he won't even know about it. Poor boy, being raised by that witch."

"Easy, Caroline," Lord Diamond soothed. "We should take Clarity's advice and not judge."

"If it weren't for Lady Aston," her mother began before sharply biting off her words. "Never mind me. Let us make young Lord Hollidge welcome and see how it goes. Shall we?"

"See how what goes, Mother?" Brilliance, the youngest in the family, asked. "Will Clarity actually be allowing him to court her tomorrow? How romantic."

"There's also Lord Brennon to consider," Lord Diamond reminded her. "He seems like a good chap."

"Not to mention Lord Mansfield," Purity added. "His cravat was perfectly tied, and he had not a hair out of place at Devonshire House."

"I wouldn't be marrying his valet," Clarity grumbled. She had danced with the man but could scarcely recall what he looked like. "Besides, I'm not as interested in tidy hair as you are."

This made Ray, who was a year-and-a-half older than Bri, and the lone red-headed Diamond sibling, giggle at the notion.

"I am not interested in tidy hair, either," she declared. "When it's my turn to make a match, I want a man who writes poetry."

"As his livelihood?" their father asked teasingly.

"Oh, no, Father. He shall be exceedingly wealthy, and thus, he can sit around all day and write sonnets."

With that particular requisite for a mate stated, they all slipped into their private thoughts while finishing their dessert. Afterward, Clarity wandered to her bedroom to work on her paper-folding skills, which she was learning from Friedrich Froebel's frustrating book, purchased for her by her dear father no matter its great expense.

Although it was in German, she had a passingly good ability to read the language, far better than her aptitude for folding paper crisply and precisely. In any case, when she got muddled by the words, she simply looked at the drawings.

She knew she ought to go back to the beginning and master the Folds of Life and perhaps make a puzzle purse. As usual, she'd gone headlong into the middle of the more amusing looking creations and was in over her head with the Folds of Beauty. Crumpling up the doglike creature, which was decidedly not beautiful, she tossed it onto her glowing hearth.

She couldn't deny a tiny ember of excitement glowed in her as steadily as the coals before her. And she could only attribute the feeling to seeing Alex again on the morrow.

Chapter Four

When Alex was shown into the drawing room, Clarity again thought how handsomely he'd turned out. He had sprouted up to be as tall as her own father. His face had lost the vestiges of boyish roundness, instead presenting slightly hollowed cheeks and a firm chin, reminding her of the Elgin marbles.

Broad-shouldered, his wavy brown hair that had forever been in disarray was mostly tamed, and his green eyes, always vivid, now seemed glitteringly attractive.

In short, he was a dash-fire man.

She hoped he wouldn't be overwhelmed when greeted by not one or two Diamond females but by five, including her mother. Adam and her father had mercifully made themselves scarce.

After Alex greeted all in turn, beginning with Lady Diamond, they took seats. Clarity poured the tea, and the normal polite conversation was exchanged regarding the weather and the streets, which were often clogged by traffic. After a few minutes, her two youngest sisters made their excuses and abruptly left.

"Don't mind them, Lord Hollidge," Lady Diamond said. "They were merely curious to see someone from their infancy whom they couldn't recall."

"And I disappointed them," he surmised.

Clarity startled. It was an odd assessment of himself. She had told Bri and Ray about the fun young man who once thought he could steal the honey from a hive only to awaken some terribly angry bees. She and Alex had enjoyed the sweet nectar on toast, despite his hand and cheek smeared in the housekeeper's vinegar balm, which she promised would ease the sting.

Maybe her sisters had hoped to witness some manner of mischief or hijinks in their Piccadilly drawing room. However, they saw merely a man wearing a snowy-white cravat and highly polished shoes. He was neat enough even for Purity's approval.

Rather than being disappointed, her younger sisters were probably bored.

Ever since her parents had brought up his aunt, especially with her mother displaying such vehemence against her the night before, Clarity thought it would be a good idea to ask after the hag, as she had failed to do during the ball.

"You mentioned to me Lady Aston shares your home? How does she fare? Is she well and...?" She stopped herself asking if his aunt were happy since the woman had never seemed to be before. She'd been nothing but a killjoy.

"My aunt is well. Thank you for asking. In fact, Lady Aston sends her regards."

Clarity exchanged a glance with her mother, who quickly took up the mantle of courtesy.

"Please give her our regards in return," Lady Diamond said.

Clarity tried again. "What did you study at university?" She recalled he'd been interested in botany when they were children. "Anything to do with plants or bugs?" She added the latter because, despite the bee incident, he'd captured his fair share of lightning bugs and once raised caterpillars until they became butterflies. But her hopeful smile was returned with a puzzled frown.

"I studied classics and read the law. My aunt thought it a favorable course of study, as there was a goodly amount of history and ancient languages involved. Although I shall never practice law, of course."

"Of course," Clarity said. Yet if he'd wanted to, despite being a viscount, surely he could practice as a barrister or even a solicitor. Feeling helpless to make the conversation flow, she sat back and nodded to her sister to try.

"Our brother attends Oxford," Purity informed the viscount, "at All Souls College. I'm sure he would appreciate having someone as well educated as yourself with whom to converse. About history and the classics."

"May I suggest he try The Royal Society at Burlington House? Now that I reside in London, I intend to go to lectures there."

"Adam's education will take approximately two years, an average time spent gaining one's degree," Clarity pointed out. She couldn't help being curious. "May I ask what else you have been doing to keep you from London after your matriculation? I sincerely hope you were able to travel the Continent as you once dreamed of doing, or at the very least made it up to John O'Groats."

Alex's glance fell to the teacup he still cradled, and she already knew the answer.

"You don't have to answer, Lord Hollidge," Purity said, reminding Clarity she'd overstepped in interrogating him. She'd been impolite.

"Take no offense," her mother added. "My eldest daughter thinks of you still as her childhood friend, one with whom she can speak familiarly. Please do not think we are prying. I'm sure we all wish the bonds of friendship had kept us close after your parents' deaths."

"I take no offense," Alex said, but Clarity thought he looked irritated when he addressed her again.

"While I was longer at Cambridge than your brother due to my studies, I then spent the past few years living at each of my family's holdings. My aunt thought it the best way to learn how to follow in my father's footsteps. I have a duty to carry out, and despite not having him here to guide me, I intend to do it well."

They all fell silent, and Clarity had the inappropriate urge to reach out and hug him.

"And now you're back in London," her mother murmured. "If there is anything you need that we can assist you with, I hope you will let us know. To me, Alex," she said, purposefully using his name, "you are family."

His eyes widened, and his face softened becoming less that of a chiseled man and more the boy Clarity remembered.

"Maybe you will come over for dinner soon, and we shall play charades," she offered. "You were always adept at sussing out riddles and at miming, and I would be honored to partner with you. My brother is very good, but I believe no one is better than my younger sister, Brilliance, except possibly you, ten years ago."

Alex shifted uneasily in his seat.

"Charades," he repeated, as if it were beneath him. "I haven't played since I was last at your house in Derbyshire, and rightly so."

Rightly so? Was he intimating no one of their age enjoyed a rousing game of charades? That could not be.

Before Clarity could decide if she'd been belittled, he addressed her mother again.

"I am in need of a wife. You have plenty of daughters, and therefore, I believe you can assist me. My aunt thinks one of them will be suitable."

Shocked silence met his words, spoken as though he were talking about borrowing a book or choosing a horse. Clarity was relieved Bri and Ray had vanished, for they would have impolitely laughed or even shrieked with mirthful delight at his words.

The silence dragged on longer while her glance went from Purity to their mother and back again.

"Well," Lady Diamond said, puffing out her cheeks, appearing momentarily nonplussed. Sipping her tea, she took her time. At last, she spoke.

"I have two daughters who might be suitable were you to form a *tendre* of the heart with one of them. The others are too young."

Alex nodded agreeably. "My aunt thinks the most important thing is a meeting of the minds and having similar temperaments in order to cohabit peacefully. That seems reasonable to me. With the right wife, she and I can offer one another support through the tribulations of life. My aunt said nothing about the heart."

Purity had begun to lean forward, appearing fascinated by this dry discourse on a marital relationship. Their mother was caught between nodding in order to be polite and shaking her head in disagreement, her mouth slightly open.

Finally, Clarity said, "Balderdash!"

"Clarity!" her mother began.

"Mother, please." Then she directed all her attention to Alex. "If I were you, I wouldn't take advice from your aunt when it comes to affairs of the heart, or in this case, of the mind and temperament. After all, Lady Aston has been a widow for longer than I have been alive. Was she ever in love? Has she ever inspired such feeling from another?"

Crossing her arms, Clarity sat back. Alex regarded her with unconcealed irritation.

"Besides," she continued, not obeying her mother who was waving her hand to silence her, "my parents have a *love* match, having developed the most wonderful *tendre* for one another almost at first meeting. As did yours."

"Lady Clarity!" Alex exclaimed, his expression darkening. "How on earth can you know what my parents felt for one another?"

"Nevertheless, she is correct," her mother chimed in. "Your parents were deeply in love, but your aunt is also right in that they were like-minded and shared the same happy, easy-going nature."

They all fell silent again.

Purity rose to her feet. "I believe I shall leave you three to discuss this further."

Alex quickly stood. "But Lady Purity, it is you who I came to court."

Clarity nearly gasped out loud. Mortified by his declaring a preference for her younger sister, she rose, too, watching Purity's mouth open and close. Her reaction would be funny if the matter weren't such a serious one.

Lastly, Lady Diamond stood. "Clarity and I will leave you two to speak privately."

Alex looked shocked. "I didn't think that was allowed, my lady. Perhaps you should send in a maid."

Their mother sighed. "Are you here to compromise my daughter?"

"Of course not!" His vehemence was out of proportion to her soft words.

"I didn't think you were. I trust all my children to behave properly. Moreover, I respect them. Since you are both adults, I shall leave you to your private discussion of courtship."

She glanced at each of her daughters in various stages of dismay. "Come along, Clarity."

As soon as the room cleared and the two of them were alone, Alex decided to press his suit formally. While he hadn't been able to take his eyes off Clarity when she was near him, Purity was the one who would be the most suitable. Her older sister was too volatile. Even as she strode out the door, his gaze following her movements, she'd appeared to be in a high tweague.

"Please," he said to Purity, "will you sit once more?"

"I will, but I must tell you, you are making a mistake."

"Am I?" Alex didn't think so. He thought things through, planned, calculated, and then acted.

"Yes. I am sorry to tell you, my lord, I have no interest in becoming your wife. I have no wish to offend you, and I am honored that you—or your aunt—considered me suitable, but I also don't want to waste your time."

"You see, that is precisely why you are right for me. You understand the importance of something as precious as time."

"Hardly a basis for a loving marriage," the young lady said.

"No, but it's a start." Besides, Alex was not interested in the "loving" part, only a successful marriage. Before he could try to persuade her, however, she shook her head, and he could see she was determined.

"I believe I am a good judge of character," Purity told him. "And I can tell you are a kind and thoughtful man. Yet you seem to depend upon the advice of an older woman. Your aunt's ways and her opinions will most likely not endear you to the young ladies ready for marriage. I would suggest you allow my sister to tutor you."

"I beg your pardon." Alex had not expected such a suggestion.

"Truly," Purity continued. "No one is more popular than our Clarity. Everyone wants her at their parties and dinners. If anyone can make you desirable enough to capture a wife, she can."

He considered. On the one hand, Clarity had already infuriated him with her casual manner and outspoken nature. She challenged him, even over his wise aunt who had made sure he didn't make a misstep in all the years since he'd had the title bestowed upon him. She hadn't done it politely as her sister had, either.

What's more, Clarity was fun-loving and silly, both useless and dangerous traits.

On the other hand, it was true that no woman he'd encountered at the ball had shown any interest in him, particularly after he spoke of crop prices and the difficulty in keeping good staff at a country estate when one wasn't in residence.

"You may be correct. Perhaps Lady Clarity can even make me acceptable to you."

Purity sighed. "I have no doubt she will be able to help you discover a suitable wife, but it shall not be me. Let me call her back in here and see if she is willing."

Alex paced while Purity was out of the room. To his consternation, he suddenly heard raised voices.

"Are you mad?" It sounded like Clarity.

"Hush!" said her sister.

Then there was a flurry of phrases he could hardly make out.

"Why should I...? insulted... wretched aunt... absolutely not... naturally, I do... no...! for whose sake...? oh, fine!"

The door was wrenched open, and Clarity stormed into the room, looking less than pleased. Coming nearly toe-to-toe, she stood before him with her arms crossed.

"I understand you need assistance."

Her eyes were flashing, and there were spots of color on her face. Both served to make her even lovelier.

"Your sister seems to think that is the case. Do you?"

"If you wish to find a wife who isn't a hundred years old or as dry as dust, then yes. At least you know how to dress, and that's a start."

Taken aback, Alex told her, "I have an excellent valet."

"Still, a pop of color would be most welcome. Do you have any purple or bright blue waistcoats?"

"No. My aunt says—"

"I will help you if you promise not to preface each statement with 'my aunt says.' Agreed?"

"Agreed."

"Good. If we can loosen you up a little, then perhaps we can find you a wife before the Season is over."

"Maybe even Lady Purity."

Her cheeks reddened further. "Unlikely," she snapped. Then she threw her hands wide, looking bewildered. "May I ask why you prefer her over me? She never even played with us when we were children."

"I don't prefer her." He stopped himself. He wouldn't lie to her. "Well, maybe I do. Only because she seems more mature, more like a life's helpmate."

She fisted her slender hands. He preferred her arms crossed, for he feared she might punch him in the nose.

"And me?" she demanded.

"And you, what?" Alex had forgotten the thread of their conversation.

"What do I seem like if not a helpmate?"

He realized he'd insulted her again. She was the elder sister after all.

"I don't know you well enough to—"

"Of course you do! You know me better than you know Purity."

He detected a hint of jealousy, which was nonsense since her sister had turned him down flat. And he hadn't any interest in Clarity. Or shouldn't, at least not for the position of a viscountess. He could easily imagine her in his bed—too easily—but that was probably due to how many weeks it had been since he'd broken it off with his mistress.

Even thinking such a randy thought was besmirching the high degree in which he held the Diamonds. He must drive her away, he decided, because her flashing eyes and her perfect lips sent desire slashing through him. And while he could picture her naked in his bed with the firelight dancing across her dark hair and pale skin, he could not envision taking her as his wife.

"If you wish," Alex said, crossing his arms as she had done. "You seem like a flutter-budgie. A tad too bold, too talkative, and clearly impulsive. While we were both merry as a grig when we were children, you have not grown out of being exactly the same."

Her mouth had opened, and he feared he'd truly insulted her beyond all repair. However, after a moment, her mouth snapped shut, and she sat on the sofa, head down, gazing at her hands in her lap. Then, to his horror, her shoulders began to shake.

Dear God! Was she weeping?

He hadn't been around a crying female for as long as he could remember. Then it struck him. She might have been the last one when she'd skinned her knee, and it had been his fault, making her descend too quickly down a gnarly tree trunk. She'd dropped the last few feet, torn her dress, and scraped her knee. Tears had coursed down her grimy face, and he'd felt helpless then as he did now.

After that, the only tears he could recall had been his own, shed at his parents' funeral. His aunt had stood stoically beside him and eventually leaned over to tell him she would do her utmost to bring him up properly. Alex had suspected that was the best she could do by way of comfort, never considering to put her arms around a grieving boy.

"Please don't," he said quietly, stepping closer. *Should he rub her back?* "I am terribly sorry."

At that moment, he would offer to marry her at once if she would give him one of her beautiful dimpled smiles.

Chapter Five

Clarity shook her head at his approach, lifting a hand to ward him off before suddenly leaning back against the striped pink-and-cream sofa. Her eyes were squeezed tightly closed. When she clamped her other hand over her mouth, Alex realized she was... laughing!

Against all odds, but to his great relief, Clarity was in a spasm of laughter, barely able to catch her breath. Despite being annoyed at how she had alarmed him, he couldn't help feeling envious. He could not recall the last time he'd laughed.

Finally, she collected herself. With her cheeks still flushed, her dark blue eyes fluttered open.

"I am sorry, Alex. I wanted to protest my flaws, but I *am* all those things you said and more! And I believe most people enjoy my company because of them. Hearing you list your reasons not to court me, it struck me as funny beyond all measure."

She took a deep breath and sighed before adding, "Especially when I think how we used to share some of the same qualities."

Realizing he'd been leaning toward her while concerned and was now too close, able to catch the delicate fragrance he'd detected when they'd danced, he straightened.

"As a child, I may have partaken in any number of ridiculous, ill-conceived actions, but one should leave such behavior in the past."

Instead of appearing regretful, she shook her head before patting the sofa cushion.

"Please sit."

"I shouldn't."

"You shouldn't sit? Why?"

"Because we are alone."

"We are still alone if you remain standing, and you're giving me a neck ache."

She stared up at him with her blue eyes as dark as midnight, and he gave in and took a seat.

"In my opinion, those attributes are some of my best. What you call bold, I call adventurous and fun. And I am talkative because I enjoy engaging in lively conversation with those whose opinion I care to hear. As for impulsive, I think I am spontaneous, and that's a far better way to live than as a stick."

"A stick?" *What on earth did she mean?*

"In. The. Mud," she clarified with emphasis. "You are far too young to be so old!"

"Old!" Surely, she couldn't object to a man behaving maturely.

"Yes. For one thing, you will find charades are enjoyed at most every party, and turning your nose up at playing shall gain you no favor." She shook her head. "Purity explained the situation as she sees it, and I agree. You will not be able to get a wife if you behave as you do. Or if you do snag one, she'll marry you for your title and fortune alone."

That seemed a rather harsh assessment, but the Diamonds were more out in society than he ever hoped to be. Thus, they must know of what they spoke.

"You think I should play charades to gain myself a wife?"

Clarity rolled her eyes. Then shockingly, she reached over and knocked her knuckles upon the side of his head. He flinched.

"What on earth are you doing?"

"Trying to knock sense into you, that's what. It's not merely charades, you dunce. It's everything. If you cannot have fun, I fear you won't like the woman you end up with. What about your children?"

This time he reared away from her. "I don't have any."

"I know that, but you will. Do you want them to have the wonderful childhood we had?"

"We had too much freedom and deservedly got into trouble."

"*Drats!* I thought I was having a conversation with Alex, but it seems I am now speaking with Lady Aston."

He was taken aback. Unsurprisingly, he repeated things his aunt said, but that was because she was a woman of good sense.

"Good day, *Lady Aston*," Clarity continued. "Would you care for tea? If I recall correctly, you take no sugar. Sadly, I cannot stir in a spoonful of bitterness to make it palatable."

Alex shook his head. She shouldn't speak like that about the woman who'd taken on his upbringing.

Suddenly, however, her words struck him as humorous. He could picture his aunt dipping her silver teaspoon into a bowl of bitterness because she often made a waspish face when eating or drinking.

"You're smiling," Clarity pointed out.

Was he? His facial muscles felt stiff.

"And it's a lovely sight to see. Now I know I am with my dear friend Alex and not his aunt. Welcome back."

"You are behaving like a pudding-head," he said, but he smiled again because it felt good.

"Maybe so, but better a pudding-head than a curmudgeon. Tell me, do you really wish to marry my sister?"

Clarity hoped the answer was no, but she wasn't as offended as she'd been at first. She realized she was dealing more with his aunt's preferences than his own. Moreover, if he wasn't taken with her, she would swallow her bruised pride and try to help him. Alex needed to smile more often, for she'd been truthful in saying his was a lovely one. More than that, it was attractive, even alluring.

He needed to learn to laugh again, certainly, and to release some of the weight he looked as though he was carrying upon his shoulders. They were broad enough, but obviously, he'd been under duress for a long time.

"I confess I have no particular wish to marry your sister over any other young lady."

"Do you want to fall in love?" Clarity pressed.

When his body stiffened, she added, "No, please don't retreat into *Lady Aston* again. Keep Alex right here beside me. Let's be honest as we used to."

He swallowed and released a breath.

"Very well. I know some people hope to make love matches. I simply don't think that's important. Instead, I see the wisdom in a wife who can help run my house in Town and the main country estate. She can hire and fire household staff and host parties. She will listen to me in the evenings and over breakfast, should I need to voice my thoughts, and I hope to listen to her and receive sound advice in return."

"And ride with you in the park to witness the first spring flowers, partake of a summer picnic, and travel in your carriage on amusing adventures while sitting on the same side as you, pressed closely against one another because you're married," she teased, watching his eyes widen slightly as if the future she described sounded impossible.

"Perhaps take a wedding trip to the Continent," Clarity continued, thinking of all the things she hoped to do with a husband. "You'll have someone to kiss and with whom to make those children we spoke of before."

The longer she tried to make him realize how much more a wife could be than a mere helpmate to pick out staff, the more she warmed to the notion.

"I am going to keep my eyes open this year for a suitable mate, too. I have a couple gentlemen already interested, although I am unsure if either is the one for me. Regardless, I think I should decide this Season. Once I am married, Purity will more easily find a husband. I don't want to be the obstruction in the line of Diamond daughters."

"Obstruction?" Alex repeated, and that ghost of a smile played around his lips. "Surely, you're the main jewel in the ring, the eldest daughter, ripe for the plucking. Every man who likes a bit of fun in his life will be lining up."

She stared at him. "That almost sounded as if you approve of me and my indecorous, flutter-budgie self."

This time, he smiled more broadly, showing a hint of a dimple on one side, and Clarity felt her insides flutter. *Oh dear!* She vaguely recalled she'd had an acute infatuation for her older friend in the year before he disappeared from her life. But it was a long-ago childhood fantasy.

"I think you will undoubtedly appeal to many men," he said, "perhaps not those who seek a serious help-mate, but those who want a beautiful bauble on their arm. Indubitably, there are many of those single gentlemen, only too happy to take you on outings and dress you up in finery for balls and parties."

Momentarily shocked, Clarity bit her lip until she could think of how to address all his insults, which she had no doubt he considered compliments. Instead of pointing out how terrible to be considered merely a bauble or a doll to be dressed, she attacked his premise.

"Are you saying you have no intention of going to a ball *after* you find a wife? If that's true, you should tell the young lady at the outset so she doesn't fall for your good looks alone, not realizing you wish to shut her away to act as a butler, a secretary, and an adviser. Oh, and a broodmare!"

"You are angry," he commented. "Yet I believe I spoke the truth. There are men who want nothing more than a pretty wife. I assure you I have spoken with them at university and at my club. I am now a member of my father's club, by the way. As for me, I see no reason why I would go to a ball once I have found the woman I shall wed."

Clarity was genuinely surprised. "Not for the pleasure of dancing with her, nor to show her off because you're proud she chose you?"

He frowned. "Wouldn't showing her off like a prized painting be treating her poorly, too? You just took offense at a woman being called a bauble."

She sighed. "We are deeply in the weeds, but I don't think there is a woman alive, particularly a newly wedded one, who wouldn't be pleased if her husband honored her by taking her out. That's different from wanting a woman *only* for her looks. And you didn't answer about dancing."

"I suppose dancing is good exercise," he allowed cautiously.

Exercise! Clarity was ready to give up. If Purity felt sorry for him, then she could be the one to make him marriage-ready. Rising again, she decided to be encouraging with her final words.

"I believe my sister made an error. You will certainly find a wife this Season because you are titled and attractive and probably wealthy, although it will *not* be Purity. As I said before, I predict the woman who accepts your proposal will be someone able to tolerate a life of solemnity and purpose. And then you will be happy."

Looking at his stoic expression, she amended, "At least, I believe you will be content."

His mouth no longer relaxed but set in a grim line, he nodded in agreement.

"Thank you." Rising, he strode from the room.

Unsettled was the word Alex would use to describe how he felt upon leaving the Diamonds' home, especially when he had passed Brennon going in.

Was the other man there for Clarity or for Purity, and why should it matter to him?

On the other hand, the longer he had been in Clarity's presence, the more he recalled how easily they kept company and conversed. They could speak to one another as equals with frankness, almost as if they were the same sex.

And now she was a fully grown woman, she had other attributes to endear her to a man. Her figure was curved in all the right places, shapely yet trim. While her eyes were the same mischievous deep blue, they held an added sparkle of allure, as did her gently arched eyebrows and her full lips.

A man could fall for a face like that. He had no doubt if she decided to find a husband that year, she would. And woe betide the man! Her type of fun, which used to be their shared amusement, led to ruin, even death. He could no longer condone it. Plainly, his aunt's notion of what type of female would make an adequate wife was correct, and Clarity was unsuitable.

More's the pity, for he felt something for her. A yearning. Perhaps it was nothing more than the familiarity of a childhood friend from a time when his life had felt complete. Regardless, he couldn't recapture that time. He'd dashed it all to pieces with his carelessness. And she served as a reminder of the dangerous actions that had ruined everything.

If only she wasn't still so immature.

Thrusting Clarity from his thoughts, he went to White's, knowing he would hear stories of how wonderful his father was and what a pity the Viscount Hollidge had been taken far too early. It was a torture Alex deserved. While he had a few friends who'd strayed away and joined Brooks's Club instead, Alex never would. Not solely because of its decidedly Whig-leaning members but for its continued emphasis on gaming. His father's club had covered its earlier air of wild gambling and an evil reputation with a more genteel patina of exclusivity, delicious food, and royal patronage. Nevertheless, one could still engage in outrageous wagers if one wished. He did not.

While he sat alone, trying to focus on reading the newspapers, he considered what Clarity had said about charades and games. He had enjoyed an occasional game of cards or chess with his friends at university. But when he thought on it, Alex couldn't recall the last time he'd played a game of anything. She had called him a stick in the mud!

Once again, he was trying to ban her laughing eyes and generous mouth from his mind—banish them completely and find himself a suitable wife.

At the next ball, upon entering, Alex steered clear of the shining brood of Diamonds. Instead, he went toward the other bachelors since there were a few familiar faces, and they quickly decided if the viscount was ready to marry, and to a man they would assist him.

"Less pressure on those of us who are still enjoying single life," said a baron's son. The other men chuckled, but Alex thought them weak.

"I don't see how you can allow yourself to be pressed into marriage."

"It's not always the young ladies," explained another. "Sometimes it's their formidable mothers or fathers."

"Don't you doubt it," said a third, "there are a number of tricksters here who appear as perfect angels but would as soon slide the parson's noose around your neck, by hook or by crook, as they would smile at you."

Alex took another look at the gaily dressed ladies.

"They appear harmless to me."

General laughter ensued before the first gentleman advised, "Don't let one request a walk outside, Hollidge, even if she's fine as fivepence, or you'll be leg-shackled in three weeks."

The men all laughed again. They were a mirthful lot, Alex decided, apt to be drawing a flask from their pockets more often than might be wise. However, they knew more than he about assemblies, and thus, he paid heed. He kept his dance partners in sight of their chaperones and danced no more than once with each. He didn't want to end up ensnared by the wrong woman.

Eventually, perhaps inevitably, he found himself near the Diamonds, who even then were talking animatedly about something. They were like bright candle flames, and he confessed to feeling little more than a dull moth.

"Greetings, Lord Hollidge," Lady Diamond was the first to acknowledge him.

In succession of age, he greeted Clarity and Purity. The younger girls were not yet out in society, but there were also no male members of the family.

"Where are Lord Diamond and your son?" he asked.

"My son has returned to university," she said, glancing past him as if Adam might appear. "I believe there is more than one unhappy young lady here tonight."

"Mother!" Lady Purity protested.

The countess shrugged away any impropriety in discussing her son's love life.

"As for Lord Diamond, he is away on business," she said. "A collapsed granary on our property in Derbyshire and a flooded bridge at our holding in Birmingham, both of which will cause our tenants great distress if not quickly mended. My husband likes to keep on top of such disturbances."

"Making him a good lord and steward," Alex said. "My own father was like that, too, and I am trying to follow in his footsteps."

"Then your tenants will respect you," Lady Diamond said.

He nodded, aware that both her daughters were eyeing him. It occurred to Alex he had been remiss, perhaps even downright rude, in not seeking them out at the ball's beginning and securing a dance with each.

"Do either of you have a dance still free?" he asked, unsure what he hoped was the answer. He knew only that Purity was far easier to be around. When he was with her, none of his thoughts twisted in his head, nor did any emotions arise, nor silly notions of laughing... or longing.

"Sadly, I do not," Purity responded immediately, "but I believe my sister does."

Clarity's eyes widened before she sent her sister an infuriated glare. Alex hoped she wasn't offended by his visit the week before.

After a long hesitation, Clarity said, "I don't think I do."

Anyone could tell she was lying. He had insulted his one and oldest friend in London, and now he regretted it. She stood before him a vision of loveliness, and in truth, he wouldn't mind dancing with her despite their incompatibility.

Luckily, her mother stepped in.

"I think Lord Burlington had to beg off. Something about indigestion. Strange for someone his age, but he stopped by while you were on the dance floor."

Lady Clarity looked none too pleased as she eyed her mother, but then she turned to him.

"If that is the case, then I suppose I have an upcoming free dance after the next."

Alex nodded, experiencing an unwelcome feathering of excitement.

When the sisters' partners arrived for the next dance, he bowed and walked away, having a curious sense of propriety over Clarity after realizing one of the men had spoken earlier about ladies in a derogatory way. The man was by no means wanting to secure an engagement of marriage if that was truly Clarity's wish.

At the other end of the room, he collected his next partner, Miss Emmeline Brambury, a viscount's daughter. Her mother was a close acquaintance of his aunt.

With her tightly wound ringlets and doe eyes, Miss Brambury was civil, pretty, quiet, staid, and spoke properly about the recent London weather and the musicians. While he did have to work hard not to yawn, he also appreciated her demeanor and comportment.

"What do you think about people who slurp their soup?" he asked her.

By her disdainful expression, he had his answer. Miss Brambury would never slurp.

After the dance, when he had escorted her back to her chaperone, he asked, "May I call upon you at your home this week?"

"Yes, you may," she said, offering him a polite smile. Not effusive like one of Clarity's beaming smiles. Instead, it was modest, albeit welcoming.

When he visited with her in a few days, he would determine if Miss Brambury was suitable in all the ways his aunt had said were important, but upon first appearances, she seemed to be. This was almost too easy, and Alex failed to see what all the fuss was about.

Strolling back to Lady Diamond and the Diamond sisters, he felt a sense of lightness. He wouldn't have to do this for weeks on end.

"I have come for our dance," he said to Clarity. She rested her gloved hand upon his arm, and they walked to their place upon the parquet floor.

"You look pleased," she told him as they began.

"Do I? That's a strange assessment when one is dancing," he said.

"You had a tension about you that has now been lifted," she observed, which he thought was astute of her.

"I see your meaning," he agreed. "It may be because I have found a lady whom I believe will be a suitable wife."

Chapter Six

Clarity stumbled but quickly righted herself and caught up to his step.

"Are you well?" Alex asked.

"Yes, my apologies. I don't think I have ever before done such an egregious misstep." But then she'd never been taken by surprise with such a declaration at the beginning of a dance.

"No harm came of it," he assured her as the dance continued.

"Here? Tonight?" She glanced around.

He narrowed his eyes. "Tonight, *what* exactly?"

With exasperation, Clarity asked, "Are you saying you have found a wife here?"

"I might have. Obviously, I cannot be too hasty."

"No, of course not," she relaxed. "She is someone you have only just met."

"Correct. Yet I hope after I call upon the lady at her home, I shall be able to satisfy all my questions and make a reasonable decision."

"After a single visit?" she asked.

"I am not looking to fall madly in love with her over a cup of milky tea," he asserted. "I merely wish to discern her sensibilities and her nature."

"To make sure she has no sense of fun," Clarity muttered.

"Pardon me?"

With a surge of exasperation, she puffed out her cheeks. "Do you think it's hot in here?"

"A little," he agreed. "But aren't all such assemblies warm and stuffy? Isn't that why you have a fan?"

"I can hardly draw it out while we're dancing."

"Do you wish to stop?"

"Yes," she said. "I need some fresh air."

"As you wish. I shall return you to your mother."

"Oh, Alex. What harm can there be in escorting me, as an old family friend, out onto the terrace?"

He stared at her, but then he nodded. They walked off the floor and toward the rear of the ballroom. As soon as they stepped out into the foggy, sooty night air, Clarity breathed deeply and coughed, feeling better.

Why his announcement should have shocked her, she didn't know. It couldn't be because she'd allowed all of her warm feelings for her childhood friend to take up a place in her heart. He was plainly not the same person. If she met him for the first time that night, he wouldn't interest her at all apart from his appearance. And she hoped she wasn't so shallow that she would ever allow a man's face and figure alone to sway her.

She kept walking until they stepped off the terrace, where many were gathered on the warm night, and continued into the shadowy area beyond.

Alex halted. "We cannot go any farther."

"Why not?" She knew, but she wanted to hear him say he might compromise her. It gave her a little thrill to tease the stuffy part of him. The youth she knew wouldn't have cared a fig about societal mores.

"Strangely, you are doing precisely what the bachelors I was speaking with earlier fear the most, trying to trap me into an improper situation."

"Trap you?" She was momentarily insulted, except she had too many young men buzzing around her like bees to believe he could be serious.

"Why on earth would I do that?" she asked. "If I want a husband, I shall simply say yes to one of the swells who already court me. I don't need to trap anyone. I would be miffed by your insult, but you are basically new to London society and thus have no idea how popular I am."

That should set him down a peg. *Trap a man, indeed!*

"Besides," she added, "we are friends, and since you've judged me unsuitable, the last thing on earth I would want is to be forced to marry a man who doesn't admire me."

He looked doubtful, which was galling.

"Never mind. You may return to the ballroom. I shall walk on my own. In fact, I prefer it to your company."

"No, you cannot do that either," he protested.

Since she'd already turned away and started walking, Alex had to catch up to her. She kept striding over the grass toward the wall at the garden's end, just to madden him. It was amusing to thwart the man who used to be the leader of their lively capers.

Finally, when there was nowhere else to go, she turned behind the perimeter's hedgerow. It was the first time she'd been alone in a garden with a member of the opposite sex. She knew what was supposed to happen, what she'd been warned of by her mother. But that was with ne'er-do-wells and rogues. This was Alex.

Irritated, he growled, "We must go back."

Grabbing her arm, he made her halt. However, instead of drawing her into an embrace and kissing her soundly as a rake might do, he scolded her.

"You are behaving like a hoyden. I must insist you return to the house with me. And I shall have a word with Lady Diamond about your behavior."

She laughed out loud. "Oh, Lady Aston, I didn't think I would be with you tonight."

"That's not funny." He was visibly seething, staring down at her. She blinked back up at him and quickly sobered to see genuine ire in his expression. It made her heart ache.

"Oh, Alex, where has my old friend gone?"

Disbelief flashed behind his eyes, and something else she couldn't identify. And then slowly, he drew her closer.

Not protesting, remaining silent, Clarity was curious to see what he would do even as her heart began to beat wildly. *Were they going to hug as two people who had once been thick as thieves?*

In the next instant, he dragged her up against him and took hold of her with his other hand, too, one clamped around each of her upper arms.

"What harm can come?" he repeated her words softly back to her, and then he kissed her.

Whatever she'd imagined, it wasn't this. As soon as his lips touched hers, a scorching jolt sizzled through her, and her knees instantly went as wobbly as aspic jelly.

The kiss was blistering! When their mouths fused, a fiery trail blazed from her tingling breasts to the sensitive place between her thighs until her body was pulsing everywhere.

Unable to help herself, she reached up to wrap her fingers behind his neck and hold on.

A sideways tilt of his head sealed their mouths more closely, and as she gasped, his tongue slid between her lips.

His tongue? The unexpected added pleasure of his silken tongue sent shivers along her spine. At the same time, his hands left her arms to caress her back.

Acutely aware of the growing yearning inside her and relishing the searing heat of his firm lips, she sighed and melted against him.

And then he groaned, a noise so low and throaty at first that she wasn't sure it came from him. If there had been bears in London, she would have wagered that was the sound one would make.

While her mouth was still vibrating from the hoarse sound, he abruptly released her.

"Good God!" he exclaimed. "Either you are incredibly naïve, an idiot, or a wanton. Have you done this before?"

Not exactly love words! Putting her fingers to her tingling lips, she shook her head.

"I don't believe I am any of those things," Clarity protested, hearing a quiver in her voice. "I am, however, ready to return to the ballroom. Sadly, the garden has made me not a whit cooler."

Surely, he would think that funny, how they'd heated up instead of cooled down.

But his expression was thunderous. He stepped aside and gestured for her to go past him.

"Hurry," he urged. "And straight to your mother's side. I will come inside a few moments after you."

At Hyde Park in the early morning before it was fashionable to be riding, when there was no one else to see or be seen, Alex exercised his horse. He remembered being there with his father. They would come at a similarly quiet hour to have as much of the park to themselves as possible. Later, his father would ride with his mother, when the popular Lord and Lady Hollidge would greet their friends and make arrangements for dinners and picnics.

Alex had no one with whom he wished to do any of those things.

Yet he did allow himself this one fun and albeit dangerous activity. Kicking his horse into a full gallop, he tore from one side of Hyde Park to the other. It was glorious. He felt free and alive, like his old self, the one that had ruined everything good in his life.

And when his horse's sides were heaving, he let it walk slowly back home.

He hadn't called upon Miss Brambury after kissing Clarity, although he still intended to. He just needed to put a little time between the disturbingly sensual tryst with the eldest Diamond sister and the placid one he hoped to have with Miss Brambury.

Too many irons in the fire probably applied to one too many ladies on his mind as much as to anything else.

On the other hand, he knew he ought to hammer his iron while it was glowing hot. His aunt, who had known Miss Brambury's mother for the past five years, seemed convinced the young lady was the best choice among those coming out this season. With Lady Brambury as his aunt's friend, the path would be easy if he wanted to court her daughter.

Thus, the following day, he gave his card to the Bramburys' butler and soon found himself seated in the viscount's drawing room opposite the demure Miss Brambury. With utmost propriety, *both* the girl's parents were also present, one on either side of her.

"The circumstances that have kept you out of London these past few social seasons have actually been a blessing," Lady Brambury said after the tea was poured. "Our daughter was not ready to come out until this year."

The message was unmistakable—if he had searched for a wife earlier, he would have missed out on this particular one. While Alex was confident another equally refined and capable woman would become available, it was exceedingly convenient to have found this one as soon as he had. He could stop going to those balls where unsuitable women like Clarity might tempt him.

Clarity, with her lovely face and kissable mouth.

"Yes," he said, realizing a silence had fallen that he ought to fill.

"Your aunt mentioned your estate is a mere one county away from my own," Lord Brambury remarked, as if this practical coincidence ought to make the union of his daughter with the Hollidge viscountcy a decidedly certain affair. "In Essex," the man added.

Alex nodded but seeing that something more was expected, he said. "I have holdings in Suffolk." The conversation was as boring as watching grass grow.

"Some fine fertile land," Lord Brambury added.

"And close for visiting," Lady Brambury added.

Alex took a second look at her parents, realizing they would become his new family, his in-laws, and consequently in his life forever after. They would be grandparents to his children. He considered their looks and their demeanor and could find no fault.

"Yes," he said again.

But a small part of him was screaming no!

Miss Brambury nodded her approval, too, whether to the close proximity of the estates or the fecundity of the land, he didn't know.

Regardless, she held out the biscuit plate to him with a steady hand. Her manners were impeccable.

"Lady Aston said you were not yet in any way aligned with a suitor. Is that correct?" he asked, not wishing to waste time. He'd already done that at the Diamond household.

When any day could be one's last, it was foolish to squander a minute on the wrong endeavor or the wrong female.

However, when Miss Brambury's cheeks pinkened and her mother coughed, he feared he'd made a misstep.

"I say," Lord Brambury spoke up. "It may be premature for you to ask such an intimate question, or indeed to press for exclusivity, my lord. We shall speak to our daughter in private about such an important step. Naturally, you are welcome to escort her around Town, in my wife's presence or with a chaperone, and to dance at the next assembly."

Perhaps he looked a little crestfallen for the next words were encouraging ones from Lady Brambury.

"Not to worry, my lord. This is simply how things are done. You must ask Lady Aston, and she will assure you it is."

"Very well." As far as he could tell, the delay was a customary formality. They spent another few minutes finishing tea and discussing the weather in detail, straying only so far into the political field as to wish the queen abundant good health, and then Alex departed.

All in all, a well-spent half an hour.

Hyde Park on a busy afternoon was a bright, colorful, crowded place. The Diamond siblings always enjoyed riding together, especially when Adam was in London as he was that month, and sometimes one or both parents came, too.

"Don't you wish we could race our horses like in Derry?" Clarity asked, patting her horse, Bonny, who loved to be given her head every once in a while and had a smooth gait while galloping.

Purity shook her head. "No, I am quite happy to amble along and see people. If I were zipping by, I wouldn't notice those flowers or that dashingly handsome buck over there."

Clarity's head swiveled. For an instant, she hoped to see Alex, the most attractive *buck* she could imagine. Yet all she heard was Adam's laughter.

"I don't see anyone," Clarity declared.

"He must have dodged out of sight," Purity said, then she too laughed, leaving Clarity unsure if there had been a dashing man or not. All three of them were constantly teasing one another.

In truth, she had been unable to drive Alex from her thoughts after their single fervent kiss. She felt warm whenever she recalled its intensity. His mouth, the pressure, his scent that had enveloped her, his hands on her body—all had been perfection. She hadn't seen him since.

Not that she'd expected him to recant his statement about having already found a potential wife, one who wasn't her! But after such a passionate encounter, she had hoped he would come calling if only to discuss the possibility of something more between them.

"I wouldn't mind a race," Adam broke into her thoughts, "but you'll have to get yourself out of bed early. If we come when the mists have yet to clear and there's still dew on the grass, then we can race."

"Don't encourage her," Purity said.

"Pish," Clarity told her. "It's a grand idea, and we'll do it the next morning when we're not out too late at a ball."

Fortunately, that turned out to be two mornings later. However, almost as soon as they began their plan, it fell into failure.

"Blast it all," Adam said, dismounting. "The girth strap has frayed. I love this saddle!" he moaned.

"You love it so much you've worn it out," Clarity declared. "I don't mind telling you I am disappointed."

"It's not the saddle, muttonhead. It's only one strap, but a damnably important one."

"I'm your elder. Don't call me a muttonhead and don't swear, either."

Adam laughed. "All right, but you don't have to let it ruin your fun. Gallop to the end of the row, give Bonny a good run, and then come back."

"You can take a turn afterward, if you wish. My Bonny won't mind you atop her."

"Wretched girl! You know I'm not going to use your saddle. What if anyone saw me riding aside like that? I wouldn't live it down until I was an old man. Anyway, it'll be practice for you, and I vow I shall still beat you next time."

"I don't need to practice to beat you," she quipped. "Regardless, I shall go straight up and back."

"Off with you then." He slapped her horse's flank.

Gleefully, Clarity urged Bonny, a lively jennet, into a trot, then a canter, and finally, a gallop. Hyde Park flew by as she bent low in her sidesaddle and held on. Unfortunately, her hat, which she had pinned herself, flew off within a few yards, but she looked back, gesturing to Adam to retrieve it.

In the next few yards, her chignon also came undone. She would have to speak to her maid Winnie about this. Pinning her hair in the same manner for a dance was not sufficient for a vigorous ride. Regardless, enjoying the sensation of flying, she laughed.

"Good girl," she murmured, patting Bonny's neck.

Approaching the far end of Rotten Row, Clarity spied another figure, a man on horseback, stationary, watching her ride.

Mindful of how far away she was from her brother and how isolated, she began to draw upon the reins and slow her horse to a walk. However, before turning and fleeing in the other direction, she had a delightful realization.

"Alex!" she exclaimed, raising a hand in salutation. Her heartbeat sped up accordingly at the sight of him, handsome and tall, sitting on a splendid gray Arabian.

After she hailed him, he started forward. Instead of appearing happy to see her, he wore his usual rigid expression of displeasure.

"What on earth are you doing?" were his first disapproving words.

"My brother and I like to race," she explained.

Pointedly, he looked around and behind her.

She laughed, breathing hard, for somehow, even though Bonny had done all the work, the exhilaration of galloping always took her breath away. And unexpectedly seeing Alex added to her breathlessness.

"Adam's saddle has a broken strap." She shrugged slightly. "Therefore, it's only me."

Alex shook his head, and she knew his next words were going to be disapproving.

"Beyond the pale, as usual. Not just risking yourself by galloping, you are alone and at the mercy of any scoundrel who comes along."

"Not yourself surely," she teased.

"When it comes to you, Clarity Diamond, and your outrageous behavior, you could push even me to behave badly. You ought to be spanked."

His words should not have conjured up a vision of herself bare, helpless, and willing, lying across his lap, but they did. Suddenly, she was very warm indeed.

Chapter Seven

Ignoring her beautiful face and how her breasts rose and fell with the exertion of her ride, Alex tried to sound reproachful.

"And then there is the matter of your appearance."

With Clarity's hair down around her shoulders, her cheeks colored with a blush that was spreading down the slender column of her neck, and her eyes sparkling with amusement, she was breathtaking.

More like a wild Gaelic princess than an English earl's daughter!

In fact, she looked like a woman who had been pleasured in bed, and well and truly satisfied. Every particle of his being yearned to take her in his arms and kiss her again. Maybe that was why he was being tweaguey.

"You are all disheveled," he groused.

"We used to race at Oak Grove," Clarity reminded him. "Even though I was years younger, I believe I beat you a few times."

He remembered it well, with her long dark braids flying out behind her. On the rare occasion she passed him, he'd wanted to grab hold of one of those braids and yank her back. They'd always laughed, especially when he'd thought nothing of tossing his cap at her head to slow her down.

Today, when he'd watched her approach with her hair streaming behind her like a Norse Valkyrie, he'd been stunned by her exquisite beauty. How he would love to see her raven hair spread out across his pillow while he made love to her.

Swallowing his desire, he focused on the dangerous game she was playing.

"When we were children, you only won because the pathways were more familiar to you, and the horses knew you, too, so they responded better."

Her tinkling laugh made him ache.

"Is that why I beat you?" Then she cocked her head. "We both know this path well enough. And each has their own horse. Shall we race back to my brother? He will be growing worried if I don't reappear soon."

"No," Alex said. "It's not safe. It is asinine to race in a public park."

"Nevertheless, are you ready?" she asked.

"No!" he protested. Knowing she was going to do it anyway, he tried to get closer to grab her reins.

She nudged her horse to dance just out of his reach.

"Oh, Alex, what harm can come of a little horse race?"

With that, she urged her horse into a quick run.

The devil!

Kicking his own horse into action, he trailed her for merely a few yards before his larger thoroughbred caught up and came astride her.

"Stop!" he yelled to her, but she hunkered down along her horse's neck plainly intent on winning, which was impossible given her jennet's shorter legs.

And then the next few moments happened too fast for Alex to say what precisely occurred. A ball came from the other side of the hedgerow ahead of them, and a young child abruptly appeared in their path.

While Alex could easily swerve to the left, he was penning Clarity in with nowhere to go except to the right, which she bravely did, slamming her horse into the yew hedge and falling onto the shrubbery, before tumbling over the other side.

In an instant, she had disappeared.

"Clarity," he yelled, yanking back on the reins before jumping from his horse and dashing past the child whose nanny had followed behind. The woman was flustered and shrieking so loudly he couldn't hear if Clarity was calling for help with her body twisted and broken.

Scrambling through the opening by which the child had come, he found her in a heap, with her long hair tangled in leaves and half her dress caught upon the dense hedge, causing her silk stockings to be scandalously on view. Her head was down, and she rested upon her forearms.

Falling to his knees beside her, he dreaded learning the extent of her injuries.

"Clarity."

She looked up at him, not a scratch on her face and no tears either.

"Gracious!" she exclaimed. "I wasn't expecting that!" Then she pushed herself up to sitting and tugged at her caught gown. "Ow!"

"Are you hurt?" he asked.

"Mostly my pride, but can you disentangle my hair from the bush? It is pulling frightfully. I fear I shall be bald."

"That's why you should wear your hair properly tied back when riding," he admonished, but he couldn't help glancing at her slender legs before he wrenched her dress free.

"Please be a little gentler with my hair than you were with my gown," she said, sounding not the least distressed. "And for your information, my hair was properly pinned and even under a hat when I started."

"That's neither here nor there. Obviously, it is undone now and in a frightful state. As soon as it came unpinned, you should have stopped riding."

"Clarity," called another male voice.

"Adam!" she replied. "I'm over here. Alex is helping me."

He cringed at her use of his given name as her brother suddenly appeared through a break in the hedge.

"Are you hurt?" The heir to the Diamond's earldom at least asked a sensible first question.

"Not in the least," she said. "Thankfully the queen's gardeners have maintained a full hedge."

Her brother started to laugh, and she joined in.

"I cannot believe you two," Alex said, thinking he should knock their heads together if he ever managed to disentangle Clarity.

"Good day, Hollidge," Adam addressed him finally. "If we took all this seriously, then I would have to call you out for being alone with my sister behind the shrubbery, in the intimate action of grooming her."

The siblings laughed again, even harder.

"Buffoons," Alex muttered, not caring if they heard him. His heart had only just calmed to its regular rate. "There. You're free and with few hairs lost."

She offered him her hand when she ought to have outstretched it to her brother. Taking it, he rose and pulled her up beside him.

"That gown is ruined," her brother pointed out.

"Agreed," Clarity said.

"She could have broken an arm at the very least," Alex reminded them. The dress was hardly important.

"Nonsense," she said. "The *very least* was no injury at all, and that's what happened. I assume the child is fine or someone would have told me."

"Yes," her brother said. "The nanny had already taken him by the hand and dragged him away as I ran up. I think she feared she was going to be reprimanded for letting the toddlekin run onto the path like that."

"The boy could have been killed, too," Alex couldn't help pointing out, knowing he sounded like a worried crone. "Trampled under your horse's feet."

"At the very least," Clarity quipped, echoing his previous words.

She was mocking him, standing in a state of disarray with twigs in her hair and her gown half-shredded. He felt a bubble of amusement but attributed it to his great relief that she was uninjured.

Her brother went first back through the hedge, and then Clarity and Alex followed. Their horses stood nearby, eating grass.

"We didn't lose our mounts," Clarity said. "There is always a bright side."

Alex wanted to tell her what a remarkable woman she was. He

couldn't imagine any other lady not in fits over such a mishap. However, he didn't wish to encourage her antics.

Instead, staring at her accusingly, he reminded her of her own words. "'What harm?' you asked directly before doing something irresponsible."

She shrugged.

"*Twice* now you've asked that same question," he added.

Her lovely gaze flew to his, and they were both thinking of their ill-advised stroll in the garden and the even more foolhardy kiss. Her cheeks, now smudged with dirt, blushed a ruddy hue.

Adam gave them both an interested look, and Alex wished he hadn't said anything.

"I will leave you," he said to the Diamond heir, "to take your errant sister home safely. Good day!"

Feeling like a coward but needing to get far away from Clarity's alluring presence and her reckless behavior, Alex mounted his horse and rode away.

He didn't miss her calling after him, "Thank you for your help, Lord Hollidge!" emphasizing his title in a persnickety way that told him she was mocking him again.

What could he do but sigh? Every meeting proved her less suitable to be his viscountess, yet each time he was with Clarity, he wanted more of her.

A conundrum, indeed!

Entering the ballroom, Clarity cast her gaze over the crowd, scanning for Alex before she even had her fan out. He had well and truly made an impression upon her with that kiss. And when he'd rescued her from the vicious yew, restraining his fury at her predicament while plainly worried, something inside her shifted from fondness to a deeper sentiment.

All she knew for sure was she wouldn't mind repeating their kiss. Unfortunately, he would never agree to walk outside with her again.

Besides, he had chosen a woman to be his wife, and for all Clarity knew, he had made a declaration of intent to the lady already.

That was, unless he wished to repeat their kiss as much as she did. He'd acted less friendly after the incident in Hyde Park when they'd both attended a dance two nights later. He'd steered clear of her. And now, she didn't know what reception she would receive when next they met.

"Are you going to stand there gawking?" Purity asked. "I nearly bumped into you."

"Then *you* should look where you're going," Clarity quipped. "That's what I am doing, looking to see which way I wish to go."

"I suggest we simply enter the fray," their mother said. "As it's too crowded to get our own table, I fear we shall have to stroll about the room all night while you girls each find your heart's desire."

"Mother!" Purity said.

"Why not?" her mother asked. "You know that's how I met your father. He was walking one way and I, the other, and we met near the musicians' dais. I couldn't hear a thing he said at first." She offered a beaming smile. "Not until we took a private stroll."

"Mother!" Purity exclaimed again. "I swear it is your red hair that makes you so devilish. What if Ray takes after you? You and Father will have to watch her like hawks."

Clarity led the way clockwise around the edge of the dance floor. Occasionally, a gentleman came up with the ball's manager who introduced him if he was unknown, first to their mother and then, with her permission, to each of her daughters.

They had their dance cards nearly filled within fifteen minutes, and then Clarity stopped accepting partners until she determined if Alex were there.

At last, she saw him. Her heart lurched. He looked remarkably handsome for such a miserable man, and misery was the expression he was projecting to the rest of the guests while standing by himself on the edge of the throng.

Shaking her head, she approached him, knowing her mother and sister would follow.

"Good evening, Lord Hollidge. You are looking well." *As well as an unhappy man could look!*

"Good evening, Lady Clarity." He bowed and looked past her. "Good evening, Lady Diamond, Lady Purity. Is this the extent of your party tonight?"

"It is," her mother answered. "And you? Not that you need a chaperone, but are you joined by your aunt?"

"She prefers to remain at home."

Clarity smiled at him, wondering if he would pay her special notice after their last encounter. When he didn't, and the conversation tapered off, it meant they ought to move on, but she hesitated. Alex hadn't offered to partner with her or Purity for a dance yet.

"Are you dancing this evening?" she asked in the next breath, instantly feeling Purity's disapproval radiating like a hot coal beside her. Clarity knew it wasn't her place to make such an inquiry, as it was generally understood the gentleman should ask the questions, particularly those related to dancing.

"I have not secured any partners as yet," he said.

"I believe you have not grasped the way this works," Clarity told him. "You must set up your dances now. If you stand here as you are doing, like a pedestal, someone will give you a plant to hold, but you shall not get any dance partners unless you ask."

"Oh, gracious!" Purity said. "Thank goodness, Lord Hollidge is an old friend and will forgive your forwardness, your condescension, and your rudeness, dear sister."

"She is only trying to assist," Lady Diamond defended her, and Clarity sent her mother a grateful smile.

"Truthfully, I am," she told Alex, "but I concede I let my tongue run off."

When his gaze dropped to her mouth, her insides fluttered.

"Would you like to dance with us?" she offered when still he didn't ask.

"Clarity," her sister warned her.

"I appreciate your kindness," Alex said stiffly, "and I don't wish to give insult, but I must decline. I see no point in partnering with either one of you."

She heard her mother heave a low groan at his awkwardness. One simply didn't say such a thing to a lady.

"I called upon you, and you know my intent," he explained, while all three of the Diamond females remained speechless and staring at him. "If I understand how this works," he echoed Clarity's words, "you want dance partners who might be potential husbands, men who will request to visit with you. Thus, I would hate to waste your time as well as my own."

"Your logic is beyond reproach," Purity said, although Clarity knew by her sister's tone she was displeased with his words.

Unable to help herself, Clarity explained further. "While I agree with my sister that you are logical, an assembly such as this one is not merely a marriage market. It serves to provide entertainment, a way to make merry and enjoy oneself," she finished.

He stared without blinking. The notion was lost on him.

Purity added, "While we shall not take offense since you have explained yourself, other ladies will not take such a pragmatic view."

Alex frowned. "How do you mean?"

Clarity jumped in again. "For instance, you might have deigned to dance with us because you enjoy our company, regardless of any future hope for matrimonial ties. Also, it is considered the duty of single guests."

She had said it as plainly as she could, trying to keep the disappointment out of her voice. Apparently, Alex could not look past his appointed task purely to have fun.

"Enjoy your evening, my lord," was all her mother had to say before ushering her girls away.

"Such a pity," Purity remarked as soon as they were out of his hearing.

"I cannot believe anyone could change so drastically," their mother said. "He used to be such a happy boy and always wanting to be in the mix, either having fun or making it for others."

Clarity knew that fact more than anyone, and her heart squeezed painfully to think of him standing alone with no better intent than to find a wife. Right then, she decided she would approach him again during the evening and at least offer some companionship.

For her own part, she enjoyed most of her partners that night. Besides Lord Brennon, she was being courted by Lord Horwood, a marquess's younger son, and he was charming, smiling, and attentive— everything Alex was not.

When she stood wearily with her sister and mother in the assembly's final minutes, she was ready to remove her dancing slippers and consider it an evening well spent. Lord Brennon, who had just completed his second dance with her, bowed over her hand and departed. The man was enthusiastically stepping up to be the favorite if she wanted to make a match that year, as she'd told Alex she intended to do.

That had been partly bravado, seeing as how he'd dismissed her out of hand as a potential wife. Truthfully, she was in no hurry unless her heart dictated otherwise. Moreover, if Purity found someone to love before she did, it wouldn't bother her in the least.

"Penny for your thoughts," her sister said.

"Not worth the cost," Clarity insisted.

"As long as you are thinking of that dashing Lord Brennon and not musing upon Lord Hollidge."

Her sister knew her so well.

"Tell me who you liked this evening?" she asked Purity, sidestepping any focus on Alex.

"Yes," their mother said. "Did some lucky buck catch your eye?"

"I had some good partners," Purity allowed, "but I didn't feel any instant tingling as you once said you did with father."

Her mother blushed prettily. "Did I say that?"

"You did," Clarity agreed. "On your last anniversary when we'd all had too much spirits, I recall. You and father danced around the drawing room without any music."

"And the dance ended with a kiss that night, as it did the night you met," Purity added.

"Naughty girls," Lady Diamond said, but she was beaming. "It would be lovely if you each experienced some wonderful surge of feeling upon meeting your future husband for the first time."

Then she laughed. "Of course, your father and I didn't simply fall in love and stroll blissfully to the church, either. We had a few matters to work out."

"Tell us in the carriage," Clarity said. "I can't stand on my feet one more—"

She interrupted herself as she realized she was staring at Alex, deep in conversation with Miss Brambury. Somehow, maybe by the tilt of his head or the way he was focusing on the lovely young lady, she knew the viscount's daughter was the one to whom he'd referred. She was his idea of a suitable wife.

Clarity had spoken to Emmeline Brambury a few times, once while waiting in the antechamber at St. James's Palace for their turn to be presented to the queen. After that, she'd come across her at a dinner solely for single ladies. Clarity could think of nothing against Miss Brambury. She'd been polite and was intelligent, a little reserved but not in a shy way.

In fact, she'd been as proper as Purity in attending to all the niceties of each interaction. In short, the perfect wife for a man who didn't want gales of laughter ringing through his house or even the slightest hint of indecorous behavior.

"Are you well?" her mother asked. "I daresay you are tired. You've gone pale. We don't have to wait until the bitter end. Let's go pay our respects to the hosts and call for our carriage."

"Yes," Clarity agreed, tearing her gaze from the couple and following her mother and sister out of the ballroom.

Chapter Eight

It was no surprise that Alex's name was linked to Miss Brambury's in the following weeks, since he was partnered with her at dinner parties and dancing twice at each ball. Not that Clarity was taking any notice, too busy enjoying being pursued by Lords Horwood and Brennon.

The former was dark-haired and devil-may-care with a saucy tongue, always able to make her laugh. The latter had a shock of blond hair, which he managed to keep smooth, light-blue laughing eyes, and usually a warm smile upon his face when looking at her.

When she danced with either, she felt content. Lord Brennon often stood with her and her family to chat between dances until he had to rush off to partner another young lady. One morning, she realized Lord Horwood had slipped into the social distance as had Lord Mansfield and her other suitors. Her name was as firmly linked with Lord Brennon's as Alex's was with the viscount's daughter. She didn't suppress her melancholy sigh.

"What's wrong?" Purity asked as they rode together through Hyde Park in their father's phaeton with Adam trotting beside on his favorite mount.

"Is it me, or have we done all one can possibly do during a Season and are now doing it twice?"

"You're bored," her sister declared. "Yet you are at nearly every event with Lord Brennon at your side. Doesn't his scintillating company keep you interested? After all, if you marry him, he will be with you each day for the rest of your life."

Clarity nearly gasped, feeling a moment of sheer terror. *Why did her sister's words worry her?* After all, there was nothing wrong with Lord Brennon. In fact, she always looked forward to seeing him and felt a distinct fondness for the gentleman.

Taking a deep breath, she considered looking across the breakfast table and the dining room table, seeing him every day and evening before sleeping beside him each night.

Would they have a relationship like her parents?

When she spied Alex on horseback with Miss Brambury beside him coming toward them, her heart sank. With certainty, Clarity knew if she could choose anyone, he would be the one. Naturally, she and Lord Brennon had shared a kiss or two over the past few weeks. Although full on the lips, they seemed chaste in comparison to the conflagration that had flared with Alex's mouth upon hers.

Undoubtedly, together, she and Alex would have had an interesting life if he'd been the person she used to know. This man who glanced at her and her siblings in turn, merely tipping his hat with his gloved hand, while Miss Brambury nodded as if she were already his viscountess, this Alex would not suit Clarity at all.

And then the couple had passed with the lady's chaperone following behind on a gentle mare.

Purity clucked in disapproval.

"What's wrong?" Clarity asked.

"Lord Hollidge was impolite if you ask me."

Clarity frowned while her brother chuckled.

"Nonsense," Adam said. "Hollidge could hardly stop and make conversation with the two of you while riding with Miss Brambury. It would be rude to the lady."

"How so?" Purity asked.

"You may be my sisters," Adam began, "but even I can see the difference between your looks and hers. She's not ugly, by any means, but she's not a Diamond of the first water." He laughed at his own joke.

Clarity ignored him. Her brother enjoyed that silly jest whenever he could, but it had long since stopped getting a rise out of her. However, Purity gainsaid him.

"Brother dear, that is all nonsense. I am not talking about our appearance, although Miss Brambury is what I would call coolly attractive without a spark of fire. But that's neither here nor there. My objection to Lord Hollidge's behavior is only that having known our family as long as he has, he should have paused and asked after our health."

Then she made a *tsking* sound and added, "What is this world coming to?" before calling out, "Good day, Lord Fenwick," as an old family friend of their father came toward them.

"Good day. Two Diamonds of the first water," he said.

Clarity cringed. If they had a penny for every time they'd heard that supposedly clever remark from someone who was not their brother, they would be rich as Croesus.

"How are you this lovely afternoon?" Lord Fenwick continued. "And you, Diamond, looking the spit and image of your sire."

"We are all well, thank you," Clarity responded. "And you, my lord?"

"Well, thank you. Tell your father I will see him at the club." Then he tipped his hat and was on his way.

"You see," Purity began. "That is how polite society passes."

Adam chuckled again. "Do you wish to hear that phrase from every acquaintance we pass?"

"No," Clarity said before her sister could. "It would drive me mad."

Purity sniffed. "That's not the point. Lord Hollidge was rude." She dug her elbow into Clarity's side. "I told you to help him behave better in public, but you refused."

How dare Purity admonish her. "You are the one who told him he wouldn't find a wife with his current churlish manners and too-serious attitude," Clarity pointed out. "And yet he has found one."

"I don't believe I said all that," Purity countered. "You must have said some of those things to him, for I never did."

They nearly fell to bickering.

Adam whistled, and they stopped at once.

"That infernal noise," Purity scolded Adam. "Must you?"

"The point is Hollidge *did* find a woman, without either of you busybodies interfering," their brother pointed out. "Everyone believes he shall ask for her hand before autumn."

Clarity knew it for the truth but didn't like hearing it.

"As predicted," she said softly. "He has found a wife who won't be much fun, but at least there is no concern she wants him for his money or his title."

Purity nodded. "Let's forget about him, shall we? I believe I see your own beloved approaching."

For a moment, Clarity couldn't think about whom her sister was speaking, and then Lord Brennon came into view.

And the greetings started all over again. But try as she might, Clarity couldn't get out of her head the fanciful idea that she would much prefer riding beside Alex, even the somber man who had replaced her old friend.

The heat became unbearable with nary a breeze in London. Ladies had their fans out at all times, trying to move the stagnant air. Some were even seen in public with fewer petticoats than usually acceptable, their gowns hanging limply against their legs. Most refused any lightweight jacket or even a shawl, leaving their arms bare, no matter the time of day.

Alex was amazed at the laxity but appreciative of seeing so much female flesh.

When he caught sight of Clarity at a charity ball at Chiswick House, west of Town, his mouth fell open. She had on a wisp of sheer lace across her sleeveless deep orange satin bodice and a matching skirt of the finest, thin silk. Every man was gawking at her beauty, enhanced as it was by her dark sable hair.

For a moment, he, too, had to stare. *How could she possibly be the same female who hadn't cared a damn about getting dirty?*

"Shameless," Miss Brambury declared, seeing where his gaze had fallen.

Alex remained silent, escorting her to the other end of the room where the doors were open to the garden. He had tried not to think of Clarity outside in a garden, especially not with Brennon, who was obviously going to be announced as her intended any day.

Although Alex had not yet kissed Miss Brambury, not feeling compelled to and content to wait until their wedding day, he instinctively knew how it would be. And he was resigned to it. She wasn't a passionate person by nature, and he could accept that in exchange for a good partner.

Somehow, she was wearing dark satin with sleeves coming to just above her elbows and a high thick lace décolletage that allowed for no peeking at the tops of her breasts. She was fanning herself constantly, and he knew she had on every proper layer, both necessary and unnecessary, despite no one being able to tell.

Glancing back at Clarity, he thought her like an exotic bird. She was waving around her matching orange fan as she spoke animatedly to those in her party. She didn't look overheated in the least, despite all the men around her being hot with desire.

Including him.

Alex, who wore the lightest-weight neckcloth and the thinnest wool jacket over his fine lawn shirt, was pleased to see the ball's manager directing all the windows to be opened to alleviate the stuffy atmosphere.

After they partook of lemonade and greeted some of Miss Brambury's close acquaintances, they moved toward the back of the house and away from the increasingly crowded ballroom.

"Let's go outside," Miss Brambury suggested. "Until the night air manages to permeate the interior," she added.

Since her chaperone was a mere two steps behind, he agreed, hoping the garden would provide a modicum of coolness. Moreover, since they were easily six miles from Mayfair and London's many chimneys, the air was lacking the usual soot and smoke.

"Better?" Alex asked as they stepped onto a spacious stone veranda, beyond which were the Italian gardens, extensive pathways, and even the estate's own lake.

Behind them, many others were exiting Chiswick House as well. Soon, there were nearly as many guests outside as in, everyone glad the gathering wasn't at a stuffy four-story townhouse in Piccadilly but a large mansion with acreage upon which to roam.

While dozens of lanterns dotted the landscape, they were insufficient to keep from leaving pockets of darkness to which some guests now hurried.

"Shall we stroll down to the lake?" Miss Brambury asked, looking toward the brightest lit path.

Together, they trod upon on a straight path through two rows of cedar trees. Then at a fork, they chose the way toward the canal-shaped lake and away from the wild Italianate gardens. At the end of the path was an arched, white stone bridge over the narrow arm of the lake.

Alex supposed it would be romantic, maybe even an opportunity to finally kiss Miss Brambury if they weren't being dogged by her devoted chaperone.

In any case, they didn't continue over the bridge as there was no other crossing by which to return. Halfway over, they turned and walked back by way of a bending, snake-like route, taking them alongside a hedgerow maze.

"It would be madness to enter at this time of night," he remarked.

"Yes, absolute lunacy," Miss Brambury agreed.

All at once, he heard Clarity's unmistakable voice cut loudly through the darkness and froze.

Since he still had Miss Brambury's hand clasped on his arm, she stumbled when he stopped short.

"What is it?" she demanded.

"Perhaps nothing," he said. But then he heard Clarity again and would swear she sounded in distress.

He lowered his arm, forcing Miss Brambury to release him.

"Will you excuse me?" he asked. "I suggest you and your chaperone return to the house." With that, he dove through the opening into the labyrinth.

As a child, Alex had liked mazes tremendously, having visited the large one at Hampton Court with his parents. He'd enjoyed the thrilling yet frightening feeling of being lost in the center of it. Eventually, his father had found him, and they'd gone for tea and cakes. Alex had begged to go back more than once.

All around him was quiet, muffled by the thick hedges. Another outburst of voices nearby made him halt, listening for Clarity's distinct tone. Then the sounds dimmed again as the other guests moved on, following a narrow path directly beside his, yet separate. At least he no longer feared Clarity had done something foolish like entering the maze alone, for there were most certainly others testing their abilities.

After a few minutes, Alex realized he was lost, but then he supposed they all were. That was the nature of a maze. Moreover at night, the disorientation and difficulty were multiplied.

Then he heard a shriek, which he would swear was her voice, and his heart began to race. *Or was she laughing?*

"Clarity?" he called out before thinking how he ought to use her title.

If she were in trouble, he wanted her to know he was nearby.

Chapter Nine

Alex's inquiry was met by silence. If she was in the maze, perhaps with Brennon or a group, they had moved on, and he was a fool. Another few minutes passed with Alex taking twists and turns, beginning to regret his rash decision.

Finally, he used his wits and looked up. He would keep an eye on the stars visible here as they often weren't in London. At least, he would know if he was going in circles.

To that end, he walked steadily in the direction of the mansion, noting the stars' placement, and figuring there would be an opening facing the back door of Chiswick House.

Around a corner at a run, someone crashed into him, someone warm and soft and definitely familiar.

Grabbing her upper arms, he held her at a distance.

"Alex!" she exclaimed before he could say anything.

"How did you know?" he asked, not letting go.

"Because you smell and feel like Alex, of course."

He couldn't argue with that, for she smelled and felt like Clarity. He hugged her tightly.

"Were you lost?" he asked.

"Indeed, I was. Isn't it great fun?"

He did think so, now that he'd found her or vice versa. In either case, he didn't want to confess to such a thought because it was incredibly childish.

"I am trying to navigate by the stars to find my way out," he informed her.

"That's genius," she said. "Then I shall join you."

Neither of them moved.

"Are you alone in the maze?" he asked, feeling her heart pounding as rapidly as his own.

"I wasn't," she said, "but I seem to have lost my party a few turns back." Her hands had crept up his jacket to rest upon his shoulders.

"Did you scream earlier?" He settled his own hands behind her, resting his fingers against the smooth silk at the small of her back.

"I admit I did," she said, pressing her breasts against him. "Lord Brennon tapped my shoulder and frightened me."

At the mention of Brennon, he knew he ought to release her. Instead, in the otherworldly solitude of the hedgerow maze, Alex leaned down and claimed her lips.

They didn't bump noses in the dark, nor did he kiss her cheek by mistake. As if they were entirely of a single mind, his mouth easily found hers.

Tilting his head, their kiss deepened, and a fiery longing raced through him like a flickering flame.

She made a strange, sweet sound, which he answered with a groan. Clarity was his siren, his weakness, despite an unwavering certainty that she was not suitable to be his viscountess. At that moment, he couldn't remember why.

Unthinkingly, he slipped his tongue between her warm lips and stroked hers. How long they stood that way with the scent of nearby lilacs wafting over them, Alex didn't know nor care until he heard voices.

"Try this way," said a distinctly frustrated male.

"I'm sure we went that way already," complained a female.

Another added, "I'm tired. I want to go back indoors."

"We're trying," said the first.

"Not without Lady Clarity," said the man, whom Alex knew to be Brennon.

Reluctantly, Alex released her before taking hold of her hand and starting to walk again.

"She is over here," he called out. "We are heading toward the house."

The voices all spoke at once.

"How?"

"Where?"

"Lady Clarity?"

"I'm here," she called out. "In the next row and going north."

"Southeast," Alex muttered, determined to get out quickly. Miss Brambury was undoubtedly concerned and annoyed.

"Southeast," Clarity called out again before laughing. "Follow the stars," she added to her friends.

As Alex suspected, when they reached the section closest to the house, there was an opening. Still, he was trapped alone with her since he couldn't leave her by herself to wait for the others, nor would it be seemly for them to re-enter the ballroom without a chaperone unless they were in a group.

"I never did find the fountain in the middle," Clarity bemoaned as they waited for the others to catch up.

"I wasn't aware there was one," Alex said.

"Oh yes," she said. "It's supposed to be rather sinful." Then she paused. "Why were you in the maze if you weren't looking for the fountain? And where is Miss Brambury?" she asked as if she'd just noticed his lady-friend's absence.

Strange how she'd kissed him back, not wondering about Emmeline at the time.

"I came into the maze because I thought you were in some distress. And I assume Miss Brambury is safely inside where you ought to be."

"Oh, Alex," she said, taking a step closer causing him to back away. "That was heroic of you. Thank you."

"There you are," Brennon boomed as soon as he exited the maze, with two ladies trailing him.

Once he got close enough to see Alex, the man halted.

"Hollidge! I didn't see you there."

"Alex rescued me," Clarity declared.

He winced at the intimate use of his first name. *Why did she persist in such impropriety?* He tried to pull farther away.

"Did you know the duke had seven hundred guests, as well as giraffes, right here in his own park two years ago?" she asked, switching topics seemingly to keep him engaged.

"I was not aware," he said.

"Oh, yes! Our famous 'bachelor duke' threw a party for Tsar Nicholas of Russia. I would have loved to see the giraffes."

He would have loved to see her seeing those giraffes, came Alex's improper thought. She would have marveled at them and been a delightful companion.

He caught himself. The past was entirely unimportant, as were the duke's giraffes. They were here tonight, and she was not his to make moon eyes over.

"I entrust Lady Clarity to you," he said woodenly to Brennon.

With that, Alex turned on his heel and went in search of the woman he hoped would still accept his offer.

———— ✳ ————

Clarity didn't think her emotions could become any more confused than they were that night. After the labyrinth, she watched Alex dance with Miss Brambury and wondered how he could continue as if nothing of import had happened.

Their second kiss had been as magnificent as their first. And while she was still content to partner with Lord Brennon for the next waltz, if Alex walked across the parquet and held out his hand to her in front of everyone, she would take it. She would go with him to wherever he wished, for a lifetime if he asked, leaving behind all she knew.

Except her family! No, never that.

Apart from the rest of the Diamonds, however, she could easily imagine slipping out of her current life to run away with Alex. Or to stay right there in London. Or to go to Belfinch Hall, his country estate in Suffolk. As long as she was with him, she wouldn't care.

At the same time, she was engaging in light prattle with Lord Brennon. How could she still dance two and even three times with him, enjoy his company, go riding with him, and let the man row her upon the Thames?

Was she a selfish person for prolonging their friendship?

Sipping the champagne he had brought her and Purity, Clarity tried to sort out how she could be clearly of two minds.

Yet more and more, she knew herself to be of only one heart—and it belonged to Alex.

As she lay awake that night, tortured at the thought of losing Alex to Emmeline Brambury, dreading the morning when she awakened to read their engagement in the newspapers, she finally sat upright in bed. A clear plan of action had come to her.

She would call upon him. A plain-speaking conversation would solve everything. Rehearsing her words a few times, she finally settled down again and fell asleep.

Early the following day, Clarity alighted from her carriage with her lady's maid in front of Alex's door on Grosvenor Square. Nodding for Winnie to use the knocker, they waited. In a short while, she'd given Alex's butler her card and been shown into the drawing room.

However, when the door opened again, it was Lady Aston who appeared and not her nephew. Clarity had to stifle a gasp at the fear and nervousness that overtook her.

Ninny! she scolded herself. You are a grown woman, not a naughty child, but why had she all but forgotten that his sour-faced aunt lived there?

A tad above average in height with gray-streaked brown hair swept up in a tight chignon, Lady Aston swept her pale green gaze over Clarity before hollowing her cheeks and pursing her lips. Her expression spoke volumes.

"Good day," Clarity said, finding her voice.

"Lady Clarity," the woman greeted her. "How you've grown and blossomed."

"Thank you," she said, thinking that was a good start. She wished she could return the compliment, but Lady Aston had hardly changed apart from appearing even sterner.

"Please, have a seat. Will you take tea?"

Clarity's stomach was pinching with nerves, and she wasn't sure she should *or could* drink anything. Nevertheless, not accepting would be rude. Perhaps Alex had sent his aunt to entertain her while he combed his hair. All she had to do was get through a few minutes.

"Tea would be lovely. I thank you." She sat on the ancient sofa, nodding to Winnie to take a chair at the other end of the room as Alex's aunt took a seat and plainly did not ring for tea service. Perhaps she'd already ordered it before she'd entered the room.

"What brings you to our home?" his aunt asked.

Clarity gaped before snapping her mouth closed. Since she'd told the butler she wished to speak with Lord Hollidge, it was highly discourteous to be asked her intent by Lady Aston.

"I am here to speak with your nephew."

His aunt's nostrils flared slightly. "Yes, I understand that. But why?"

Clarity's heartbeat sped up, and she wished she'd sent him a private letter instead. Perhaps she ought to tell the busybody how after two breath-stealing kisses, she wanted to ask Alex if he would like to try for a third.

She took a deep breath, hardly able to believe what she was about to say.

"I don't think it is any of your business." Clarity managed to keep her tone even, despite quaking inside.

His aunt nodded. "Then I fear my suspicions are correct. Now that my nephew has found a suitable wife, you want to shove a cane into his carriage wheel."

What a terrible accusation! As if Clarity had come to interfere with the smooth path of Alex's courtship of Miss Brambury. Although, without a doubt, she had.

"I can see by your expression I have hit the nail on its head with my first guess," his aunt said smugly. "And I must tell you, Lady Clarity, your efforts shall lead to fiddlestick's end."

"Is Alex here?" Clarity asked boldly.

"*Alex!* How dare you?" Lady Aston said, finally showing the irritation behind her calm, cool demeanor. "Lord Hollidge is not at home."

"To me, or to anyone?" Clarity asked.

"You were a troublesome little girl," his aunt said, ignoring her question. "Honestly, I had hoped you would have matured enough to be the Viscountess Hollidge. Believe me or not, it's the truth. Nevertheless, my nephew saw how you have stubbornly maintained a nature of untamed immaturity. Thus, he tried to court your sister, but she apparently doesn't have the taste to know a good man when she sees one. And therefore, he has moved on."

Clarity didn't think it the time to defend herself, but she would always stand up for her family.

"Lady Purity is allowed to choose whomsoever she pleases. There is not a person in London who doesn't agree my sister is a discerning lady. She could not help but notice that *Alex*," and Clarity said his name with robust emphasis, "grew up to be just like you, a hum-drum old lady without an ounce of the jolly dog."

"Lady Clarity!" This came from Alex who had entered unnoticed. "You owe my aunt an apology."

She rose to her feet, trembling with anger. *Had he been at home all along and ignored her calling card or, worse, sent his aunt in his place?*

"I owe her nothing," she vowed, wondering at her own reprehensible breach of decorum and civility. As an earl's daughter, she had been raised better than she'd behaved. But now, having failed at her task and Alex angry with her, she couldn't seem to pull back onto the path of polite discourse.

"I bet there wasn't even any tea ordered," she said, plainly confounding him by the expression upon his devilishly handsome face.

His green eyes glittered. "Tea?" He looked toward his aunt. "You didn't tell me Lady Clarity had been invited to tea."

"Because she hadn't been," his aunt said, rising slowly to her feet.

Clarity waited for Lady Aston to humiliate her and tell Alex how she had come practically begging to speak with him.

"But the young lady is not at fault," his aunt continued as the maid brought in tea service, making Clarity feel rather small for having doubted its existence.

"I owe her an apology," Lady Aston continued. "I inadvertently said something unkind about Lady Purity and set off her quick temper."

About to protest that she didn't have a quick temper, Clarity realized what a back-handed apology Lady Aston had delivered. His aunt had won the field, gaining her nephew's sympathy and making Clarity appear unhinged.

"I spoke out of turn," Clarity said, wishing she had never come. But the only apology she could come up with was a thin one. "Apparently, there *was* tea being offered, and I am sorry I doubted you. However, I am no longer thirsty. I wish you both good day."

She hoped she'd ended in a civil enough manner even Purity would approve. Nodding to Winnie, who was already on her feet, Clarity couldn't even look at Alex as she strode past him.

What a disaster!

"Lady Clarity," his voice followed her into the entrance hall.

She didn't stop. Luckily, the butler was there to yank open the door and save her doing it herself.

When she reached the narrow pavement in front of the granite-block street that encircled the square's green center, he was directly behind her.

"Clarity, please wait. What is this about?"

Unacceptably, tears pricked her eyes, but she was determined not to let a single one fall. To distract herself, she spoke to Winnie.

"You may climb into the carriage. I'll join you in a moment." She watched her maid disappear inside the enclosed carriage with the Diamond coat of arms emblazoned on its side. Then, having gathered her emotions, she finally looked at him.

"I made a mistake in coming." Then she realized there was nothing more to say.

Alex ran a hand through his hair, messing it up for the first time since she'd seen him as an adult.

"I should have contacted you," he said, surprising her into silence. "After... after what happened in the maze, you deserved a missive at the very least containing my sincere apology."

He was sorry for kissing her? She had not expected that, nor did it sit well. She had no regrets at all, and it stung to find out he was sorry it had happened.

"I would have expected your father here to demand an apology, not you. Or maybe to blister my hide and force us into marriage."

He said the words as if it would be a punishment to marry her. This was worse than his aunt's censure.

"I should have known the intrepid and outrageous Clarity Diamond would come and demand my contrition herself."

Intrepid, outrageous, and unsuitable. "I accept your apology," she said, her voice little more than a whisper.

She even let him touch her hand and help her into her carriage without the least show of emotion. And as they rode home, Winnie was smart enough to keep her eyes averted as Clarity finally let her tears fall.

Chapter Ten

A country party in late July to escape the heat of London was ideal. The Diamonds all felt cooler as soon as they left Town from the Euston Grove station. Breathing a sigh of relief as they got under way, Clarity relaxed in their first-class carriage, fashioned with mauve velvet seats and the darkest, polished wood. The only inconvenience was the noise of the train itself.

In quick succession, they crossed the elegant iron bowstring suspension bridge over the Regent's Canal and found themselves in the modern wonder of a 1,120-yard-long tunnel through Primrose Hill.

After coming out the other side and after passing through the much shorter tunnel at Kensal Green, they were truly on their way, leaving the outskirts of London and the bells of Westminster behind.

Clarity was more pleased than any of them to get away from the bustle of the Season, now grown tedious. While her second kiss with Alex at Chiswick House had made her knees buckle, causing her to want more from him, their interaction both inside and outside his home had made it abundantly clear that was not to be.

And then in case she didn't clearly understand his position, Alex had sent her a brief note on the thickest writing paper, which like a fool she'd sniffed to see if it held his cologne. It didn't. It was not a *billet-doux* after all, but further apology for his "lunatic actions at the labyrinth," as he called their delectable kiss.

On the other hand, he had suggested they try to return to their old footing as friends, which he said he valued. That was something, at least. She'd tried folding the missive into a heart shape, but it looked like a potato, and she put it in the bottom drawer of her wardrobe.

Clarity tried to relegate Alex into a small, bottom drawer of her heart, too.

Sadly, Lord Brennon seemed more tepid and wanner than before, although she knew it wasn't his fault. He was still the best choice of the gentlemen who remained on the field of suitors. And she knew she didn't have to marry him. She could wait and see if someone else caught her fancy, while simultaneously fearing Alex had ruined her for loving any other.

The warring emotions inside her, as well as the sticky late-July temperatures, had left her vexed. Leaning back upon the lace-clad headrest, with her closed eyes, she listened to her family chat.

"A fortnight is a perfect amount of time," Purity said. "And four days is the exact recommended length of a stay for guests."

"A single night is too long to have most guests," their father grumbled, but he was always a welcoming host and enjoyed playing cards with the men whom his wife invited to their house.

"Purity is correct," her mother agreed. "People have a chance to lose the stress of the journey, forget their worries from Town, and get excited for the ball. And then they're ready to return home directly after."

"How many?" Lord Diamond asked.

"From London?" Lady Diamond clarified, because unquestionably there would be locals coming to the dance at week's end. "Three couples. No, four, come to think of it. And enough singles to match up and dance with our daughters. Adam, your friend from school is coming, isn't he?"

Adam nodded.

"Lord Brennon accepted, of course," her mother continued, seemingly ticking off a list in her head.

Clarity startled, ignoring Purity's questioning expression, and raised an eyebrow. Logically, the man they all thought she would marry had been invited, but Clarity would have enjoyed time away from him in order to better understand her emotions.

Before Purity could ask if aught was wrong, Ray sighed loudly.

"I suppose Bri and I are supposed to stay in our rooms."

"Don't be silly. You will attend the evening amusements, Thursday and Friday and the ball on Saturday, but you shall not dance." This from Purity, whose bossiness sprang from her love of order.

"Is she right, Mother?" Ray asked.

Their lovely red-headed matriarch turned to her only red-headed daughter.

"It's for the best, dear one. You'll have your turn."

"When you have officially come out!" Purity added.

Clarity hid a smile. Her sister would make an excellent mother one day, or a soldier in the Queen's army!

"Also, because of his re-entrance into society recently, I invited Lord Hollidge," Lady Diamond said, looking now at her eldest daughter. "I thought it was the least I could do for my dear friend. His mother would enjoy knowing we'd renewed our connection and her son was once more at Oak Grove, which the Hollidges adored."

Momentarily speechless, Clarity finally found her voice.

"My understanding is he is not single. If not already engaged, then expected to be shortly. I would imagine a house party with single women without his intended would not be acceptable."

Certainly not in the eyes of his aunt!

"I don't know about that," her mother said. "I extended the invitation to Lady Aston, too." Her voice trailed off, sounding subdued.

An almost palpable quelling of any future amusement settled over the large family in the luxurious train car.

"I am ready for a cup of freshly brewed tea," Purity said, knowing she could not have one.

"I'm ready for a glass of brandy," her father quipped.

Their brother, who until then had been silently looking out the window on the other side of the train carriage, reached into his pocket and handed his father a silver flask.

"Bless you," Lord Diamond quipped.

"Really!" their mother said. "Do you condone our son carrying brandy upon his person?"

"Of course I do," their father said. "As long as it's not gin, what's the harm? Besides, I have more if his supply runs out." With that, he took a long sip and returned the flagon to his son.

While Clarity was enjoying the odd sensation of a blurred landscape going by, thinking as she always did how marvelous train travel was, her sister made a *tsking* sound that was quintessential Purity.

"I vow I saw another cloud of smoke and ash float past with cinders the size of walnuts," Purity said. "It will go right into the open sides of third class. Is this train run by savages or civilized people?"

None of them could help laughing at their proper Purity.

"Mother, did you bring sandwiches and lemonade?" asked Ray.

"Indeed I did, and Cook packed cold tea and cake, too."

"Cold tea," Purity spat out the words with palpable distaste. "I would rather not, thank you."

"I swear you are the oldest nineteen-year-old alive," Clarity declared, "and I love you for it."

Purity crossed her arms and looked smugly superior.

Clarity closed her eyes again and considered her newly found interest in the gathering that began on Thursday. Her anticipation greatly lifted now she knew Alex would be there. However, a whisper of doubt floated into her brain. From what she knew of his recent behavior, taking off four days in the country seemed out of character.

"Mother, you said Alex had been invited. Did he accept?"

"Not in so many words, but his aunt did. And I believe she is his social manager until such time as he finds himself a wife."

Hm. It seemed strange that Lady Aston had agreed to be a part of the Diamonds' country party. Yet if Alex's aunt had accepted the invitation, there was no doubt he would appear.

After her family had settled in and were enjoying the routine of their country estate, it seemed far too soon when the guests began to arrive the following week. Doing their duty, Clarity as eldest daughter and

Adam as heir met each carriage along with their parents to welcome their guests. Few arrived in their own conveyance. Most were in the Diamonds' own country coach, which they sent between their home and the Derby Midland station.

Three trains each day branched off from the main London to Birmingham railway at Hampton in Arden, which sent them on a short ride into Derby. Between private carriages and the first two trains of the day, Clarity was constantly summoned to the front of the house, all the while still wondering whether Alex and his aunt would come.

Lord Brennon had already arrived, along with the majority of the party-goers, when the butler announced the coach had returned from the last train of the day.

Finally, as their carriage pulled up to the house and emptied its occupants, Clarity had her answer.

Alex descended first and nodded in the direction of his hosts before turning to assist his aunt. As soon as Lady Aston's shoes touched the gravel, she looked past the Diamonds toward the house, perhaps recalling the times she'd been there with her brother and his wife many years earlier.

Maybe she had unpleasant memories, Clarity thought, walking forward with her family. *Maybe she recalled her gown being worn by their old hunting dog.*

Then they all halted as Alex turned to assist another from the carriage. A fawn-colored traveling gown came into view and then the placid visage of Miss Emmeline Brambury.

Sweet Mary! Clarity wished she'd had warning. No one had mentioned this paragon of perfection coming to the party. Even though her own beau was currently inside in the drawing room, drinking some of her mother's famed citrus and rum punch and amusing the other guests, burning jealousy at seeing Alex's intended roared through Clarity, stunning her with its ferocity.

At last, the three new arrivals and the Diamonds offered an exchange of greetings. Alex appeared if not exactly grim, then solemn. Perhaps it was merely the long journey by train. More likely, it was being in the dreadfully dour company of both Lady Aston *and* the coolly reserved Miss Brambury.

Not nice, Clarity chastised herself, making eye contact with Alex and smiling in an attempt to cheer him up. He nodded toward her without warmth.

Thus, despite his presence, this had become the worst country party ever. She would be spending four days with one lady who had already told Clarity of her blatant disapproval and the other who had taken the man holding Clarity's heart. And Alex, himself, appeared as if he were at his own funeral.

After all proper salutations had been given and received, they went indoors as a group. With her parents leading, Clarity and her brother brought up the rear, giving her an excellent view of the moment Alex took Miss Brambury's arm, as the couple lagged behind his aunt.

While footmen hurried to bring in the trunks that had been deposited upon the drive, a maid escorted the latest arrivals upstairs. Less than ten minutes later, upon removing their coats and hats and changing their shoes, the newest guests returned to join those gathered in the drawing room.

Momentarily pinned by Purity's discerning gaze, Clarity knew she must remain. She would give a year of pin money to exchange places with either of her younger sisters at that moment. They were free of hosting duties and could disappear up to their rooms if they chose. Naturally, they wanted to remain in the thick of things, whereas if Clarity could, she would leave the drawing room and keep her own counsel until dinner.

As eldest daughter, she should be the one to make introductions while her parents were otherwise engaged with Lord and Lady Fenwick, the eldest couple at the gathering and long-time friends of her father's father. Regardless, while reeling from the surprise guest, Clarity eschewed her position and welcomed Purity taking Alex, his aunt, and Miss Brambury around the spacious drawing room to introduce them to the other guests.

Staying where she was beside Lord Brennon and another couple who were friends of her mother, Clarity couldn't help noticing Alex said very little, letting his aunt do most of the socializing while he took in his surroundings.

Was Oak Grove Hall still familiar to him? she wondered.

Finally, Purity led the three directly to her.

"I am glad you could come," Clarity said, despite having said a similar vacuous phrase outside on the gravel drive. Instead of asking anything remotely untoward, she stayed with the safe and the inane. "I hope your journey was smooth and uneventful."

"It was," Lady Aston replied. "Hopefully this evening, we shall be excused from the fullness of social duties usually expected of guests. We are exhausted by the trip."

With that, she turned away to locate a seat on the sofa.

Despite how Alex's aunt had spoken for all of them, both he and Miss Brambury remained, not appearing in the least exhausted nor inclined to sit.

"It was good of her to use up her energy on my behalf," the latter spoke. "Obviously, if she hadn't, I would not have been able to attend."

"Lady Aston is playing the part of your chaperone?" Clarity determined. "But *she* was an invited guest," she added, leaving it hanging in the air that Emmeline was not.

Silence met her rudeness, as well it should. Clarity had erred egregiously. She could only be glad Purity hadn't overheard her.

Lord Brennon cleared his throat while Alex visibly clenched his jaw. It was up to Clarity to smooth it over.

"And we are fortunate Lady Aston had the foresight to know you would be welcome as Al... as Lord Hollidge's friend," she concluded, hoping that sounded genuine.

"Thank you," Miss Brambury murmured, her cheeks a little pink. She lifted her chin slightly and turned away.

Clarity gave Alex an apologetic half-smile, which he returned with a disapproving shake of his head before following his lady love.

Lord Brennon leaned down and whispered, "Don't fret, Lady Clarity. It is the height of discourtesy for Lady Aston to have brought an extra guest, and Hollidge knows it. He should have put his foot down back in London."

He should have, she agreed silently, *but he hadn't. He must really love Emmeline Brambury.*

Chapter Eleven

Clarity stayed well away from the three of them for the remainder of the reception, noting when Purity took them to exercise their legs by offering a tour of the house. Other guests joined the little group.

Alex could probably have been the guide if he'd desired, having at one time been over every square foot of Oak Grove Hall.

In any case, as soon as they were out of sight, all Clarity could think about was when they would return. Thus, with barely half her attention fixed upon the newlywed couple, the Baron and Baroness Marston with whom she was conversing, and the other half upon the open drawing-room door, she noticed the instant Alex returned. He was alone.

"You are correct about that," Clarity said to Lady Marston. "Our dinner has been delayed due to the lateness of the last train. I shall go determine the situation."

With that, she left the couple and intercepted Alex.

"Welcome again, *my lord*."

He made a wry face at her sarcastic greeting, and she rushed into her apology that really ought to have been given to Miss Brambury.

"I apologize for earlier. I was not at all gracious."

"Duly noted," he said. "Having Miss Brambury thrust upon your family was a surprise to you, I take it."

Clarity waved his words away, hoping she appeared unbothered. Besides, she didn't want to speak about Emmeline anymore. Alex was there for the first time since they were children. It was rather momentous.

"Can you believe we are now invited to the main table," she asked, "instead of being fed early and told to stay out of sight?"

Alex frowned. "Is that why we used to eat *before* the main seating?"

She laughed, reaching out and touching his arm. "Of course. My parents and yours couldn't risk you bringing another stray Tom indoors as the centerpiece."

He was staring at her strangely.

"What is it?" She thought about her day, recalling the sandwiches she'd eaten with her siblings. "Dear God! Do I have a piece of watercress in my teeth?"

"What?" He shook his head as if to lift the cobwebs. "No! You simply laughed, and it was lovely."

Her heart ached. Clarity would vow there had been little laughter during his journey.

"I hope we shall share some amusing times over the next four days," she said.

He looked far too somber when he nodded in agreement.

"Where are your traveling companions?" she asked, albeit reluctant to bring them up. She could only hope Purity had sent them away for an infraction of civility.

He shrugged. "Your sister has taken them to the conservatory. I felt strange being shown around by someone who used to be eating pap and watery gruel while I was already riding horses and shooting arrows, so I begged off."

"Understandable," Clarity agreed, unable to stop staring at his firm lips, recalling the pleasurable heat that sizzled through her when his mouth pressed against hers. He would know of her feelings if she wasn't careful, and she couldn't bear the idea of him apologizing again for leading her on with a kiss.

"Lady Clarity," he said.

"Yes." How she longed to see his single dimple again when he smiled.

"Lady Clarity," he repeated.

"Yes, Alex," she said, lifting her gaze to his emerald eyes.

He frowned. "You mustn't call me that. And I asked you a question," he said.

"Did you?" She hadn't heard him, but she had seen those perfect lips moving. "What was it?"

"I asked what is first on the itinerary?"

She could think of far better things he might have asked her, such as "May I have your hand in marriage?" or "May I kiss you again?" or even "Would you help me toss Miss Brambury into the river?"

"My parents are the best of hosts," she said. "This will not be a party packed with endless activities, like a Michaelmas goose overly crammed with stuffing."

"A stuffed goose?" Alex *nearly* cracked a smile.

"I only meant tonight between dinner and supper. You may do absolutely nothing if you wish. Would you care for a beverage, by the way?"

"What are you having?" he asked, his green eyes dancing over her.

She would swear he looked as if he were relaxing already.

"Nothing as yet since I have to keep making trips outside to greet guests, but I recommend a glass of Father's splendid port."

"That's sounds perfect. As for doing nothing, I expect I will do whatever my aunt and Miss Brambury wish me to do for the next four days."

"Hen-pecked already?" Clarity asked before almost clamping her hand over her mouth and instantly wishing she could call back the words.

Alex merely raised an eyebrow, without looking too insulted on behalf of the women in his life.

"Sorry," she mumbled. "That wasn't a nice way for me to speak about your aunt and your... your friend." She couldn't get herself to say *fiancée*. It was too final. Quite possibly, after his marriage, she would never see him again.

Just then, her mother nodded in her direction. "I'm being summoned outside again. The last of the guests must be arriving. I will make sure you are brought some port on my way out. Our butler's name is Mr. Dun—"

"Dunley," Alex finished. "Still? He seemed ancient when I was a youth. I vow he wanted to tan my hide a few times."

"He has a superb memory and may still want to. Thus, I suggest you keep your backside against the wall."

His eyes widened, and she felt her cheeks heat. Clarity could well imagine what Purity would say if her sister knew she'd been discussing a gentleman's backside.

What was wrong with her, especially around Alex?

With more a wince than a smile, she left him. Across the room, she asked Mr. Dunley to take a glass of port over to Lord Hollidge, and then she joined her family at the manor's entrance.

<hr />

His backside! Alex nearly laughed. Aunt Elizabeth would be appalled. Miss Brambury would wonder what type of household he had brought her to. In truth, he hadn't brought her at all. His aunt had insisted it would be good for him to experience Miss Brambury outside of London and in a different setting to better determine their compatibility.

It sounded like good advice until they arrived, and he could see the Diamonds had been unaware of the extra guest. He couldn't imagine why his aunt had behaved with such uncharacteristic impoliteness. But worse had been Clarity making mention of it.

Glancing around the elegant room, updated with a different paint color and new furnishings from when last he was there, it still had a welcoming familiarity. The only thing missing were his parents, enjoying the hospitality of the Diamonds.

Instantly, he felt sick to his stomach. Better they should be alive than him.

As he turned, thinking to retreat to his room until he could collect himself, his aunt appeared and with her, Miss Brambury.

Despite him not having personally asked her to accompany them, Emmeline had acted during the journey as if he had already proposed. Not that she had behaved in too familiar a manner, nor was she emotional or forward, but she'd had a calm certainty about her while discussing the latest interior fashion for his London home. Moreover, she had asked him pointed questions about his country estate.

Clearly, she was picturing herself in both settings.

Sighing, he moved to greet them as Mr. Dunley brought his drink on a silver tray, along with drinks for some of the other guests.

"May I bring you a refreshment, my ladies?" the aging butler asked.

"Tea is perfect for this time of day," his aunt declared while looking around to see what others might be imbibing. Then her gaze fastened on Alex's tawny plum-colored drink.

"Lady Clarity said it was very good," he told her, wishing he hadn't felt the need to defend himself like a child.

"How polite of you to go along with her suggestion," Miss Brambury praised. "It's always the best practice not to begin by insulting the host or the host's family, especially Lady Clarity who is erratic in her manners."

"A sensible statement," Aunt Elizabeth pronounced. "Still, I shall have tea," she told the butler who waited patiently.

"I shall as well," Miss Brambury said.

Alex thought Mr. Dunley was probably thrilled to be released. He undoubtedly had a hundred and one things to do, and hearing a discourse on manners or tea was not one of them.

"We're standing in an awkward spot," his aunt said. "Let's clear the entrance." She ushered them to a place near the hearth.

Alex sipped the port, closing his eyes a second as the fruity wine slid down his throat. And then he heard her laughter again. His eyes snapped open as Clarity entered with her arm linked through another woman's. For a second, he saw the lively girl who'd been his playmate and his friend, eyes sparkling, laughter bubbling easily from her lips.

Then she transformed before his eyes to the stunning woman he'd first seen at Devonshire House. Her hair was dressed into a soft chignon with curls hanging down behind her. A ribbon of blue to match her gown was threaded through her dark tresses like a silken coronet. She was breathtaking.

"Don't you?" Miss Brambury asked.

Egad! Fortunately, he was saved from answering a question he hadn't properly heard by a maid appearing with a tea tray. She set it upon the long table behind the sofa. The young woman poured and handed his aunt and Miss Brambury each a cup.

"It was an interesting tour. You missed the end of it," the latter said.

He didn't point out to Emmeline that he knew every inch of the house and every furlong of land around the house down to the river.

"I'm looking forward to seeing the grounds tomorrow," she said.

"I shall be happy to show you them myself," he told her, appreciating that she showed an interest. That was a good sign. She was not a retiring violet who had to remain indoors.

Emmeline nodded her agreement to this plan, but his aunt coughed and shook her head.

"I cannot show you around. Not without a chaperone. What was I thinking?"

Adam Diamond appeared as if on cue.

"Greetings, Hollidge," he said before clapping Alex on the shoulder. "Journey good? The trains running on time? Are you going to introduce me properly?"

"Of course. This is my aunt, Lady Aston." Alex didn't know where the desire to make the little jest came from, perhaps simply being back at Oak Grove Hall.

Adam laughed uproariously as if it was the funniest thing he'd heard, having known Lady Aston all his life.

Aunt Elizabeth broke in. "I believe he meant Miss Brambury." She spoke with utter seriousness, as if she thought Alex truly didn't understand.

"Yes, Auntie. I spoke in jest." He turned to the sole Diamond brother. "Lord Adam Diamond, this is Miss Brambury, the eldest daughter of Lord and Lady Brambury."

Adam didn't take her hand since she was holding her teacup in one and, most sensibly, a handkerchief in the other. He bowed toward her instead.

"Enchanted."

"I am pleased to meet you, my lord," she replied.

Alex listened to them chatting, hearing his aunt question the heir to the earldom on all matters of his upbringing over the past decade before he had to greet other guests.

"A nice young man," Aunt Elizabeth said, surprisingly. "He has turned out well for his age. I believe he will handle his responsibilities with astute capability one day."

Was Alex imagining some sort of comparison? His aunt's next words confirmed she was comparing, but not him and Adam, rather the siblings themselves.

"A good thing Lord Diamond has a mature nature, despite not being the eldest. One can only imagine the utter disarray of the Diamond earldom were Lady Clarity the heir."

Wisely, Miss Brambury said nothing to this remark, nor did Alex. Inside, he felt the wish to defend her but couldn't. Even then, he heard Clarity's voice, a little too loudly, across the room.

Alex glanced toward her and choked slightly upon his next sip. Clarity was leaning close to Brennon, her hand on his arm and gesticulating wildly with her glass of wine. Brennon appeared enchanted, nodding and smiling.

The lucky slag! He and Clarity must be on a path toward an engagement for Brennon to have been invited as one of the bachelors.

Over recent weeks, it had been impossible not to notice the two of them keeping close company. Brennon must think he could get away with having such a flighty and blithe wife to run his household. Probably her beauty was an acceptable trade. Or maybe the man cared nothing for safety, propriety, or sanity! He didn't appear to mind when she spilled a few drops of wine upon his shoes.

And when her laughter also spilled forth, Alex felt it—his heart squeezed and his groin tightened.

The devil take him!

His reaction was bloody inconvenient, especially when he wanted to leave Miss Brambury's side and join Clarity's discussion to find out what was eliciting her laughter. More than that, deep down in his gut, he knew a desperate desire to steal her away from the baron before it was too late.

As a dutiful member of the hosting family, Adam finished going around the room and returned to them.

"Tomorrow, some of us are going to do a bit of fishing," he said. "Would you care to add to our number?"

The last time Alex had fished at River Derwent, he'd done so with Clarity and their parents, but Adam had been too young to join them.

"Will it be only the men?" he asked.

"I definitely don't want to go fishing," Miss Brambury said.

Lady Purity happened by. "No one will force you," she assured her. "My mother, who is also not a fan of fishing, has devised many methods for our guests to entertain themselves during the day. If fishing isn't to your liking, then you may paint or sketch or stroll the grounds. We have every manner of instrument if you like to play, and there is a library at your disposal. And we have excellent horses if you enjoy riding."

"How kind of you," Miss Brambury said. She turned to Alex. "If you don't mind my begging off and doing something more suitable to the female nature, then I shall not join you."

"Nor I," said Aunt Elizabeth, as if Alex had thought for a single moment his aunt was going to pierce a worm on a hook and cast her line.

Clarity appeared at her brother's other elbow.

"Did you ask Alex about fishing?"

Both his aunt and Emmeline visibly startled, and Alex pierced her with what he hoped was a suitably disapproving look. *Why did she insist on being outrageous?*

Clarity didn't appear to notice. "I was telling Lord Brennon about our extraordinary haul of trout last year. The fish were as easy as picking apples."

She turned to Alex. "You would have loved it. Remember when we were fishing the summer those stray cats showed up?" Turning to

Emmeline, she added, "Not that they have anything to do with the story."

Emmeline nodded, while wearing a censorious expression that she might have mastered from his aunt. Clarity either didn't notice or purposefully ignored it.

She continued her account. "Alex said, 'I vow there aren't *any* fish in that stream,' and then I caught one directly." She glanced at him again. "You broke your rod in disgust over your knee and then tossed it into the water."

"I remember," he said tightly.

She chuckled with only Adam joining in. Even Purity pursed her lips in disapproval. Clarity was unpredictable, and Alex was beginning to wish she would find someone else to share stories with and about.

Where was that Brennon chap?

"Then you declared it must have been a faulty rod and took mine," she continued. "Still, you didn't catch anything that day." She beamed at him so genuinely, any annoyance at her embarrassing story slipped away.

"You gave your fish to the cats," he said, suddenly remembering her kindness. She hadn't wanted to show up at the house with a fish if he hadn't caught one, too.

Clarity clapped her hands. "I did, didn't I? I had forgotten." She turned to Aunt Elizabeth and Miss Brambury once more. "Then I was wrong. The cats are part of the tale."

"Lady Clarity," her sister said stiffly, attempting a modicum of formality in the midst of the chaos of her sister's familiarity. "I believe another carriage is pulling up."

"Excuse me," Clarity said. "I thought everyone had arrived. I must go greet the newcomers."

She offered a perfectly acceptable curtsy all around, regardless of rank and despite hers being higher than Miss Brambury's. Then Adam gave a shallow nod and followed her.

"Well!" was all Aunt Elizabeth said in their wake.

Miss Brambury locked gazes with him, widening hers and at the same time, giving a roll of her shoulders and a shake of her head as if to say, "How odd!"

On the surface, Alex agreed. Compared to the other women, Clarity might seem strange in her forwardness and her relentless insouciance. Beyond that, though, she was one-of-a-kind in all the right ways, too. He would scoop her up in an instant if she behaved the way he wanted a wife to, as Emmeline did.

On the other hand, then she would not be Clarity Diamond.

Chapter Twelve

At the dinner which had been pushed back an hour for late-arriving guests, Clarity was seated between the elderly Lord Fenwick and a married man, Lord Branton, whose wife was seated opposite and already round with child. Since that gentleman was distracted, constantly gazing at his adoring wife through the flowered centerpieces, she was free to converse with her parents' old friend. His Lordship was good company over the fish soup, followed by roast beef and potatoes, and all the way to the sponge cake with cream and strawberry jam drizzle.

Afterward, the ladies retired to the drawing room, able to chat more easily than at dinner across the long table. Each guest had their own tidbits of news to share, be it weddings, births, or deaths in their extended families. Then came the usual discussion of the latest fashions as dictated by the magazines most of them read. Some had even thoughtfully brought copies to pass around.

With utmost politeness, no one spoke of anything too personal in their own lives, especially the single women who would never dream of disclosing if they might be developing a *tendre* or for whom.

Nevertheless, more than one of the married ladies directed pointed questions toward a blushing Miss Brambury regarding Lord Hollidge, setting Clarity's teeth on edge. The gossip rags of London had made it known they were keeping company even if absolutely nothing scandalous had been detected.

The *ton* enjoyed a love match among equals, and the disclosure of which sold many papers. If they had *not* been equals, many more papers would have sold!

About halfway through a tedious discussion of whether the mineral waters at Bath were really good for one's health, with Alex's aunt coming down firmly on the side of yea, and another woman, a young wife, being just as firmly of the opinion that it was not, Clarity realized Purity was attempting to catch her eye.

Giving her sister her full attention, she watched Purity gesture with a lift of her head while wrinkling her nose. Clarity knew the signal, rose to her feet, and excused herself before exiting the room. She waited on the stairs, and soon, her sister came out to join her.

"Don't tell me," Clarity guessed. "You were unimpressed with your dining partner."

Purity had been seated next to Lord Kilbey, a titled bachelor whom her brother had invited. Only a little younger than Purity but worlds less mature, he'd probably been repeatedly chastised over some perceived failing in etiquette.

"Indubitably," Purity said. "It was like dining with a boy who ought to still wear leading strings."

Clarity laughed until her sister pierced her with eyes that were the mirror of her own.

"But this isn't about me. It is about you."

"Me?" Clarity asked. "What did I do now?"

"Don't you blink those innocent eyes at me, sister dear. Why were you all 'Alex this' and 'Alex that,' during the afternoon reception, knowing it is not done? If I didn't know better, which I do, I would think you were trying to get under Miss Brambury's perfect creamy skin. And why would you be doing that?"

Clarity opened her mouth, but her sister filled in the answer.

"I'll tell you why. Because you don't think she's good enough for your old friend. But you must let Hollidge make his own choices and above all be gracious to our guests."

With those sound words of advice, Purity returned to the drawing room, and Clarity had no choice but to follow.

In a short time, the men rejoined them.

"Was everything satisfactory?" Lady Diamond asked the male guests, most of whom now wafted the nutty, earthy aroma of cigar smoke.

"Perfectly satisfying," came murmurs of approval.

"Diamond's port was as smooth and buttery as... well, as butter," declared one chap who'd perhaps had a glass too many.

Then her mother rose from her chair. "Dear guests, I am aware many of you traveled long distances to come, and my husband and I are grateful." She glanced at Clarity's father, who made a good show of appearing grateful.

Clarity caught Adam's eye, and he nearly started to laugh. They both knew their father would be as happy, if not more so, for a peaceful fortnight in the country without a single guest in sight.

"Therefore," Lady Diamond continued when it was obvious her husband wasn't going to perjure himself with an effusive welcome, "I am going to make the mildest of suggestions on how to pass an amusing hour or two before we have a light supper and go to bed early." She cleared her throat. "Would anyone care to play charades?"

There were more claps and yeas than groans and nays. Thus in short order, the evening's entertainment was decided.

"Please feel free to watch if you don't wish to play," she added graciously.

"Or if you think you shall be beaten soundly," Brilliance Diamond spoke up for the first time in hours.

With that challenge from such a young person, all the adults rallied to play.

"Acted charades or riddles?" asked Adam's friend, Lord Kilbey.

"Both," said Lady Diamond, "until we grow weary of each. I've taken the liberty of creating teams." Then her mother grouped people, being certain to mix up the married couples and also the singles.

To Clarity's delight, instead of Alex being partnered with Miss Brambury, he was on her team, along with one each of her parents' male and female married friends, Lord Trent and Lady Fenwick, who had a special grandmotherly relationship with Clarity. The dear woman had even brought Clarity a stack of thick colored paper for folding and another slim volume upon the same subject. Her enjoyment of the game had increased tenfold.

"I am thinking of a number between one and fifty," her father said. "Each team must pick a number and the closest will go first. After that, we shall continue clockwise if the team doesn't guess correctly."

"Pick the number five," Clarity suggested to Alex, who'd been named their team's leader.

"Why?"

"Because he loves his five children."

Perhaps because he thought she was cheating, he chose twelve. When the winning number turned out to be five, guessed by Purity's group, Clarity glared at him. He didn't care in the least and only shrugged.

Her sister's team went first and easily solved the well-known riddle, read by Lord Kilbey:

"My first doth affliction denote,
Which my second is destin'd to feel.
And my whole is the best antidote
That affliction to soften and heal."

People clapped and whistled to distract, but Purity calmly said, "The answer is 'woman'."

However, their next charade was for three of the four to act out *The Fall of the House of Usher*. No matter how many times Lord Kilbey and Lord Branton, whose expectant wife was in Adam's group, fell to the floor amidst much laughter, Purity and Lady Aston, who was the fourth member, could not guess.

Clarity's team also had a riddle to begin with, and she was allowed to ask it.

"When is nine plus nine equal to six?"

"Absurd," someone called out. "The math of a lunatic."

People laughed.

"Give us a chance," Clarity said.

Hoping it wasn't cheating, she looked directly at Alex, who seemed to be pondering, and she moved her eyes, left to right and back, like the pendulum of the longcase clock in the front hall.

When they were children, it was an easy signal to indicate silently it was time to vacate a room or ask to be excused from the table to go have fun.

His eyes widened in response.

"Repeat the clue," he ordered. And she did.

The others on their team remained silent, mystified until Alex said, "Add nine hours to nine o'clock and you get six o'clock, so the answer, Lady Clarity, is a clock."

"Indeed," she said, and people clapped their approval.

Their next charade was a *tableau vivant*, or living picture. The two older team members nominated Alex and Clarity to perform for them.

Looking at the slip of paper in her mother's handwriting, she saw three words: *The balcony scene.*

Her cheeks warmed. Showing it to Alex, since they weren't allowed to speak, she saw him react with the merest hint of his jaw clenching. When he looked at her, she saw a resolute determination to win.

Dragging the chair he'd vacated to the front of their group, he turned it to face the guests. Then he offered Clarity his hand and assisted her to step onto the chair. She hoped her mother didn't mind her feet on the furniture.

Glancing over, she saw Lady Diamond smiling softly to herself. Apparently, she would enjoy the spectacle of her daughter playing the famed Juliet.

Thinking how best to mime the balcony, Clarity pretended to lean her forearms on an invisible railing and then rested her chin on one of her hands. It was a little awkward, and if she leaned over any farther, she might pitch forward onto the laps of her team members.

Getting into position, Alex went down on one knee and gazed up at her, then for added effect, extended his arms upward and looked at her adoringly.

"Romeo and Juliet," said Lady Fenwick at once.

"More specific," called out Lady Diamond, adhering to the rules to make it harder.

"The balcony scene," added Lord Trent, who was Clarity's father's close friend from school.

The clapping began in earnest.

"I object," Lady Aston said, and the clapping trailed off. "There *was* no balcony scene in *Romeo and Juliet* as written by the Bard."

An awkward silence ensued. It was only a parlor game, and they had succeeded brilliantly.

"But everyone knows it as such, Aunt Elizabeth," Alex said, breaking character and rising to his feet.

Clarity stood straight because her back was starting to ache, holding her pose.

"Your nephew is right," she chimed in. "From Otway's first staging to Garrick's famous revival, we all think of it as 'the balcony scene.' Besides, that's what was on the paper."

"Well, it is wrong, and the point should be deducted," Lady Aston insisted.

"I am afraid it is my fault," Lady Diamond said. "I assumed most people *saw* the play performed on stage rather than reading it."

"*Hm!*" Lady Aston said. Perhaps realizing she was arguing with the hostess and a countess at that, she suddenly sighed. "You are right, of course. Bravo to my nephew and your daughter."

With that mishap averted, they reached for their next charade, this time another riddle that none of them could guess no matter how hard Lord Trent tried. The answer was a hat, which made Clarity laugh at the simplicity that eluded them, although Alex looked disgruntled at losing.

Miss Brambury and Adam's group went next, along with Lord Fenwick and Lady Trent. They began with an easy one they'd all heard before, which Clarity thought seemed a bit like cheating.

Rolling her eyes as her brother began to speak, she crossed her arms and waited.

"A box without hinges, key, or lid, yet golden treasure inside is hid. What is it?"

The other two on the team looked at Miss Brambury, who made a great show of puzzling it out before saying, "I believe the answer is an egg."

Everyone clapped, however they lost on the next one.

The turns continued with Lady Diamond's group, which also contained Lord Brennon, gaining three points and beating Clarity's.

Before they knew it, it was time for tea or coffee, and then the guests broke into groups for cards or chess, or merely sitting and chatting. There would be no more organized events that night as people were feeling increasingly weary.

At ten, the announcement of a light supper was welcomed, as was the sparkling champagne that accompanied it. Afterward, people happily went to their rooms, almost floating on the good will and the bubbling French wine. No one would ever say the Diamonds couldn't throw a good house party.

Clarity and her family stayed up until all their guests were settled and then bid each other goodnight. Ray and Bri had long since disappeared with some of the fashion magazines and were probably fast asleep. Purity and Clarity went arm-in-arm up the stairs.

"I'm glad this is only three nights and four days," Purity said. "It's a little taxing."

Clarity couldn't help laughing. "No, it's not. It is all good fun, and you need to relax and remember that Mother and Father are the hosts. Don't try to take it on, dear sister, and have it rest upon your shoulders."

"You're right. Tomorrow, I shall endeavor not to worry if we have perfectly even numbers for the games or if each person gets a new partner for dinner."

"That's a start," Clarity said. And she kissed her sister's cheek and watched her close her bedroom door. Her own room was directly next to it, but then she remembered Lady Fenwick's book and folding paper. If she left it lying around, one of the guests might easily take it to his or her room for an interesting read or help themselves to her folding paper as if it were stationery.

"Drat!" In two shakes of a lamb's tail, she was back downstairs, recalling she'd set the bundle down on the round table in the main drawing room. Fortunately, it was still where she'd left it.

However, as she retrieved her gifts, she heard someone nearby in the adjacent salon. Not expecting to hear footsteps, when she did, she assumed it was her father or Adam.

What other male would be prowling after hours?

"Greetings," Alex said, coming into view through the open doorway.

Chapter Thirteen

Clarity's heart beat a tattoo of excitement. Despite having spent the better part of the day in close quarters, now they were alone, butterflies took flight in her stomach.

Clutching her book and package of paper against her, she realized her hands were trembling.

Stop it! she admonished herself. It's only Alex.

Handsome, tall, sweet, kind, green-eyed, Alex. *The man I love!*

"I thought everyone had retired," he admitted, leaning on the door frame, arms crossed.

"I nearly had, but I remembered I'd left behind my gift from Lady Fenwick. It's a book and some paper, not for writing but for folding," she added, wishing she could stop yammering like a ninny. "What about you?"

He hesitated, then said, "This may sound strange, but I wanted to see your home when it was quiet and empty. It's a little disconcerting being here without my parents. My brain keeps telling me I'm a boy and they are here."

"I understand," she said. "It is strange for me, too, to see you here as you are now. I half expect to turn the corner and come across you as my childhood friend. And then, as you said, you were never here without Lord and Lady Hollidge. How wonderful this party would be if your parents were here today."

Alex nodded. "I suppose I wouldn't mind being a boy again since we had such good times, but I wouldn't want to go through all the years in between then and now."

Of course he wouldn't. "I am sorry," she whispered.

He shrugged, pushing away from the doorway and coming farther into the room.

"There are ghosts everywhere," he said. Walking to the piano, he trailed a finger across it.

Clarity shivered. "Ghosts?" she repeated.

"Of our past. I suppose more mine than yours since you continued to grow up here, but for me, each room holds a distinct memory. My mother sat at that piano and played one night, and I was in the window seat, wishing she would hurry and finish so I could go and explore."

When his voice thickened, Clarity's eyes filled with unshed tears.

"If I could," he continued, "I would now gladly sit for hours to listen to her and to talk with my father, too. There is much I wish to hear from them."

She tried to imagine the awful emptiness of not being able to speak with her own parents ever again. And then she had an idea.

"I know it's not the same, but my parents were very close to yours. I wonder if it might be helpful to you to speak with each of them."

Silently, he stared at her, his jaw clenched, and she couldn't tell what he was thinking. Perhaps she had overstepped.

"You could ask them what your parents thought about different things," she added, "maybe even if they had dreams for your future."

She almost wanted to tell him how his mother imagined them married, but that was an unfair secret from a long-dead woman. The last thing Clarity wanted was to manipulate Alex into making an irrational decision based on the past.

Nevertheless, if he took her in his arms that moment and invited her to spend her life with him, she would do it without hesitation. Something about him, even changed as he was, spoke to her heart so strongly she feared he alone could bring her happiness.

Because her knees weakened at that moment, Clarity sat on the piano bench. To her delight, he joined her.

Yet, when he still said nothing, she added, "You can think about it. Besides, I suppose you can ask your aunt many of the same questions."

Idly, she pressed a key, and a pure tone rang out into the silence.

Finally, Alex spoke. "I think your idea is genius. I will act upon it tomorrow. As for my aunt, she is more likely to talk about my father as a boy but little of him as an adult. They didn't exactly see eye to eye."

"Really?" she asked, blinking up at him as if that was a secret. Lady Aston had snapped waspishly at her younger brother, Alex's father, in mixed company.

He nodded. "I guess that much was obvious. Anyway, Aunt Elizabeth probably feels strange being here, too."

"She seemed precisely as she always has," Clarity said, making sure not to use any of the negative descriptions that popped into her head.

"No, truly, she grew quieter the closer we came to Oak Grove. If not for Miss Brambury, I think not a word would have been spoken for the last two hours of the journey."

Stiffening at the lady's name, Clarity wished his newfound romantic association didn't cause her such sadness. Envy and jealousy were petty emotions, but they were real just the same.

"Miss Brambury," she echoed, striking the black key under her finger. A flat, despondent note rang out.

"That's a melancholy tone," he said. "Is it your commentary upon the viscount's daughter?"

Did he want her opinion?

She ought to keep it bottled up. After all, what good would it do to have him think she disapproved of his choice?

"It is merely the note under my finger. Nothing more. It was gracious of you to invite Miss Brambury here to show her where you spent time as a youngling."

"I did not invite her."

Finally, she took her gaze from the keyboard and looked at him.

"Didn't you?"

"No," Alex spoke softly, "although I suppose I should have thought of it. But it was my aunt's doing."

"Thoughtful of her, then," Clarity said, trying to sound sincere.

Strangely, her words made him grunt. It might have been what now passed for his laughter.

"You don't sound convinced," he said.

"I do not wish to speak ill of Lady Aston. Thus, I shall say nothing more. It's getting late. Time for all sane folks to be in their beds."

Not really wishing to leave him, she rose from the bench anyway. His hand gripped her arm as he stood to join her.

"And what about all the not-so-sane? Is that what we are and why we are both here?" he asked.

Looking from where his bare hand held her arm, sending flames of heat flickering deep within her, and then back to his beloved face, she was speechless. When she licked her lips, he groaned. Worse, his eyes flashed a message she thought was the same deep longing she felt.

But he had Miss Brambury, and while Clarity might be considered the easy-going, playful Diamond daughter, she was not foolish. At least, not all the time.

"I came for my gift." She eased herself out from behind the bench, and he had to release her. Otherwise, the intent would have been clear and entirely inappropriate.

"Tomorrow, I hope you will speak with my parents and gain some peace. But please, feel free to wander around as long as you wish. No one will disturb you. Good night."

With that, she went toward the door.

"Thank you," he said.

If she turned to speak again, he would see her tears. Hence, she kept walking.

<hr />

Alex could not recall when he had enjoyed himself more. In truth, he couldn't think of the last time he'd done something simply for fun. That morning at Oak Grove, the sun was sparkling upon the gently moving river, and he was surrounded by relaxed, happy people, including Adam, Clarity, and the earl himself, Lord Diamond, who'd given most of his family their dark-haired, blue-eyed looks.

What's more, Alex had just pulled a fish from the River Derwent, his first one since he'd been a boy.

He heard Clarity clap her hands before she laughed in her delightful way.

"Better than the last time, my lord."

He smiled back at her, using muscles that had seen little use in the past decade.

"You've stocked the stream and given me a good rod this time," he teased.

"I assure you it is entirely your skill," she said. "In any case, I intend to catch more."

"It's not a contest," Adam pointed out.

"Of course not," Clarity agreed, "but I still intend to win."

"You were never this competitive when we were children," Alex said. "Not that I can recall."

She jiggled her fishing pole impatiently.

"It was pointless when I was six or seven or even eight," Clarity said. "You were older and thus taller, faster, and stronger. Regarding most of the things we did, I couldn't hope to compete with you and win, except fish."

"And charades," he added. Then he remembered something she was very good at. "And hiding. Dear God! If you set your mind to hide, I could never find you. I used to give up and go have biscuits in the kitchen."

"Sometimes, I fell asleep waiting for you to find me," she confessed.

They looked at one another in silence.

Then Adam spoke, reminding them there were other people around.

"Perhaps I will catch the most, or Kilbey, or Brennon."

At her brother's words, Clarity's glance left Alex, and the strange moment passed. Before he knew it, she'd left him to see whether Brennon was any good at fishing. And then everyone settled in at the stream's edge, occasionally stepping away from their rod for a glass of lemonade or a Shrewsbury biscuit.

There was only one other female, Lady Fenwick, who professed to have been fishing since she was a wee lass. Sure enough, she patiently caught more than her husband, who spent more time chatting with Lord Diamond.

Suddenly, Clarity laughed loudly at something Brennon said.

"Hush! You'll scare the fish," said a crotchety voice, which Alex realized was his own when the others turned to look at him.

He felt his face warm with shame. It had been seeing Clarity leaning on Brennon's arm that had upset Alex far more than her laughter. He could well recall the feeling of her soft, full breast pressed against him, and it irked Alex to think of Brennon as the recipient of such delight.

"Nothing but a jest," he called out. "I don't think the fish have ears, anyway."

Truthfully, he'd been paying more attention to the people around him, a merry group, than to the trout. Alex couldn't deny a longing for such camaraderie in his daily life—a disquieting desire given how he hadn't let himself experience any such lightheartedness in years.

At university, it was no secret he preferred to remain at his studies while other students got up to the occasional mischief, usually directed at one of the hapless dons trying to lecture sense into them.

Beyond that, he found it nearly impossible not to keep an eye upon the dark-haired lady who was like an exotic flower in their midst. In full bloom, Clarity was waving her colorful petals over the entire fishing party.

What a muttonhead! Alex rolled his eyes until he could see whether he had a brain in his head, and then he felt a tugging on the line.

"I've got another one," he called out, feeling a foolish rush of excitement over something so trivial. It wasn't as if they needed his meager contribution to survive.

"Well done," Clarity exclaimed, before dropping her own rod and hurrying to his side.

"I haven't actually got it yet," he explained, pulling steadily and walking backward. "It seems to be bigger than a whale."

Her tinkling laugh distracted him. Looking at her smiling deep-blue eyes and generous mouth, he wanted to kiss her right then and there. *Outrageous!*

Suddenly, he was yanked back toward the water.

"Let me help," Clarity insisted, getting in front of him and wrapping her fingers around the pole.

"Stop! What are you doing?"

They were wrestling and moving toward the water. She tripped him with her slender leg as she tried to brace herself, and he fell over her while at the same time pushing her forward down the slight incline at the water's edge. In the blink of an eye, they both went into the shallow river.

A roar went up from the others, mostly guffaws of laughter.

"It's all right," Clarity called out over her shoulder. And in the same good humor, told everyone, "It's not deep at all."

"I can attest to that," Alex agreed, for he was sitting on the pebbly river bottom with water up only to his elbows. "But it is rather cool. You lunatic!" he added.

She shrugged, dismissing his insult with a flick of her hand, which sent more water droplets spraying his way.

When a fuse of hilarity lit inside of him, Alex couldn't put it out. Feeling the chortle start deep down in his gut, he let it rise to the surface, releasing a loud burst of laughter. Clarity joined in, and he laughed harder.

Strangely, after a few moments, he had the urge to cry, which sobered him swiftly. Regardless, he was still unable to stop until he developed a sudden bout of hiccups.

"Hold your breath," she advised. "And perhaps we should stand up. I'm not very comfortable."

"Nor I," he agreed, rising to his feet. In fact, soggy wool between his legs and on his nether regions was a nightmare, but he kept his mouth closed in case she mentioned his backside again. "Why didn't you drop the rod?" he asked.

"Why didn't you?" she retorted, taking the hand he offered and rising from the water like Venus.

His glance dropped to the bodice of her gown. On clear display were her nipples, or at least the outline of them, pearled against the sodden fabric. And he would swear he could actually see a shade of deep pink against the cream-color of her day gown.

"Um," he began. While his heart began to pound, he could think of only one thing. *Two things actually!* Clarity's breasts, naturally, but a third thing, too—protecting her. Swiftly, he unbuttoned his jacket.

"What are you doing?" she asked.

"Take this so you don't grow chilled," he said, shrugging out of it and shoving it toward her.

"But it's damp," she protested, pushing his hands and his dripping coat away.

"Is everything all right?" This from Adam, who didn't sound the least bit concerned by the mishap.

Luckily, Lord Diamond was in conversation again with Fenwick and paying them no mind.

"We're fine," Alex called over Clarity's shoulder.

Yet as she started to turn toward her brother, he grabbed her arm.

"Stop," he ordered, and she went still. "Take the blasted jacket," he insisted.

Her chin tilted and her gaze found his. "What is the matter?" she hissed.

"Look down," he urged, "and be careful not to poke your own eyes out."

Chapter Fourteen

A lex was behaving very peculiarly, but Clarity did as he suggested, looking down at herself.

"Oh!" she shrieked, snatching at the garment he offered.

"Is aught the matter?" Lord Brennon asked.

"No," Clarity declared. Mortified, she allowed Alex to reach around and drape his coat over her shoulders. Then she eased an arm into each sleeve before holding it closed over her chest.

Knowing her cheeks must be burning, she could do nothing but make light of the situation.

"I suppose that is why women walk out in a rainstorm with a coat and an umbrella," she said, at last turning to the embankment.

"I don't think that's the reason," Alex replied. "Although now I firmly believe it ought to be illegal for a woman to be wet in public."

She laughed again, relieved he hadn't let her turn toward those on the shore in such an exposed state. He was a gentleman, indeed.

"I am sorry about your fish. I was just trying to help."

"I know. But I don't think there ever was a fish. It felt more liked I'd caught my line on a sunken log, or maybe an old boot."

"You may be right," she said. "Perhaps we can recover your rod downstream."

"Since it belonged to your family," Alex said, "I shall certainly hunt for it later. It was a nice willow one, too."

"If it's anywhere, it'll be at Dead-Man's Crook."

He shook his head. "I cannot believe you remember that."

Clarity smiled. It was a simple bend in the river, which he'd christened with a name of fanciful dread after reading aloud to her from Defoe's *The King of Pirates*.

"I have called it that ever since," she confessed, "and all my siblings do, too, even Bri and Ray, though they don't know you're the reason."

He was staring at her in a way that made those butterflies take off in her stomach again. She was still in disbelief at hearing how heartily he'd laughed, so familiar and yet different, too, in the tone of an adult male.

"Take my arm," Lord Brennon offered beside her, making her jump. She hadn't noticed his approach. "I'll escort you back to the house," he continued. "Would you care to remove Lord Hollidge's jacket?"

"No!" she protested, clutching it more tightly at the closure.

"I will give you mine," Lord Brennon promised, looking wounded. "Besides, he may not wish to go among mixed company without his coat. He is half-dressed."

"Let the lady wear it back to the house," Alex intervened. "I'm sure no one will mind me in my shirt-sleeves just this once." He tugged on his wet waistcoat as if to tidy himself.

"Of course they won't," Clarity said.

"Are you unharmed?" her father asked. Clearly, she was fine, but if her mother found out he hadn't shown some concern, Lord Diamond knew he'd be in trouble.

"Yes, Father. I shall leave you and my brother to be hosts for the remainder of the fishing party."

"We could never be as gracious as you, sister dear," Adam teased. "Tripping and plunging one of our esteemed guests into the river for an unwelcome bath. I am sure Hollidge appreciates his soggy trousers."

She shot Alex another glance, but he was already heading back to the house, having relinquished her care to Lord Brennon. He must think her no better than an awkward child.

Sighing, she allowed Lord Brennon to escort her back, following in Alex's path.

After she'd changed, she sought out their housekeeper and gave her Alex's coat, hoping it could be restored to its former perfection.

"I've already got Master Alex's pants," Mrs. Cumby said, which made Clarity shake her head. Even their housekeeper couldn't think of him as *Lord Hollidge*.

"Seeing as how he hasn't got his valet with him," Mrs. Cumby continued, "I shall make the attempt to clean and dry his suit. Try not to have as much fun with the guests, my girl."

After a cup of tea with Lord Brennon, before he went with Adam and some of the other men to shoot at targets for sport, Clarity decided to take a stroll along the river and look for the lost pole.

Bri and Ray accompanied her to enjoy the fresh air since both had been cooped up with the other ladies, sketching and practicing their watercolor painting.

"I wish I had seen you and Lord Hollidge fall in the river," Bri said.

"Don't be mean," Clarity rebuked. "It was cold and wet."

"Obviously it was wet," Ray said. "It was water."

They laughed. When Clarity was in Purity's company, she tried to match her polish, but with her two youngest sisters, she fell easily into their enthusiastic manner and good humor.

When they reached Dead-Man's Crook, Alex was already there. He didn't appear to be looking for a fishing rod, nor for anything else. Facing away from them, he was staring down the river to where it disappeared into the trees.

Clarity put a hand on each of her sisters' arms to stay them.

"Maybe we should leave him in solitude."

"But we've walked all this way," Ray protested. "What do you suppose he is doing?"

By the way he stared out into the distance, given their recent conversation, Clarity assumed he was pondering the past. He'd had a discussion with her mother already that morning. And while Clarity hadn't pried, Lady Diamond had disclosed that she'd satisfied Alex's curiosity on any number of topics, such as his mother's favorite food, flower, and book, and even Lady Hollidge's favorite color, which was quite naturally the color of Alex's green eyes, the same hue as his father's.

"The little tidbits I recalled meant a lot to the dear boy," her mother had said.

"I am glad for him."

"For me, too," Lady Diamond had agreed. "It was comforting to discuss my good friend with him, with someone who loved her even more than I did. It brought Daphne back to me for a little while. And although Alex's eye color might be his father's, his facial expressions remind me very much of his mother."

"Let's go back," Clarity insisted. "The fishing pole can wait. Besides, you ought to get your questions ready for the fortune-teller. Mother said it will be an extremely entertaining evening."

"Do you think the seer will know our future husbands?" Bri asked.

"Maybe," Clarity said, although she knew it was their midwife from the village, hired more to amuse their guests than to provide actual predictions. Still, it was known locally that Mrs. Boswell had the gift of being a seer.

Bri gave a squeal of delight, grabbed Ray's hand, and spun about to race home.

"Don't forget it's a secret until dinner," Clarity called after. Watching them dash ahead, she had the impression of springtime colts in the field.

"Lady Clarity," came Alex's familiar voice, sending tiny tremors down her spine.

She glanced to where he stood, now facing her, and went over to join him.

After picking her way around the prickly brambles, she stepped onto the promontory that had built up where the river curved. They were able to stand practically in the middle of the Derwent and see all the debris that the bend collected.

"Why did your sisters leave?" Alex asked when she was beside him.

"We didn't want to disturb you, but I fear we did."

"Not at all. I was glad to see you there," he said. "Three Diamond jewels at once."

Her insides fluttered at hearing his teasing, relaxed tone.

"It sounds terribly odd whenever you call me *Lady* Clarity," she mentioned, looking away from him to the riverbank where they'd played as children.

"Frankly, it feels a little odd to say it," Alex confessed, "since part of me still thinks of you as a girl with pigtails and freckles."

Her glance came up to lock with his.

"I never had freckles," she protested. Those were the domain of the redheads in the family, and neither her mother nor Ray were thrilled with them.

"Actually, you did," he argued, "before your skin became the porcelain satin it is now."

Porcelain satin! It was a compliment any woman would be thrilled to receive from a gentleman, but he was nearly engaged to Emmeline, and she was supposed to be falling in love with Lord Brennon. Besides, coming from Alex, it made her want to giggle.

Clarity stifled the laughter, knowing Purity would disapprove and say she was being rude.

"I am lucky to have my father's Irish skin," she agreed.

"And his hair and his eyes," Alex pointed out.

"You're listing my features as if seeing me for the first time."

He said nothing, then looked away. "I am merely appreciating how we children carry on something of our parents."

Ah, she understood now. He was, as she'd guessed, pondering the past and undoubtedly thinking about the conversation he'd had with her mother.

"Certainly, you remind me of both your parents," she agreed.

"Do I?" He still didn't look at her. "Aunt Elizabeth used to say she couldn't see them in me."

Clarity nearly gasped. *Why on earth would the woman say something that hurtful and cruel?* Not only was it incorrect, it was undoubtedly the wrong thing to tell a grieving son.

"Perhaps Lady Aston needs spectacles," she said. "You are the image of your father but with your mother's smile and hair color. I was eight, I believe, when last I saw them, yet even I can see that."

He smiled at her, giving evidence of his dimple, and the earlier flutter returned, although it had grown to more of a quaking all the way down to her knees. She needed to give herself a stern talking to when next she was alone. It was ridiculous to have such a reaction to Alex. But how wonderful to see him wearing a real smile.

"I found it," he said.

She stared at his mouth. He had very attractive lips, and even watching them form words was mesmerizing.

"It?" she asked, unable to tear her gaze away.

"The rod," he explained. "Caught in the Dead-Man's Crook, just as you thought."

His words broke the spell.

"Is it?" She peered past him into the water. Sure enough, one of their willow poles was securely out of the water.

"No damage done," Alex added.

"Did you find anything else?" she asked.

"Such as?"

"I might have lost a shoe or two," she confessed.

He chuckled, but she had more to add. "Also a hat, a pair of lace gloves, and a parasol."

"Were you trying to open a shop?" he asked.

When the laughter bubbled up, Clarity couldn't stop it. He didn't join in, but he watched her with an amused expression that warmed her heart.

"I didn't lose all those things at once, silly," she pointed out. She thought of how many times she'd left something on the bank or dropped it as she strolled by the water.

He shook his head. "Still, careless once or twice is understandable, but that's excessive."

"You were careless, too, in the past," she said, thinking of how he'd once fallen off the garden shed roof, lucky there was a pile of snow to break his fall.

Yet when his expression darkened and all traces of humor vanished, she wished she'd curtailed her words. *Was he thinking of the many scrapes they'd got into? Or something else?*

Whatever it was, she had ruined the companionable moment.

"I am sorry. I can see you are taking my words to heart. But they were said in jest."

He shook his head. "It's the truth," he ground out, taking a few steps and snatching up the fishing pole. "Besides, I would not want you to *think* before you spoke. At least not around me. We are too familiar with one another for anything but the brutal truth."

Without waiting for her, he brushed past, heading back toward the house.

Closing her eyes, Clarity cursed her loose tongue.

"Idiot!" She'd ruined a perfectly lovely encounter. That night, she would attempt to be on her best behavior. At the very least, she wouldn't drown Alex or insult him.

Chapter Fifteen

Alex wished he hadn't stormed away. Despite knowing Clarity hadn't intended to hurt him, her words stung. The carelessness of his youth was precisely what he had spent years trying to overcome. It was why he could live easily in the same house with his persnickety Aunt Elizabeth, who wanted everything done in a precise, particular manner.

It was also the reason he could see himself married to Emmeline Brambury, who would provide a steady, calm existence. Even their children would be quiet, serene children, he imagined, not prone to falling in the river or racing their horses too fast. He wouldn't have to worry, and they would be safe.

But none of that reasonable thinking erased the fact that when he'd realized they were alone, far from the house and the other guests, a wicked notion had taken root. He had wanted to kiss Clarity again, exactly as he'd wanted to at the piano the night before.

It was clearly wrong-headed. *How could he kiss her when she had Brennon, and he had Emmeline?*

While he'd told her the truth about thinking of her as the child she'd been, he also saw her clearly as the stunningly desirable woman she'd become. Without trying, she was alluring beyond all tolerance, causing him to tingle when she was near.

Moreover, he felt mirth bubble up within him at her presence, even when she was wrestling with his fishing rod and sending him into the river.

A life with Clarity would always mean uncertainty and worry, he reminded himself as he reached the stables and returned the pole. She was the opposite to what he wanted in a wife, and he had best remember that the next time those wayward urges danced through his brain and his body.

To that end, he kept his distance during the four o'clock dinner that lasted until six. While remaining with the other men, he was a silent, unexceptional guest lost in thought. He nearly begged off joining the ladies in the drawing room at seven, but he could picture his aunt's disapproval and Emmeline's disappointment if he abandoned them.

Thus, instead of feigning business correspondence and retiring to his room after the cigars and port, he returned with the others to the drawing room. Unlike the night before, the room was dimly lit, and the ladies were practically buzzing with excitement.

In the middle of the room, seated on a chair was a gray-haired woman, dressed in the garb of a Romany traveler with a red kerchief around her head, wearing a colorful blouse and skirt.

A fortune-teller! He groaned at the utter foolishness before taking up a spot near his aunt and Emmeline.

All the Diamond ladies were standing in a half-circle on his other side.

"She has just arrived," Clarity told him, fizzing with excitement. "You haven't missed anything yet."

He nodded, but when he didn't react, she added, "Alex, don't you remember the fair at Castle Donington when the fortune-teller scared us by knowing my name?"

Speaking of names, he flinched when, in her enthusiasm, she'd used his given one again. He felt his aunt bristle, and a glance at Emmeline showed she'd raised a delicate eyebrow.

"Yes," he said quietly, wishing Clarity would focus her attention on someone else. "I recall. But I don't believe she truly knew your name. As children, we mistakenly took it that way."

"She said she would speak with clarity, and she was looking directly at me."

Alex shook his head. At the time, the hair had stood up on the back of his neck, and he had grabbed Clarity's hand and run off to the hot cider tent.

"Without roots and without honesty," his aunt suddenly spat out. "I cannot believe Lord and Lady Diamond allow such a transient, independent creature into their home."

Independent! That seemed a strange condemnation, but Alex supposed the Romany travelers, who were famous for being self-sufficient and living life on their own terms, must seem threatening to his aunt's view of British rule and order. After all, not that long ago it was still a criminal offense even to speak with them. Luckily, British laws had changed.

"It is only for entertainment," he reminded her. The woman must be in costume, he concluded, for one couldn't command one of the genuine traveling folk to be anywhere at any particular time. Not even Lady Diamond could do that.

"Keep your wits about you," Aunt Elizabeth advised Emmeline, "and if you have any valuables, hold them tightly when near that light-fingered diddler."

"Gentle guests," Lady Diamond began, drawing everyone's gaze. "We are lucky tonight to be in the presence of Mrs. Boswell, a gifted teller of fortunes. If any are interested, you may sit down with her, and she'll tell you what she sees."

"Balderdash!" Aunt Elizabeth exclaimed loudly.

"Why, then you needn't sit with her, Lady Aston." Lady Diamond's sharp tone was one Alex had never heard from Clarity's mother before.

"Well!" his aunt muttered before retreating to a chair at the far end of the room.

In a far more organized fashion than Alex would have thought possible, people began to take turns while staying in a ring around the fortune-teller, with the one closest to the chair opposite going first.

Most of the seer's words were ambiguous with general promises. However, since her predictions were pleasant and benign, the other guests were in good humor, clapping at each new proclamation. They also laughed when the fortune-teller seemed to get something oddly accurate, such as telling Lady Branton a second helping of dessert was in her future. Indeed, the lady had mentioned wanting another portion of custard trifle directly after polishing off the first at dinner and eagerly looking forward to supper. But given her expectant condition, it was a safe guess.

For most of the soothsayer's proclamations, Alex could have easily said an equally bland and truthful declaration. Nonetheless, he found his interest piqued when Emmeline took the seat in front of Mrs. Boswell.

"A lovely lady with everything ahead of her," the fortune-teller began. "Do you have a question for me?"

Emmeline glanced at him first, then asked, "Can you tell me something about my future husband?"

Many of the guests looked at Alex, and suddenly his cravat felt too tight. When he saw Clarity also watching him, he was rewarded with her encouraging smile. At the sight of her dimples, the tension inside him released a little.

Mrs. Boswell remained silent for a moment, as if dredging up some answer from the mystical recesses of her brain.

"He will adore you, and you will feel the same."

Alex felt a shiver of shock race through him. He definitely did not *adore* Emmeline Brambury. He wasn't even sure what adoration would feel like, but it didn't describe the practical admiration he felt for her as a sensible female.

Emmeline opened her mouth, looking equally stunned. He doubted she adored him, either.

"And I see chickens," the soothsayer added.

"Chickens?" Emmeline repeated.

"Yes, many of them. Many, many feathers. And eggs."

The guests laughed. Emmeline pushed her chair back a little harshly.

"All in fun," Lady Diamond reminded everyone.

Nevertheless, Emmeline went to sit with Aunt Elizabeth, who wore a less-than-pleased expression.

Eventually, the Diamond ladies had their turns. With the youngest ones, it was all giggling and silly questions about the handsomeness of their future spouses.

Naturally, the fortune-teller promised each they would meet their heart's desire in the coming years.

"You may not recognize him as such at first," she told Radiance.

"He will need something from you," she told Brilliance.

Purity sat down looking reluctant. "Whatever you wish to tell me will be welcome," she said politely.

The fortune-teller nodded. "Your heart will be much affected and soon. You will be surprised, I think. But don't let your rigid notions blind you."

Purity squirmed and rose to her feet. Alex thought it was starting to get interesting, especially when Clarity took the chair next.

He watched her profile as she gazed steadily at the soothsayer.

"Your eyes are like your sister's," the woman said, "but inside, you are different."

Clarity's family laughed softly at the plain truth. Alex couldn't take his gaze off her, for she glowed with excitement and had a delicate blush to her cheeks. The seer reached out a hand, and Clarity placed hers on the upturned palm.

"Your husband is near," Mrs. Boswell said, her voice dropped to a serious whisper. "He is in this very room."

Brennon coughed, and many laughed again, but Alex noticed Clarity's face grew serious, even as her cheeks became redder.

"And will he adore me?" she asked in a whisper.

The fortune-teller closed her eyes. When they popped open, she smiled. "He already does."

Alex felt as if he'd been punched in the stomach.

Clarity's glance found his before she rose to her feet and rejoined her family.

"Will some of the men have their futures told?"

"Not unless Mrs. Boswell knows who will win at Epsom Downs," Adam's friend, Lord Kilbey quipped.

Regardless, a few men did in fact take the seat before the sooth-sayer, happy to play along.

When Brennon took a turn, the mystic told him, "You will soon take a journey."

"Perhaps a wedding trip?" the man asked to the other guests' amusement.

"No," Mrs. Boswell said. "Not likely."

"Oh." Brennon rose with a frown.

When offered a turn, Alex declined, unable to shake the fear the woman would see into his soul and know him to be trouble. *And if she saw into his heart, then what?*

Adam was the last to receive his fortune.

"A happy life," Mrs. Boswell assured him. "And an answer to your heart's yearning where you might least expect it."

"Bravo," Lord Diamond said. "That's what happened to me with Lady Diamond."

The crowd, who by this time all had a drink in hand, raised their glasses in a jolly cheer.

Relieved it was finished, Alex wandered over to where his aunt and Emmeline were chatting together.

"That wasn't so bad, was it?" he asked. Both pairs of eyes looked up at him.

"It was horrid," Emmeline said. "Chickens, indeed. I cannot but think she wanted to humiliate me."

He sighed. "Doubtful." Suddenly, he needed to give in to his earlier longing to be alone in his room. All this social interaction was wearing upon him. "If you ladies will excuse me, I shall see you at supper."

Despite their displeased expressions, he turned heel and left them. Nearly at the door, he realized Clarity had appeared by his side.

"You aren't staying for the piano recital?"

"I'm afraid I wasn't paying attention earlier when the evening's entertainment was described, but if no one minds, I will beg off."

She nodded. "No one minds. I only wanted to make sure you were well."

He was not well, at least not peaceful in his mind. He could hardly tell her she was the reason, although it was the truth. Coming back to the place he'd spent many happy and carefree moments had been a mistake.

He nodded, turned, and walked away, which was harder than he'd imagined. Actually, Alex wished to grab her hand and bring her along. Each footfall he took in the Diamonds' home was retracing a step he'd taken in the past, usually with her tagging along beside him.

He'd been a hopeful youth, dreaming of a future perhaps with plants and travel, as Clarity had reminded him once. He hadn't imagined the plants would be ordinary crops, and the travel would be no farther than the reaches of his own holdings.

It was somewhat painful to return to Oak Grove Hall, feeling all his hopes had been dashed. But he had become an adult with responsibilities, the sole Hollidge heir and a viscount, and his path no longer had room for the dreams of a boy. He had to try not to see his younger self around every corner, nor wish to trade places with him.

And the dreams of a man were even more dangerous where Clarity was concerned. He, more than most, needed stability in his life, not her capriciousness.

Halfway through the first piano piece being played impeccably by the ancient Lady Fenwick, Clarity realized Purity was widening her eyes and wrinkling her nose again. They met once more upon the stairs.

"Don't tell me—you were unimpressed with your dazzling fortune," Clarity concluded.

"Obviously. No one wants their 'rigid notions' mentioned in mixed company, but that's not what this is about. It is about you."

Clarity sighed. "I tried not to call Alex by his name, but still it slipped out. Won't you overlook my impropriety?"

"I was wrong yesterday," Purity said.

"Were you?" Clarity asked with interest. Her sister hardly ever admitted to fault, mostly because she almost never made a misstep of any kind. "When was this?"

"When I accused you of trying to rub Miss Brambury's nose in your old friendship with Lord Hollidge and get under her skin. It's not that at all, is it?"

Clarity felt her cheeks warm. "What are you thinking?"

"I am thinking that my oldest, darling sister is in love with the Viscount Hollidge."

Chapter Sixteen

Clarity wondered whether to deny it. In fact, she thought about telling her younger sister to mind her own business. She did neither. She merely shrugged.

"You seem to have all the answers, so why did you call me out like this?"

Purity took a deep breath, looking a little sad. "To tell you to stop."

"Stop?" Clarity repeated. "Stop loving someone? Just like that?"

Purity twisted her fingers, looking unsure, which was unlike her.

"Then I was correct. I hoped I wasn't. But you must cease with your infatuation, if at all possible, before you embarrass yourself or become tremendously hurt."

"*Oh,*" Clarity said softly. "Am I embarrassing you and the rest of the family?"

"I may be the only one to notice, although Mother has a keen eye. You looked directly at Lord Hollidge when Mrs. Boswell mentioned your husband was in the room."

Clarity gasped. "Did I? I didn't mean to."

Her sister patted her shoulder. "I don't want you to appear desperate, nor allow Miss Brambury to stomp on your feelings with her perfect silken slippers."

"Is *everything* about her perfect?" Clarity demanded.

"Hardly. She is boring and humorless."

"Are those really her *only* bad traits?" Clarity knew she, herself, had many more than that. At the moment, she was jealous, too, and feeling decidedly petty regarding Emmeline.

"I am certain the lady has many more," Purity said. "Probably she has exceedingly long toes or a wart on her backside, but the ones I mentioned are the most apparent. I think Lord Hollidge can hardly keep his eyes open whenever she speaks to him."

"Then you don't think he loves her?" Clarity asked.

"He might," Purity said, dashing Clarity's hopes until her wise sister added, "but not with his heart. He may love the idea of the proper, serious, attentive, capable wife, but he doesn't really want to live like that."

"He doesn't?" Clarity thought that was precisely what Alex did want.

"Don't you think he seemed far happier when he used to visit?" Purity asked. "I was younger than you and didn't spend nearly as much time with him as you did, but I recall a laughing, joyful boy."

"That's what Mother said," Clarity agreed. "It's hard to imagine he could turn out as he has or that he wishes to grow ever more staid with someone like Miss Brambury at his side. Think of their children's lives."

Purity shuddered. "Maybe they'll raise solely chickens," she mused, recalling what the fortune-teller said.

Clarity clamped her hand over her mouth to stop the laughter, and then, wretchedly, for the briefest second, a sob escaped her instead. Her sister's slender arms encircled her.

"Try to spend your time with Lord Brennon. You looked happy at dinner. Were you?"

Clarity nodded, having been seated between Lord Brennon and Lord Kilbey. "I was. He is ever such good company."

"Well, then, he shall make you a good husband."

Her sister might be correct, but she didn't love him the way she had expected to love the man she married. *The way she already loved Alex.*

Luckily, Lord Brennon hadn't yet asked her for her hand, and Clarity continued to hope she could persuade her heart in his favor.

And then unexpectedly, she ran out of time.

"A word in private, Lady Clarity, if I may," Lord Brennon asked abruptly as the late-night supper ended.

He'd been quiet during the meal, and now she realized he'd been thinking of making this grand gesture. A moment before, they had stood up from the table, with the guests set to retire to the drawing room for a recitation by her father from one of Jonathan Swift's satiric works. The Irish writer was a favorite of Lord Diamond.

Taken aback, Clarity was momentarily silent.

"That is," Lord Brennon added, "if your parents would allow."

He'd spoken in front of everyone, and each pair of eyes had gone from his face to Clarity's to their hosts'.

Lord Diamond looked at his wife. Almost simultaneously, her parents nodded at one another, and Clarity knew they were expecting Lord Brennon to propose. With her insides trembling—or more accurately, heaving—she feared she would lose her recently eaten supper.

"Yes," her father said. "You may speak privately in the library."

Her mother coughed, and he added, "With the door open, naturally."

Clarity nearly laughed. Her dear mother had prompted her father to save her reputation in front of the other guests, not because either of her parents feared she would ever do anything untoward. They would never believe she'd already kissed Alex ever so passionately in a dark garden—twice—or that she longed to do more with him if he were willing and an opportunity presented itself.

Wrestling her thoughts back to the gentleman at hand and away from the one who was staring at her from the other side of the table, she nodded.

However, she did not tuck her hand into the crook of Lord Brennon's arm, which he offered, but simply led the way out of the room.

As soon as they entered the library, going to the far wall of windows where they wouldn't be easily overheard, Lord Brennon spoke.

"Lady Clarity, I hold you in high esteem and admire you greatly."

That would be an excellent start, she considered, *if she felt the same way.* Except in place of the excited fluttering she experienced with Alex, she felt ill. That could not be an auspicious sign.

"Thank you, my lord. You are a kind man." He would make someone an excellent husband but not her. She should have stopped spending time with him as soon as she realized she wasn't falling in love.

"Thank you," he returned. "I believe I have made my intentions clear over the past weeks."

Clarity held up her hand, and he stopped, open-mouthed and mid-speech. She should not have been caught unawares. She hoped she could prevent Lord Brennon from proposing because she would have to turn him down, which was a grave thing, indeed. The fault was entirely hers, foolishly believing a grown man could be content to remain as they were for the remainder of the Season, for no other reason than because they were having fun.

"You have been clear," she agreed. "Were I to pretend otherwise, it would be a lie. And I have happily kept company with you because you are charming and witty. I hoped by this time..." She trailed off as he began to frown. "That is, I fear your attachment has grown stronger than my own."

His forehead smoothed. "That may be true since you are easy to grow fond of."

How sweet of him! And yet, searching her heart, Clarity couldn't dredge up a spark indicating she would ever feel more for him than she did at that moment. Maybe he was overestimating his own feelings for her. If so, they could return to the party and pretend they had conducted a private conversation about... about...

She couldn't think of any reasonable excuse they could offer. And with him continuing to gaze tenderly at her, there was nothing she could do now but end their association. She saw that as clearly as looking through a freshly vinegared window pane.

"It is easy to become fond of someone with whom you spend a great deal of time," she began. "Nonetheless, that doesn't indicate—"

She gasped as Lord Brennon grabbed her hands in both of his in a gesture of passion that she hadn't witnessed from him before.

"Clarity, I love you!" he declared.

Oh, dear! Her stomach sank.

"I am terribly sorry," she said, watching his expression change from hopeful to crestfallen. "It is entirely my fault. I know that men and women make attachments during the season with the idea of a proposal at the end. Frankly, I didn't think you would wish to become engaged this quickly." *Rather pell-mell,* she thought, *like a runaway horse.*

Again, his expression grew placid. "I understand now. I have rushed you. You aren't averse to an engagement between us but are only concerned by the haste."

She swallowed. That would be an easy way of putting off hurting him until they returned to London. Like a coward, she could send him a missive, telling him they should no longer keep company.

However, she was no coward.

"I am sorry," Clarity repeated. "I do not think I... no, you deserve utter honesty. I will never fall in love with you, my lord. If I were going to, I am sure I would know it."

Frozen for a moment, Lord Brennon finally sighed. Then he nodded.

"I am disappointed. Some might say devastated, but I am not a complete fool. I did keep a little of my heart in reserve in case this didn't work out as I had hoped."

"I didn't realize that was possible," she said, admiring the man even more. If the situation was reversed, she had no doubt she would be crushed.

In truth, she knew deep down to her bones such a horrible experience awaited her when Alex and Miss Brambury made their own announcement.

"As I said, you are kind, my lord. I wish my feelings were otherwise. Moreover, I cannot express how appreciative I am that you never once said I was a diamond of the first water." Her voice broke with a hiccup of sadness, and she knew she was going to cry.

"I thought it," he said with a small melancholy smile, finally releasing her hands, "and I still do because you truly are."

Her tears started to fall, and as the gentleman he was, Lord Brennon produced a handkerchief and handed it to her.

"I shall gather my things and leave at once."

"You don't have to," she said, although they both knew he did. Everyone would know what had occurred.

"Yes, I do. While I can say I am not entirely devastated, I am also unwilling to endure the torment of being in your presence a moment longer, knowing now that you will never be mine."

She nodded. After all, it was the same reason she half-wished Alex had never come, while at the same time relishing each minute in his presence. It was, as Lord Brennon said, the very definition of torment.

"In that case, my lord, because we have been friends and because I wish you the best, I urge you not to travel at night. I would not be able to sleep if you did. There is a well-appointed inn in the village, and I will make sure our driver takes you there directly." She hoped he would at least think of her as a caring person, even if she'd trampled his heart.

"I will not snub you when we meet in London," he said, which put him head-and-shoulders above most.

She sniffed again as fresh tears threatened. "I shall alert my parents as to your departure."

And then he was gone, not only from the library but from her life. How strange to have been spending so much time with a man suddenly to realize she never would again.

A wave of loneliness crashed over her as she blew her nose on his handkerchief. She had, in fact, grown fond of Lord Brennon.

What a pity she couldn't have loved him. Nor could she have married him without love, grateful he hadn't asked her to compromise.

Chapter Seventeen

Brennon was absent at breakfast. Alex was not the only one to notice, but maybe he was the only one to feel a sense of relief. That did not speak well of his selflessness. However, since Clarity didn't appear distraught, he thought it acceptable to be the smallest whit pleased she hadn't accepted the man's marriage proposal.

What was Brennon thinking, making such a public spectacle of himself?

More importantly, Alex wondered why he was damned relieved she hadn't tied herself to him.

If her face had been ruddy and her eyes swollen with crying, he might have felt otherwise. Because much to his surprise, Clarity had become as dear to him as she had been before, in the youthful days when he'd cherished their friendship. Moreover, her happiness was important.

While Clarity didn't have the look of the brokenhearted, she was quieter than he'd observed previously. Keeping her attention on her food, she let those around her carry the conversation while she poked at her coddled egg disinterestedly.

Alex spent the better part of breakfast trying to catch her eye. He had no right to pry, nor was it his place to comfort her should she need it, but he wanted her to know... *what precisely?* He supposed he wanted her to know he cared.

When he finally succeeded in gaining her attention, she gave him her smallest smile and turned quickly away.

Later, as they all parted ways, some to change clothing depending on their chosen activity or lack thereof, his aunt sidled up to him, leaning close.

"What happened last night was exactly as I expected of Lady Clarity, a muddled and public failure, causing derision instead of respect. Maybe you and Miss Brambury can take up the mantle of the suitably engaged couple." She tapped her chin. "You could make an announcement tonight at the ball to make up for Lord Brennon's debacle."

He winced at her words. "That seems a tad premature."

"Whatever do you mean?" Aunt Elizabeth frowned at him, her nostrils flaring. "There is no reason to wait, especially if you hope to have your affairs organized by year's end with a wife installed on Grosvenor Square, one who can capably run your household. Think of the ease with which Miss Brambury will arrange a festive Christmas dinner and a Twelfthtide party. And then before you know it, you will be the proud father of an heir."

Wordlessly, Alex stared a moment, but all he could summon himself to say was, "We'll see."

In his room, which was the same one his parents used to occupy, he sat upon the bed and mused over his aunt's words.

Marry in order to have his holiday parties organized and a child in the new year?

Strange advice from the woman who had never been particularly festive during the Twelfthtide or anytime, nor did she like children if he recalled correctly.

More than most, though, he knew how everything could end in the blink of an eye, and he must remind himself his aunt was only looking out for his future as she'd done since the accident.

What if he didn't have an heir because he dallied and something happened to him? Ending the Hollidge viscountcy by dawdling would be yet another way he disappointed his parents.

Aunt Elizabeth was right, after all. There was no reason not to choose Miss Brambury if all he was looking for was a competent mate. No reason at all.

Certainly not because of the unwelcome rekindling of some silly childish emotion, for an unpredictable female who had repeatedly demonstrated how impossibly unsuitable she was.

And also how impossibly delightful, sweet, and passionate, too. She sparked an avid and relentless craving in him each time they were close. Tossing himself back onto the counterpane, he closed his eyes and considered. He would be a happy man to be alone with Clarity Diamond, holding her close, feeling her heartbeat against him. Even if they did nothing else, he would be content.

Of course, there was a lot more he wanted to do with her!

And by her mouthwatering kisses and the way her eyes sparkled when they looked at him—not to mention how she'd given Brennon the mitten—Alex could dare to believe she felt an intense craving for him, too.

He groaned. If he could go with his heart and not worry about the consequences, it would be an easy choice, although not necessarily a good one. All he had to do was get through the next twenty-four hours without making a dreadful mistake, and then he would be on the way back to the sanctuary of his study.

Meanwhile, he'd agreed to an archery outing. Unsurprisingly, Emmeline declined to attend, and just as expected, Clarity was enthusiastically eager to participate. Since her glum demeanor at breakfast, her effervescence had returned when he met the group on the back terrace.

Some might say that spoke of a fickle nature. In fact, his aunt said that very thing before he bid her good morning and headed out with the party toward the targets.

Most of the gentlemen were with them and also Lady Fenwick, again keeping her elderly husband company, and Radiance, the redheaded younger Diamond sister.

"Only wait until you see how much I've improved," Clarity boasted, as if they had last drawn bows the week before.

She'd never been one to sing small about herself, but he liked that. It had made the difference in their ages less relevant as the somewhat plump girl tried to keep up with him in all regards, out of sheer determination.

"Your improvement cannot be difficult since you never once hit the target last time we let arrows fly," he reminded her.

Adam spoke up. "My oldest sister is quite good, Hollidge. We joke she could join the Grand National Society if she wanted."

"Is that so?" Alex asked, impressed.

"I may decide to join Queen Victoria's St. Leonards Archers," Clarity said. "Thanks to Father."

"I have given her and her brother many lessons," Lord Diamond said. "And Ray, too, now that she's shown an interest."

Alex felt a heaviness in his chest. He tried to recall every minute his father spent passing along advice and lessons, cherishing each one. Still, he wished he'd come to visit after his parents died, for gladly, he would have accepted the earl's tutelage.

"And how are *you* as a bowman?" Alex asked Adam, realizing Clarity was staring at him as if she knew his thoughts—how many memories had been made freshly raw by returning to Oak Grove Hall.

"I'm passing fair, am I not, Father?" the heir asked.

"You are better than Ray and worse than Clarity," Lord Diamond concluded.

"Too much talking," Clarity said. Then she looked at Alex. "How about a wager?"

"Clarity!" her father said. "Your mother would be appalled." But he grinned, and the others in their merry party chuckled.

"And why isn't Lady Diamond with us?" another of the guests asked. "I've competed with her before, and she is an excellent archeress."

"She is indeed, but someone had to stay and handle the watercolor activity, and it couldn't be me," Lord Diamond said. Then he nodded toward his daughter. "Ladies first."

Alex was impressed when Clarity drew her forty-pound bow and shot a 26-inch arrow, hitting close to the middle of the nearest target, which was fifty yards away.

"Bravo!" he said before anyone, and she offered him a pleased smile.

They all took a turn on the near targets, with the men using sixty-pound bows. Alex, who hadn't practiced much in years, was by no means the best. Yet it was enjoyable, and he decided he would take it up again at his country estate.

Soon, they'd all progressed to the farther targets, apart from the younger sister who declared herself ready to sit with old Lady Fenwick and watch. However, Clarity continued until the end, and as Lord Diamond had said, she was consistently good.

What's more, she handled the bow and shot the arrow with grace and femininity combined with unexpected strength. She was both womanly and competitive!

Alex found it difficult to focus on anything except her. Perhaps that was why he was shooting worse even than young Adam.

"A pity we didn't wager," she said, removing her shooting gloves.

"Indeed," Alex agreed. "You would be much the wealthier."

Although full of admiration for her, he was shocked when they returned to the manor, and in the midst of the other guests, Clarity crowed about her accomplishments.

His aunt glared disapprovingly, although it was Lady Purity who gave the subtle set-down.

"Didn't you think your fellow archers would give an accurate account of your skill, dear sister?"

Clarity's mouth snapped closed, and her cheeks turned crimson before she added, "Each one of the shooting party performed very well."

"I wouldn't say that," Lord Fenwick disagreed, entirely oblivious to the undercurrent of disapproval over the poor manners Clarity had displayed. "I shot like a ten-year-old girl, but I can hardly see past the end of my nose. Thus, I am sure I am forgiven."

"You shot like Odysseus, my love," said Lady Fenwick. And the two wandered upstairs to change from their outdoor clothing.

Clarity followed, looking morose, and Alex couldn't help feeling sorry for her. She had a joyful nature that overtook her good sense in some instances. He recalled being the same way.

"Tea and cake in the drawing room," Lady Diamond announced.

Some guests went to change from their outdoor clothing, while others headed directly for the promised refreshments.

Aunt Elizabeth approached with Emmeline.

"How was your painting session?" Alex asked.

"Even if either of us was as talented as the famed Mr. Sandby, I'm sure we couldn't compete with Lady Clarity's self-proclaimed ability."

"She was merely excited," Alex defended her. "She has a remarkably accurate aim, even at a distance."

"She was conceited!" Aunt Elizabeth declared. "Humility is a wonderful trait in a female, and that young lady lacks even a wisp of it."

Alex was pleased Emmeline had not piled on the insults. But then she spoke.

"Lady Clarity's pride and lack of humbleness are undoubtedly due to being doted on by her loving family. One can and must forgive her for knowing neither her limitations nor the agreeable nature of polite meekness."

Alex sighed. Both ladies were making a mountain from the smallest mole hill and painting Clarity to be gloating and pretentious.

Unsure why they were still discussing the matter, he pointed out, "I believe tea is being served in the drawing room." Giving them each a short bow, he strode away.

Chapter Eighteen

"It is as though Purity is the older sister," Clarity moaned almost as soon as Alex entered her mother's private sitting room on the second floor.

Seated on the sofa with her feet tucked up under her, she was folding sheets of paper to distract herself. Sadly, she couldn't deny they all looked abysmally like the same freakish winged dog, and not one like the delicate bird she intended.

She hadn't been the least bit surprised when Alex found her. As children, if he came looking, she was usually in this room where her mother had the most glorious trinkets and whatnots. And if she was ever looking for him, he was in the stable, all the way up in the hayloft.

"Why don't I have more sense? Why must I be so frivolous?" she asked when he came to stand in front of her.

"Not frivolous," he corrected. "Playful and frolicsome."

"And rudely boastful," she added. "I swear I didn't intend to turn all my geese into swans."

"You didn't say anything that wasn't true," Alex protested. "Your sister was harsh," he added.

It was kind of him to take her side.

"I bet Purity wasn't the only one to say something." Clarity sent her latest attempt at a bird dashing to the rug with the others piled there.

When he looked uncomfortable, she knew the truth.

"Your aunt thinks I'm a crow. Admit it. And Miss Brambury does, too."

He shrugged, confirming the worst. As the eldest daughter of the hosts, she ought to have behaved better.

"I admit I was overly pleased at having done well." She snatched up another piece of paper and began to fold back the corners for wings.

"It's your exuberant nature," Alex said. "Besides in a way, I'm the oldest son, albeit the only one," he added, making her smile, "and I was beyond exuberant if you'll recall. I didn't have an ounce of sense when I was younger."

"You grew up to have it," she pointed out. "The good sense to earn an Oxford degree and handle your father's land. Accordingly, you earn the respect of all who know you. And then to top it off with cream, you sorted out your personal life by choosing a suitable female at your very first dance."

"I think it was the second ball," he corrected, crouching at her feet and examining the folded bits of paper.

She had a good look at the top of his head and thought he had lovely hair for a man.

"Besides," he said, "I had everything playful knocked out of me by tragedy that I wouldn't wish upon my worst enemy. I envy you your family. Eldest or youngest or in between, how lucky you are to have your siblings."

She nodded. "Your situation would have been far more bearable if you'd had a brother or sister to share your grief. But we were here. Why didn't you ever come back to visit?"

"My aunt said I wouldn't be welcome because of how much your mother cherished my mother."

Shocked, Clarity's mouth fell open as she tried to make sense of his words.

"I'm sorry, but I do not understand," she said after a moment.

"Because I would be a painful reminder of whom Lady Diamond had lost and why."

Another confusing statement. "And why is that?" Clarity asked, dropping her feet to the floor and leaning toward him as he spoke.

"Because it was my fault." Alex's words were dropped into the air between them like heavy, sharp rocks into a smooth pond.

"Nonsense," she said when she recovered.

"You hesitated because it is not nonsense," he said, rising to his feet and pacing to the window. "Amazing to think my parents looked out upon this same view."

But she wouldn't let him change the subject.

"I hesitated because I was greatly surprised by your wrongheaded thinking. Your parents died from a broken wheel causing their carriage to career over a steep bank, and nothing to do with you at all."

How had his aunt made him believe otherwise?

"The journey was undertaken because of me. They would have been safely in London, living their happy lives, if they hadn't had such a wayward son whom they had to drag to boarding school to put on the straight path."

He turned to face her. "If I had been a serious and proper heir, they would be alive today!"

She'd felt her eyes grow larger with his words. *What a terrible burden he carried and so pointlessly!*

"I tell you again, Alex, that is nonsense. Moreover, it is inaccurate to lay the blame at your own feet."

He gave a bark of derisive laughter. "Then whose?"

"Your aunt's!" she insisted.

He shook his head, and his shoulders flagged. "I know you don't care for Aunt Elizabeth, but she means well and has raised me as best she could."

"Out of guilt, I warrant. And she didn't raise you," Clarity pointed out. "She shipped you off immediately to that horrid school where you were beaten."

"It wasn't that horrible, merely a shock after my earlier life. Other boys were beaten, too," he dismissed with a shrug. "And I came home on holidays. Besides, why would my aunt feel guilty? She wasn't even in the carriage."

Clarity took a deep breath. She had to tell him, wishing her mother were there to do it instead.

"After your parents died and it had been ages since I'd seen you, I asked my mother why you couldn't come to visit. She became distraught."

Alex's mouth tightened in a line.

"Not because of you. I caught her at a bad moment. Normally, she is the epitome of patience and serenity. At that instant, however, she raised her voice and said you couldn't come because you were at that 'miserable school' Lady Aston pressured your parents into sending you."

She fell silent. Alex appeared hardly able to breathe.

"If you don't believe me," she said, "you may speak with my mother. She told me Lady Aston convinced your parents you should attend Eton. My mother recalled it specifically because your aunt said it would be worth every penny of the £300 it would cost per term. Lord and Lady Hollidge didn't like the idea of being parted from you and were determined to see if it was a jolly place before committing to anything. And that is why they were going," Clarity insisted. "Not to send you away because they were disappointed in you."

She placed her hand on his forearm.

"After they died, I suppose your aunt didn't bother to find out whether it was jolly or not."

"It was not," he said softly. Then his gaze lifted from the floor to hers. "Well, I'll be damned."

That wasn't something she'd expected the stuffy, proper viscount to utter. It nearly broke her heart. She put her other hand on him, too, now grasping both his upper arms. He didn't shake her off.

"It does put things in a different perspective," he said, his green eyes unwavering as he gazed into hers. "Then why did she keep me from visiting all of you?"

Clarity shrugged, wishing it were her place to put her arms around him.

"Perhaps she worried my mother would tell you the truth if you ever mentioned your feelings of guilt."

"I can scarcely believe this. It doesn't excuse my behavior—"

"You were a child doing childish things," she insisted.

He nodded. "It doesn't excuse my pushing the limits of childish behavior," he amended, "but what you've told me does bring me a sense of relief." He paused. "I didn't push them into the carriage and force them to ride to their deaths."

It wasn't a question, but Clarity gasped and answered anyway.

"No, of course not. How awful for you to have ever thought such a thing!"

Before she realized it, she had pressed herself against him, laying her cheek on his shoulder and sliding her arms around his waist purely to embrace his motionless form.

After the briefest hesitation, his arms went around her, hugging her to him as tightly as she could imagine. Neither attempted to turn the gesture into anything more, and Clarity had no idea how long they stood there. All she knew was she wanted to give him as much comfort as she could. She didn't expect to experience such a sense of well-being in return.

When at last they broke apart, with him loosening his hold first, there was no embarrassment. He smiled down at her, and she returned it.

As usual, being the more sensible, he turned away and walked toward the door.

"Thank you for not using your considerable feminine attributes to turn this," he gestured at the two of them and the room in general, "into something improper and compromising. It's wonderful to know we can still be friends."

She nodded, yet her heart pinched. She would be his friend always if he would allow it, but she could still wish for more.

"Regardless, I suppose we had better not be found unaccompanied," Alex added, while not sounding as inflexible as previously he might have.

"I suppose not," she agreed, letting him walk away without another word, obviously needing to be alone with his thoughts.

Saturday morning, Clarity awakened with a sense of dread. It was the last full day of the house party, which would be capped with the ball. Their guests would all leave on the morrow, including Alex.

Being a bit of a crow herself, the previous evening, Lady Aston mentioned to the other ladies in the drawing room after dinner how she expected her nephew to be married before the year's end. Miss Brambury blushed accordingly, looking pleased as Punchinello.

Clarity had felt ill. If Alex seemed his vibrant self, full of interest, vim, and vigor when in Emmeline's company, it wouldn't pain her so, but the tepid interactions she had witnessed saddened her further.

What a colorless, paltry life he was condemning himself to! Unless he truly loved the woman.

Clarity decided to ask him outright. If he said he loved Emmeline, then she would let him alone. If his heart was not engaged, then she might try to convince him the entanglement was nothing but an error.

At breakfast, she did not change her mind. Guests were offered a casual arrangement, taking their morning tea and eggs either in the salon, the dining room, or outside on the veranda since the weather was fine.

Clarity enjoyed the veranda, and it seemed Alex was of a similar opinion when Miss Brambury was overheard to worry about gnats and too much sun. With a rueful glance to where Clarity and her siblings were eating, he turned heel and escorted the lady back inside where undoubtedly his aunt was already enjoying the gnat-free interior.

Wolfing down the remainder of her breakfast, Clarity went to find him, determined to ease her mind long before the evening's ball. Luckily, she caught him descending the stairs, wearing a lightweight jacket. Apparently, he was going out.

Twisting her hands in the skirts of her green gown, a pale version of his verdant eyes, she looked at his handsome face. When he peered expectantly back at her, for a moment, her thoughts scattered like dandelion fluff.

"Were you looking for me?" he asked finally.

"Yes." She coughed.

He waited patiently until she took a deep breath and plunged ahead.

"Are you free or otherwise—?" Clarity cut herself off mid-sentence. She'd nearly said the word *engaged*. "Or otherwise committed to some activity?"

"Miss Brambury and my aunt went upstairs for their wraps and sturdier walking shoes. I was going to take them to the knobby hill."

"Are you?" She took a step back. Clarity didn't want him taking those women anywhere but especially not there. "To *my* knobby-kneed giant?"

Long ago, they'd made up a tale of a giant lying down, and the two hills on the Diamond land were his knees.

"The knobby-kneed giant," Alex repeated, offering a small smile that seemed larger than it was due to its rarity.

Clarity bit her lip. Maybe he was going to ask for Miss Brambury's hand on top of the hill, a sunny, beautiful place with a view of the river. Glancing up the stairs, seeing no one but Lord and Lady Fenwick starting their descent, she hoped she still had time.

"Lady Aston and Miss Brambury are taking longer than you anticipated to get ready. Maybe they have a touch of indigestion. Cook's breakfasts can be very rich."

Taking hold of his arm, she began urging Alex toward the door, hoping to get him out of view before the women came downstairs.

He looked behind him, concerned. "Do you really think so?"

She did not but heard herself saying, "Absolutely. Perhaps they're even having a bit of a lie-down."

"Surely walking is better for digestion than lying down," Alex said.

"I don't know about that." Clarity had succeeded in getting him out the front door, and now they would have to walk around the side toward the back.

"I probably shouldn't go far," he said.

"I know I should leave you to a walk with Miss Brambury, and you can have time for that later, but I was having trouble falling asleep last night—" she began.

"As was I," he said.

They looked at one another, and her breath caught. *Please let him agree to walk with me,* she prayed.

Chapter Nineteen

"If we take a stroll, perhaps I can tell you what I was thinking, and you can tell me what was keeping you awake," Clarity suggested, hoping he didn't start to squawk about impropriety and chaperones. Not here on her family's estate.

Alex blinked, seemed to relax, and finally nodded. They fell into step, going along at a quick pace, her because she was trying to get him as far from Miss Brambury as possible and him because he had long legs.

When they had gone through her mother's flower gardens, nodding to other guests, and then past the vegetable gardens and through an arbor, they were on the path to the wooded copse.

She grabbed for his arm. "Can we slow down a bit now, please? I am not a brown hare."

"My apologies. It felt good to strike out without the others."

"Like the old days," she said.

He slowed a little. "You don't really believe both my aunt and Miss Brambury have indigestion and are lying side-by-side recuperating, do you?"

A bubble of hilarity escaped her lips at the picture he painted.

"Of course, not side-by-side," she said.

"Not at all," he affirmed.

"Perhaps not. I wished to speak with you."

"All right," he agreed. They were in the middle of the woods, and he began to look around him. "I recognize this area."

"You should. There's the climbing tree." She gestured to an elm that wasn't really any different from any of the other elms.

"That tree is taller than I recall," Alex said. "Are you sure that's the one we climbed? The one you fell out of?"

"I didn't fall so much as get pushed," she reminded him.

"God, I was a terror. I could have broken your neck."

"Nonsense," she said. "I think children bounce."

He looked at her as if she were a different species. Then he shook his head. "I'm not convinced it was this tree."

"It was," Clarity promised. "We ran from over there"—she pointed back toward the stables—"toward that hill where my kite finally took flight, and then as we were heading to the pasture, the wind wrenched it from my hands and took it into this tree. See, there are the two hazel trees. Remember collecting the nuts?"

He nodded. "I suppose you're right."

"After all," she said as she patted the elm's rough gray-brown trunk, "we have grown up, too."

"You have become a lovely lady," he blurted.

She felt her cheeks warm with pleasure.

"And you have become a handsome man," she said, wanting to lean toward him and kiss him before recalling his earlier compliment about her not using her feminine attributes. *Friends first and foremost.*

"But you are also now a viscount with a head full of responsibilities and worries."

He nodded, looking suddenly morose.

She touched his arm. "I would take some of your worries if I could."

His eyes widened and he wrinkled his nose. Shocked, she realized his eyes were glistening. However, when she would have wrapped her arms around him and consoled him for whatever pain was torturing his thoughts, he turned away and looked up at the tree.

"A good solid tree," he proclaimed, also touching the fissured bark.

"It was," she said, "until it was struck by lightning. You can't see from here, but there are a lot of dead branches on the other side." She looked up into its jagged, hairy leaves. "We discovered the best view that day when we went up and reclaimed my kite."

He nodded, still not looking at her.

Clarity was determined to help him regain his good humor before she asked him about his heart's true intent.

"Come along," she said, "give me a hand up to the first branch. I've got my boots on, so I can climb rather well. I need merely a helping start."

"No," he said. "Children might bounce, but grown-up earl's daughters most certainly do not."

She laughed. "We most certainly do. Remember the hedge in Hyde Park? I bounced right over it."

She heard him chuckle, and her heart gave a painful squeeze. *How she loved the sound!* How she wished she could coax it from him more often.

"A leg up, my lord."

"No," he repeated but less sternly.

"Please. I will sit upon the first branch and enjoy the view. What harm is there in it? And you'll keep me safe. That is, if you'll join me?"

He hesitated, then she watched him strip off his jacket and flex his arms.

"Easier to climb when unencumbered," he declared. Stooping low beside her, he laced his fingers together and looked up at her.

She clapped her hands. "Thank you." With that, she put her booted foot upon his gloved hands and launched herself onto the first low branch. "As easy as mounting a horse," she avowed.

Pulling herself up to standing, she put her hand over her brow and surveyed the countryside.

"Good but not good enough." Looking up, she found the next branch was within easy reach, almost like a step. In the next instant, she was a few feet higher. "That's better."

"Stop right there," Alex said as he leveraged himself into the tree. "You said you would only ascend the first branch."

"Did I?" Without hesitation, she went higher. "This is the perfect tree for climbing because the branches are evenly spaced. Come up, Alex. It's beautiful."

He did as she said, not seeming to mind that she kept going higher, with him following a bit below her. Either he didn't notice their rapid ascent, or he was enjoying it too much to put a stop to it.

Then abruptly, she was stuck, held fast by a small twig of a branch that snagged her hat.

"I think I am going to forego hats entirely after this, both for riding and for climbing. They are more trouble than they're worth."

"Stay still," Alex ordered.

"I have no choice. It's a good thing this branch is sturdy. It will easily hold both our weights. I think." She snickered.

"Why is that funny? If you were alone, you would have a devil of a time getting yourself free. Eventually, when it was winter and all the leaves had drifted off, they would find your skeleton clinging to the trunk."

She laughed harder. "Stop. When I laugh, I close my eyes, and that's not good in this situation."

He climbed closer.

"Besides," she said when he joined her on the branch, "I wouldn't do this alone. I am not a lunatic."

"Truly?" He grinned at her, and the breadth of his smile seeped into her like sunshine to a flower. Then he looked out over the land behind her. "The view is worth the climb. I agree."

"I *would* agree," Clarity said, "except I cannot turn my head and see it. Please, Alex, free my hat."

"Please, *Lord Hollidge*," he corrected.

She laughed again, closed her eyes, and swayed. Naturally, his arms went around her.

"*Ow,*" she said. "The hat pins are tugging my hair. It's most uncomfortable. Please, Lord Hollidge, Viscount of the Hollidge estates, won't you free me?"

"I shall." And he did by snapping off the small twig and drawing it out from under her hat.

"I am eternally grateful." She gazed out around her family's land. It had been a long time since she'd seen its beauty from such a lofty vantage.

"Isn't it lovely?" she asked.

"It is," he agreed.

She turned to look into his jade-green eyes. One of his arms was still around her, while the other held the branch beside them for support. He drew her close against him.

"Are you looking at the view?" she asked, even though their gazes were locked.

"I am," he said.

Clarity went absolutely breathless with wanting him.

Lowering his mouth to hers, Alex claimed her lips in a searing kiss. Throwing caution to the wind, she let go her grip of the tree and put her hands upon his shoulders, able to feel his muscles through the fine lawn of his shirt.

Tilting her head, she fused her lips more firmly to his, and he groaned.

With her pulse quickening and her body beginning to throb with desire, she heard a strange sound. If she didn't know better and wasn't deliriously happy to be in a tree kissing Alex, she would think it was her heart cracking. Her eyes popped open.

Surely, if he broke her heart, it would sound exactly like—

"Christ!" he exclaimed as they dropped, nearly spilling off the old branch until it caught on the branch below.

Alex flailed his arms wildly, managing to catch hold of the trunk, anchoring them.

Rocking, she realized she was hearing the same cracking sound.

"The compounded weight of our bodies and the broken branch is breaking the next one," he said. "I think this whole tree was weakened by the lightning strike."

"Won't it keep happening all the way down?" Clarity asked as the branch they stood on creaked, groaned, and began to bend.

"What harm is there in climbing a tree?" he mimicked. "For God's sake, woman, let go of me and climb sideways."

For the first time, she felt a sizzle of fear. They were fairly high after all. And if something happened to him, it would be entirely her fault.

"Hurry," he urged. "This is not the time for the impetuous Lady Clarity to become a dawdler."

Doing as he said, she reached out and grabbed hold of another branch to the side, using it to swing down to the next closest one that could hold her. Even as she got settled, the branch she'd vacated broke, and Alex dropped down another few feet.

She shrieked.

"I'm fine," he said. "And also getting closer to the—" The next branch went down with the weight of the two on top of it. Alex disappeared, and she yelled again.

"Still fine," he called up after a moment.

She giggled, despite the somewhat dire circumstances.

"Poor old elm," she yelled to him.

"Poor, indeed! It withstood lightning but not you," he returned. "I seem to be stable now and nearly at the bottom. Wait for me to stand beneath you, and then you can start your descent."

"Oh, *pish!*" she said and began climbing down.

"Blast it all, Clarity! Must you always be so blasted pigheaded?"

Not considering herself at all pigheaded, she continued making her way steadily from branch to branch until she was on the lowest one, with nowhere to go but a five-foot drop to the ground.

Glancing over, she saw him jump the last few feet, landing and stumbling forward before he turned back to her.

"Why don't you sit first," he asked, "and then jump into my arms?"

"If you insist. This gown is utterly ruined," she added, letting her exposed, stocking-clad legs dangle over the side toward him. "I am glad I'm too old to be sent to bed without supper. Cook is making my favorite roast chicken with a citrus glaze tonight."

And then she dropped onto him.

Alex didn't catch her as much as he broke her fall before they both toppled over. As a gentleman, he made sure to take the brunt, ending up on his back with her cushioned on his front.

"Thank you," she said, looking down at him, her hair cascading into a curtain on either side of their faces.

"Your hair has come down again. Maybe you should shave it like those last-century ladies with their wigs."

She laughed. "Maybe I will."

"No!" he said suddenly serious. "Your hair is glorious, like black silk, and you should never cut it."

His tone caught her attention, as did how delightfully warm she felt atop his strong, hard body, not to mention the way his hands were roaming up and down her back.

"What about when my hair has changed to gray?" She wanted more than anything for him to still be her friend to see it.

"Then it will be like a silver waterfall and still glorious," he promised.

"A silver waterfall," she repeated. "That's far too frivolous a thing for the Viscount Hollidge to say."

His fingers sank into her hair and drew her head down until their lips met again. With her heart thumping against his chest, she was a wild thing, sprawled atop him, able to feel the heat of his arousal pressing low against her stomach. *This must be a dream!*

Pulling back, she gazed down at him. She should tell him how she felt.

"What is going on here?" Lady Aston's voice was unmistakable. And she was not pleased.

Guiltily, Clarity rolled one way and Alex, the other. Raising her head, she looked at his aunt and his intended, who appeared more confused than perturbed.

Had their kiss been witnessed? Clarity guessed not.

Alex was quickly upon his feet, reaching down to assist her.

As soon as she was upright and brushing her gown, hopelessly dirty and torn, she shrugged.

"I fell out of the tree and landed on Al—on Lord Hollidge," Clarity explained, hoping to keep him out of trouble.

They were adults, but her need to protect the boy who'd always taken the brunt of responsibility for their antics was as keen as ever.

There was no reason for his aunt to know he'd been climbing the tree with her.

"What were you doing in that tree?" Lady Aston demanded of her. "No doubt awaiting my nephew's passing so you could spring upon him."

Clarity should have taken offense. And deep down, she did. However, the notion of her waiting on a branch under the cover of leaves, in order to pounce upon her prey, tickled her tremendously.

"Like a big cat?" Clarity asked, glancing at him.

She couldn't tell if Alex recalled the time he put the large barn cat in the empty porcelain tureen in the middle of her grandmother's sideboard. The tabby had fallen asleep, giving the housekeeper a shock when she lifted the lid.

Yet he didn't appear amused nor reminiscent. All vestiges of the lighthearted man had disappeared. After all, the woman who would become his wife was eyeing him with a measure of disapproval.

"Lady Clarity's branch collapsed under her," Alex said, which was the truth. "Luckily, I was in the right place to be of assistance." Knowing how improbable that sounded, he added, "We had walked out together to see the view."

"But why are you in a state of undress?" his aunt demanded.

Alex glanced down, patting his waistcoat, and then looked around for his jacket, which he retrieved.

"You don't have to explain any further, my lord," Miss Brambury said. "I know you are covering for Lady Clarity's high-jinks. I have been warned." She looked meaningfully at his aunt.

"I say," Clarity began, then thought better of protesting.

While he ought not to have been kissing her, she should cease tempting and teasing him. And while she hadn't had a chance to ask him if he truly loved Emmeline, if Alex was choosing that lady and the life she represented, then there was no point in putting up a fuss about his aunt casting aspersions.

"I believe I shall leave the three of you to enjoy your walk and the lovely afternoon," Clarity said, feeling magnanimous and mature.

Turning to Alex, who appeared uncertain if she had to name his expression, she added, "I thank you again for saving me, and I apologize for involving you in my tomfoolery."

And she *was* sorry. *For him!*

As she strode away, feeling three pairs of eyes fixated upon her back, Clarity realized that any man who wanted Emmeline Brambury would never suit her. She only wished it didn't seem as if by abandoning the field of battle, she was condemning her good friend to a life of endlessly dull tedium. And a lack of passion, too.

Chapter Twenty

lex felt like a caged animal. While knowing he and Clarity had conducted themselves irresponsibly, even dangerously—for broken bones were no laughing matter—he couldn't shake the notion he'd behaved in keeping with his genuine nature.

Instead of thinking first, considering the ramifications and consequences as he'd done since his early days at boarding school and which had been lodged deep into his brain while studying law, he had simply acted.

Proceeding without pontification and doing something that might make one smile.

Whatever had gotten into him?

It was a rhetorical question for he knew what had got into him. Or rather, *who.*

But his aunt had made promises to Miss Brambury, maybe even to her parents. And she'd invited Emmeline to the Diamonds' house party with the hope of bringing them closer together. Fortunately, there was nothing on paper. Moreover, Alex personally had made no verbal avowal. At least, he couldn't be taken to court to plead in his own defense over breaking his word or a contract.

Truthfully, he had no cause not to choose the lady his aunt thought best. Emmeline was precisely what he'd imagined he wanted in a wife. Even then, as they trod through the pasture back toward the manor, she had not a hair out of place, nor a hint of a smudge, or even a stray leaf or flower petal on her.

Yet now, he couldn't stop thinking of what he most desired. Clarity was visible ahead, about to turn up the path to the rear of her family's home. Her hair was a fright, she was dirty, and had so many leaves stuck into the gauzy outer layer of her day gown, she was more tree than woman, practically ready for a costume ball.

"I completely understand what occurred here this morning," Miss Brambury said as Clarity took a turn in the path, disappearing from sight, and Alex could direct his attention back to the lady at hand.

"Do you?"

"Yes," she insisted. "When I return to my family's estate in Essex, I find myself not only behaving more immaturely but also cleaving to the things from my happy childhood. Why, I might gaze fondly at the porcelain dolls arranged on the shelf in my room."

"Might you?" he asked, thinking that made for a poor childhood.

"I have sometimes asked our cook to make me her porridge with sultanas, which I loved as a child. There is nothing quite like the food one remembers fondly. Or I might ask the maid-of-all-work to whip me up a batch of clay in order to sculpt something. Even when very young, I was talented."

"Whip you up a batch of clay?" Alex repeated, feeling a feather of amusement tickle him. Obviously, Emmeline had no idea where clay came from, and thus, he doubted her story of being a young Michelangelo. Clarity's boasting must have irked her more than he'd realized. It was no matter, but he suddenly had a question.

"Do you wish to become a mother?"

Behind them, his aunt gasped, and he wondered if such a question were inappropriate. He sensed it was slightly vulgar, as it evoked *how* one became a mother.

"If you don't mind my asking," he added to soften the query.

Emmeline blinked. "Lord Hollidge, I am a normal female with the natural inclination to bear children. I know my duty to give you an heir, and I know my duty to have extras in case our eldest is not fortunate enough to survive to maturity."

He faltered a step. Good lord, but the lady sounded exactly as he might have a few weeks ago. There was a lot more to having children than bringing them up merely so they could survive and then have their own children.

The three of them had turned onto the path, but Clarity had vanished already into the house.

"What of fun?" Alex asked Emmeline.

"Fun?" she echoed.

"Yes. *Fun.*"

"What do you mean, my lord?"

"I don't know what you're asking," he chided. "You know the word, do you not?"

"Hollidge!" his aunt chastised him.

Without heeding her, he added, "It's a perfectly good word meaning amusement. And I am wondering what you think about children having fun, and you with them, for that matter."

Emmeline gaped like a fish, then answered. "I suppose I haven't thought about it at all."

"Not once?" he asked. "Not once in your whole life have you thought about fun?"

Emmeline smirked but didn't really smile.

Had he ever heard her laugh?

"Assuredly, I have thought about fun," she insisted. "I like to take tea with my friends or even have a glass of wine with them."

"Yes," he urged, "and what else?" If she didn't at least mention charades, all hope was lost.

"There are drawing room games, as long as they're not too boisterous," she allowed.

He recalled the evening with the Diamonds lately when it had dissolved into hooting and howls of laughter. Emmeline's games sounded dull. Perhaps he could remind her of things she liked that were fun, and it would spur other activities.

"You enjoy riding," he said.

To his astonishment, she made a face. "I do, but it's not because it is amusing, my lord. I do it to see others who are out riding. Not only for their fashion, but for their pairings."

"Pairings?" he repeated.

"Yes, my lord. To see who might be a couple. That's fun."

Was it? He didn't think so.

"How about a fast ride for the excitement of it?"

She shook her head, appearing shocked.

"For the benefit of physical exercise?" he persisted.

"Physical exercise?" Emmeline repeated, frowning again.

Alex knew their association was over. Emmeline was the stickiest stick, and he no longer could bear it.

They stepped onto the Diamonds' paved terrace, and he ought to usher her inside. However, he was determined to finish the telling conversation first.

"Yes, Miss Brambury. Fresh air, deep breathing, moving your body, and all that."

Her brow cleared. "Oh, I don't believe in any of that nonsense."

"You... don't... believe... in... fresh... air?" Each word came out slowly, incredulously. The feather tickling his insides became an entire bird, clucking its amusement. Before he could stop himself, he barked out a laugh. Then he snorted and laughed harder.

"What is it?" Emmeline pleaded. "I fear you are having a fit, my lord."

His aunt, well aware he was in a paroxysm of good humor, made an exclamation of frustration and walked past him into the house.

Still, Alex didn't answer since he was laughing too hard to breathe. Then he wheezed and finally coughed before he could stand up straight once more and catch his breath.

"My apologies, Miss Brambury. I was gripped by a bout of that amusement we were speaking of, and I am out of practice. Anyway, where were we? You were explaining how you don't believe in air."

"Not at all, my lord. I meant that I do not hold with this fiddle-faddle about needing to take in great gulps of it or to exert one's body. I believe the Town air is perfectly fine, nourishing in its hardiness, indubitably created from the rich minerals of the coal being burned. And I certainly don't think it's a good idea to tire out one's body, risking early old age and advanced deterioration."

He shook his head. "It is a wonder how much thought you have given to *not* exercising and yet how little you have given to having fun."

She opened her mouth, then shut it. Finally, she gave a delicate shrug.

"You needn't worry, my lord. I shall always behave in an entirely appropriate manner. You will never have to worry about my embarrassing you or causing you a moment's misgiving by doing anything childish."

"I believe you," he said. "I am sorry to say that is the main reason I must let you know I cannot go along with my aunt's wishes regarding a union between us. I may as well tell you now *before* your heart grows in the least attached to the idea of becoming my viscountess."

He had little fear she would actually become attached to him personally.

She blinked at him. "But we are perfect for one another," she protested. "Perhaps when Lady Clarity fell out of the tree and landed upon you, she damaged your skull."

"On the contrary. When Lady Clarity fell upon me, she knocked some sense back into my head." He held the door open, but she didn't move.

"Are you seriously rejecting an engagement between us?" Emmeline demanded with more passion and heat than at any moment since he'd met her.

"I am," he said, and the relief Alex felt at no longer having to pretend to wish to marry her was like a sweet, cleansing rain. "And may I point out we are alone without a chaperone? Your parents would not be pleased."

Emmeline gasped, looking around her. "They most definitely would not. I cannot believe you have allowed me to be compromised in this fashion."

"Never fear. I don't think anyone would consider you capable of being compromised, not with your rigidly incorruptible morals and your unyielding disposition."

With that, Alex gestured for her to enter, but he didn't follow.

Slowly, he wandered toward the stables, almost without realizing it. Once there, he climbed the ladder into the hay loft and lay down his body, bruised from being attacked by an elm tree and providing a cushion for Clarity.

There, in the sweet-smelling clean hay, he had a great deal of thinking to do.

Chapter Twenty-One

"I have gone too far!" Clarity moaned while Purity brushed her hair.

"Why did you push your luck in such a manner?" her sister asked.

"I thought to remind him again of how good life can be."

"In a tree?" Purity shook her head. "You always knew how to have fun, but you were never reckless, at least not since you donned stays. What has gotten into you?"

Miserable, Clarity felt tears well up.

"I am in love with Alex."

Purity barely hesitated in brushing before she nodded. "And you're trying to show him by nearly getting you both killed?"

"Of course not! I simply want him to like me the way he used to." She broke into wrenching sobs.

"Nonsense," Purity scolded. "You don't want him to like you as a boy likes a girl. You want him to love you as a man loves a woman. I admit I find Lord Hollidge a bit stiff, but he's better than he was a month ago at the first ball. You have done wonders already, and he will see your suitability."

"I have done nothing," Clarity said through her tears.

"You have been a good friend to him and reminded him how to laugh. Being around you has awakened his latent sense of fun."

Clarity dabbed at her face with her handkerchief.

"Do you think so?"

"Yes. Now that he is nearly ready to fall for you, instead of falling on top of the man, why don't you show him what a fine lady you've grown to be?"

"I won't pretend to be a Mrs. Princum Prancum," Clarity protested.

"No one would believe it if you did. You don't have to become like his Aunt Elizabeth, just a little less of a tomboy."

"You know I never liked that term. I am female through and through." They used to squabble when children about this same issue. While Clarity was out having her own kind of fun, flying a kite or braiding the horses' manes, Purity practiced the pianoforte and became adept at painting.

"I know you are, dear sister. And a rum doxy, too," she said, not using the most acceptable of terms except between sisters. "But perhaps with the fishing and the archery, Lord Hollidge has forgotten what a prime article you are. If you want the man to worship you, you must dazzle him."

"Dazzle him?" Clarity repeated.

"Dazzle him!" Purity concluded. "Wear your blue silk dress to the dance, and let Mary do your hair in the pink of the fashion with ringlets to spare."

"But Miss Brambury," Clarity reminded her, "is the paragon of placid perfection."

"*Pish!* She has nothing you do not have."

Then why had Clarity never felt more inferior in her life?

"Emmeline is a little taller, and she has that tawny-colored hair, currently in fashion, not black as a crow's wing."

"I like to think of our hair more as a raven's wing," Purity said, touching her locks, "or even rare obsidian."

"That does sound better than an old crow." Clarity put her arms around her sister. "Thank you. *You* should be the eldest."

"I should be," Purity agreed, "but no matter our order, never forget, we are Diamonds of the first water."

Her sing-song voice caused them both to start laughing over how many times they'd heard the phrase since coming out into society, and each time spoken by a man who thought he was saying something beyond clever.

"Very well," Clarity agreed. "I shall dazzle him!"

It was hard to show off one's gown and hairstyle to a man who wasn't there. Alex had disappeared, vanished after she'd fallen on him and walked away. Clarity feared he might have left Oak Grove Hall, but their butler confirmed his things were still in his room.

He hadn't shown up for the light buffet dinner before the dance, nor was he there for the opening grand march. Neither was Miss Brambury.

"They have run off together," Clarity predicted miserably. "Probably to Scotland."

"No, dear," said her mother. "Such people as Miss Brambury and, unfortunately, the young man Alex has become do not dash off to Gretna Green. They have banns and announcements and parties. Then they get married in the heart of London, have a staid wedding breakfast, and go off on a short, honeymoon somewhere extremely ordinary, such as Norwich or Leeds. Bath, if he's lucky, but only for his new wife to attend to her health. Moreover, because they know little of one another, which is painfully obvious, Miss Brambury will insist on a female companion to ease the transition to wedded life."

Clarity's eyes widened. "Mother, are you clairvoyant?" For surely, Alex had mentioned such a plan for his marriage, barring the part about another woman going on his wedding trip.

"No, sweet girl. It's simply predictable and dull, neither of which describes you. I wish Alex wasn't, either. His parents most definitely were not, and I am sorry he turned out that way."

Clarity recalled the conversation in her mother's sitting room.

"Because he blames himself for Lord and Lady Hollidge's death." She wasn't divulging any secrets by explaining it to her mother. "Since the age of thirteen, Alex has carried guilt over being too rambunctious and high-spirited, thinking he caused his parents to want to send him to Eton. I know it's not the case, and I even told him, but I'm not sure he believed me."

"Poor man," Lady Diamond said. "No wonder he became so serious."

Clarity nodded. *If he hadn't run away with Miss Brambury, where was he?*

"I have to get back to the ball. These things don't run themselves," her mother said.

"May I search for him?" Clarity asked.

Her mother's brow furrowed, a rare expression for her usually carefree face.

"I suppose. But not out on the grounds alone, and no farther than the stables."

"The stables!" Clarity repeated. "Mother, you're brilliant!"

Clarity knew with certainty Alex would be there. Whenever they had got themselves into the suds, he retreated to the loft, and sometimes she followed him. And often on the morning before his family was to leave, he went there. Sometimes Clarity thought he might try to hide up there in hopes his family left him, especially when his aunt was sharing their carriage.

In five minutes, she was at the base of the ladder.

Softly, she called up to him, but there was no response. With her gown draped over her left arm and her legs exposed up to her knees, Clarity climbed the ladder.

A sigh of relief escaped her when she saw him, stretched out in the hay. He'd removed his coat and balled it under his head and had one arm over his face, apparently sleeping soundly.

Rolling her eyes, she smiled, wishing she could capture this peaceful moment and look at it whenever she wished to see him. Instead, she committed it to memory and then dropped to her knees beside him.

"Alex," she said. "Wake up, please."

He stirred, slowly lowering his arm and opening his eyes, until he was peering up at her. Then he grinned, and her heart lurched against her ribs.

"You look beautiful," he said. "Am I dreaming?"

Before she could answer, his hand snaked out and grabbed hold of her arm, dragging her across his chest.

"You feel real. Very warm and soft."

Her pulse racing, blissfully happy to be in his arms again, Clarity could hardly speak.

"I am real."

"I was dreaming about you. Thus, I'm not sure," he said. "Let me test."

With one of his hands at the back of her head, and the other at her back, he pulled her down for a kiss, agonizingly tender until the moment it wasn't.

Like oil in a hot pan, their mouths sizzled, and her body burned where it rested atop his. She wished she could strip off all her garments and his, too, and feel his bare skin against her own. It was her greatest yearning, to be naked with him.

When his mouth opened under hers, she slid her tongue inside, and he groaned. In a dizzying motion, Alex rolled her over until she was on her back, and he loomed above her.

"My Diamond," he murmured.

A shard of bittersweet memory pierced her as she remembered him calling her by that same name. Although there were five siblings, she was *his*, the one who would play his games and get into trouble with him.

"Come along, my Diamond, we shall see what we can do with this rare find of milk paint." They had wickedly turned one of the brown horses dappled white.

"The day is fine, my Diamond, and we shall sail to the West Indies." They'd made a wretched raft that broke apart as soon as they put it in the river beyond the pasture.

"Alex." His name came out as a whisper of wanting, and she closed her eyes, thinking she might cry.

Lacing their fingers, he captured her hands in the straw on either side of her head, and then his mouth claimed hers again. Every particle of her body was tingling with urgency. Where their hips met, she pulsated maddeningly, and squirmed beneath him, trying to ease her plight.

His lips left hers to scorch a path along her chin and down her neck, and she arched to give him better access. Releasing her hands, he levered himself on his forearms so he could gaze down at her.

Her thin silk gown had a fashionably low neckline that gave him pause.

"I like this dress," Alex murmured against the upward swell of her right breast. "Very much." Then he licked her heated skin.

Gasping, she bit her lower lip as liquid heat pooled at her core.

"It's almost too easy," he said, tugging gently at the décolletage until both her breasts were exposed.

Wild and wanton, and nearly desperate, Clarity wanted his mouth on...

"Yes!" she hissed.

His lips had closed over one of her nipples. When he sucked and soothed it with his tongue, her body jerked at the sensual assault. And when he treated the other nipple in a similar fashion, she couldn't help sounds of pleasure from escaping her while shivers danced down her spine.

But she wanted more.

"You must touch me," she begged, writhing against the prickly hay beneath her.

"I know I have been a tedious bore," he said, drawing her skirt up with one hand until the cool night air caressed her silk stockings and the bare skin of her thighs above them.

He'd never bored her, yet she couldn't find her voice to gainsay him.

"But I hope you will do me the honor of marrying me, anyway?" he added.

She didn't hesitate. "Yes! Just touch me!"

His husky laugh caused the junction of her thighs to throb with need. And when his fingers tantalized the soft curls between her legs, her body hummed with anticipation. Finally, the pad of his thumb touched her pulsing bud.

"*Oh!*" she breathed out on a sigh.

In the space of a heartbeat, the long-simmering yearning blazed through her veins while every muscle coiled and tensed. Alex stroked her again and again, rapidly yet delicately sending her into an exquisite euphoria.

Gripping him tightly, she clenched her fingers into the fabric at his shoulders.

Lifting her hips to give him better access, she couldn't control her movements or stop the thundering tremors that shook her. Eyes closed, arching against his hand, her legs splayed farther open, and then she keened as a quivering release took hold of her.

With her body trembling from the power of it, she was grateful he kept touching her while the sensations peaked and then began to ebb.

For a long moment, she could do nothing but breathe deeply as his fingers slowed their blissful movements. Her heart was still racing, but her body calmed and stilled.

"Sweet Mary!" she muttered, opening her eyes.

Alex had a half-smirk on his handsome face. It made her chuckle.

"I bet you want to sleep now," he said, brushing his knuckles against her cheek.

Part of her did, but there was another part that knew there was more.

"No, I want... you." She cupped her palm against his face.

"Clarity," he warned.

She lifted her hips. "All of you. I've waited long enough."

"Proper ladies don't do that until *after* they're married."

"Proper?" she repeated, wishing the word had never been invented. "Like Miss Brambury."

"She's gone," he said. "Before I fell asleep, I heard a footman ask the stable boy to hook up the carriage to take one of the guests to the station. By the way, I am eternally grateful you are nothing like her."

She digested this fact—*Emmeline was gone!*

"You sent her away because you don't want her?" she asked, needing to be sure.

"Correct."

"*Hm.*" The evening was getting better and better. "Well, I *am* a proper lady, yet I still want all of you. That is, if you are truly going to marry me."

"Oh, you remember that, do you?" He pretended to wince.

She giggled. "I do. And it's the only time in our whole lives I shall ask if you were being serious?"

"I was. I am! Desperately serious, in fact. I cannot imagine a life without you by my side." Then he cupped her breast. "And under me. And sometimes astride me."

"You are *not* being serious!" she scolded.

"I am. I love you, Clarity Diamond. And you cannot take it back. You said yes."

"I love you, Alexander Hollidge. I don't want to take it back. I cannot wait to marry you." She stroked his cheek again. "And I cannot wait for the other thing, either."

"As you wish. I have grown into a responsible man. I cannot leave my lady wanting more. It would be grossly irresponsible! Why, the code of gentlemanly behavior practically dictates I concede to your wishes and make love to you!"

And he did, slowly penetrating her before beginning a steady rhythm of his hips until she couldn't catch her breath and would swear she saw stars swirling behind her closed eyelids.

Gracious!

Chapter Twenty-Two

"Why didn't you tell me the moment you awakened me?" Alex asked as he hauled Clarity to her feet. "I had lost all notion of the time."

After the most intensely glorious climax of Alex's life, Clarity had casually announced they ought to return to the ball. It was already in full swing, like the many bells in "Oranges and Lemons," which they all learned in the nursery.

"I thought it was obvious," she explained, smoothing down her skirt. "After all, I'm wearing a party dress, am I not?"

Pulling the neckline back into place, she hid her beautiful breasts, which was the sole reason he was able to speak coherently.

"I am still wearing my day clothes," he pointed out, reaching for his crumpled coat.

Shrugging into it, he stood before her.

After she brushed at it and made him spin around, she did the same and let him brush her off. They ended in an embrace that caused a bonfire of desire to blaze through him again.

"Let us skip the party," he suggested.

She didn't reply before tossing the hem of her skirt over her arm and stepping onto the ladder.

"You should have let me go first," he grumbled, but she was already halfway down to the wood planks of the stable floor. "If you fell, I could have caught you."

"I think tumbling on top of you once in a day is enough."

He jumped down beside her, grinning, with a pointed glance back up to the hayloft. Clarity's cheeks turned rosy.

"Very well," she said "*Twice* tumbled is enough."

"Not nearly enough," he protested.

Taking her hand, they ran like children to the main house and in through the side door.

"Let me go change," he pleaded.

"If you must, but I shall wait outside your door," she insisted. "I am not going into the ball without you, nor can I change as everyone already saw me. They would wonder at my disappearance *and* at my appearance in a new gown."

Alex sighed and made a decision. It would be unfair to make himself neat and tidy while allowing her to remain disheveled.

"Never mind. If you are going in all scruffy, I shall, too."

"Scruffy?" she repeated, glancing down at her obviously wrinkled skirt. "Am I too rumpled?"

"You are perfect," he said.

Of all the things they'd ever done, showing up in a state of disarray was probably the most outrageous. He could only pray it wasn't painfully evident they'd been rolling around in the hay. To that end, he tried to pick the last few pieces of straw from her hair, but the damage had been done.

He would be lucky if her father didn't shoot him on sight.

Offering Clarity his hand, they strolled through the hallway and entered the ballroom. He would swear the musicians faltered and a hush went over the room for a few seconds, but it might have been his imagination.

However, there was no imagining Lord and Lady Diamond's stare, nor how swiftly they were approaching.

When Clarity's parents were close, her mother's eyes widened. Amazingly, she smiled.

"What the deuce!" her father said with a shake of his head, his still raven-black hair lifting and falling.

"I apologize, my lord. I know I am not exactly cutting a bosh figure tonight."

"Not your natty self, to be sure," the earl agreed. "But then my daughter also seems to have been through the mill and let the cat drag her in."

"Geoffrey," Clarity's mother addressed her husband, "it looks like we're going to have a wedding."

Instead of demanding a duel at dawn, Lord Diamond clapped Alex on the shoulder.

"Welcome to the family," the earl said. "And God help you!"

"Father!" Clarity exclaimed. But her beautiful smile was in evidence, and Alex couldn't remember ever feeling happier.

"Lady Hollidge got her wish, after all," Lady Diamond said, threading her arm through Alex's. "Would you like me to tell you about it?"

And he let the woman who would become his mother-in-law take him for a stroll around the room as she explained how his own mother had wished for him to marry Clarity.

At the same time, despite his untidy appearance, she proudly introduced him to one and all as her eldest daughter's fiancé, turning the party into an engagement celebration.

The single blemish on the evening was the blue-deviled face of his aunt, standing alone. And although she accepted a glass of champagne in his honor, she looked anything but congratulatory.

As soon as he'd made the rounds and had his health and Clarity's toasted a dozen times, he broke free of the throng and went to the side of the woman who'd been a steady presence in his life.

"I hope you aren't too disappointed by the departure of Miss Brambury. We never would have suited, you know."

With a twist of her lips, Aunt Elizabeth took his measure, head to toe.

"Perhaps not, at least not as you are lately."

"I fell asleep in the hay," he explained, brushing his hand over his coat, even though he knew it was hopelessly wrinkled.

She shook her head. "I didn't mean merely tonight, although you should have changed before strolling in here like a plucky peacock."

Alex cocked his head. "I am sorry you disapprove."

His aunt startled. "I didn't expect you to apologize to me."

"I know you have a heartfelt interest in my future. I appreciate how you've tried to guide me."

To his amazement, tears glistened in her hazel eyes.

"What's wrong, Auntie?" he asked. "Are you that upset over my engagement? I assure you Lady Clarity makes me happy, and I, her."

"It's not that. I, too, wish for you to be happy, more than you know. Yet I fear falling in love with Lady Clarity will cause you misery in the end."

Of all the things his aunt might have said at that moment, those words were the most unexpected.

Handing him her empty glass, she drew a handkerchief from her sleeve and dabbed at her eyes.

"I loved my brother very much," she said. "And I know at times I was an unwelcome appendage to the family."

He started to gainsay her, but she cut him off.

"When you were a small boy, my husband had only recently died."

"Yes, Lord Henry Aston. I know. My mother told me once that was why you went on holiday with us."

His aunt nodded. "Lord Aston was—" she interrupted herself. "Your fiancée appears to be looking for you," she told him, gesturing with her handkerchief behind him.

Glancing over his shoulder, his heart squeezed when he looked at Clarity. Her sister Purity was surreptitiously pulling a piece of straw from Clarity's sleeve.

When he thought of how she'd become in such a state, he couldn't help smiling. He would try to show more restraint until their wedding night, but it would be difficult. Joining with her had been *the* most joyful experience of his life.

"Go to her, Alex."

Nodding, he took a step and then halted. Lady Diamond was smiling over something her husband said, and they were holding hands. Adam was rolling his eyes over the antics of his youngest sisters, who had been allowed to attend the ball but were trying to snatch his glass of champagne.

And Clarity—*his dear Clarity*—was whispering in Purity's ear, making her younger sister burst out in uncharacteristic laughter. Purity was usually so proper.

"Come along, Auntie. We are all going to be family. We might as well start acting like it."

He offered his arm, which she took, and they crossed to the jubilant side of the room.

Chapter Twenty-Three

The wedding was everything a Diamond marriage celebration ought to be, large, lively, and filled with laughter. Even Clarity's two sets of grandparents came. Her father's parents arrived from their estate on the mild Cornish coast. James Diamond had retired there upon being honored with the title of marquess years earlier, at which time he passed on his earldom and title to Clarity's father.

Her maternal grandparents, Lord and Lady Chimes, came to Town from their country estate in the Surrey Hills. Despite enough room in either the Diamond or the Hollidge homes, the tendency of the grandparents to get along like badgers fighting over elderberries, made it fortunate Lady Diamond's parents kept their townhouse on Upper Brook Street.

Other relatives came for the marriage of the eldest Diamond daughter, as well as many friends. Clarity had never imagined feeling such joy as she did when she stood with Alex in the church and became his wife before the many people who loved her and wished her well.

Looking up into her husband's beloved face, she knew she had been blessed with the perfect man. At the wedding meal that followed, she could hardly recall what she ate. And then they were off on a trip to John O'Groats, just as they'd once discussed many years earlier.

"The Continent *next* time," Alex promised. Yet two weeks into the journey, with much cajoling from Clarity, they decided to extend their trip.

"Why not?" Alex asked, trailing a finger around his wife's navel as they reclined in bed in a Scottish inn.

"Why not, indeed?" Clarity asked. "You have years of amusement to make up for. And what better time than at the beginning of our married life?"

Alex didn't respond. He was too busy kissing his way across and down her bare skin. She giggled.

Thus, after a ten-shilling-and-six-pence ferry ride from Dover, they spent three more weeks traipsing around France and Italy. When they'd barely set foot in Florence, he began to appear distracted.

"Most people travel the Continent for months," Clarity reminded him as they stood in the octagonal Tribuna room of the Uffizi Palace, staring wide-eyed at the antiquities and Renaissance paintings.

Tearing his gaze from the wall, he looked at her. "You know I cannot do that."

"I know. Let's enjoy today." Over dinner, she promised she would ask him to go no farther than Rome. From there, as promised, she forsook seeing Naples, and they took a boat to Barcelona.

Clarity was seated on a beach overlooking the Mediterranean. Despite wearing a large hat, she also had her parasol up to protect her from the late September sun. Seated at her feet on a cotton blanket, Alex was fidgeting instead of relaxing.

A child came along selling shells, and she bought a bag.

Alex lifted his hat off his eyes. "You know we have seashells in Britain, don't you?"

"I do, but they aren't Spanish shells, are they?" She tucked the pouch into the sack she carried, holding all the bibs and bobs she acquired each day. "Now tell me why you aren't enjoying either that book or the splendid view of the sea." She'd purchased a book in English about Greek and Roman antiquities before they started their "grand tour," as she liked to call it.

"I appreciate the book, my love, but I've already seen the same as it describes. And frankly, I have had enough of the old." He tossed it down onto the blanket. "I'm thinking of the future and the responsibilities awaiting me back home," he confessed. "I have people who depend upon my estates for their livelihood. And the longer I am away, the more chance things can go wrong."

Clarity was racked by guilt. She'd been extending their wedding trip due to her own anxiousness at what awaited them when they settled down in London. For whenever Alex mentioned it, he grew serious, pensive, and even morose. But she could put off their return no longer as it was distressing her husband.

"Tomorrow," she said, "we shall start for home."

"London first," he agreed, removing his shoes and stockings. "But then I must travel around to all my holdings."

Clarity bit her lip. They would be apart for the first time. Anticipating an empty bed beside her, she sighed.

Laughing at her melancholy expression, he reached up and stroked her hand.

"Naturally, you must come with me, Lady Hollidge, so I can introduce my wife to my estate managers and to my staff."

This was the first she'd heard of accompanying him, and joy coursed through her.

"I thought you were tired of me already and wanted to leave me in London while you roamed England."

"I could never grow tired of you. You are my heart." He rolled up his pant legs and stood before capturing her hand and tugging her to her feet. "Come along. We are going to paddle in the sea."

Snatching her parasol from her, he tossed it to the sand. Then sweeping her into his arms, Alex ran into the warm water lapping at the shore.

Clarity didn't care if her splashing husband soaked her shoes and the hem of her dress, for she couldn't stop laughing.

It seemed inconceivable that the Lord Hollidge she'd met at the beginning of the Season could have turned into the one now able to play in the sea.

"Please don't drop me," she ordered, making him threaten to do exactly that.

That evening, over supper at a seaside inn, she vowed, "I shall never grow tired of being your wife."

"I'll hold you to that as a woman of your word," he said.

Alex intended not to introduce any bad luck to the beginning of their wedded life and carried Clarity over the threshold of his home in Grosvenor Square.

"We have returned," he announced to his butler, setting Clarity on her feet in the entrance hall. "Mr. Berard, this is Lady Hollidge."

As he said the words, he turned and looked at Clarity, whose rounded eyes mimicked his own.

"That still sounds wonderful," he said. "Doesn't it?"

She nodded, her cheeks blushing softly.

Letting Berard take their coats, Alex gave him instructions to bring in their trunks. The sour look from his butler told him he oughtn't have done so.

"Sorry, my good man. I know you have it all under control." And he gave his butler a warm smile.

Mr. Berard looked at Alex as if he were not himself. And he wasn't. Alex felt lighthearted, and when he took Clarity's hand, everything around him seemed fresh and new.

"What shall we do first?" he asked her. "Do you want tea? Or a meal? Or—?"

"How about you give me a proper tour of my new home," she suggested.

"Splendid idea," Alex agreed. "Isn't she splendid, Berard?"

"Splendid, my lord," the butler agreed before disappearing outside to direct his footmen.

"You embarrassed him," Clarity protested.

"Did I?" Alex asked. He didn't care. "But you *are* splendid!" He grinned at her. *How was it possible this glorious woman was his wife?* The fact hit him anew now that they were back on Grosvenor Square where they would settle in and start their married life.

"Now what precisely did you mean by a 'proper tour'? Did you mean we must be on our best behavior, or that we go over every inch?"

Those words put a decidedly wicked thought into his head—of going over each soft inch of her skin with his tongue. And since they were alone with his pulse speeding up, and since she was his lawful wife, he drew her close.

"May I kiss you?" he asked. "To welcome you home?"

"Yes, please," she said.

Their lips met and heat coursed through his body, from his heart to his groin. Maybe the tour should start in his bedroom. Sliding his hands down her back, he grasped her round bottom in each palm, squeezing gently as he pulled her hips against him.

She gasped into his mouth, and he took the opportunity to slip his tongue between her lips and stroke her.

"Well!" came his aunt's voice from the staircase.

Despite their wedded state, they broke apart like guilty lovers.

"Aunt Elizabeth, we're home," he said, not letting her disapproving expression dampen his spirits.

"I can see that. Luckily, the staff didn't have to bear witness." She turned her gaze to Clarity. "Welcome, Lady Hollidge. I hope you find your new home to your liking."

He felt Clarity startle. Perhaps that was more welcoming than she'd expected.

"Thank you, Lady Aston. I look forward to learning my way around here and settling in to my new responsibilities."

"You need do nothing but attend to your husband. The house runs like a perfectly balanced top."

Alex nodded, for it did. His staff was most efficient.

"I see," Clarity said, and he wondered at her lack of enthusiasm. Maybe she was tired after all.

"Do you still want to see the whole house, or would you prefer to rest?"

"I wish to see everything," she said.

A few minutes later, they were on the second floor, coming out of Alex's study, which he'd confessed to leaving as it was when his father used the room. Next to it was a closed door.

When Clarity put her fingers upon it, Alex stayed her hand.

"That's my aunt's sitting room," he said, leaning past her and knocking with a sharp tap.

When there was no answer, he hesitated before pushing open the door.

Without setting foot inside, Clarity surveyed the comfortable interior with a small sofa and a chair before the hearth, some bookshelves, and a little table. In the corner was a writing desk.

"My aunt brought these furnishings from her own house, except for the desk," Alex said in answer to her unspoken question. "That was my mother's."

Clarity nodded, half expecting Lady Aston to pop up from behind the sofa and chastise them for entering her private domain.

"I suppose this ought to be your salon," Alex said.

Clarity thought for half a second about what upheaval that would entail.

"No, thank you. That won't be necessary," she said. "Let Lady Aston keep her sitting room. I will find another room to make my own."

At the tour's completion, including her bedroom adjoining his, they dallied for an hour, giving them an excuse to change out of their traveling clothes. Finally, they sat in the drawing room drinking tea.

Nothing in the house was the least bit shabby. It was clean and dusted. Everything that ought to shine was polished or oiled. The decorations and furnishings of Hollidge House, however, were quite out of twig compared to the Diamond home on Piccadilly, which was universally considered to be pink of the mode from cellar to attic.

"Are you attached sentimentally to all the furniture and the way it is decorated?" she asked, trying to tread carefully in case he was keeping his home like a shrine to his parents.

"Not at all," Alex said. "I look forward to your sprucing things up as well as you have brought a sheen of Clarity Diamond to my life."

After those encouraging words, Clarity sought out the housekeeper first thing the following morning after Alex retired to his study.

"I would like fresh flowers delivered once a week," she explained to Mrs. Rigley after finding her in her domain, a small sitting room in the basement.

The woman was still recovering from the fright of the new mistress of the house coming downstairs.

"You ought to have rung for me, my lady. You shouldn't be down here. Lady Aston never comes down here."

"That's no matter," Clarity said, hoping to soothe the housekeeper into complying without any fuss. "The flowers, Mrs. Rigley. I don't want them in bouquets, mind you, as I shall arrange them myself. I'll need a good assortment of fragrant blooms—roses and pinks, of course. And when you can get them, peonies and lilacs, too. Even the humble daisy will be most welcome."

The woman nodded, but asked, "Have you consulted with Lady Aston?"

"What for?" Clarity asked, mystified. *Did Alex's aunt have a flower preference?*

"Lady Aston oversees the household accounts."

"I will be taking over the accounts," Clarity said, fully intending to. "Were you here when Lady Hollidge was alive?"

"Yes, my lady."

"Then you recall the flowers. I wish to revive her lovely practice. If you are still in possession of her vases, then I would like you to bring those to me after the first flower delivery. I need enough for the front hall, the formal drawing room, the breakfast salon, Lord Hollidge's study, and our bedroom."

She tried not to blush on saying the last words.

Mrs. Rigley nodded, yet two days later, no flowers had arrived.

Clarity sighed. Deciding not to browbeat the housekeeper, she knocked on Lady Aston's door, which was ajar, and even poked her head inside.

Alex's aunt was seated and reading a newspaper with an empty teacup on the table beside her. Wearing spectacles, she lowered them immediately, frowning at the interruption. A second later, her forehead smoothed.

"Come in, Lady Hollidge. How are you finding your new home? Is everything to your liking? Perhaps you would like more towels?"

Lady Aston had a way of making Clarity feel like a guest, despite the word *home*.

"Everything is fine where towels are concerned. I would like to have fresh flowers brought in for me to arrange."

"I see." His aunt narrowed her eyes, and Clarity could tell Mrs. Rigley had discussed the matter with her already.

"They can be costly," Lady Aston remarked.

Clarity nearly laughed at her. It wasn't as if a few flowers were going to cause them to starve or even to cut back on wine.

"Nevertheless, I intend to have flowers. Alex's mother had them, and he recalls the lovely aroma throughout the house when he was a boy."

Lady Aston nodded. "Yes, I remember. Well, if *Alex* wants flowers, then that's all right. I shall make sure they are ordered once a month."

"Once a week would be preferable," Clarity said, "or at the least, every fortnight."

"Very well," Lady Aston said, leaving Clarity in doubt which it would be.

More than that, she wondered at this strange process of having to consult with Lady Aston. Surely, Alex and the staff didn't expect her, as the new Lady Hollidge, to kowtow to his aunt.

Thus, before excusing herself from this encounter, which felt like a pupil coming before a headmistress, Clarity said, "I believe I should take over the household accounts."

Lady Aston's nostrils flared. "That won't be necessary."

"I beg your pardon," Clarity asked. *Were they going to war over this?*

Alex's aunt smiled benignly. "What I mean to say is that as soon as you are settled and learn the ways of this household, as well as how much stock we go through and who our suppliers are, then naturally, you must take over. For the time being, I urge you to settle in and enjoy the early days of your marriage, remaining as carefree as possible."

Clarity supposed that sounded reasonable.

Lady Aston added, "I did not have a lot of time with my late husband before his passing, and I cherish each moment of our marriage. I wish someone had told me at the time to concentrate more on pleasing Lord Aston and less on worrying about the flour bins and barrels of wine for the cellar."

"Sound advice, indeed," Clarity agreed. "I thank you for it."

When she left, her heart had decidedly softened toward Lady Aston. The woman was only trying to ease Clarity's way into the household and allow her to spend more time with Alex. When the first flowers arrived the next day, she was grateful for the woman's cooperation.

Chapter Twenty-Four

Alex heard happy voices coming from the drawing room and stopped to listen at the uncommon sound in his normally quiet home. One voice was Clarity's, and the other he recognized as Purity's. Just as he'd been drawn to their joyful group at the Devonshire House ball many months earlier, he now couldn't help going into the drawing room.

"Husband," Clarity exclaimed, jumping up to greet him.

He wondered how he could ever have thought her too forward. It was a distinct pleasure to witness the outward signs of her affection.

"Wife," he returned, meeting her halfway across the room, not even cringing when she threw her arms around him in front of her sister.

"Excuse me for witnessing this," Lady Purity said with mock horror, shielding her eyes with her hands.

Clarity laughed. "Stop teasing," she said. "I know you don't mind if I embrace Alex."

"Truthfully, I don't," Purity agreed. "How are you, Lord Hollidge?"

"I am well. What brings you to our humble abode?"

"Merely a brief visit. It's nice to get out of the house and come to a place that feels as comfortable as home. Clarity makes it such."

He nodded, glancing at the table before them, strewn with publications and odd scraps. He knew what the scraps were, more of Clarity's folded paper creatures.

"I brought some of the latest magazines for home decorating," she added, seeing his glance.

Before he could comment or release his wife, his aunt entered behind him.

"That will never do. Even if Lady Purity is family, I know she is also a woman of discernment and cannot possibly appreciate being subjected to your public impropriety."

Alex slowly released Clarity, noticing both the sisters looked as if they were about to burst out laughing.

"That's better," Aunt Elizabeth said when Clarity resumed her seat beside Purity. Then his aunt frowned. "Moreover, I didn't realize we were having company. If I had, there would be tea and cake already on the table."

She glanced at the pile of crumpled paper.

"Lady Purity's visit was *not* on the house schedule." Bending down, his aunt grabbed up two handfuls of Clarity's paper-folding detritus and tossed it onto the hearth. "That nonsense is a terrible waste of precious paper," she added.

Clarity's cheeks turned pink, and Purity at once came to her defense.

"On the contrary, Lady Aston. The meticulous and minute practice of the art of paper folding should be considered beneficial to the female brain, which is known to have a tendency toward imprecise and unfocused thoughts."

Alex's aunt didn't fall for any humbuggery. Taking a seat, she said, "Be that as it may, we now have a shortage of writing paper in this house."

"Shall we all take tea?" Clarity offered, going toward the bell-pull.

"I ordered service as soon as I heard voices," Aunt Elizabeth said, and Clarity's face fell. Yet Alex couldn't help but think his aunt had helped.

While they waited, now in silence except for his aunt discussing the weather, which she'd always insisted was the single safest topic,

Purity absently picked up one of the remaining sheets of paper and began to make little folds.

As the conversation regarding how warm was too warm and how cool was too cool progressed, Alex realized Clarity was staring as hard as he was at her sister's fingers—quickly, methodically, and effortlessly turning the rectangle into a square and then folding the square into a delicate bird.

Clarity actually winced as Purity tossed it onto the table in front of her when the maid came in with the tea.

Aunt Elizabeth leaned forward and picked it up. "How clever! Look, Alex, isn't that a pretty thing?" Then she looked at Clarity. "Is this what you've been trying to do?"

His poor wife! Purity had not done it on purpose, but she'd embarrassed Clarity beyond measure.

"How did you do that?" Clarity asked, her voice near to trembling.

Purity gaped as if she hadn't realized what she'd done.

"I… I," she began, then she coughed. "I only did what *you* taught me."

"Poppycock," his aunt said. "I've watched Lady Hollidge, and she hasn't folded a single page that looked like anything but a bowl of porridge."

"Aunt Elizabeth!" Alex cautioned.

But true to form, his Clarity offered a smile.

"Lady Aston is correct. While I appreciate my sister trying to cover up her own aptitude while bolstering mine, I agree with Lady Aston's assessment. But I must know how you did it, dear sister?"

"I read the book you left behind," Purity said. "I'll bring it next time. It is much easier if you follow the written instructions precisely."

Feeling pleased with the results of the flower arrangements, Clarity made sure one could catch the joyful aroma of roses from nearly every room on the first two floors of the house.

Mrs. Rigley even remarked how it was just like when the former Lady Hollidge was alive.

"She used to sketch her arrangements," the housekeeper recalled.

"Where are those sketches now?" Clarity wondered. "Are all the previous viscountess's things stored in the attic?"

"Yes, my lady, although there might be some drawings in the desk in Lady Aston's salon."

At least Mrs. Rigley hadn't recommended Clarity ask permission to search the attic before she curtsied and went about her business. Regardless, Clarity would ask Alex's aunt if she had come across them before she went on an attic expedition.

When her husband's strong arms slipped around her waist from behind while she was standing quietly enjoying the drawing room, she squealed in surprise, then delight.

"Did I startle you?" he asked, nuzzling her neck, making her body tingle.

"I wasn't sure for a moment if it was you or Mr. Berard."

They both laughed. The sound of Alex's laughter was a boon to her soul. Knowing she had helped conjure it after all these years tickled her. Turning in his arms, she slid her hand up and laced her fingers behind his neck.

"Do you like the flowers?"

"I *love* the flowers. And I love you for bringing them back. I would never have guessed that their scent would make our house smell like home again. The air seems lighter even while being perfumed."

She beamed at him. "I am very happy."

"As am I."

He bent to kiss her. As always, when his lips touched hers, she experienced a firestorm of pleasurable fluttering in her stomach while sizzling desire heated her, seeming to turn her muscles and bones to molten liquid. Nor could she deny his simple, perfect kiss caused her to grow damp between her legs now that she knew what swiving felt like.

Relaxing against him, Clarity relished his large hands roaming across her curves, molding the fabric of her day gown.

"Let's go upstairs," he whispered. "I can think of nothing more important than making love to my wife."

In minutes, she was spread across their counterpane in broad daylight, bare as a newborn with Alex's mouth upon her. Sinking her fingers into his thick brown hair, she closed her eyes and accepted his worship of her body.

When he swirled his tongue around one nipple and the other and then continued down her body, searing a path toward her soft thatch of curls, Clarity held her breath.

"Ow!" he exclaimed, his mouth against her womanly mound. "You're tearing out my hair, woman!"

She giggled, releasing her hold, not realizing she'd been fisting and tugging his soft mane in her excitement.

With Alex's hands under her bottom, tilting her toward him, his talented tongue worked a familiar magic that always brought her to the brink of release quickly enough to steal the breath from her lungs.

"Yes," she said, sailing over the peak as his tongue teased and flicked her most sensitive spot. "Yes!"

After he delighted her with a final suck upon her little throbbing nubbin, he rose above her before nestling his hips between her legs. She felt safe, cherished, and wildly aroused when he pinned her to the bed with his strong, naked body.

Parting for him, she was eager for his rigid arousal to enter and fill her. From that moment, Clarity held on to Alex's back while he set the rhythm of their tupping and brought her once more to climax before finding his own shuddering release.

She could not imagine that it could be this perfect with all couples, but she hoped so.

When she had redressed and accompanied him to his study, leaving him with a kiss, she knocked on Lady Aston's sitting-room door.

With no answer, Clarity pushed it open and entered. Alex had said the desk was his mother's, and she could see no harm in looking inside it for the sketches Mrs. Rigley had mentioned.

To that end, she approached the mahogany desk in the corner, which sat sturdily upon reeded, tapering legs. It had a polished, green-leather inset and three shallow drawers. A lamp and a blotter were all that cluttered the top.

Clarity tried to open the middle drawer, but it was locked, making her think failure of any meaningful discovery was imminent. However, when she tugged on the left-hand drawer, it opened smoothly. Unfortunately, it contained merely the usual writing implements, a pot of ink with a pipette for filling the fountain pen lying beside it, a stick of green wax, another of black, and two silver seals.

She picked up the one with the initial *H* and shivered, thinking of the Hollidges who might have used it before and their connection now to her. She would forever after represent a single knot in the long rope of this lineage. The other seal was an *A* belonging to Alex's aunt.

Pushing the drawer closed, she was reaching for the right-hand drawer when Lady Aston entered the room, halted, and gasped with her face turning florid.

"How dare you?" she demanded.

For the briefest instant, Clarity was eight years old again. A frisson of fear trickled down her spine, and she imagined Lady Aston demand she be thrashed or caned. Then she recalled who she was and where she was and straightened.

"How dare I what?" Clarity asked.

"Rifle through my personal belongings."

"That was not my intent. The locked drawer, which I assume contains anything of a personal nature, remains secure," Clarity assured her, although now she wondered just what might be in there. "I was looking for Lady Hollidge's flower sketches. Mrs. Rigley said they might still be in her desk."

"Then you should have waited until I was here and asked me."

"I meant no offense, but I apologize sincerely, nonetheless. There was nothing of import in the drawer I looked in."

If the lady couldn't accept her apology, Clarity could do nothing about it. But she was still determined to see Lady Hollidge's arrangements. She had a mind to frame and display them.

"Have you seen the drawings I seek?" she asked, determined to change the course of their discussion away from being made to feel like a naughty snoop.

"As a matter of fact, I have, but they are *not* in that desk." Lady Aston strode to the bookcase. On the bottom shelf was a wooden case, which she withdrew. Without ceremony, she shoved it toward Clarity, ramming it into her midsection.

"You may take them with you when you depart my sitting room."

Despite the rude invitation to leave, Clarity still managed to thank her before turning to the door.

"I shall see you at dinner, Lady Aston."

"Yes," the woman hissed.

As Clarity strolled along the corridor to her bed chamber, she heard Alex's aunt slam the door.

That was the single most satisfying noise she'd heard in a long time. Not that she wanted to be a thorn in the older woman's side. But it certainly was rewarding not to be the one who'd been left thwarted and annoyed.

Having no place to call her own besides her bedroom, she sat in a chair by the window next to her bed to examine the treasure she'd gleaned

Seated in his study, Alex couldn't shake the anxious feeling of dread. It had crept into his brain almost as soon as they'd returned from their wedding journey. After meeting with his accountant and his banker, he was ready to strike out for Suffolk with Clarity by his side, yet he was hesitating.

As usual, she was fizzing with excitement, ready to leave at a moment's notice, unmindful whether the coach wheels had been inspected or if any of the horses had thrown a shoe.

Normally, he liked the quiet, solitary journeys by carriage, regardless of the length of the journey. But riding with Clarity had its benefits.

"With the curtains drawn," she mused, "we could be doing anything inside while traveling."

That made him laugh, but then the unsettling doubts and the recurring nightmares drove out the promise of enjoyment. Abruptly, for her safety, he decided they should take the train instead. Seated upon the red upholstery of the train to Suffolk, Alex still hadn't told her about the return of his nightmares, which always ended with an overturned carriage.

He hadn't had them for years. Now, nearly every night, he sprang awake with his heart racing, breathing hard, feeling the sheen of sweat upon his skin. Beside him, Clarity slept peacefully, unawares.

"This is Lady Hollidge," he told the manager at his largest farm in Ipswich. "I think she would enjoy it if you showed her around." And he didn't have to say anything else. Clarity jumped in with questions, pointing out what interested her and making a joke about the sheep sounding as if they were laughing.

By the time they departed to return to Belfinch Hall, as they did each night while touring the area, she'd clearly delighted his manager.

She did that everywhere he took her. They spent their days walking the land and exploring villages, and each night they were entwined, satisfying each other. Everyone liked her, and nothing was wrong.

And yet the nightmares continued, along with the growing anxiety.

Only when he emerged from the same dismal dream and stared at her—watching her breathe, occasionally sigh, or even smile in her sleep—only then did the worry leave him temporarily. He had his Diamond, and all was right in the world.

He reminded himself of that every day and night.

But what if one day he didn't?

That awful thought had him awakening one night, realizing in the dream, she had been inside the carriage with him when it overturned. Unthinkingly, he gathered her sleeping form close in his arms, startling her awake.

"Alex," she exclaimed.

"Sorry, my love. I didn't mean to wake you. But I needed to hold you."

She had chuckled softly. "You may hold me anytime you like without apology."

And when he drifted off to sleep again with her pressed against him, he slept peacefully.

The following day, as they traversed the bridge beside the largest mill he owned, with Clarity prattling on about everything she saw, a board cracked under her feet. The rotted wood split, she stumbled, and to his horror, nearly pitched toward the waterwheel, catching herself on the rustic railing.

He grabbed her to him. "You must be more careful." His tone was harsh with terror.

"I'm fine, Alex. I can hardly be careful about a board beneath me, can I? But I'm unharmed."

"Come along," he ordered, keeping her hand in his.

"Mr. Johnson," he yelled as they reached the mill's office.

The manager, whom Clarity had met an hour earlier, rose from his desk when they entered.

"Yes, my lord."

"There was a rotted plank by the waterwheel. My wife could have died."

The man blanched. "I thought I told you about that, my lord. We have a carpenter coming tomorrow."

"Not good enough," Alex fumed, too easily able to imagine Clarity plunging to her death. "You are sacked!"

Chapter Twenty-Five

Clarity gasped.

"Please," the man began, and she saw desperation flash across his weathered face.

With her hand still held captive in her husband's, she tried to pull herself free, wanting to speak on the manager's behalf. After all, no harm had been done.

"Alex, don't do that on my account."

He turned on her. "You will address me as Hollidge or my lord when we are in public!" he snapped, breathing hard but finally releasing her.

She gaped at him, then collected herself, looking around to see the scene they were making. Not only was Mr. Johnson there, but also two workers who'd followed them inside to see what the fuss was about.

"Yes, of course, my lord. I ask that you reconsider. Mr. Johnson has been with you many years. This was a mistake of my own making. I should have—"

"You did nothing wrong," Alex insisted, but he looked angry at her as well as at everyone else in the room. "Wait in the carriage," he ordered.

They had never been in this situation before, but she could tell his mind was made up and to gainsay him, at least right then, was pointless. Sending Mr. Johnson a look of regret, she turned and walked out. Hopefully, Alex would get over the fright, which was surely what had precipitated his outburst, and allow his manager to keep his job.

As soon as he climbed into the carriage and they were under way to the inn, she asked him, "Did you actually terminate his employment?"

"I did," he ground out, leaning miserably against the side and crossing his arms.

"Such unfairness is unlike you," she said. "I hope you will reconsider. He probably has a wife and children."

"He should have thought of them before endangering my wife."

She rolled her eyes. "You cannot blame him. Blame me."

"You did nothing wrong. That is, except contradict me in front of my staff. Don't do it again."

To this, she said nothing. Clarity didn't like Alex's behavior or his tone. An hour later, when they had left their coats in their bedchamber and changed out of muddy shoes, they entered the inn's dining room in silence. She still had not forgiven him for behaving like a merciless tyrant.

Alex, however, seemed to have put it behind him.

"What is the cook's best dish?" he asked the waiter and placed their order.

When the wine was poured, he smiled at her, looking like his normal self. Her insides fluttered as they always did when his green eyes gazed into hers.

"I hope you enjoy sheep," he quipped. "Tomorrow, we shall be seeing a great number of them and little else." Then he took a sip. "The farmer and his wife are good people. I like them very much."

"That's what you said about Mr. Johnson this morning," Clarity pointed out.

He froze before lowering his glass. She held her breath. *Was he going to take her to task again?* If he did, he would find himself sleeping on the floor.

After a moment, he nodded. "You're correct. The man is an excellent mill manager."

She sighed. "And your mill needs a manager," she agreed.

"I put Mr. Flemming in charge."

Clarity shrugged. The name meant nothing to her.

Alex gave a lopsided smile that showed his single dimple.

"He was the one with the floppy hat."

She frowned, thinking over the people she had met. "Wasn't he a hundred and twenty years old and nearly blind?"

"Yes," Alex said, and he started to chuckle. "He's kept on because he's devoted his life to our mill. And he's only a hundred and two if he's a day."

Clarity shook her head, and soon they were both laughing over the ridiculousness of putting him in charge over the capable Mr. Johnson.

"I'll send word first thing in the morning," Alex promised. "I overreacted, but my heart stopped, I swear it, when you stumbled."

She reached out and took his hand. "I appreciate your caring for me—"

"I don't care for you," he interrupted. "I adore you. You are my wife and my responsibility."

"I would rather remain my own responsibility," she chided. "I am not a child. But anyone could have stepped on that board. You cannot control everything that happens to me."

"I know."

They released each other's hands as their plates were put before them.

"And I think you should put poor Mr. Johnson's mind at rest and send word to him tonight. Please, Alex."

"Anything you ask," he said, "I shall always grant if I can."

That night, in the aftermath of their lovemaking, Clarity lay awake in the darkness. They'd been married nearly three months, although most of that time had been spent playing at being married while merely enjoying one another's company while traveling .

Moving into the Hollidge townhouse had not been as she'd expected. Well run under the exacting thumb of Lady Aston for many years, it had been difficult to take over as its mistress. In fact, Clarity had not managed to take the reins before they'd come away again.

Moreover, Alex had told his aunt she could reside with them forever. And thus, she hadn't made any effort to find other lodging.

Clarity didn't want to begrudge the woman her long-time London home, but as she blinked in the darkness, she thought of Alex's words.

Anything you ask.

Surely, he would want some privacy for their new marriage, too. His aunt was quite the presence at the breakfast table, in the small salon, in the drawing room, and at the dining table—always there, always with an opinion.

Oddly, hers seemed to contradict any opinion Clarity had, especially if it was regarding changing something at Number Thirty, Grosvenor Square.

"We've always kept to this schedule," Lady Aston had informed her, opposing Clarity's suggestion to have dinner later during the week and to skip supper, at which they mostly nibbled with little actual hunger. This not only put the kitchen staff to extra work but kept the newlyweds up later than they wanted, eager to retire, strip off their clothes, and devour one another. None of which Clarity could tell Alex's aunt, so she'd conceded.

"It's always been that color, even when Alex's parents lived here," Lady Aston had protested over changing the wall paint in the drawing room or dining room.

"Then it's time for a fresh color," Clarity suggested.

"We shall ask Alex," his aunt had promised, as if the new Lady Hollidge couldn't redecorate her home without her husband's permission.

And now, Clarity had missed her monthly flow. Twice. She couldn't see her husband in the darkness, but she could hear his steady breathing. It was an intimate and pleasurable privilege to be the one lying beside him while he slept. She wouldn't disturb him. When they returned to London, she would tell him the good news just as soon as she was certain.

Thinking of his warmth and intelligence, she knew he would make a superb father—although the slightest of doubts lingered in the recesses of her mind. True, he was much more like the Alex of childhood, quick to laugh and full of winsome smiles that melted her heart each time.

But he was also the Viscount Hollidge now, with all the responsibilities and worries that went along with his title. She'd seen how easily he could transform from her loving husband into a stranger when dealing with the outside world.

In her mind, Clarity tried to separate the two, the man who worshipped her body in bed, who loved her and whom she loved in return, and the viscount who had taken up the mantle at too young an age and keenly felt the full weight of his title and of keeping the family solvent for the next generation.

Rubbing her stomach idly, she yawned. The next generation was coming whether she and Alex were ready or not. But she would be damned if she would let Lady Aston stop her from redecorating the musty, outdated nursery.

Suddenly, Alex moaned, thrashed out, and awakened with a gasp.

"Alex? Did you have a nightmare?"

His calm breathing of moments ago was now ragged, and she could feel the tension of his body.

"Did I awaken you?" he asked, reaching out and clasping her hand. His own felt damp beneath hers.

"No, I was already awake. What was the dream? Do you want to tell me?"

He shuddered. "No, thank you. Better to leave it behind me. I'm glad you're here," he added.

With their hands joined, she soon fell asleep.

⁓

"I am going to host my first dinner party," Clarity told her mother and sisters over tea and sandwiches upon her return to London.

Seated in the Diamonds' Piccadilly home, she could relax entirely, without fear Lady Aston would pop up and tell her she was doing something if not wrong, then "differently from how it should be done."

The party would be done her way!

Clarity's mother nodded, and Purity dove in instantly with questions, "When and for how many?"

"Including Alex and myself, perhaps six other couples."

"Couples?" Purity asked. "Are none of us invited besides Mother and Father?"

"Actually," Clarity began, glancing at their beloved matriarch. "I wasn't going to invite you and Father, if that's all right."

"Perfectly fine. I understand completely."

"I don't!" This from Ray. "Isn't it an insult?"

"It's not meant to be," Clarity assured her. "I want this to be a Hollidge party and not a Diamond one. If our parents come, then I will still feel like a child and probably start asking Mother for all sorts of help."

"She's correct," their mother said, then turned to Clarity. "We have plenty of time to enjoy meals at your table."

"Besides," Clarity added, "I know this sounds odd, but I think I would be more anxious with you and Father watching. If no one is there whom I care about except Alex, I can be more focused."

All her sisters considered this. Then Purity asked, "What about Lady Aston?"

"What about her?" Clarity asked. *Was her sister asking if her husband's aunt fell under the category of people she didn't care about?*

"You said only couples would attend. What will you do with the widow?"

"Oh dear!" Clarity had overlooked Alex's aunt. She could hardly not invite Lady Aston since the woman lived under the same roof. Nor could she have an uneven number with an extra female.

"I suppose I shall have to find a man for her."

Bri giggled.

"Matchmaking is a difficult task," her mother said. "I suggest you ask Lady Aston if she has a gentleman friend whom you can invite to partner with her."

"Yes, thank you, Mother. That's a grand idea."

"What if she doesn't?" Purity persisted. Her sister liked to be organized and prepared, but Clarity couldn't worry about that right then.

"I'll deal with that if I have to. And while I am happy to do work with my new household staff, I would love to talk over my ideas with you now."

They spent an enjoyable hour working out the details of an amusing dinner party for a young couple to host, one as unpretentious and unstuffy as they were.

"And just like Queen Victoria, we shall have some Atholl brose to delight our guests," Clarity said.

"Can you get that in London?" Purity asked.

"I doubt we shall need to send to Scotland for it. Our Cook can make it."

Once back home, as she wished to think of Hollidge House, she went in search of the housekeeper.

"Mrs. Rigley, I am putting on a dinner party."

"Are you, my lady? Have you spoken yet to Lady Aston?"

Sweet Mary! Not again! "No, I haven't. Why?"

"It's just that she keeps the schedule for the household. She would know if there is a conflict."

"That's a clever idea," she told the woman, although Clarity thought it odd indeed that there might be a party scheduled in her own home, maybe in her own dining room, that she didn't know about.

"Regardless of the schedule," Clarity continued, "I intend to speak to Cook about the menu."

Mrs. Rigley frowned. "Wouldn't it be best if Lady Aston were with you?"

Clarity felt a prickle of alarm. "I believe Cook and I can handle it," she told the housekeeper and dismissed her.

Pushing open the door at the back of the basement, she was met with damp, warm air reminding her of her own family's kitchen. Water was always on the boil for washing, for tea and coffee, and for cooking. A scullery maid was peeling potatoes, and one of the housemaids was setting tea things on a tray, probably for Lady Aston.

In the midst of it was their middle-aged cook, who was portly and red-faced. The first time Clarity had been introduced to Mrs. Wheaton, the woman had apologized for her appearance, saying she'd been tasting too many things her whole life, from scullery maid on up.

Clarity hadn't known how to respond beyond saying she would be worried if she met a skinny, sallow cook.

"Good day, Mrs. Wheaton."

"Good day, my lady. What brings you down here?"

"A dinner party. Probably the two words you most dread."

"Not at all," their cook said. "I like to show off my talents as well as the next."

"Very good. I was reading in the newspaper about Queen Victoria's love of pale consommé, and that seems like a nice starting course instead of a heavy pottage."

"Yes, my lady. That's clarified veal stock. Not easy, but I can do it."

"The queen also likes a buffet table covered in a variety of meats, and she allows her guests to rise from the table and choose from among them."

Mrs. Wheaton appeared shocked. "Like at breakfast?" She shook her head. "How many people, my lady? I'm asking because I cannot imagine it's a good idea to have too many guests milling about and getting up from their seats. They'll be tripping the footman."

"There will be fourteen of us, and I thought it might be fun to call the ladies first to the buffet table with a footman putting whatever each chooses on her plate. Venison, beef, and chicken, prepared any way you wish. There's a new butcher shop opened in Holland Park. Lidgate's, it's called. My mother says they serve superior cuts, and I should like you to try them. The side dishes can be served as usual when everyone is seated."

"As you like, my lady."

"For dessert, I think both a hot pudding and a chilled one. Perhaps a sponge cake, too."

"Of course,"

"I don't suppose you know anything about Atholl brose, do you?"

"No, my lady. Is it a soup?"

"It's a Scottish drink, very creamy and festive, made with uncooked oatmeal, honey, whisky, and cream."

Mrs. Wheaton narrowed her eyes. "You want to drink porridge, my lady?"

Clarity realized the scullery maid had stopped peeling to stare at her.

"No, not really. The oatmeal is mixed with boiling water, but not really cooked into porridge. I think it might be strained after."

The cook shrugged. "If you give me a recipe, I can whip it up, I guess, just as well as the next person."

"Whip what up?" came Lady Aston's voice behind Clarity, causing her to jump.

Chapter Twenty-Six

To Clarity's ears, Alex's aunt sounded much like a scolding headmistress.

She hoped Cook hadn't noticed Clarity roll her eyes, but when Mrs. Wheaton looked away with a smile, she feared the woman had.

Turning, Clarity faced Lady Aston. Dithering directly behind her was the housekeeper. Apparently, Mrs. Rigley had summoned the person she considered to be in charge, and Clarity could not refrain from sending the housekeeper a withering glare before she answered.

"Queen Victoria enjoyed a cup of Atholl brose near Perthshire. I thought we could have it at my dinner party."

"What dinner party?"

Again, that supercilious tone grated on Clarity's ears.

"I am hosting a party for five couples, as well as yourself, naturally, and the guest of your choice."

"I see." Lady Aston flared her nostrils, then asked, "What is the occasion?"

Clarity was stunned by the question. After all, she was the new viscountess. "Do I need one?"

Lady Aston's pause was a trifle too long. "I suppose not. Including you and my nephew, there will be fourteen people."

"Yes, that's right. Do you have a gentleman in mind? If you give me his name and address, I shall send out an invitation."

"I will handle that myself," she said.

Clarity wondered if Alex's aunt would have trouble scaring up a man to be her partner. She wasn't bad looking, but her demeanor could best be described as off-putting.

"I will need to know the date," Lady Aston said.

"Yes, of course. Mrs. Rigley told me you keep the house schedule. I would like to see it and transcribe it into my own diary."

Lady Aston's nostrils flared even larger. "That won't be necessary."

Clarity took that as a negative. She would *not* be seeing Lady Aston's schedule, and consequently, she considered herself free to plan whatever she wanted, whenever she wanted.

"I will let you know the date shortly." She might as well play coy and make Alex's aunt wait and wonder.

Two days later, Clarity knocked upon Lady Aston's private sitting-room door, having not yet figured out a way to summon the older woman to her. She supposed it was a petty matter, who went to whom, but it tipped the balance of power toward Alex's aunt.

As expected, Lady Aston thwarted her at once.

"That will not do!" she said upon hearing the date, which was a week and a half away.

Clarity had been prepared for resistance. *And why not?* Apart from the cook, everyone else she'd spoken with regarding the party mentioned deferring to Lady Aston, including the butler with whom she'd tried to discuss the wine.

Thus, hearing Lady Aston's words was no surprise.

"Whyever not?" Clarity asked.

"Because Alex will be busy that night. We shall all be at Garrick's on Leman Street."

Clarity was taken aback. "We shall not, for the theater burned down last month. Hadn't you heard?"

Lady Aston's lips became a straight line, and she stared without wavering. Finally, she blinked.

"My mistake. We shall be attending a play at the Haymarket."

Sighing, Clarity supposed her party date was flexible, but this inconvenience was irksome, nonetheless.

"I wish you had shared your schedule with me beforehand. Perhaps the night following?"

"That's not a good party night," Lady Aston declared. "No one likes to go out late on a Thursday."

Clarity frowned, but she would have to take Alex's aunt at her word.

"The following night is Friday, and everyone loves a Friday party," she declared, practically daring Lady Aston to gainsay her.

"I agree. That will work perfectly. I will begin on the invitations."

"No, thank you," Clarity said. "I shall do them myself."

"If you wish." The words barely made it past Lady Aston's gritted teeth.

"I do wish, except the one for your gentleman guest. May I know his name?"

"Major Grover. And I do hope you decided against the Atholl brose. Your party is *not* the Grand Caledonian Ball. Therefore, I think it would be grossly inappropriate."

"I shall take your advice into consideration," Clarity promised. Silently she added, *And I consider it worthless.* She intended to have the special drink, regardless.

Having settled that, she took her leave and popped next door to Alex's study.

"There's my lovely wife," he intoned as soon as she saw her.

Swiftly, he came out from behind his desk, banged the door shut with his heel, and took her into his arms.

Instantly, he put her in a good humor. "I must come bother you more often."

"You are never a bother. And I prefer holding you than wrapping my arms around that pile of papers."

"I came to tell you've I've decided on a date for the dinner party I mentioned, and if you tell me to talk to your aunt, I shall scream."

He laughed. "Doubtless, you can handle a dinner party, but she has hosted many, so I know she would be useful."

"I can do it all myself if only—" Clarity held her tongue. She was about to mention the lack of cooperation from the staff. Yet she was mistress of the house, and as such, she would deal with it. "If only I can borrow your seal for my envelopes."

"Is that all?"

"Yes. Although it would be handy to have a proper desk, I can make do in the dining room."

His brow furrowed. "We must have a spare room or a nook where you can have a desk."

Assuredly, he was correct, and she would eventually find somewhere to set up a little desk.

"For now, the dining room table will be fine," she told him. "I don't have many to write."

To her astonishment, while still holding her, he moved her backward until she felt the edge of his oak desk against her rear end.

Then he leaned over her, forcing her back, until she was nearly resting upon the ink blotter. All the time, he was gazing down at her, his eyes sending a wicked message.

"What on earth are you doing?" she asked.

"Reaching for my signet," he said innocently.

But he now rested between her thighs, and she could feel his burgeoning interest.

She smiled up at him, and then slowly parted her lips.

Swooping down like a falcon on a mouse, he claimed her mouth with his. Resting his hands on either side of her, he pressed his manhood to the apex between her thighs, making her skin prickle with heat.

At once, she felt damp, warm, soft, and very feminine, throbbing at her core.

"Yes," she said simply.

"Yes?" he asked, nuzzling her neck.

"Oh, yes." Wrapping her hands around the back of him, she tried to draw him closer.

"Hold on, my love," he said, starting to undo his trousers while she leaned upon her elbows and watched.

"Can we really engage in relations here, upon your desk? It seems brazen."

"I believe we can," he said, letting his arousal spring free.

When he put his large hands on her skirts and drew them up her legs, she shivered and lay back again.

With his fingers at her exposed entrance, he brushed against her mound, causing her to arch up for him and splay herself open.

Without hesitation, Alex fitted his shaft to her canal and penetrated her softness with a long, searing stroke. Gasping at how quickly and ardently her body raced toward the peak of release, she closed her eyes and gripped the edge of the desk as he thrust and retreated.

Arching her neck, she urged him onward, feeling her climax just out of reach.

"Good?" he asked, drawing out slowly, torturing her with his length.

"Mm," she answered, unable to form thoughts, let alone words, relishing the hard desk at her back and the firm muscles of the man she'd married at her front.

When he slid his hand between their bodies and touched her aching bud, she reached her climax easily, let go, and flew like a hawk.

"Oh," she cried, too loudly for a study with Lady Aston next door, earning her Alex's hot mouth quickly covering hers.

With her husband stroking her relentlessly, her body shuddered, tightening and releasing over and over, taking every last sensation he offered. Then he sheathed himself again, spending his warmth deep inside her.

They both fell still and silent as he rested his forehead upon her shoulder, breathing hard. Finally, she opened her eyes and groaned.

"I hope I don't have ink on the back of my dress."

As he laughed, their connection broke. As a gentleman, he swiftly lowered her skirts before tucking himself in and doing up his trousers.

"As I said, come and bother me anytime," he quipped, offering her his hand and drawing her up and off his desk.

Showing him her back, she asked, "Am I presentable?"

"Completely," he said, but she felt his hands smooth her skirts a little. "Although maybe your hair wasn't quite as loose when you entered."

She bit her lip. "I think I had best go to my room and tidy up before I wander the house." Then she held out her hand, palm up.

Leaning down, he kissed it, letting the tip of his tongue tickle its center and causing her knees to weaken and her body to start tingling again.

"No, silly man," she said. "The seal, please."

"Oh, yes." Leaning over his desk, he retrieved it.

"Good luck with your invitations."

"And you with your paper work," she returned, wondering how she could manage to return to the humdrum of life after such a spectacular ravishment.

⁓⁓⁓

Alex had never been happier, and it wasn't solely because he had access to his wife's body practically any hour of the day or night, with the exciting knowledge she relished their encounters as much as he. Truthfully, that might be one of the main reasons, but he also immensely enjoyed her company at breakfast, dinner, and supper, as well as whenever they took a stroll or a ride or simply lay in bed talking before or after swiving.

He was even glad she hadn't taken the customary place all the way at the end of the dining table but instead was seated halfway along. Easily, each evening, he could see her smile and the laughter in her eyes.

Moreover, he was immensely pleased Clarity was throwing a party as the new Viscountess Hollidge. He would show her off to their guests, and she would make him proud.

An hour later, his aunt appeared at his door, bringing him a glass of brandy.

"Am I going to need that?" he quipped, for she usually came bearing only tea, and occasionally, before his marriage, they used to sip port together after dinner over a game of chess.

"If you don't, then I shall," she said. "Your bride tried to send these out."

He looked at the envelopes sealed in blue wax. The seals were small and appropriately glossy.

"What's wrong?" he asked.

"That is not Hollidge green," she protested.

He laughed, which felt good. Normally, before Clarity, his aunt would have had something troubling to tell him, perhaps one of his friends passing away or some new war having broken out that had just reached London's newspapers. And he would have let it sit heavily upon him, even if he could do nothing.

But this? "That's no matter. It doesn't bother me." It wasn't as if Clarity had used a cheap wafer seal, which would have shown great disrespect to her invitees.

Aunt Elizabeth's eyes narrowed. "It should. As your wife, she should represent you in public, and both of you ought to be unified in all things to do with the title."

He frowned.

"If it bothers you, then tell her. I'll give her some new wax."

"I've already taken care of it. I didn't want to embarrass her, so I redid her invitations. I thank God I noticed the hideous seal because the contents were even worse."

He was uncomfortable with his aunt opening Clarity's sealed envelopes but also curious.

"What was wrong with her invitations?"

"She is determined to have couples, but she tried to invite the Merediths without Lady Meredith's cousin, Lord Bedington, and his wife. It would have been a dreadful insult to the latter since the Bedingtons have known you longer."

"Have they?" Alex couldn't put a face to any of the four she'd mentioned.

"And then your Lady Hollidge invited the Gilstraps, who I know are out of Town next Friday."

"Strange. I thought she'd said it would be next Wednesday. People like a Wednesday dinner party to break up the week."

His aunt gave an uncharacteristic shrug. "We are going to the theater on Wednesday night. It has long been arranged."

"Has it?" He didn't recall.

"Yes! Besides my guest, Major Grover, was not free on Wednesday."

"I see. Then the party is on Thursday?" he asked. "People are often free."

"It's too late now. Lady Hollidge chose Friday." His aunt waved the invitations in the air. "And she also intended to invite the Duke and Duchess of Hambleton. They were unlikely to show. In the end, I had to swap out three of the five couples."

"I wish you had come to me first. Or better yet, spoken to Clarity directly."

"I didn't want to bother you with things that you ought not to have to worry over," Aunt Elizabeth pointed out. "And as I said, I had no intention of humiliating her when I could easily sort it all out without her ever knowing."

"She'll know when different people show up at her party," Alex said.

"Yes, but by then, she'll be delighted it wasn't ruined through her own ineptitude."

"I suppose. In that case, I thank you for looking out for her and her first party."

Aunt Elizabeth nodded. "Shall I continue to help and advise, such as with the food and drink? And what of the entertainment?"

"I am certain she has that all in hand," he said. "But no doubt she would welcome your offer of assistance."

On the night of the gathering, it was a relief to realize all he had to do was show up. During the day, the staff were like horses waiting for the start of Ascot.

After his valet had dressed him, Alex knocked on Clarity's bedroom door. She used her chamber only for dressing and climbed into his bed each night. It still felt like a dream when he awakened in the morning to find her beside him.

The door opened and her maid came out first, curtsied, and hurried past. Pushing it open wider, he got his first look at her.

"Beautiful lady," he said, taking in her appearance from head to toe. She wore a shimmering satin gown in sapphire blue that matched her eyes and set off her nearly black hair to perfection. "How did I get so fortunate?"

A sweet pink suffused her cheeks.

"I suppose you are lucky," she teased. Then she turned in a circle. "All good?" she asked.

"Far better than good," he answered. "Let's go have a drink in the drawing room before the first guests arrive."

"I have a surprise to start off the evening," she said, taking his arm. "A special concoction."

He looked forward to it. However, when the maid brought in a tray, it was ordinary French wine—claret and burgundy—in carafes directly from the casks in his own cellar.

Clarity stared at the glass offered to her but accepted it as did he.

"I can see by your face this isn't the surprise."

"No," she said. "I wonder if Cook decided it would be better after dinner."

"Maybe. She is skilled at pairing food and drink."

"Perhaps, but I wish she'd told me. Now there is nothing special to start the party."

"Yes, there is." And he leaned down and kissed her. "There is you."

A cough heralded his aunt's entrance.

"That is unacceptable in public," she said as if they were disobedient children. He wondered what she would think about their activities in his study.

But all he said was, "Yes, Aunt Elizabeth, but you are not public. You are family."

"True," she said, helping herself to a glass of burgundy.

Was it his imagination or was she wearing an expression of satisfaction?

Whatever it was, it was vastly different from his wife's look of utter shock when the guests arrived.

About five minutes after the last couple had been greeted, Clarity signaled for him to join her in the hall.

"Husband, I am bewildered. Most of these people are not the ones I invited," she said in a whisper.

He was glad to be able to explain. "These must be the ones Aunt Elizabeth substituted."

"Substituted? How could she have done that? I wrote the invitations myself."

"I asked her to tell you herself. She was concerned about the seal and then discovered some of your guests were out of town, I believe."

With each word he told her, she appeared angrier and angrier. This was not a good beginning to their first hosted event.

Chapter Twenty-Seven

"The seal?" Clarity snapped. "You mean the wax seal on the envelope?"

"Don't think about it now," Alex urged. "We have an even number of couples, a delicious meal, and good company. Everything is fine."

Everything *was* fine. But since they were no longer *her* guests, she imagined as the evening progressed, it might no longer be *her* party.

"This was not the group I had planned for," she said. "Why, I think she chose *her* own friends. Most of the guests in there are your aunt's age."

"Not true," he said. "Well, maybe it is. But there will still be pleasant conversation. And the best part is at the end of it all, we can retire together. I'll make you forget anything that has displeased you tonight. I promise."

Clarity tried to hold on to that promise all evening as things began to go badly. Lady Aston lorded it over the drawing room conversation, making a toast while standing center stage by the hearth. It was followed by her guest, Major Grover with his face full of white whiskers, drinking to her health and thanking her for helping to put on the splendid gathering.

To make it worse, when they were finally called to dinner, Lady Aston and the major led the way.

Clarity looked at Alex, who merely shrugged, appearing entirely unbothered at being usurped in his own home. She half expected the major to take Alex's seat at the head of the table and fervently wished she'd told his aunt ahead of time that she wanted the seat at the other end. There was no way to do it gracefully once the major drew out the chair and slid it under Lady Aston, before taking a seat at her right.

Two of the couples who had exchanged a few withering glances now began to trade snide remarks. One was on Clarity's original guest list, but the other had been invited by Lady Aston. It seemed someone had kissed someone else's wife if she was correctly interpreting the jagged innuendo.

When the two couples had verbally fenced into hostile silence, mortifying the rest of the diners, another guest complained about the thinness of the consommé.

"A nice thick pottage is what's needed," one male guest without better manners proclaimed. "Remember what you served last time," he said, looking to Alex's aunt. "That was delicious."

"I remember," she replied. "However, Lady Hollidge handled the menu." She looked to Clarity as did all the guests around the table.

Feeling as if it were her first time at an adult dinner, Clarity did the unthinkable. She squirmed and knew her cheeks were probably flaming.

"I think it is a perfect start to a long dinner," Alex said.

She could have kissed him until he added, "If you have a richer, tastier pottage, then you might fill up."

Inwardly, she groaned. That was like saying she'd served them all something nasty to keep them from gorging. She nearly got up to stave off the footman from serving the meats *à la Victoria*, as she'd come to think of it. It was too late.

In came a footman followed by a maid, each holding two platters, which they placed on the high sideboard table against the wall.

"What's happening?" Lady Aston asked.

In that instant, Clarity knew Alex's aunt was fully aware of how the meats were going to be served and was drawing attention to it so she could gloat.

Sure enough, instead of enjoying the novelty of the buffet table, it was universally panned as an inconvenience, having to rise from one's seat, and also in poor taste. Too loudly, she heard Lady Aston mention to the major how it was strangely "crass" but understandable from an inexperienced hostess.

If the guests had been her original ones, she knew they would have enjoyed the novelty and been interested in the queen's custom. Unfortunately, the meat selections were mediocre at best, which shocked Clarity due to her mother's recommendation of the butcher.

By the time the females returned to the drawing room, Clarity considered the evening a disaster, and that was before she discovered the musicians had not arrived. While her guests found places to sit, Clarity spoke with the butler.

"They came highly recommended," she said to him, as if there was some way Mr. Berard could produce two violinists, a viola player, and a cellist from the cupboard under the stairs.

"I am sorry, my lady."

"What's the problem?" Lady Aston asked, coming up beside them.

"The musicians never arrived while we dined. I had hoped for a short concert to end the evening."

"I hope you aren't referring to Mr. Ella's string quartet."

It was obvious Alex's aunt already knew. Clarity didn't need to answer, but she did.

"Yes," she said, trying to keep her tone neutral.

"Their bill arrived the other day, wishing to be paid ahead of time."

"That's what I agreed to," Clarity told her.

"I didn't know," she said, utterly unbothered. "I tore it up."

Clarity wondered if one could actually expire from a fit of the red devils.

"Did you not think to speak with me about it? Now we have no entertainment."

"Maybe *you* should have spoken to *me*," Lady Aston insisted, "and then I could have directed you to a better choice. What next, a tavern singer?" She gave a dismissive shake of her head.

Clarity was stunned, only glad no one else could hear.

"Mr. Ella plays *popular* music. What we want," Lady Aston continued, "is music as art, not merely entertainment. Our guests shall not be subjected to an amateur quartet for hire. When we pay, we want professionals such as those who play in the concert halls. In any case, artistic music is now considered to be that played upon a piano or at least accompanied by one."

"We don't have a piano," Clarity pointed out, trying to be reasonable while seething mad.

"Then we cannot have a proper musical concert. Thus, we should either let our guests perform to the best of their amateur abilities, as in my day, by singing, or we should have invited them out to a proper concert."

Clarity's fingers were curled into fists. With nothing else to say, she returned to the drawing room where the guests were amusing themselves with prattle and gossip, except the two hostile wives who were gnashing their teeth at one another.

Save for those two, Clarity was confident her guests would have been happily entertained with the quartet she'd heard in her parents' drawing room at the beginning of the year.

Soon, with Alex leading the way, the seven men entered to rejoin the ladies' company. Her husband came directly to her side.

"We hurried with our cigars and brandy in order not to miss the evening's entertainment."

"Oh, no, no, no, my love. Your aunt says we are not to expect *entertainment*. Only *art*."

He smiled uncertainly. "I don't understand."

She sighed. "Nor do I, but there is no music unless you wish to sing."

"I do not," he said.

"Should I ask if any of the guests wish to perform?" She folded her arms, wanting to stamp her foot but managed not to. "I suppose we should obtain a piano if we're going to have parties more often."

"I don't fancy asking a guest to sing for his or her supper, do you? Nor do I know of any place we can get a piano on short notice. I suppose we could knock on one of our neighbor's doors and ask."

She didn't find anything funny about the situation, no matter how hard Alex tried. She hadn't set up tables for cards, nor had she planned out any charades.

Luckily, two footmen entered with trays, each holding a pitcher of creamy white beverage.

Clarity relaxed. "At least my surprise beverage is finally being served."

"I implore you all to take a glass," she invited.

When everyone had done as asked, with Alex's aunt's nostrils flaring when she sniffed the concoction, Clarity announced it to be "genuine Atholl brose."

"My Scottish grandmother used to make porridge and call it brose," Major Grover said. "Funny this should share the name."

"History and a good dose of rumor states the Duke of Atholl used a well filled with this creamy beverage," Clarity informed the room, "all the way back in 1475 to capture his enemy, the Earl of Ross, who was overly fond of drinking it. Lured to the well, he somehow fell in."

A few people gasped, but Clarity continued, "It is, as Major Grover said, oatmeal but it is blended with honey and whiskey."

Some guests set their glasses down on nearby tables, apparently unwilling to try it.

"Don't be shy to taste it, I beseech you," Clarity continued. "Just as some of our meal was inspired by our gracious monarch, so too the queen and the prince consort were served Atholl brose about three years ago when visiting Perthshire and greatly enjoyed it."

"How clever of you to come up with it," Alex said, and she wished his tone wasn't condescending, although she knew he was trying to help.

Those still holding their glasses took sips. A few coughed.

"*Hm,*" Clarity said doubtfully. It was lumpy, tangy, and unpleasant.

"I think you'll find it was supposed to be strained after curing for a week," the major said. "At least, that's how I have had it before."

Clarity felt her cheeks grow hot again. Her mood didn't lift when Alex joked to the guests.

"I guess my wife decided to present us with the stodgy version to capture us as firmly as the Earl of Ross in that dratted well."

"I, for one, would prefer a nice glass of sherry," came Lady Aston's icy tone.

"I would like some port," said one of the gentlemen. "And then we must be on our way. If there is no music, then I have a card game to attend at my club after dropping my lovely wife home."

⁂

Alex had expected better. After all, Clarity had been around dinner parties all her life. Moreover, Lady Diamond was considered a renowned hostess. He could even remember his mother saying how wonderful her dinner parties were.

Yet this had not been wonderful at all, nor smooth and polished. And if his wife repeated such a poor performance in party-planning, she would get a reputation as a poor hostess, which was the last thing he wished.

"A calamity," his aunt declared when she sailed into his study the following day, wearing her sourest expression. "She even tried to use a new butcher! A new butcher for a party, can you imagine? Fortunately, Cook mentioned Lady Hollidge's wish to use some upstart in Holland Park, and I made sure our meat came from our usual man. You must dissuade Lady Hollidge from any more of her parties until she has been schooled in what's proper and what is decidedly not."

"Agreed," he said. "For her own good, I will suggest she let you instruct her. Maybe she can take notes and then after watching you host the next one, she'll be ready in a month."

His aunt rolled her eyes. "You think I have nothing better to do than provide tutelage to your inexperienced viscountess. You ought to have married a woman who could step in and immediately run this household."

"Don't start with that again, Auntie. I love Clarity beyond reason. And if we have to have a few failed dinner parties now and again, I don't care. On the other hand, if you're too busy to help," he began.

"For you, I shall make time. But she must listen and do as I say, not protest and argue."

Alex thought of Clarity's nature. "I am sure if you are friendly and not demeaning, she will be happy to receive assistance."

"Very well. But if she makes a fuss, I shall leave her to her own missteps and mistakes."

"Fair enough."

When he saw Clarity later, he broached the subject, knowing he must persuade her when she wasn't in the same room as his aunt. For some reason, even though Aunt Elizabeth was reserved and reasonable, he could detect an underlying current of animosity between the two females.

Thus, after seeing his wife spend with a shudder of passion, calling his name before he, too, released, Alex cradled her in his arms. Then he broached the subject.

"Would you allow Aunt Elizabeth to assist you in—" Before Alex had even finished his question, he felt Clarity stiffen.

"Do not ask me what I think you are going to ask me," she protested, bristling like an alley cat.

"But she is experienced. She can help your next dinner party to go more smoothly."

Clarity slammed her palm onto the rumpled sheet.

"I would rather we had an uneven number of guests and ate nothing but boiled cabbage than ask for her help. Don't you understand? Everything would have been fine if she hadn't interfered."

"The Atholl brose was your idea, wasn't it?" he reminded her gently.

"Yes, but—"

"And the meats presented on the sideboard?"

"Well, yes, but with younger guests, the ladies wouldn't have minded getting up from the table to choose. If it's good enough for the queen," she insisted.

"The queen can make her guests stand on their heads and eat roast horse if they wish, but that doesn't mean we should try to make them dine on thin broth, stand for their meat, and drink whiskey-spiked porridge."

"The brose was supposed to be strained," she said mulishly. "Anyway, I thought it was tasty, if unusual."

"Guests don't come to dinner for the *unusual*," he pointed out, stroking his fingers along her arm, hoping for the return of her good humor. "Aunt Elizabeth had to change the meat order for that very reason. Dinner served to guests must be practiced, tested, and approved."

"Then the gristly beef and stringy chicken were not from Lidgate's," she said. "I knew my mother wouldn't recommend such average fare. Your aunt switched the butcher and invited guests who were at each other's throats. I tried to provide superior food and invite our contemporaries, both friends and would-be friends."

"I know you did."

"Don't speak in such a fashion, as if you're patting me on the head. Why did you think it acceptable for your aunt to intercept my invitations and open them?"

"I told you, it was the wax," he said.

"The wax?" she repeated.

"It was the wrong color."

Clarity closed her eyes and growled like a she-wolf. When she opened them, he could see the anger glittering in their cobalt depths.

"The wrong color! The seal was the wrong color!"

She was yelling and behaving like a child, so he covered her mouth with his hand.

"It wasn't Hollidge green," he explained.

"Mm mmm mmm," she mumbled against his palm.

"Please don't yell," he beseeched before removing his hand.

"It was my favorite blue," she insisted, her tone still too loud. "My Diamond blue wax. Am I required to use green?"

"Aunt Elizabeth thought we should show unity as the Viscount and Viscountess Hollidge."

"I used your seal. That should have been sufficient. My parents don't always use the same blasted wax. Did yours?"

He recoiled at her vehemence. "I don't know."

"If you don't know, you shouldn't assume your nosy aunt knows either. I enjoyed writing those invitations, using one of the first wedding presents my mother gave me, decadently thick cream-colored card stock with my new initials embossed upon it. The task of writing and signing each one gave me great enjoyment." She wriggled away from him. "And your aunt ruined it!"

"Where are you going?"

"To sleep in my own room in my own bed."

"Clarity, please—"

"I am insulted, not only by Lady Aston but by your complicity. You should have told me she had opened my outgoing mail and altered my invitations. Nor should Mr. Berard have given them to her in the first place. I am your wife and mistress of this household, not her."

With that, she scrambled away as he tried to reach for her. In a flash, she was at the door that connected their rooms.

"Good night, Lord Hollidge!" And she slammed the door behind her.

Alex lay on his back, looking at the top of his canopy for a long while. Even though they'd shared a bed for mere months, not even a whole year, he felt her absence keenly.

She was undoubtedly correct. He ought to have told her about the invitations. Moreover, he hated for her to be upset. And with her pride having been well and truly bruised, he predicted in the morning, she would be sulking and sullen.

Chapter Twenty-Eight

In the days and weeks that followed, Clarity kept her visage perfectly placid. She had seen just such a mild expression on Emmeline Brambury and could imitate it perfectly. Using it, she would not give Lady Aston the satisfaction of knowing how she'd destroyed Clarity's confidence, nor how she'd caused a rift between the newlyweds.

The latter was probably an accident. For Clarity couldn't see how Alex's aunt gained anything by driving a wedge between the spouses. Yet she was certain of one thing—the woman wanted to maintain her control of the Hollidge household. And while Alex considered his wife to be incompetent, he would allow his aunt to remain in charge.

In any case, for the time being, with the change that was taking place inside her, Clarity was not only willing to cease trying to wrestle control of her new home, she was going to heap every task she could think of upon Lady Aston.

Except one—redecorating the room that had once been Alex's nursery and now would belong to their baby.

In short order, Clarity stopped doing anything. When the flowers arrived for her to arrange as she had been doing since she'd moved in, she left them to die until his aunt started putting them haphazardly in vases.

When the butler asked if she wanted to continue the weekly purchase of port that was the same as her father's and brother's loved drink, which she'd first ordered for Alex, she declined.

"Whatever Lady Aston used to buy is fine."

And when at last the draper came to discuss fabric for new curtains throughout the house, she showed him to the sole room she was interested in redecorating.

With her remaining time, she folded paper into abstract shapes that looked nothing like she intended, visited with her family and friends, and with her lady's maid, Winnie, accompanying her, took endless walks in Mayfair.

When Alex tried to broach the topic of her doing more regarding the household, she merely shook her head.

"Your aunt has it all under control," Clarity reminded him.

But when he reached for her in their large bed, she could not deny either of them the pleasure of slaking their hunger for one another.

Alex knew something was changing with his whimsical wife. Something besides her inexplicable refusal to take up the mantle of being his viscountess. She'd had a single bad experience and needed time to lick her wounds before she would try again.

But the real change was something else. Where previously, Clarity had boundless energy, she was now prone to bouts of fatigue, and more than once, he had found her napping like a cat on the sofa, snoring softly in the parlor.

Also, her breasts, which had always been full, had grown plumper.

At first, he thought it to be his imagination. But as she rode rantipole atop him one night, he reached up to cup her breasts. When they spilled over from his palms, he knew they were larger.

Grabbing her by the waist, he stilled Clarity's enthusiastic movements, anchoring her in place.

Her heavy lids fluttered open, and she looked down at him, her blue eyes glazed with desire.

"Is there something you wish to tell me, wife?" he asked.

"Now?" She tried to defy him and continue her pleasure ride, but he wouldn't let her move.

"Yes, now," he insisted, resting his fingers on her gently curved stomach.

She sighed deeply, and her glorious bosom rose and fell before him. *Definitely larger and more spectacular than before.*

"I am expecting," she confessed, "and I was going to tell you soon. Maybe even tonight *after* we finished! Please, Alex." Her teeth sank into her lower lip, and he couldn't resist her.

He pulled her down onto his chest and then rolled her beneath him. After a few firm strokes, she was arching back and tightening around him. Her body's rapid response caused his own climax to swiftly follow a heartbeat behind as he drove into her warmth.

However, he was careful not to collapse atop her. Instead, he stretched out next to her, took Clarity's hand in his and with his other, drew the bed clothes up and over them.

"I am going to be a father," he said.

"And I'm going to be a mother," she added. "I cannot tell from your tone if you're happy."

"Of course I am happy. I'm only surprised."

"Well, we have enjoyed ourselves often," she reminded him. "You shouldn't be that shocked."

He chuckled at her words. "Not overall, no, but in this moment I am. I assume you've had some time to get used to the idea."

She nodded, then asked, "How did you know?"

"A man knows his wife's breasts," he told her.

She giggled.

"Have you told your family?"

"I would tell no one until I told you." She yawned. "I suppose we should tell your aunt tomorrow."

"A built-in nanny," he teased.

But Clarity didn't laugh. She turned on her side and stared at him.

"Lady Aston will have no part in raising our child," she said vehemently.

Thinking of his life before and after his parents, he said, "Agreed."

"And I intend to paint the walls and change the wallpaper in the nursery," she declared.

"I would prefer you have a professional do it," he said, "unless you're particularly good at it, but I don't want you up a ladder until after the baby is born."

She punched him in the shoulder. "I cannot tell if you're joking, but I do not need permission to redecorate the nursery or any room," she said, although she spoiled the forcefulness of her declaration by asking, "Do I?"

"Obviously not. You are Lady Hollidge. Do whatever you wish to make this house into the home of your dreams."

"Thank you," she whispered and yawned again.

Soon, his adorable wife, mother of his unborn child, drifted off to sleep, and Alex was right behind her, traipsing into the land of Nod.

Until the damn nightmare started, and he found himself in the carriage with his parents, knowing what was about to happen, unable to stop it, and as terrified as the child he had been at the time. Clarity was there, too, laughingly changing between the child he grew up with and the woman who was his wife, and back again.

Desperate, frantic, he tried warning them, but they couldn't hear his cries. Thrashing, he awakened to glaring moonlight streaming through a slim parting in their curtains, slashing directly across their counterpane.

With his heart pounding, Alex climbed out of bed, making sure not to disturb the woman who had his heart, and went to his study where a decanter of French brandy awaited.

<hr />

"What are you reading so intently?" Alex asked her. He'd come late into the informal salon where they often took their breakfast, and she hadn't even looked up.

She giggled. "My goodness, dear husband. I didn't hear you come in. Kiss me, and I'll tell you."

He grinned. In her expectant state, she went between smiles and tears each hour. She cried if he said something too kind or romantic and laughed uproariously at the silliest things. But what she didn't do was attempt again to run the household. She seemed utterly content to let his aunt handle the entire winter season, including Christmas and the Twelfthtide.

The only festive gathering Aunt Elizabeth hadn't attended was a Stir-Up Sunday celebration at the Diamond's home. Alex enjoyed their tradition of going over the year's accomplishments on the last Sunday before Advent. His and Clarity's news had been blatantly obvious with her blossoming figure.

Leaning down on the chilly February morning, he kissed her full on the lips, no matter the footman standing nearby awaiting an order for tea, coffee, or chocolate.

"You know we kissed a few minutes ago." As usual, when they awakened, they kissed. When one of them left the bedroom ahead of the other, they kissed.

"I know," she said.

"I only ask because you've been a bit distracted, even forgetful lately."

"I haven't!" She declared. "Have I?"

This time, he laughed. "You have but never mind. I'm here to remind you of anything you need. Anyway, you were going to tell me something."

"I was?" she asked, looking mystified. "About what?"

He rolled his eyes. "About what you were reading."

"Oh, yes! There's a robber entering some of the best houses, not a nibbler, either. He's taking as much as he can get away with."

"May I?" he asked.

She handed him *The Times* as he sat down. Before he could read a word, she started to speak.

"The Bedingtons were robbed this week, and the Wolstenholmes on Mount Street a few days prior. At first, they were keeping it quiet to avoid public panic, but now Scotland Yard is investigating. Inspector

Field thinks it best to let people know about the threat. Thus, we can all be watchful."

Alex scanned the story. Both the robberies were within a few blocks.

"It's rather exciting," Clarity declared, breaking into his thoughts. "Remember when we pretended to be highwaymen and held up my parents' carriage?"

For a moment, he smiled at the memory, crystal clear of the both of them on horses with handkerchiefs over their faces. Her parents, riding in an open curricle coming down their long drive at Oak Grove Hall, knew it was them as soon as they burst from behind the hedge on familiar horses.

Regardless, Lord and Lady Diamond played along and gave them each a silver coin.

Then he sobered. "It's not exciting. It is bloody dangerous. I shall make sure Mr. Berard looks over the latches on all the windows and the door locks, too."

She merely shrugged. "I always feel perfectly safe when I am with you."

He felt a constriction across his chest, as if a band of iron was tightening around him. More than anyone, he knew he couldn't keep her safe. And yet, he was determined to do the impossible.

That night, the nightmares awakened him, not once but twice. The second time, he went downstairs with a lamp to patrol the windows, making sure each latch was fastened.

The following day, while his wife was bubbling with vivacity as usual over breakfast, glowing with her condition, Alex felt weary and cranky. He could barely keep his eyes open at his desk while trying to answer correspondence.

When she came into his study with a maid behind her carrying a pot of tea and some of his favorite shortbread biscuits, he snapped at her.

"I cannot concentrate on these accounts with you popping into my private space every five minutes!"

Shocked by his vehemence, Clarity took a step back, nearly

knocking the tray out of the maid's hands. Instinctively, her arms went around her now-protruding stomach.

Alex felt like an ogre.

Jumping up, he rushed around his desk before she could escape.

"I am exceedingly sorry," he said, taking hold of both her hands, ignoring the housemaid's shocked expression. "Please forgive me."

Clarity appeared close to tears, but she nodded.

"Set the tray down," he told the maid-of-all-work, "and bring an extra cup for Lady Hollidge."

"Yes, my lord." The girl retreated from the embarrassing scene.

"I will have tea only if you'll have it with me," he vowed. "Besides, you've brought enough biscuits for an army. Please stay."

"I will," she agreed, allowing him to lead her to the chair by the fire, then dragging his from behind the desk to sit beside her.

"It's not like you to yell at me," she said.

"It's inexcusable. There is no reason for it." He didn't want to tell her about the nightmares. Instead, he added, "I had trouble sleeping last night."

"I didn't notice," she said.

"Because you were soundly sleeping as you should," he said.

"That is one thing about carrying a child. I can sleep better than I ever have before. Mother says I had best enjoy it because when I get bigger, I shall not be as comfortable."

"It's hard to believe you will get bigger," he marveled. His slender wife was beginning to look as if she'd swallowed a gourd.

"I shall. I have been through this four times," she said, "although I only recall the last three."

For a moment, he was mystified by her words. Then he understood. "With your mother carrying your siblings?"

"Exactly. Her stomach grew too big for me to be able to sit on her lap, and it made me very cross."

"I just realized the first time we met that you were an only child like me," he said.

"I don't remember that meeting."

"Nor I. I think I was five. But the next time I came back, Purity was in the cradle, and you were toddling around."

"I don't remember that, either."

"Who would have thought that grungy tot in leading strings would grow up to be my beautiful viscountess?"

The maid returned with another cup and saucer, then left them alone again.

"Our mothers thought, that's who," Clarity reminded him.

"Smart ladies," he muttered, pouring for both of them and handing her a biscuit, which she dunked into her tea before eating it in two bites.

Soon, she'd polished off all but the one he ate.

"Shall I call for more?" he asked. "Or have you had sufficient to hold you over until dinner?"

She laughed. "You haven't forgotten the dinner party at my parents, have you?"

Of course he had!

"Of course not," he said. *How had he forgotten?* He wanted to weep with the thought of what lay ahead that night, about four hours of being a good guest. At least it was merely a dinner and not a dance, but it would be long and exceptionally merry, as only a Diamond party could be.

Perhaps he could dash upstairs and take a catnap before they left.

Brushing off her hands, unmindful of the crumbs falling on her skirt and on the floor, Clarity rose.

"I have a few more things to do before I change for dinner. Maybe I shall even lie down for a few minutes," she added, stealing his idea.

At the door, she turned. "Perhaps we could do so together."

He almost groaned. Her pregnancy was having a strange effect on her about which he'd had no prior knowledge or warning—making her extremely randy. Normally, that wouldn't be a problem. Today, however, if he stretched out upon the bed, he feared he could do nothing to satisfy her. His eyes would close, and he would find himself dead to the world.

"Perhaps," he said.

She frowned. "You don't sound particularly enthusiastic."

"I'm distracted. Nothing more. I have a lot to get through before we depart."

In the end, he was rushed and without having napped, he felt needlessly nettled. He didn't wish to go eat with his in-laws. When his valet was doing his best, Alex griped about everything. Eventually, the man lowered his hands from adjusting the cravat for the third time and uncharacteristically sighed.

"My lord, perhaps you would prefer a simple necktie."

"No! I'm not appearing at Earl Diamond's dining table in such a slovenly fashion. Just get it right this time, Mr. Lawson."

"Yes, my lord."

Painstakingly, his valet tied the cravat again. It still looked wrong, but Alex stormed out and hurried downstairs to find his perfect, happy, smiling wife in the front hall, already wearing her thick mantle against the chill night air.

"You look especially handsome tonight, my love," Clarity said.

With her words, Alex plastered on a smile, swallowed his unwarranted peevishness, and decided to be joyful along with her for the remainder of the evening.

But that night in bed, when he felt her turn to him, murmur a passionate endearment, and lay her hand upon his chest, he could not respond with anything but a broad yawn. In the next instant, his eyelids slammed shut, and he knew nothing again until the nightmare began.

Chapter Twenty-Nine

I n the space of a fortnight, to Clarity's dismay, her husband reverted to the stranger she'd met at the Devonshire House ball at the beginning of the prior year's Season. Not that he wasn't still loving, but he no longer laughed nor even barely smiled.

Alex had dark smudges under his eyes and a pinched, haunted look. When she asked him what was wrong, he said he was merely a little tired. She wasn't sure how that could be when they retired at the same time, had a long night's sleep, and rose together for breakfast.

And then one day, his unsmiling demeanor became harshness, and he was sharp with her. They were out together, and with the sunlight in her eyes, she stumbled on a cracked granite pavement.

As if she'd fallen down an uncovered well and broken every bone in her body, he raged against the City of London and even the unfortunate shop owner outside whose business the pavement was situated.

"Get this fixed," Alex demanded of an elderly tailor after dragging her inside to complain. "My wife is expecting the heir to my viscountcy, and she nearly sprawled on the street."

"Yes, my lord. I'm sorry. I shall bring it up to the city's commissioners."

"See that you do. I will be back in a week's time, and if it's not repaired, I shall sue."

"Sue?" The man's brow furrowed for what. "Your wife is perfectly fine."

"I have a law degree, and I shall sue nonetheless."

"Yes, my lord." The man looked shaken.

All the time, Clarity was trying to pull him by his sleeve and get him to stop his blustery attack on the shopkeeper.

"I've fallen out of a tree. Twice!" she reminded him. "I believe I can trip without injuring myself."

But his expression was thunderous all the rest of the day. That night, he was still thinking of it.

"I will stop off at William Haywood's office tomorrow. He's the new engineer and surveyor for the blasted commissioners. I shall make sure they're going to do something about it."

"Oh, Alex, don't you think—"

"I do think," he cut her off. "I also look where I am going. Please, Clarity, try to be more careful while you are carrying our child. I know you enjoy fun and games, but don't be selfish right now."

She closed her mouth and bit her tongue to keep from lashing out at him. He cared for her, and now he had the baby to care for, too. And plainly, he was worried.

"I will be more watchful," she promised.

"Thank you," he said. As if realizing he'd overreacted, his expression became sheepish.

"I apologize. You are not in the least selfish, and I am a dunce. Ignore me." Then he added, "Except do not ignore the part about being careful, or I shall have to swaddle you in a large bunting to keep you safe."

That brought her good humor back, imagining a baby's swaddling cloth large enough to envelop her.

"It sounds cozy," she admitted.

However, the next day, not only did he snap at her for coming down the stairs too quickly, he wouldn't allow her to go out in the carriage with her maid unless he accompanied them.

"But Alex, I want to go to the office of Mr. Crace, the decorator, and look at the wallpaper samples, and then I'm going to choose fabric for the baby's first gowns at the linendraper's."

"That's what I wish to do, too."

She sighed. He obviously didn't want to do either. He rushed her at the first place and stayed in the carriage reading a newspaper at the second shop. Yet seeing how he wouldn't leave her, she hurried through her choices, unsure whether she'd made the correct ones.

The following day, she told him she was going to her parent's townhouse to consult with her mother.

"I shall go with you."

"No," she put her foot down. "This is a ladies-only tea. My sisters will be there, but not Adam or my father. You would stand out like a sore thumb amongst the female fingers."

He frowned, and she could see she'd nearly convinced him. All that was left was to go up to him, look him in the eyes, and kiss him.

To that end, she stood before him. When Alex's arms came around her, she leaned against him, went up on tiptoe, and claimed his mouth with hers.

"*Mm,*" he said.

"*Mm,*" she sighed.

After a few minutes, because her toes and legs were aching, she had to break it off. He grinned down at her.

"That was unexpected."

"At nearly every moment of the day," she confessed, "that's what I want to do. It's simply not always appropriate. And you know, I am nothing if not proper."

He laughed.

"Any time you wish to kiss me, please do. I didn't marry you for your attention to propriety."

With that, he put an arm behind her knees and swept her off the ground.

She squealed with excitement.

"*Oof,*" he said, swaying slightly. "You are gaining a little, and it's not solely your bountiful breasts anymore."

With her cheeks feeling hot, she ordered him to put her down.

"No, wife, I am going to carry you upstairs and make love to you before you go to tea."

"Maybe we should enjoy ourselves in the dining room or in the parlor," she advised as he staggered on the fourth step up the staircase. "For goodness' sake, Alex, put me down."

"No!" he said. Soon, with him practically on his knees, he'd breached the landing outside their bedroom. Lurching forward, he carried her over the threshold. But after placing her carefully upon the bed, he lay down beside her breathing hard.

"Are you going to ravish me or have a restful slumber?" she teased.

"Both," he said. "Give me a minute."

True to his word, after a minute, he was ready to ravish her. An hour later, she left him stretched out on his stomach, his magnificent bare back and buttocks presented to her.

"I will see you later, my love."

"Not too late. Promise."

"I promise." And she slipped away to her parents' mansion on Piccadilly.

"My husband is immensely caring. I fear he's about to put me under glass like an upside-down apple-and-orange jelly," Clarity told her mother and Purity five minutes after sitting down to tea. Her younger sisters had gone with friends to Kew Gardens and then to a show about "Industrious Fleas" at Covent Garden.

"Did Father become overly protective each time you were carrying one of us?" she asked. "Alex is becoming like a Newgate jailer."

Her mother cocked her head and considered. "Your father is not an anxious man by nature, but when I was carrying you, because you were the first, he demanded I curtail some activities toward the end of my lying in. No horseback riding, for instance."

"How about walking on a London pavement?" Clarity asked wryly.

"Oh dear!" Purity said. "That does seem unreasonably protective."

"In jest, Alex said he would swaddle me, but I think he might actually try it if he can find enough soft wool or bunting."

Her mother and sister looked at one another, raised brow to raised brow, and Clarity felt badly for talking about her husband behind his back. After all, he was only being cautious.

"I wondered if we three could go to the mercer's. I went yesterday, but my dear husband was hovering, and I am not at all certain I made sound decisions, nor at the decorator's, for that matter."

Afterward, they went to Gunter's for ice cream. By then, she knew her husband would be missing her and dashed home, deciding to go directly to his study.

Alex was pacing, running his fingers through his hair when he turned at her footfalls.

"Thank God!" he exclaimed, rushing to embrace her.

"What's the matter?"

"When I went to your parents' home, you weren't there, and neither was our carriage."

"You came to Piccadilly? Whatever for?"

"To make sure you were all right. When I awakened, you had already gone."

"That was unnecessary," she told him. "And you worried yourself needlessly."

"No," he said sharply, "*you* worried me. You said you were going to your parents' house. Where were you?"

Clarity didn't like his tone or being questioned, but to ease his anxiousness, she answered.

"After tea, we went to Gunter's." No need to tell him she had also returned to the same places he'd taken her the day before.

"You never said anything about gallivanting all over town."

Since she could not imagine a sensible response, she said nothing.

"Anyway, I am relieved you're back," he said.

She left him before she said something that would annoy him, something about his smothering tendencies. More than ever, she missed the Alex who had once tossed her into the River Derwent simply because he could.

The following week, their strained conversation long forgotten, she hurried along the hall to find him. Rushing through the open door to his study, she waved a newspaper at him as he rose to his feet.

"Did you see the advertisement for *The Last Days of Pompeii* at the Adelphi?" Clarity asked her husband. "I would love to go at week's end."

His expression had quickly changed from interested to scowling.

"What are you wearing?" he asked.

"I told you I was starting the nursery today."

"I thought you meant you were *starting*, as in the workmen were starting with you telling them your wishes and then leaving them to it. Surely you don't think you can do any of it yourself."

"Not all of it, but I have nothing to do and thought it might be fun to..." She trailed off at his look of horror.

"What if you overexert yourself?" Alex demanded.

"I won't," she promised.

"What about the noxious fumes?"

Was he serious? "I won't breathe any."

"What if you spill some paint, and it gets in your eyes or mouth?"

She stared at him.

"It is possible," he insisted. "That is why we hire people to do these things. People who are *not* expecting a baby."

"I was simply going to try my hand at tearing off the wallpaper. I've never removed wallpaper before, but it seems a most satisfying endeavor."

"You will not. You'll be in the way of the workers, and it will cost more if you slow them down."

"But Alex—"

"I suggest you take that handkerchief or whatever it is off your head and change out of that awful frock and apron. You don't look like a viscountess. The workers will think you're a maid and start asking you to bring them cups of tea."

That made her giggle. In truth, the men had already arrived and something like her husband's imagination had in fact occurred. Clarity hadn't minded the request for coffee, not tea as it turned out, but she most definitely had not cared for Lady Aston's attempt to take over.

After they'd nearly engaged in a quarrel, Clarity had banned Alex's aunt from the nursery.

That had gone about as smoothly as spreading rocks on bread. She didn't want to get into a similar argument with her husband.

"If I change and stay out of the workmen's way, may we go to the theater?" she asked.

"Yes," he agreed. "To see the lighthearted, wildly amusing *Last Days of Pompeii*."

She laughed at his tone. "I know it sounds grim, but the novel was good, and reviews of the performance say the spectacle on stage is most entertaining."

"I said we could go," he reminded her. "Now keep up your end of the bargain."

"Fine, I will leave you to your work." Clarity hesitated by the door. His aunt was livid with being thwarted over interfering in the nursery, and Alex ought to know.

"By the way, I argued with Lady Aston and called her overbearing and bumptious. She may be in a bit of a tweague if you see her. Rather testy, in fact. Just a warning."

And then before he could ask her anything, she blew him a kiss and retreated.

"Carriage rides are as perfectly safe as ever they were," Clarity found herself arguing with Alex in bed the night of the theater. They'd thoroughly enjoyed the live drama of Pompeii, and she'd had no idea telling him she was going to Twickenham the following day would start a quarrel.

"I only wish to explore Marble Hill," she insisted, referring to a famous old Palladian style mansion that had twice been the home of a royal mistress.

Now standing vacant, she and her sisters wished to poke around the old house and the Italianate gardens with the pretty river view.

To her consternation, Alex had told her she couldn't go.

"Not in your present condition," he said.

"I wasn't really asking permission," she muttered. "Besides, think of all the people out upon the roads even now."

"Now? At two in the morning?" he asked, rolling over, apparently ready to end their discussion and go to sleep.

"Granted, they are not there this minute but tomorrow. And think of all the trips you have taken in your lifetime."

Clarity implored him to be reasonable. The alternative was his crippling fear for her safety, which was restricting her beyond all measure. Despite his parents' accident, most carriages managed to go from one place to the next without incident. And while she hated to keep bringing up carriage rides, she was not going to become a prisoner.

Tapping his shoulder to make sure he was still awake, she continued, "I am as safe in a carriage as I am here in our home."

No sooner were the words out of her mouth, than they heard an unfamiliar thump. Perhaps it sounded louder in the Stygian darkness of their bedchamber, but it made her jump nonetheless, especially as it was so unexpected.

Alex was on his feet and reaching for his dressing gown before she could gather her wits.

"It sounded as though it was directly below us," she whispered, leaning over to light the oil lamp.

"Stay here," he ordered. But when he drew a pistol out of his bedside table, she gasped.

"Don't you think it might be Mr. Berard?" she asked.

"In all the years I've known him, my butler has never made such a sound, particularly not at this hour."

With her heart pounding, she watched her brave husband rush barefoot from the room, his robe hanging behind him like a cape. Chewing her lip, Clarity tried to stay put as ordered. Yet when she heard another noise from the room directly below, she donned her slippers and reached for her own dressing gown. Cinching the belt closed, she crept silently from the bedchamber.

The house was quiet on their floor. Apparently, Lady Aston at the other end of the hallway had not been disturbed. As Clarity went down the stairs, the hair on the back of her neck rose upon hearing more noises. In the foyer, the housekeeper approached from the back of the house, her hair in a cap, wearing a robe, and yawning broadly.

"What is happening, my lady?"

Before she could answer, Mr. Berard arrived, holding a fire iron. She would have found his appearance humorous if she weren't terrified. Robbers were common, especially pickpockets. People were desperate, but some were career thieves. And those who dared break into houses were bold, indeed. Moreover, some worked in gangs. Alex might be facing more than one cracksman.

"Lord Hollidge is in the—"

She was interrupted by a gunshot.

Chapter Thirty

Without hesitating, beating both senior members of the staff as well as the maids who had come along after them, Clarity ran down the hall and through the open library doorway.

It was dark, but a man was groaning.

As a scream welled in her throat, light flooded the room.

Alex was beside the reading table, having leaned over to light the lamp. As he straightened, she saw blood staining the front of his amber-colored dressing gown. Giving in to the impulse, she shrieked, despite him staring back at her with clear, alert eyes, and despite another person on the wool rug at his feet.

"I'm not bleeding," her husband reassured her, and she relaxed, although still lightheaded from the initial terror.

"Send for a doctor and a constable," Alex ordered his butler.

Mr. Berard rushed from the room, and the rest of them gave their attention to the man on the floor, dressed in coarse clothing, with a bloom of blood on the front of his shirt.

Clarity recognized him at once. "Mr. Chimes?"

"You know this man?" Alex asked, shocked.

"He is one of the Mr. Crace's workmen."

"Is he?" Alex asked. He went to the sash window casement. "He must have broken the latch before he left to allow himself easy access."

Then she saw the long, wicked knife where it had fallen from his grasp.

"You fought with him?"

"I did," Alex said. "Mrs. Rigley, perhaps you have something we can press against the man's wound, although I..." He stopped speaking, looking uncharacteristically uncertain. The housekeeper vanished as quickly as the butler had.

"Go back to bed," Clarity ordered the two maids who were staring at their master and the felled intruder. "At once."

They did as she said. Then she turned to him, now crouched beside the robber.

"Tell me what happened."

"I don't think he will live," Alex said. "I had to shoot him. He came at me in the dark like a fool. I felt his blade."

"What do you mean you felt it? Alex, stand up!"

When he did nothing, she yanked at his arm. He hissed in pain, but he stood. On his left sleeve, blood was seeping through, and without doubt, it was her husband's.

"He cut you," she insisted, starting to shake. "You *are* bleeding!"

"I suppose I am," he agreed as Mrs. Rigley returned.

Quickly, Clarity grabbed one of the cloths from the housekeeper's hand.

"The robber may not live," she said over her shoulder, "but we will need that doctor. Mrs. Rigley, will you press a cloth to the man's side?"

Meanwhile, she wrapped the one she held tightly around Alex's arm over the blood stain, tying the ends in a knot.

"No point, my lady," she heard from behind her. Mrs. Rigley's voice was trembling. "He's not breathing no more."

Clarity and Alex locked eyes. Alex groaned, whether from pain or from hearing he'd killed someone, she didn't know.

"Sit," she ordered and practically pushed him backward into the comfy wingback chair. "And stay. There's nothing more you can do."

Alex wondered how a delightful evening at the theater could end with him finally getting back to bed, bandaged, in pain, and having killed a man in his home.

The constable had arrived and taken the dead man away to the morgue. The capable staff had already rolled up the Persian rug. Whether Mrs. Rigley would clean it or throw it away, he didn't particularly care.

But Clarity had disobeyed him, and it stung. She had come directly downstairs and entered the library right behind him, seconds after the fight.

What if she'd come in before he'd shot the man? The robber might have run for the door and stabbed her.

He shuddered. *How could he keep her safe if she wouldn't obey him?*

At that moment, she slept deeply beside him, which was a wonder in itself, considering all that had happened. She'd made sure he was comfortable after his doctor had cleaned and dressed the superficial gash, and then she'd yawned so broadly, it looked as if she would split her face. In seconds, she was asleep.

Lately, as his baby grew inside her, she was exhausted by bedtime and usually drifted off as soon as he put out the lamp. And then she snored as she was doing then, something he didn't recall from when they were newly married. He could only conclude it had something to do with her pregnancy.

That made him smile in the darkness. His ever-larger wife, growing rounder in face as well as belly, snuffling and snoring beside him. He went to put his arms around her, knowing it wouldn't awaken her as she was such a sound sleeper, but he winced upon moving, having already forgotten his wound.

There was no question of her going to Twickenham. He didn't think he could let her out of his sight, not until after the baby had arrived. And he knew it was going to cause an argument. Closing his eyes, he prayed for dreamless sleep, providing him the strength to stand up to a willful Clarity.

In the morning, as expected, they went toe-to-toe.

"Are you actually telling me I cannot go to Marble Hill?" She was fuming over her morning cup of chocolate, which was not a good sign.

"You do realize even the queen herself has had assassination attempts that did not keep her from going out."

"I am telling you," Alex said with as much patience as he could muster, "I would like you to wait until I can accompany you."

"Which will be when?" she asked. "And while you look at reports of cattle sales and the price of grain, I am to do what precisely?"

"If you hadn't pushed aside my aunt's offers of assistance in learning the ways of Hollidge House, then you would have plenty to keep yourself busy."

It was a sore spot, but as far as he could tell, Aunt Elizabeth still ran everything. And the one thing Clarity had done recently, hiring workmen, had brought a thief into their midst.

"And each time you cause problems with Aunt Elizabeth—"

"*I* cause problems?" Clarity echoed, setting down her cup. "You have that the other way around, I assure you."

He hated to gainsay her. Mostly, he didn't want to upset his expectant wife, but facts were facts.

"We had no issues in this house before your arrival. Certainly no nighttime robbers, nor people refusing to come to dinner." He had heard from his aunt that one of the couples from the previous party had refused a repeat performance.

"Of course you had no issues," Clarity insisted. "You lived like a lifeless ghost or a tamed lion with Lady Aston as your overbearing keeper."

"You must grow up," he told her, ignoring the insults. "How are the preparations for St. George's Day?"

"It seems early to worry about that," Clarity protested. "We only recently celebrated the Hocktide and Easter."

He waved away her words. "My parents used to host at least a party a month, especially for the traditional festival days, and I expect you to take up the tradition."

"I am well aware of that. But your aunt said she—"

"You cannot expect her to do it all. *You* are the viscountess."

"I know but she—"

"Clarity, please stop arguing with everything I say. I married you, trusting that you would become mature enough—"

"What are you saying?" She rose to her feet from the small table in the salon where they took their morning meal. Thus, he did the same.

"On the day we married, we were blissfully in love," she continued, resting her clasped hands upon her burgeoning stomach. "You said nothing about wanting me to change. How can you be such a beast?"

A beast! What an odd thing to call him. After all, he was trying to protect her. Indeed, he'd shot a man for her.

"I don't want you to change," he said, but he didn't sound convinced, even to his own ears. "Merely do not be so..." He halted abruptly.

"So much myself," she finished, her tone flat.

Or maybe that was finally the sound of his wife speaking reasonably. If she were more like his aunt, there would be no drama. If she had handled all her duties with aplomb, then Aunt Elizabeth wouldn't have had to step in and try to fix things, bringing it to Alex's attention, rubbing his nose in the fact that he'd chosen a wife with his heart instead of his head.

"I understand what you're saying, Alex."

He almost snapped at her to call him "my lord" before realizing what an ass that would make him. In fact, he loved hearing her say his name. He loved her beyond reason, which was why he wanted everything to go smoothly.

If one tempted fate, then the wheel of that mythical lady Fortuna might spin dizzyingly around and send their happy life into one of wretchedness and turmoil.

"I'm glad you understand," he said. "Let me finish what I'm working on, and we'll go to Gunter's for ice cream this afternoon."

She shook her head. "You don't want ice cream. You probably consider it a childish thing to eat."

"I don't," he protested. "I love ice cream."

"How often did you go there before we were married?"

"Never," he admitted.

"You see," she said softly. "Another compromise in your orderly life that you made on my account."

"Ice cream isn't a compromise," he said.

"In any case, I don't want any, and I no longer want breakfast, either," she proclaimed.

The red devils had got hold of her, whipping her up until her eyes were flashing and her cheeks deeply flushed.

"I shall leave you to eat hurriedly and then get on with your work."

"I hope you change your mind about Gunter's," Alex said when she reached the doorway.

"Another thing to change," she muttered and stormed out.

As it turned out, Alex didn't finish until it was nearly the dinner hour and already growing dark. Sticking his head into the drawing room, he searched for Clarity. She wasn't there, nor in the library, nor in the informal salon, which was the scene of their morning altercation. At that moment, he couldn't even remember how or why it had escalated so quickly into the worst argument they'd had since getting married.

Upstairs, she wasn't in either of their bedrooms. He even opened the door to the nursery, but the curtains were drawn closed. It was dark and empty, giving him an unsettled feeling.

Wandering back downstairs again, he looked in the dining room before going down another flight of steps to the kitchen, knowing how Clarity loved to snack. Cook gave him one look and shook her head.

What on earth? Alex should have asked Mr. Berard directly. Against his wishes, his wife had gone out, but his butler would know the when and where of it.

Retreating to the front of the cellar, he tapped on Mr. Berard's sitting-room door.

"Yes," the man said, sounding aggravated. Alex figured that was probably how he sounded when the butler interrupted him in his study.

Pushing the door open, he caused his butler to jump to his feet and spill his cup of tea.

"My lord?" Mr. Berard queried, looking and sounding shocked at this breach of the servants' quarters.

"I didn't mean to disturb your break," Alex began. "I am looking for Her Ladyship."

The man nodded. "Lady Aston is—"

"Not that lady," he snapped, annoyed the first woman his head of household thought of was his aunt. Annoyance was swiftly followed by a blanket of guilt. Alex hadn't done enough to make sure they understood Clarity was in the superior position as lady of the house. That was *his* fault.

"Where is Lady *Hollidge?*" he asked again.

"I don't know, my lord. As far as I know, Lady Hollidge is within as I've had no indication she was going out, nor did she call for the carriage."

"Is Mrs. Rigley above stairs?" Perhaps he should have started with her. The women tended to stick together, from the lowest scullery maid all the way up to his capable housekeeper, knowing everything that went on at Grosvenor Square. If Clarity had gone out on foot, she would have taken her lady's maid, and Mrs. Rigley kept a careful eye upon all the maids.

"I believe Mrs. Rigley is in the pantry, my lord. I shall ask her at once about Lady Hollidge," Mr. Berard began.

"Never mind," Alex snapped. "I'll speak to her myself." Luckily, as he turned, he spied the housekeeper coming along the passage.

"Mrs. Rigley," he hailed her. "I was on my way to see you."

"And I, you, my lord. I've been looking all over for you. Lady Hollidge has left."

"Left?" Alex repeated, his mind going blank on the meaning of it.

"Yes, my lord. She has left us," Mrs. Rigley confirmed, her voice sounding thick with emotion, which served to alarm him further.

"Left for where?"

"I don't know, my lord. But her lady's maid spoke to the maid-of-all-work, asking her to give me a letter."

"Let me see it," he commanded.

Nodding, Mrs. Rigley drew a paper from her apron pocket, which he snatched with impatience. The handwriting was barely legible.

"Lady Hollidge wrote this?" he asked, continuing to scan it for its intent.

"No, my lord. Winnie, her lady's maid did. It says they've gone away because... because..." But the woman broke down crying. "I did so want to see the little 'un."

Alex's gut twisted as if she knew somehow that he would never see his babe. Glancing again at the unreadable missive, he gave up.

"The devil! I can barely read it, and what I can make out is all slum and slang. Am I correct in interpreting they have gone to Lady Hollidge's parents' home?"

"Yes, my lord."

"Dammit!" he swore. "Berard, get my horse. On second thought, see if there's a hackney outside." After all, he couldn't bring Clarity home on horseback, not in her condition.

The butler hurried to the front door.

"Why did she leave us, my lord?" Mrs. Rigley asked, her face entirely forlorn.

He didn't answer as he knew in his gut it was their heated discussion over breakfast. He had caused his pregnant wife to run away.

Chapter Thirty-One

Back upstairs, having donned his overcoat, Alex was yanking on his gloves when his aunt came through the front door.

"Mr. Berard is holding my taxi for you," she said. "He mentioned you're in a hurry. Has something happened?"

"Clarity has left me."

His aunt gasped, her nostrils flaring. He was glad he didn't see even the smallest glimpse of gladness or triumph. Instead, surprise was rapidly replaced by disapproval.

"It certainly doesn't look good to have one's wife up and leave. You had best go after her and bring her back."

"That's what I'm doing," he said through gritted teeth, dodging past her, resenting her seeming more worried about appearances rather than Clarity's safety.

Twilight had given way to darkness when he reached Lord and Lady Diamond's home on Piccadilly. Foregoing any semblance of calm propriety, he knocked on the door and then opened it, not waiting for the butler.

"Alex," came Lord Diamond's voice at the top of the staircase. "Head into the drawing room. I'll join you in a minute."

"I came to see Clarity." He didn't have time to sit with his father-in-law.

"I know," His Lordship said.

"She is here, is she not?" he asked, dreading the answer if she wasn't.

"She is," Lord Diamond told him.

Relief, pure and simple, took hold of him, and he had to look away before he unmanned himself before the earl. Alex hadn't realized exactly how scared he was that she'd gone some place where he couldn't find her.

Without another word, he strode across the foyer and into the drawing room.

After an excruciatingly long minute, Lady Diamond entered, followed by her husband but not by Clarity.

"I would like to see my wife," Alex persisted. He hadn't needed to study law at Oxford to know he had every right to be given access to Clarity whenever he wished, and even her parents couldn't keep him from her.

"She's napping," her mother said.

Alex paused, thinking of how sweet Clarity was when she fell asleep anywhere in their house like a dormouse.

"She gets fatigued often," he conceded. "I shall wait until she awakens and then take her home."

Lord Diamond sighed. "She doesn't want to go back to Grosvenor Square tonight," he said. "Since she's now a married woman, she has put us in a predicament." The earl knew as well as Alex that they shouldn't interfere, at least in the eyes of the law.

"Geoffrey," Lady Diamond said, as if speaking to her husband in private. "Our daughter is not the one who has brought this about, at least not by herself." Then she eyed Alex, reminding him of his own mother's discerning gaze.

Alex swallowed, fully comprehending that he was being chastised. "What has she told you?"

"She doesn't have to say anything," Lady Diamond added. "But she is clearly unhappy. And an unhappy Clarity breaks my heart."

Alex considered this. "She didn't tell you why she came?"

Lord Diamond leaned back and crossed his arms. "Why don't you tell us why she is here, napping in her old room, looking as if she just lost her best friend? Again."

"Again?" Alex asked.

"She was a distraught little girl when you stopped visiting us after your parents' passing."

It wasn't as though he'd wanted the terrible tragedy to happen. In any case, he couldn't change the past, and it didn't matter anyway.

"She's no longer a little girl. She's my wife, carrying my child, and I want her to come home."

Both her parents remained silent. Finally, under their scrutiny, he confessed.

"We had a quarrel earlier today. I inadvertently offended her."

"I see," her mother said. "It seems strange she would run away after a single *inadvertent* offense." She had a single eyebrow raised in a way that Clarity had perfected.

Yet he refused to explain any more. The intimate matters of their marriage needed to stay between him and Clarity.

"Shall I return later or will you accompany her home yourself?" he asked her father. "Obviously, she can't come alone in a hackney."

"Of course not," her father agreed. "When Clarity awakens, we'll determine her wishes."

Her wishes! That sounded ominous and not at all as if they were cooperating.

"If we need you to return," her mother said, "we'll send word."

Short of storming the staircase and upsetting his sleeping wife, Alex didn't know how to break this impasse. Rising, he bowed and was nearly out of the room when Lady Diamond halted him with a question.

"Do you regret marrying our daughter?"

"Caroline!" Lord Diamond said, shaking his head at the bold, personal query.

Alex flinched. *Had Clarity said something to her parents, indicating her own change of heart?*

"I don't mind answering. I have no regrets. I love her."

"Precisely as she is?" her mother pressed.

He didn't hesitate. "I promise you she has my heart. If sometimes I might hope she were less exuberant, it is only to make life easier."

"Yours or hers?" Lady Diamond asked, her tone becoming slightly sharper.

"What my wife is trying to say, Hollidge," the earl interrupted, "is that Clarity has always been a joyful person. From a happy baby, she has grown to be a jubilant adult. Anything, or *anyone*," he added pointedly, "that dims her sunny nature is cause for our alarm."

"I have no wish to diminish her natural joy," Alex asserted, "but she is a viscountess now and soon to be a mother."

"And thus, you believe she should be *less* happy?" her mother asked.

"No, I..." Alex began. He hadn't said that. Lady Diamond was twisting his words. He was tired. Too many interrupted nights, too many worry-filled days.

Surely, they understood their daughter needed to show more caution, more maturity, more restraint, more gravity.

How could he keep her safe if she were reckless? Not that being safe meant not being happy, merely being more thoughtful. At least, that was his intention.

"Clarity must rein in her high-spirited tendencies and embrace her new roles, all of them, as I had to do at age thirteen. Otherwise, who knows what might happen?"

"What might happen?" her mother asked.

He could not live in constant fear of losing her to some silly lark, to climbing a ladder, falling into a river, or even allowing a robber into their house, for God's sake. It was bad enough knowing she might not survive childbirth.

Nonetheless, he could hardly express his fears, particularly to the mother of five healthy children. Lady Diamond would dismiss them out of hand.

"She might continue to fall short," he said lamely, knowing it didn't say all he meant.

"Fall short," her father repeated, frowning and turning to his wife whose eyes had widened considerably.

Alex knew he'd said the wrong thing.

"Our eldest daughter is not living up to your expectations?" Lord Diamond asked, his tone one of astonishment.

"I did not mean that," Alex said quickly. "We had a dinner party, and when it went badly, she stopped doing anything expected of a lady of the house, even arranging flowers. And early on, she spoke of redecorating the common rooms in our home, but I think she became overwhelmed."

They stared at him as though he had sprouted an extra head.

"Our daughter has been making lovely floral arrangements since she was old enough to go into our garden and pick blooms," Lady Diamond said. "Your mother had a great fondness for flowers, you may recall, and complimented Clarity when she was about seven years of age. As for organizing a dinner party, my daughter has well been able to since she was fourteen. And as to the redecorating of your home, the last I heard, she had been encouraged not to change anything by another member of your household."

Alex knew to whom she referred, but he knew nothing of his aunt telling Clarity not to change the interior of their home.

"If you have not already, you might take a look at the one room she did decorate to prepare for your forthcoming child."

Alex rose to his feet. "You must excuse me. Like my wife, I am tired, although for different reasons. Naturally, you heard about the intruder."

Her parents also stood. "Yes, we did," Lady Diamond said, sounding more like her congenial self. "We're very grateful for how you handled the dreadful situation."

"In your place," Lord Diamond added, "I would have done the same thing."

That was kind of them, to ease his conscience about what had happened.

"I haven't slept soundly since that night," Alex acknowledged, not bothering to tell them he hadn't slept well prior to the cracksman's break-in, either.

Not with the blasted nightmares having returned full force since his marriage!

"It is late," Lady Diamond pointed out. "Why don't you return home and let Clarity stay here tonight? She probably won't want to get out of bed again this evening. You can return home and rest, too."

He hesitated. It didn't sit well to leave his wife behind and not have her under his roof. On the other hand, her parents' home was the one place he knew she would be as safe as if she were with him.

"Very well." Alex took his leave and hoped his aunt had retired. He had no wish to explain why he'd returned empty-handed.

It had been an easy decision to leave London. Upon hearing Alex's voice the night before, Clarity crept downstairs and listened at the drawing-room door.

A grown woman and a wife, eavesdropping on her own husband! She ought to be ashamed.

Moreover, it served her right to hear him say she wasn't measuring up to his standards. Alex had told her own parents how she had fallen short of his expectations.

Clearly, neither of them was happy with her being Lady Hollidge. At first, she had assumed Alex would loosen his cravat and laugh more. And he had done exactly that, at least for a little while. However, his return to the easy-going nature she'd recollected hadn't lasted long.

Even before he found out about the baby she carried, Alex had begun to take everything too seriously again. Knowing life was precious and fragile was one thing. Tamping down each bit of amusement the way one snuffed out a candle was quite another.

No longer did she look forward to their meals together, whether with Lady Aston or by themselves when Alex's aunt was out. During the months since Clarity moved in, Lady Aston had kept her seat at one head of the dining table for dinner and supper. In the beginning, Clarity saw the lopsided and ugly arrangement, sitting midway between Alex and his aunt, less as a slight to her status and more as a fortunate way to be closer to her husband.

Now she wondered if she ought to have insisted on taking her rightful place. Even when Lady Aston was at a concert or at the theater with Major Grover, Clarity didn't assume the end seat. It would feel as if she were an interloper or worse, a child playing the part of an adult. Besides, the following night, there would be an awkward stand-off if Clarity challenged the older woman.

Unfortunately, even allowing Lady Aston to remain in charge of the housekeeper and the maids had not made the woman any more pleasant to live with. If anything, she'd become increasingly waspish.

After putting up with all of that and still hearing Alex voice his disappointment, Clarity had made up her mind to go away. It wasn't enough to stay at her parents' home. It was too close and too easy for Alex to cajole her into returning to Grosvenor Square—or force her, which would not only be embarrassing but would alter the tenor of their relationship forever.

As she traveled along in the luxurious train carriage with Purity and Adam for company, along with Winnie and one of her father's footmen, she tried to dismiss the pointless thoughts. Yet it was irksome how the blame for any mistakes made since she'd become Lady Hollidge had been laid at her feet, while any small successes had been snatched by Lady Aston as if she'd managed to triumph *despite* Clarity's bumbling.

Sighing, she felt the tears gather. She was no bumbler. As the eldest daughter, she'd watched her mother run both their home in Town and their country estate to which she now journeyed. Moreover, she'd helped her on many occasions. Clarity was confident she knew how to do both. For some reason, she'd relinquished her confidence along with her maiden name.

She sniffed. Adam, seated opposite with his back to the direction in which they traveled, looked up from his book. Beside her, Purity took hold of her gloved hand and leaned against her. They were her support as she left her unhappy husband to carry on in London, with his imperious aunt continuing to clench the reins at Grosvenor Square.

"I am relieved to be going to Oak Grove," Clarity said, trying to keep the waver from her voice. "I can relax and enjoy the remainder of my lying in."

"I, for one, intend to catch up on my correspondence and reading," her brother said. "Maybe I'll even go hunting, though it's almost too late for foxes and far too early for grouse."

"You should invite a friend, maybe Lord Kilbey," Clarity said, then recalled the last time they were all at Oak Grove with Alex, and the tears started to trickle down her cheeks.

Purity handed her a handkerchief. "Please, dear one, don't grow melancholy. Adam and I couldn't bear it. For our sakes, try to think happy thoughts."

Clarity nodded. "How generous of Father to agree to open the house. I know it's a great expense for only the three of us."

She had dragged her brother from his London interests while in between terms at Oxford. Normally, he would either shadow their father or attend the gallery of the House of Commons, where he studied the debates with particular interest this election year. As for Purity, she was now the most eligible Diamond sister with a full calendar of spring and early summer events. Yet they had both come willingly.

"It will be fun," Purity said. "We shall stay up late reading aloud to one another, play music and sing off-key with no one to judge us, and eat our meals at any hour we choose. That is, any hour that Cook allows."

Clarity smiled. Her sister was trying hard to cheer her.

"You sound like me," she said, "without once mentioning what propriety or society dictates we *ought* to do. Besides, it's not Cook. It will be Mrs. Dilbert."

They fell silent, and Adam wrinkled his nose. Mrs. Dilbert, who oversaw the house when Mrs. Cumby was in London and the family wasn't in residence, was also in charge of the kitchen when their regular cook wasn't there. Occasionally, they'd sampled her best efforts, but nothing had been quite right.

"Her cooking isn't terrible," Purity said finally, and they all laughed.

"It bloody well is," Adam protested. "She's fit to clean the stove, not whip up meals at it."

"We'll help her," Clarity said, bringing stunned silence from her siblings. "Why not?" she demanded. "If nothing else, we can at least tell her what something is supposed to taste like. Maybe it will be fun. Besides, we can't do any worse."

"You ladies can play in the kitchen," Adam said. "I shan't be doing any such thing, but I pledge to eat whatever you concoct without fussing."

Despite the circumstances, Clarity was determined to look on the bright side. Sometime soon, she would bring a new babe into the world, and she was determined to surround him or her with joy.

"I am thrilled to think of my little one in our old nursery," she said, glancing out the window as they approached the Derby Midland station. A coach would take them the few minutes to the hall.

Feeling the silence grow thicker, she glanced at her two siblings, who were eyeing each other.

"What is it?"

"Do you think we'll be here that long?" Adam asked.

"We don't mind, of course," Purity said, "but I would think your husband will come after you and..." She trailed off.

"Try to drag me home?" Clarity said. "I would like to see him try."

Adam shook his head. "Poor Alex, marrying the oldest, most stubborn Diamond sister."

"That's not a nice thing to say about your own kin," Purity scolded, and the train car rocked to a halt.

"Maybe he'll be glad to be rid of me." Clarity tried to say it in a teasing voice, but it fell flat.

"You know that's not the case," Purity said.

"Never mind. Let's not talk about it anymore." Descending from the train, the two sisters strolled along the platform to where taxis awaited, with Winnie in tow. Clarity realized she was at a stage where she waddled more than walked. Alex sometimes, when in a good mood, quacked rudely as she went by, making her laugh.

Trying not to think of her husband, she waited while Adam secured a carriage and their footman arranged for the trunks. Then she had a cheering notion.

"Let's enjoy Oak Grove Hall," she said to Purity, "and pretend we are children again, and our parents have gone away and forgotten us."

Chapter Thirty-Two

Alex couldn't remember ever being so furious. Clarity had run away like a child. He'd done the same when he was six or seven years old, departed the Hollidge country estate with a bread roll and a piece of cheese tied up in a kerchief. Their old Cook had given him the food, and he later found out his parents had watched him go about a furlong, keeping an eye on him until he sat down under a tree. They'd brought a picnic and joined him. He couldn't even recall why he'd run away.

Clarity was not six or seven, and she was carrying his child. She'd left London with two of her siblings, sending a short missive sealed with a purposefully large glob of blue wax, delivering the wretched message by way of one of Earl Diamond's footmen.

Opening it in his study, Alex felt a surge of anger, followed quickly by his least favorite emotions—fear and loss. At least she'd bothered to write the note herself this time.

Before he knew where he was going, he'd left the sanctuary of his study and wandered upstairs to Clarity's bedroom, hoping against hope that this was all a dreadful dream. She would be in the chair by the window with her lap-desk situated on her knees, either writing or reading.

She wasn't there. What's more, the room exuded a profound empti-ness, reminding him of when his parents had died. In a way, it had been a relief to live at school until he was better able to deal with being in the house without them—or at least until the last of his mother's perfume and his father's tobacco scent had faded.

Soon, he would be the parent with a little one depending entirely on him and on Clarity for everything. *How bloody odd!*

Closing his wife's door against the stillness, Alex went upstairs to the room that had allowed the robber entrance into their home and had taken up much of Clarity's time.

Pushing open the door to the nursery, which still smelled of fresh paint and lemon oil, Alex entered the newly decorated room. Seeing it in daylight, he was unable to keep from smiling. Any child would love the room. *Blazes!* He wouldn't mind it for himself.

Cheerfully painted from floor to chair rail in pale yellow with a bird-and-butterfly wallpaper for the rest of the wall up to the ceiling, it made him want to sit in the rocking chair and read a book from his own childhood. More than that, it made him want to hold his baby in his arms and rock him or her to sleep. He couldn't wait for the infant to arrive. The room would be a place to sing that damned song, which if he thought about it, would be stuck in his head all day. *Too late!*

Oranges and lemons,
    Say the bells of St. Clement's.

You owe me five farthings,
    Say the bells of St. Martin's.

When will you pay me?
    Say the bells at Old Bailey.

When I grow rich,

Say the bells at Shoreditch.

Humming the tune, he examined the crib—his own—that had been brought down from the attic and refinished. A new blue and yellow rug rested underfoot. Under the window, ready for the baby to become a toddlekins, was a rocking horse with a soft woolen mane and a real leather saddle molded to its wooden body. And on the sill, as if Clarity had been reading it, was a book he'd never seen before.

Picking it up, he examined the thin volume. *The Book of Nonsense* by Edward Lear, it had been published a mere few months earlier. Flipping through the pages to see entertaining illustrations and silly verses, Alex smiled.

How he wished his parents were there to meet their grandbaby. He could easily imagine them sitting in the nursery, reading aloud the funny poems. He would do it in their stead.

Proud of what Clarity had created with this now-perfect room, he couldn't fathom why she hadn't done over the whole house. Touching the window curtain, a cheerful gold-colored damask, he recalled Lady Diamond saying something he didn't want to dwell on, that Clarity had been discouraged from making this house into her own home.

There was only one person who might have done that. And he had turned a blind eye, allowing it to happen right under his own nose while he was too busy worrying over things he could not control.

Putting the toe of his boot to one of the hobbyhorse's rockers, he sent it teetering gently and left the nursery. Finding his aunt in the drawing room, reading the morning papers, he sat down at one end of the sofa. Clarity once said the room looked as though it had been decorated when the last king was a baby, and she had been correct.

Aunt Elizabeth gave him an inquiring look, and he filled her in on Clarity's unexpected trip to the countryside of Derbyshire.

She pursed her lips and set her newspaper down.

"At least your wife saved you the humiliating scene of returning to her parents' house again to collect her and finding her gone."

Alex didn't give a fig about humiliation. He wanted Clarity home with him where she was safe.

"Anything could happen to her out on the road. Lord and Lady Diamond should not have let her go."

Aunt Elizabeth folded her arms, looking disapproving. "I doubt they had much choice. Lady Hollidge is a grown woman."

"She is not acting like one," he fumed, then instantly felt disloyal for speaking ill of his wife to his aunt.

However, Aunt Elizabeth overlooked his unkind words. "I had no idea the two of you were unhappy," she continued. "Lady Hollidge must have been extremely forlorn to leave behind her new life as your viscountess."

He disliked how she always referred to Clarity as *Lady Hollidge*. While accurate and even respectful, it put up a barrier to true familial affection, which he'd hoped would have already bloomed between the two women.

"Clarity never cared about being a viscountess. It takes more than that to impress an earl's daughter," he said. "But you're correct about her not being happy, and I believe it was all my fault."

"Yours?" his aunt seemed confounded. "What did you do? Nor did anything occur in the household that would warrant your new wife being discontented."

"That's exactly it," Alex said. "Nothing changed, yet she believed I would be like the youth she remembered."

"That's absurd. You're a grown man with responsibilities. And usually, you behave appropriately."

"I do, don't I?"

Why, then, did he feel as if he'd failed the most important person in his life?

"I led her on by behaving as..." He tried to come up with who he was when he was with her. "I was my old self, meaning my *young* self, when we were at her parents' country party. We fell in love over fishing and climbing trees and laughing until we cried. She believed I would keep behaving in the same manner because I all but promised her I would."

His aunt shook her head. "Then Lady Hollidge was naively holding on to unrealistic expectations. It is obviously easier to be carefree when away from the demands of running an estate and handling a vast fortune with staff and farmworkers and millers and brewers and herdsmen and the like, all depending upon you."

At that moment, Alex would trade it all for a glimpse of Clarity. His Diamond was worth more to him than any fortune or title. Even her smile was precious beyond jewels.

"I know you are correct," he said, "but I should be able to handle both my viscountcy and my marriage. My wife makes me happy."

"Then why have you become increasingly cross and doleful?"

"Wasn't I as I've always been?" he asked, wondering at his aunt's characterization of him.

"No," Aunt Elizabeth declared. "Naturally, you grew serious once you took up the mantle of your father's title, but you never seemed particularly dispirited. I thought you had grown into a mature, responsible young man, satisfied with your lot in life. I am proud of you."

"I honestly didn't realize how unhappy I was," Alex admitted, "until I renewed my acquaintance with Clarity. In fact, I believe I would have been happier if I had never stopped visiting with the Diamonds."

His aunt shrugged, glancing away. "All in the past," she said.

He might as well tell her what he had learned months earlier.

"It has come to my attention that my parents didn't want to send me away to school, at least not at that age. Instead, it was you who wanted me to go."

Aunt Elizabeth hesitated, her lips pursing as her cheeks paled. Then she nodded.

"It's true."

"Yet you told me not to visit with the Diamonds, neither here in Town nor in the country because seeing me would upset Lady Diamond in particular. That she blamed me for their deaths."

"Well!" she said with exasperation. "I guess I have been the topic of much tongue-wagging."

"Some perhaps, but mostly because I was trying to explain to the Diamonds last autumn why I had never returned to Oak Grove. They were astonished that I might think they held my parents' death against me."

"And they blamed me," Aunt Elizabeth concluded.

He remained silent. After all, while his loss of both parents was devastating, she had also lost her beloved brother. There was no reason to dwell on the why of it.

"They were right to blame me," she added, surprising him. "Your mother hugged me before you three left. She thanked me for the advice and said even if you didn't end up attending the school, you would have a cheerful time on the trip. But my brother rolled his eyes and was far more frank. 'We're only doing this to appease you, Elizabeth. We want to keep our boy home.'"

Alex's mouth fell open, even as an enormous weight lifted from his shoulders. As it did, the room tilted around him.

Dear God! It truly wasn't his fault. They hadn't wanted to send him away. They hadn't been disappointed in him for being something of a madcap.

"You should have told me," he said, unable to keep the hurt from his voice.

All the years of guilt and pain had been unnecessary. What's more, he'd nearly missed out on loving Clarity Diamond.

His aunt hung her head. "I know," she whispered. "I was ashamed. But then I tried to ease your pain by sending you away to avoid living in this house without your parents."

"I hated it," he told her.

She gulped in air, and he had to soften his tone for fear she would dissolve into sobbing.

"Although I learned a great deal," he added, trying to think of some benefit to being tormented daily by those who were either cruel, jealous, or both, and seeing himself as the recipient of too many flogging-day Fridays, not to mention being disciplined by the senior boys who were heavy-handed. "And you brought me home for the holidays."

She nodded, her eyes large and sorrowful.

"I did feel bad for Lady Diamond," his aunt confessed. "It was as if she'd lost a sister. But that's not why I kept you from them. *You* are my primary concern. I didn't want you to go back and be reminded of all you had lost," she said. "Amongst the happy Diamond children and their parents, I thought it would be harder on you."

"Consequently, you made me want to stay away from them, as if it were for their sakes?"

She raised her chin unapologetically.

"Then you don't dislike the Diamonds or disapprove of Clarity," he concluded.

His aunt's pinched visage didn't alter, and it dawned on him her usual severe expression had been forged through the tragedies of life, and not necessarily indicating peevishness at all.

"I feared your particular choice of a wife would drag you back into the dangerous waywardness of your youth," she said.

"I believe I was the one dragging her into trouble when we were younger, but now, I am beyond grateful she's helped me to feel happy again."

Aunt Elizabeth lowered her eyes. "Seeing how things turned out, I might have handled some things differently," she allowed. "At the time, since I was your only family, I didn't want you to hate me for your parents' accident. Then you would have felt alone, indeed."

"We shall muddle through," he said, using an old saying of his mother's.

Also at that moment, he was also struggling to determine if her disclosure did make him hate her, even a little. But he didn't. She, too, had suffered. Moreover, for the first time, he could accept that the carriage accident had been precisely that, an unforeseeable twist of fate.

Aunt Elizabeth sighed softly. "I told you I lost my Henry," she said.

His aunt rarely mentioned her late husband, Lord Aston, but Alex knew she'd been a young, childless widow.

"Henry Aston was a joyful creature," his aunt stated softly, "but very careless. Reckless, even. Not a day went by that he didn't seem to have a mishap. I believe he needed spectacles," she added.

"One day, he went riding, which he loved to do." She sniffed. "When it grew dark, I sent our footman out to find him. He'd fallen off his horse and broken his neck."

This shocking statement was nearly as bad as reading Clarity's letter. No one had ever told him how his uncle died, nor had he thought to ask.

Reaching an arm out, he touched his aunt's shoulder. "That must have been dreadful for you."

"Yes, it was." She sniffed again, drew a handkerchief out of the pocket of her skirt, and dabbed at her eyes. "After my brother let me become a close part of his young family, I'm afraid I grew more and more concerned by your mischievous ways."

"I was merely a boy," Alex reminded her gently.

"I know. But I feared you would grow up to be reckless and die tragically. I wouldn't wish that on anyone, not on your parents, but then..." She paused, looking past him into the distant long ago. "Then tragedy happened again, anyway."

His stomach twinged uncomfortably.

"We both lost everyone," he said.

"Untrue," she protested. "You always had me, and now you have a wife. At least you did until you chased her off with your churlish behavior, like a wild boar."

He crossed his arms. Her attack would not stand.

"A wife whom *you* have disapproved of from the beginning, I must remind you."

"Nonsense," his aunt declared. "I was trying to spare you the heartache of loving the wrong person and enduring future loss. If you had married Miss Brambury, your heart would have barely been engaged, certainly not shattered should anything happen to her."

Alex gaped at her twisted logic. "You hoped I would have a loveless marriage in order not to endure any more pain?" That was a topsy-turvy way to look at life. Then he recalled that had been his precise plan before meeting and falling in love with Clarity.

His aunt gave an awkward shrug. "I acknowledge how pushing you in Miss Brambury's direction was a mistake. Instead, you followed your heart. I warned you on the night of your engagement how such a course of action could lead to misery. You cannot go back and fall out of love. However, you also cannot go forward as you are, with both of you so miserable."

Damnably miserable, Alex thought, longing to see his lovely wife again.

Aunt Elizabeth shook her head. "Your parents would be most disappointed in what has occurred. Don't forget they liked your Lady Hollidge. Your mother even wanted you to marry her, if I recall."

"She only knew her as a child. And I doubt my mother was doing anything more than lighthearted matchmaking with her friend."

"Perhaps," she agreed. "Regardless, you liked the child Lady Hollidge was, and you liked the woman she became well enough to marry her. Now she's expecting your baby. What do you intend to do? Let her leave you on a whim while you hide in this house until the babe is old enough to come see you?"

"Of course not!"

What did he intend to do?

"I shall give Clarity some time to regain her happy disposition, considering how Oak Grove Hall and being with her siblings always put her in a good mood. Then I will ask her forgiveness. Somehow, I got it into my head she wasn't up to the challenge of running this household or even of looking after herself competently. I can't even imagine how I got it all cocked up, can you?"

His aunt widened her eyes, looking innocent. He wondered if she would accept some of the blame, but she said nothing more.

"When she returns, Auntie, I intend to give her full head to be lady of the house. You can no longer be its mistress. Will you be able to remain living here while behaving thusly?"

Her eyes widened farther, then she added, "Once Lady Hollidge has proven herself able to run this household, I will bow out gracefully. I may continue to live here if I feel welcome, or I may set up my own residence."

That had gone better than Alex expected. Now he simply had to get his wife back.

Chapter Thirty-Three

"You look the pinnacle of health, my lady," Mrs. Boswell said in her role as midwife, when she was summoned to examine Clarity's progress two weeks later.

Clarity knew it for the truth. She felt marvelous, not nearly as fatigued, and ravenous but without the space in her stomach for all the things she was craving.

"You married the one who used to come visit, the laughing boy, now the man with the sad eyes. I told you your husband was in the room that night, didn't I?" Mrs. Boswell reminded her.

Clarity gasped. "You did! I'd forgotten. Yes, I married Lord Hollidge. At the time, everyone thought you meant another man who was at the party."

"I could see the connection between you and your Hollidge, like a golden thread, plain as day."

Clarity knew her eyes were as big as saucers. "Could you really?"

Mrs. Boswell chuckled and touched her own forehead with two fingers. "Always could see things."

Clarity nodded. Then she recalled what else the woman had said.

"You said he adored me." She wished her voice hadn't cracked with emotion.

"I did, and he does, as much as you love him."

"Then why am I here without him?"

Mrs. Boswell shook her head of black and gray curls.

"Young people!" she muttered.

At that moment, more than anything, Clarity wished Alex had come after her. She wanted to be a wife he admired. And loved. She wanted him to look at her with the adoration the midwife said he felt.

"I disappointed him," she said softly.

"Nonsense. You are all he needs," Mrs. Boswell said. "Things will work out." Then she frowned. "But not if you are here and he is in London."

"I could go back," Clarity said, struggling even to rise from the chair, large as she was.

"I don't recommend it, my lady. Not in your advanced condition."

"How long before the baby comes?" Clarity asked, considering that London was only as far as a short carriage ride to the station, followed by the relative comfort of a velvet-cushioned train seat.

"That's hard to say. This little one might want to meet you tomorrow or next week. No longer is my best guess."

"Then that's enough time to return to London."

"Absolutely not," Purity said, entering the room. "That's precisely the type of action your husband would label as unbearably reckless, and I would agree."

"But Mrs. Boswell said I need to be with him to fix my marriage."

Purity pierced the midwife with a narrowed gaze. "I am sure she didn't mean for you to run off willy-nilly."

"Your sister's right," Mrs. Boswell said. "I didn't intend for that. Once your wee one arrives, there'll be time enough to get back with your husband."

"But Alex should be here," Clarity moaned, tears pricking her eyes. "He should be at the birth. Father was at each of ours."

"Was he?" Adam asked, entering in time to hear. "News to me."

"I was there for many of them," Clarity declared, "and I know Father was, too, or at least he was pacing in the hallway beyond."

Tears started to fall, thinking of her beloved parents and the happiness of having babies.

"Why am I this impossibly weepy?" she asked.

"Probably a boy child," Mrs. Boswell said.

Purity rolled her eyes, and Clarity was glad her sister hadn't been there for the pronouncement of a golden thread between her and Alex. Yet at that moment, she could practically feel it tugging at her heart because she had gone too far and been away from him for too long.

"Adam, will you drive me to the station?"

"Of course," he said amiably until Purity's head whipped around so she could glare at him.

"No, I won't," he amended. "Foolish idea because...?" He ended with a question.

"Because we don't want her baby being born in a carriage or on a train!" Purity snapped.

"Right," Adam said. "A very foolish idea."

With that, knowing he was outnumbered by three women and too many emotions, he turned heel and disappeared from the room.

"Your baby will be here soon. I am not a midwife, and even I can tell that," Purity said. "As soon as he or she has arrived, and you feel strong enough, we will return to London."

Clarity nodded. "Mrs. Boswell said it could come anytime now."

"Why don't you write to Lord Hollidge and ask him to come quickly?" Purity suggested.

Her sister made a great deal of sense. But Clarity wasn't feeling sensible. She was feeling emotional and vulnerable, and she wanted to be with Alex.

"I shall take what you say to heart," Clarity agreed.

⁓

Alex was certain he had fallen asleep on the train to Derby, lulled by the rhythmic rattle of the tracks, and was now having one of his usual nightmares.

As he approached a carriage, which appeared undamaged but was stopped on the side of the road, he plainly heard Clarity screaming as she often did in his recent terrifying dreams.

Having paid to borrow a horse from the stable by the station, Alex was about a mile from the Diamonds' country estate. Or he was soundly asleep on the train.

Silently, feeling sick inside, he glanced at the coachman, who was standing on the road with one hand resting on the carriage.

"Lord Hollidge!" the man exclaimed, white as a sheet. "Thank God! Lady Hollidge is inside. I didn't know what to do, so I pulled over when she cried out."

Alex shook his head uncomprehendingly. *Why was his wife screaming?* With a shaking hand, he took hold of the carriage handle just as she yelled again.

Yanking it open, he expected to see her and his parents in a mangled heap with broken necks. That was how the nightmare often concluded.

With her head down low, Clarity was on all fours, rocking gently. When the door opened, she looked up. Her face was flushed a ruddy color.

"Alex!" she cried. "Our baby is coming!" He would swear she sounded happy, despite the circumstances.

Abruptly, he knew he was wide awake.

"Here? Now!"

"Not by my choice," she said, breathing hard, her features pinched with pain. "It's happening again." Then she went silent, lowered her head again, and in the next instant gave a keening cry of pain.

"What can I do? Why are you here?"

This was a nightmare, indeed. He didn't know the first thing about childbirth.

She said nothing, continuing to moan. And then she stopped and lifted her head again.

"How far?" she asked.

At first, he didn't know what she meant, but it dawned on him quickly.

"Less than a mile but too far, surely." He feared he would have to help her birth his baby on the roadside.

"No, it's not," she insisted. "The pain comes in waves. I watched my mother do this. Can you get me home?"

By God he could and he would!

"Yes," he said. "What about the midwife?"

"She's in the village."

Alex thought quickly. "Can you be by yourself during the journey?" Since she was taking up most of the carriage floor, he didn't think she would argue, and he had a plan.

She lowered her head and didn't answer except for the merest of nods.

"Hold fast, my Diamond."

Another nod.

He closed the door on the woman he loved more than his life.

"Driver, take my horse. Go straight to the village and get the midwife. Do you know her?"

"Yes, sir. Mrs. Boswell."

"Good. Bring her quickly to the manor. I'll drive the carriage back to Oak Grove."

The coachman hesitated, but Alex didn't. Climbing onto the dickey, he snatched up the reins as Clarity yelled again.

"Hi-ya!" he called. As soon as he got the team moving forward, he turned them. By the time they were heading in the correct direction, the coachman was a cloud of dust going around the bend in the road.

"Can you hear me?" he called out when Clarity went silent.

There was no response. Either she couldn't hear him and the wind was taking his words, or she had collapsed.

"I love you," he shouted.

When there was no answer, he willed Clarity to be all right, and then he started to pray.

As the road to the Diamonds' country estate came into view, Alex turned down between the elm trees and tried not to think of what might await him when next he opened the carriage door.

What he found at the house's entrance was pandemonium. Maids and footmen were scurrying hither and yon with trunks and cases. Purity was ordering everyone around including her brother, who was trying to listen and to speak with the estate manager.

When Alex drove into the midst, all movement stopped for a moment and every person stared.

Finally, recognizing the carriage as the one from their own estate,

Purity ran toward the horses before the carriage had even come to a halt, Adam at her side.

"Hollidge? Is that you?" The heir was the first to speak.

Then Clarity let out a cry, and Alex nearly wept with relief. Hearing her was better than not hearing her, even if she was in pain.

Leaping from the seat, he was at the door before either of her siblings could beat him to it, and for the second time, he yanked it open.

"Clarity!"

No longer on all fours, she was on her side, still on the carriage floor.

"Help me get her upstairs," Alex ordered, climbing into the carriage and trying to get her onto her knees while Adam yanked down the metal step. Between the two of them, they soon had her feet upon the gravel, and then Alex swept her into his arms.

She moaned loudly, keeping her eyes closed.

"Sorry, my love," Alex said. "I know you're uncomfortable."

"No matter," she whispered, and her eyelids fluttered opened. "It's lovely to see you."

"Send for the midwife," Purity said to the nearest footman as she hurried along in front, thrusting aside anyone in their way.

"Already done," Alex ground out, not wasting words with the burden of his bulky wife clasped high against his chest.

Dropping Clarity and his unborn child was out of the question. Therefore, he let the sweat trickle down the back of him as he took to the main staircase as swiftly as he could.

"In here," Purity directed him when they reached the second floor, and he followed her inside a sunny bedchamber.

As gently as he could, he lowered Clarity onto the silk counterpane.

She sighed. "That's much better than being in the carriage."

"Why on earth were you in a carriage?" he demanded, trying to keep the severity from his tone, even though he'd had the wits scared out of him at discovering her in such a state.

"That's what I would like to know," Purity said.

Leaning over her sister and wiping a strand of hair from her forehead, she added, "When we discovered your note, we were packing up the household to follow. What if you'd begun to labor on the train?"

Alex couldn't even imagine such a situation. "Thank God my train arrived early."

Clarity looked abashed, but then he could tell by her changing expression that pain was rolling through her again.

"Where is that blasted midwife?" Alex asked as his wife closed her eyes and began to pant.

"I need to sit up," she said.

"Indeed she does," came a voice from the doorway.

He turned to see a woman who looked vaguely familiar.

"Help her, both of you," the midwife ordered. "Take an arm each and get her to a seated position."

They did as they were told, and the curly-haired woman stuffed the pillows from the other side of the bed behind Clarity's back to keep her propped up.

"Now, my lord, you must vacate the room and let us get to our woman's work."

"But I—" Alex began.

"You can help by fetching some tea and a few plain biscuits for your missus to keep up her strength. Actually, get enough for all of us."

She looked at the maid, whom Alex recognized as Winnie, and seemed to be giving her the list of more important things than tea. "I'll need a pail of clean water and some clean towels, and something to spread over this fancy counterpane, unless no one cares if it gets soaked."

"Soaked with what?" Alex asked, looking from the apple-cheeked midwife to Purity and then to Clarity.

Winnie had already darted from the room, but the midwife rolled her eyes. "Never you mind. Now kiss your wife and do as I say."

He hated to leave Clarity until he'd told her everything that was on his mind, but he could see he was in the way.

"*Oohh,*" she cried, then gave a long hiss.

Regardless, he leaned in and kissed her forehead, then her cheek, and finally, her lips.

"I love you," he told her, wishing he could look into her gorgeous eyes, but they were scrunched tightly closed.

"Love you," she managed on a brusquely expelled breath.

"Off with you," the midwife said, "and don't forget the tea and biscuits."

As he reached the door, he heard her add, "Well, ladies, shall we birth a baby today?"

Chapter Thirty-Four

Exhausted but happy, and feeling satisfied with her labor since Mrs. Boswell said she'd done very well for her first time, Clarity looked down into the ruddy face of her newborn son. He had a fuzzy covering of the softest black downy hair on top of his little head.

While not remembering Purity's birth, she knew from seeing Adam and her younger siblings being born that everything about her baby looked perfectly normal.

The door opened, and Alex entered. Mrs. Boswell had gone to fetch him and take out the detritus.

Upon seeing her sitting up and fully awake, he yelled, "We have a son!"

Purity, who was still seated beside the bed, arose and stroked Clarity's cheek.

"You are a marvel, dear sister. I'll go send word to Mother and Father." She turned to Alex, who seemed mesmerized by the swaddled baby in Clarity's arms.

"Congratulations, Lord Hollidge. Does your son have a name I can tell my parents?"

His gaze found Clarity's, and she smiled at him.

"We don't have one yet," she told her sister. Then she wondered. "Do we, Alex?"

He shook his head.

"How terribly remiss of the two of you," Purity said in jest. "It wasn't as if you didn't know the little lord was coming. I will call him 'the healthy baby boy' for now. I'm sure our parents will be here with our sisters in a few days."

And then she was gone, leaving the two of them to stare at one another.

"We have a baby." His tone was softer now, sounding awestruck.

"We have a baby," she agreed. "With Mrs. Boswell's help."

"I think I recognized her. Isn't she the traveling fortune-teller?"

Clarity felt tired, relaxed, and so giddy with relief, even his question made her laugh.

"Fortune-teller, yes. Traveler, no. She lives in the village and put on that costume in order for our guests to believe in her gift as a seer."

"Then she was a sham?" Alex asked.

"No! Not at all. Mrs. Boswell has the gift of seeing. Everyone in the village has always said it is true." She paused, then decided to tell him. "She knew we were going to marry. She told me that's what she meant the night she said my husband was in the room."

"How strange," he murmured, but his glance was fixed upon their child again.

"May I?" he asked, gesturing to the space beside her on the bed.

"Of course." Clarity could scarcely believe he was at Oak Grove.

After sitting on the edge of the mattress, he leaned over to better see their son.

"Hold him." Immediately, she thrust the baby toward him, swaddling blanket and all.

Alex flinched slightly before taking the bundle from her, his large hands dwarfing the infant.

"Hold him close," she said. "We must keep him warm."

Nodding, he tucked their boy against his chest. "He's tiny."

"He is perfect," she said, touching her son's small forehead.

"Yes, I can see that," Alex agreed.

Clarity had already memorized the baby's face, but she hadn't dared to think of a name for him until Alex was next to her.

"My sister is correct. We should have chosen a name."

Alex nodded, not taking his eyes off his son.

"We can give him your father's name if you like," Clarity offered.

His gaze flew to hers, tears glistening.

"Yes." He cleared his throat. "I would like that."

Clarity paused. "I confess I don't know what it is. How remiss of me. I know you've told me in the past, but my brain is fogged, and I cannot recall. Besides, I always think of your parents as Lord and Lady Hollidge."

"*We* are Lord and Lady Hollidge," he reminded her. "I think my father's name will suit him perfectly. Young Osbert."

Clarity stifled the gasp of dismay, determined not to let him know she didn't like the name. After all that Alex had been through with his parents, she could give him this gift.

"A good, strong name, don't you think?" he asked.

"Yes," she said, keeping a false smile on her face while wondering if she could call him Bertie, at least while he was little.

To her amazement, Alex started to laugh.

"I'm teasing you, wife. My father was Thomas and, if you're amenable, our son shall be Thomas as well."

"Yes, of course! Now I remember." She giggled. "You teased me!"

"I did," he agreed.

"And you laughed," she pointed out.

"I did that, too."

They beamed at one another before a large yawn snuck upon her.

"Can he have my father's name as a middle name?" she asked, before a wave of tiredness nearly made her close her eyes while they were talking.

"Yes. Thomas Geoffrey," Alex said. "That sounds grand, doesn't it?"

"It does." This was all too easy and too pleasant.

When was he going to start berating her again for her idiotic actions?

Now that she'd produced a healthy baby, she could scarcely recall how desperately unhinged she'd felt to get to Alex.

"I'm awfully pleased you're here," she told him.

He shook his head. "You say that as if I arrived back from a pleasant trip in time to hold our son, rather than finding you on the road about to give birth in a carriage."

"Mrs. Boswell said we wouldn't be able to solve our problems until we were together. I should have listened, though, when she said to simply wait."

"Mrs. Boswell makes a great deal of sense. Your coachman looked positively green. Imagine what you put the man through."

He shifted his position, standing up and going around to the other side of the bed before sitting beside her and leaning against the headboard.

"You were returning to London, and I was racing to get here," he pointed out.

"Yes, I forgot that. Why were you?" she asked. "Racing here, I mean."

"Because I adore you, and I cannot live without you."

Clarity couldn't suppress a gasp this time, although it ended in another large yawn.

"That's wonderful," she said. "I thought you were disappointed in me." Leaning her head upon the many pillows still behind her, she closed her eyes.

"I was disappointed in myself, actually."

She heard Alex's words but couldn't summon the strength to look at him or respond.

"We will talk more as soon as you've slept," he promised, and then she slipped into blissful oblivion.

⁓

When Clarity awakened, it took her a moment to remember all that had occurred. *The baby! Alex!*

Neither were in the room with her, but she knew they had both been real. They were all at Oak Grove Hall together, despite her reckless flight the day before. Or had it already been two days?

But where were they now?

"You're awake," came Purity's voice when she stirred.

"My mouth feels as though I've been sucking wool."

Her younger sister smiled. "I've got lemonade for you."

"Bless your heart. That's exactly what I want."

"I know my sister." Purity poured her a glass from the pitcher and brought it over. "Or I thought I did before you did such a silly thing."

Clarity knew to what she referred. Since it had all worked out for the best, she wasn't going to dwell on her stupidity, nor keep apologizing.

"Love will make you do something foolish someday, too. I will wager upon it."

Purity appeared shocked.

"Does falling in love mean losing one's common sense?" she asked.

"It's more like you have horse blinders on. Suddenly, you don't care what is to your left or your right. All you can think about is the one person your heart has thrust front and center."

Purity cocked her head, looking thoughtful. "Yet you are married to the man you love, and still, you left him."

"I was wrong," Clarity confessed. "I should have stayed to attack our difficulties head on, but I'm confident we shall work through any issues between us. Where is he?"

"Your husband was here for hours, and finally, I told him to go get some proper rest. He is sleeping next door."

"And Osbert?"

"Who?" Her sister frowned.

"Sorry, I mean where is Thomas, my son?"

"In our old nursery with Winnie playing nursemaid. Thomas is a good name, by the way."

Clarity felt relieved. "For a moment I thought you would say you'd found a wet nurse."

Purity raised both eyebrows. "Is that what you want? We'll have to ask in the village if you do."

"No, I shall nurse him myself." In a short while, Clarity was propped up again with pillows, trying to get Thomas to suckle, grateful when Mrs. Boswell returned.

"How are you doing, my lady?"

"I am beyond frustrated," she declared, as Thomas began to cry again.

The midwife merely chuckled. "These things take time. Your milk doesn't come in right away, dear. He'll fuss a bit, but in a couple days, there will be plenty of nourishment for him."

Clarity closed her eyes. "What do I do until then?"

"You're doing fine," Mrs. Boswell said. "That's the correct way to go about it. Let him suck, and he'll get something. Moreover, the more he sucks, the faster your milk will come. And you'll need plenty of rest and keep quenching your thirst. And the good news is your milk will come in more quickly next time."

Clarity nodded. It was hard to think of a *next time* after what her body had just been through.

"And in a few days, when your nipples are sore and red and cracking, don't lose heart!"

Clarity's eyes popped open. "Sore nipples?" she asked. "I don't remember Mother mentioning that."

The midwife chuckled. "I have some excellent salve you can rub on. Or maybe your handsome husband will rub it on for you."

Clarity felt her cheeks heat.

"Speak of the devil, and here he comes," Mrs. Boswell said when Alex entered, looking as if he had come directly from the land of Nod. His hair was mussed, and he wore only trousers and his shirt without a jacket or even a waistcoat.

His gaze locked immediately with Clarity's. And then dropped to her chest. One breast was bare while her other was covered with a piece of linen.

She raised her chin and continued to fidget with their baby until Thomas latched on. Not for a minute did she want Alex to think she couldn't handle this any better than she had run their household.

"There you go," Mrs. Boswell said. "You and the little one are getting the hang of it now."

Clarity was grateful for the midwife's words of encouragement. Even more grateful when she swiftly vacated the room, leaving them alone to chat.

"How are you feeling?" Alex asked.

"Fine. I slept deeply. Although now that I think about it, I am famished."

He smiled. "I imagine what you went through would make anyone hungry. I don't think you should get up, however. It's best if you remain resting and take a meal in bed."

Clarity had watched her mother go about her business more quickly with each baby, but she didn't mind being pampered.

"If you would ask the kitchen staff for some soup and bread and butter. That's what appeals most. And maybe a coddled egg."

He nodded and went to the door.

"You could ring them from here," she pointed out.

"It will be faster if I go ask directly."

"Will you come back and eat with me?"

"If you wish, I would like that," he agreed.

"Yes, I would. And I would also like a few rashers of bacon, please."

He grinned, and the sight of it made her heart bloom nearly as much as the fact that Thomas was quietly sucking as if he knew what he was doing.

Their new routine was interrupted the next day by the arrival of the rest of the Diamond family, which Alex sorely wished had been delayed. He enjoyed having his wife and baby almost to himself, while Purity and Adam stayed out of the way for the most part.

Besides, he and Clarity had put off a deep discussion of what had driven her away from London, and he knew they ought to tackle it before they returned home to engage in more of the same strife. When they did return to Town, more than anything, he wanted them to go back as a family.

"Congratulations." Lady Diamond was the first through the front door of Oak Grove Hall, putting her arms around Alex. Immediately, he felt like a small person for wishing even for a moment that Clarity's family hadn't come.

After his wife released Alex, Lord Diamond stuck his hand out and pumped his arm fondly. The two younger sisters were practically jumping up and down.

"Can we see the baby now, please?" Brilliance asked.

"We'll be ever so quiet," Radiance promised.

"I am sure Clarity will love seeing all of you," Alex said.

"Then lead the way," Lady Diamond said, as if he were the host instead of being a guest in her country home.

With a nod, he turned and went up the stairs with four pairs of feet following him. Knocking on his wife's door, he opened it gently and peeked in. Clarity was awake, with Purity sitting nearby.

"You have visitors. Are you ready?"

She smiled, showing her dimples. "Yes, please, send them in."

Opening the door wider, he stepped back and let the close-knit Diamond family reunite. Only Adam was out of the house, riding.

Alex watched them all circle the bed and walked quietly away. His steps led him to the kitchen. Lately, he'd been entering their culinary domain at will. It gave him something to do, to be helpful by giving a direct request from his always famished wife, since there wasn't much he could do for Thomas.

Each time he put his hand to the familiar smooth door, he couldn't help but think of when he and Clarity would sneak in there for treats.

Wandering in, he wondered what the staff would do if he sat on the cook's stool and asked to stay for some small bite.

"Can I help you, my lord?" came the query from the scullery maid.

"The Diamond family has arrived. They are in Lady Clarity's... that is, in Lady Hollidge's room. I suggest tea and biscuits for all of them."

"Yes, my lord. At once." True to her word, she grabbed two teapots from the shelf and began to scoop in leaves from a nearby tin. Since water was almost always kept at a boil, tea would be ready within minutes.

"Anything for yourself?" she asked.

"Thank you, no." He took a step toward the door, then looked back. "That is, unless you have any of those spiced sultana buns I recall from childhood. I expect not. Foolish of me to ask."

Just then, Mrs. Dilbert came in from the store room, overhearing him.

"I know the very ones you mean, my lord. I wasn't the cook when you were here as a lad. Mrs. Davis was. She stays in London with the family now. But I was here in the kitchen at the time. It won't take long to whip up a batch."

Startled by the long speech from the woman who had previously barely spoken to him, Alex nodded.

"If it's not any trouble," he said.

Mrs. Dilbert looked at the scullery maid, and they both burst out into laughter.

"Sorry, my lord," she managed when she reined in her humor, "but that's the funniest thing anyone has ever said to me. That's my job, you know. That's what I'm here for. That's what we're all here for, to take care of this family, and that includes you."

"Yes, of course," Alex returned awkwardly. "Thank you."

His extra politeness threatened to have the woman in gales of laughter again, and thus, he promptly left.

Halfway down the corridor, he heard the scullery maid's voice call after him.

"No need to come back to the kitchen, my lord. I'll bring the buns to you."

Alex merely waved over his shoulder and continued on his way. He'd had an idea sometime between ordering the tea and being laughed at by the jolly kitchen staff.

His next stop would be considered outrageous by anyone who knew him, but he was determined to go see Mrs. Boswell. Previously, he could have hoped to catch the midwife alone in the house, but now that all the Diamonds were milling about, he knew he would have to seek her at her home.

To that end, Alex saddled a horse and was on his way. Running into Adam who was returning, he told him of his family's arrival before continuing on the only road. At the pub, he asked for the midwife's residence.

Fortunately, when he knocked on her door a few minutes later, Mrs. Boswell was at home. Immediately, she claimed it was not purely good luck.

"I've been expecting you," the fortune-teller declared.

Chapter Thirty-Five

"Nonsense!" Alex nearly blurted, but wasn't that why he was there? If she did *see* things or *know* things, ludicrous as that seemed, then she might be able to tell him what he needed to know.

"I can tell by your face you are skeptical. That's all right, my lord. Come in and sit down. How's the little Lord Thomas?"

When they were seated in her small parlor and he'd declined the offer of tea, she said, "Tell me why you wanted to speak with me."

Suddenly, he felt beyond foolish. He didn't believe in fortune-tellers or mystics. Wouldn't she *know* why he was there? Yet her kind eyes were staring into his with interest, and so he answered.

"I want to know why my parents died."

She cocked her head, looking unruffled. "They died in a carriage accident, did they not?"

"But *I* didn't. Here I sit."

"I think I understand," she said. "I cannot tell you that they were destined to die, and it was the natural way of things. That's not for me to know. But you lived, and now you have produced a son. That means the thread of your life was not meant to be cut along with your parents'."

"Can you tell me if Clarity and our son will be safe?" That was uppermost in his mind.

She sighed. "You want me to tell you they will live long and happy lives, yes?"

He nodded. When a shadow passed over her face, a stitch of fear threaded itself into his heart. But Mrs. Boswell did not make a pronouncement of doom.

"The length of someone's life depends on a great many things. But I can *see* much happiness for many years if that gives you comfort."

Again, he nodded.

"I notice you didn't ask me about the longevity of your life," she said, looking bemused.

Alex shrugged.

"You care more about those you love than you do for yourself. That's admirable. But if you've learned anything from your parents' accident, it should be that we have little control over our fate."

He disagreed. "Surely, we can be careful instead of reckless."

"Yes, my lord. But there's nothing reckless about enjoying your life each week from Monday through washing day. And since you did survive, it would behoove you not to waste the time you have, don't you think? Nor try to put limitations on those you love. That won't keep them safe, only make them miserable."

Mrs. Boswell knew a lot, he decided. But not anything more than any other sensible person. He rose to his feet, ready to get back to the manor and reclaim his sanity.

"Before you go," she said as she, too, stood, "I'll tell you something else. I remember your parents when they visited. I was at the manor more than once doing midwifery duties for Lady Diamond when Lord and Lady Hollidge came. They had a distinctly happy nature, light and pleasant. People wanted to be around them. Do you agree?"

"I do." He still heard from members of his club how much they missed his father's company for those very reasons.

"You can be that way, too, my lord, as you were when you were a boy. Your happiness is in here." She tapped her chest over her own heart.

Alex swallowed hard. No one had said those words to him before, and yet they made profound sense.

"I do think it's interesting that you found Lady Clarity going into labor in a carriage, don't you?" Mrs. Boswell asked, as if she knew about his nightmares.

Alex caught his breath. He had spent no small amount of time pondering that fact. And even though a few nights had passed since then, he hadn't had a single terrifying carriage dream. He could almost imagine his parents had arranged it in order that one incident would eradicate the tragedy of the other.

"By the way, you and Lady Clarity will have more babies."

"A safe prediction," he said, but his heart felt warm with the notion of a house full of their children.

"Mayhap, but I am usually correct, and I would say sooner, rather than later. Just as I knew she would be your wife and no one else's."

"Thank you," he said.

"No need, my lord." Then she smiled. "Keep your wife close and treat her the way your heart wants to, with utter adoration. She is worthy of it."

Mrs. Boswell had a twinkle in her eye as she saw him to her door.

"And in case you forget again," she added, raising a round eyebrow, "Lady Clarity is as strong as her family name."

On the ride back to the manor house, Alex considered how he'd treated Clarity like fragile, thin glass instead of like an enduring diamond. He wouldn't make that mistake again.

Half past midnight, the house was quiet, but Clarity had spent so much time resting, she couldn't sleep. Besides, after months of being wedded, it still felt strange to be in bed alone. Baby Thomas was asleep in the nursery, and she decided to go along and see him. Yet strangely, she ended up outside Alex's door.

Hesitating, she decided not to knock before entering. He was her husband, after all. If she wanted to see him, she could, even if he was fast asleep.

Pushing the door open, in the light of the moon, she saw Alex sprawled in bed, one arm over his eyes. His other arm was stretched out with his hand pressed upon the mattress where normally she ought to be.

Longing, sweet and strong, curled inside her. Approaching the bed, she gazed down on the peaceful, handsome face of the man she loved. It was difficult to remember why she had ever left him.

Except she did recall. He thought her incompetent and weak. And his aunt was the female who controlled their household. *Would it be any different once she returned with the new heir, or would she be pushed further aside?*

With her womanly parts still sore, she couldn't even make love to him the way she wanted to. With a sigh, she turned away.

"Clarity," his voice broke the silence, sounding rich and warm. Its timbre sent a sizzle of desire dancing down her spine.

"Come to bed with me," he said.

When she looked back at him, he was raised upon his elbows, with the bedsheets and blanket fallen down, exposing his chest.

How she loved to run her fingers over his chest!

"What if the baby needs me?" she asked, although she desperately wanted to slip under the covers and nestle close.

"Winnie will come find you. It can't be that difficult to figure out you're in my room."

Deciding he was correct, Clarity returned to the bed. He slid over and lifted the covers, allowing her to climb under.

As soon as she was beside him, he turned on his side and tucked her against his warm front before wrapping his strong arm over her hip.

Since her family had arrived, they hadn't had a moment alone. Lying quietly, held against his body, she wanted nothing more. Feeling his breath on her neck and his chest rise and fall, Clarity closed her eyes and let her own breathing match his.

"Did you want to speak to me?" His voice seemed to rumble against her.

She did, but right then, she didn't.

"Not really. I didn't think I could sleep, but now I'm with you, I feel relaxed."

He pressed his mouth to the top of her head and spoke against her hair, making her smile.

"With you in my arms again, everything seems as it should be," he said, his lips warming her scalp.

And then neither of them spoke again until many hours later. As Alex expected, her maid Winnie awakened them with a tap on the door before her head of curls poked into the room when he bid her come in.

"Master Thomas is up and roaring for his mother," she said cheerfully.

"Bring him in," Alex said.

In short order, Clarity found herself in bed with both her husband and her son, not to mention a beaming maid looking on.

She knew they were both waiting for her to lower the side of her nightdress and let the baby latch on. For some reason, it was not the same as when Mrs. Boswell was there, or perhaps it was because she and Alex were in bed. Whatever it was, it seemed indecent to expose herself in front of both her maid and her husband.

Whatever it was, she needed to get one of the other adults out of the room.

"Please ask Mrs. Dilbert to send up a pot of tea and some buttered toast?"

"Yes, my lady." Winnie disappeared in a swirl of her skirts and apron.

Clarity could see out of the side of her eye that Alex was watching her as Thomas pressed his face to her breast still covered by her gown. Moreover, Clarity couldn't help noticing her breasts felt decidedly different from when she'd lain down the night before.

When she hesitated still, Alex said, "Don't pay any attention to me. Go ahead."

She glanced at him. "Stop staring at me, and I shall."

He grinned.

"And stop smiling like that," she snapped. "You look too desirable, and this is a serious matter of me feeding our son."

"Serious?" He looked puzzled.

"In case I cannot do it. I don't want him to starve."

He shook his head while she slid her nightgown down one side and fumbled with Thomas, who was rooting against her skin until she led him to her nipple. He latched on with ease.

"Mrs. Boswell said my milk should be in any day now and—" Clarity interrupted herself. *"Oh!"*

"Is aught wrong?" Alex asked, leaning closer.

"No, quite the opposite." Clarity experienced a tingling sensation in both breasts, precisely as Mrs. Boswell had described. "I believe he's feeding at last."

At that moment, Thomas made a distinct slurping sound as he sucked.

Her gaze flew to Alex's again, and this time they both smiled.

"He's a noisy little babe," her husband said, sounding delighted.

For her part, relief trickled through her, and then she realized while Thomas was upon her left breast, milk was trickling from her right nipple.

As she glanced down at her nightdress growing damp, Alex followed her gaze. Clarity cheeks heated with embarrassment when her husband brushed his knuckle against the milk-sodden, fine cotton chemise.

"It seems you need another baby," he said.

She shuddered at the notion of having one on each breast.

"I vow I would feel like a cat with kittens," Clarity remarked. "When Thomas has had about ten minutes, then I shall put him on the other side. That's what Mrs. Boswell told me to do."

They both looked at the mantel clock, which the housemaid would dutifully wind when she tidied the room.

Alex leaned back against the headboard. "Now that you can put aside the silly notion you might be incapable of feeding our son, I guess we have some time to talk."

Clarity had hoped for the chance to do exactly that, yet faced with a frank conversation, she almost wished they could simply remain silent. If he was going to tell her how she fell short of being a good viscountess, then she would have to tell him firmly to go jump in the river and soak his head.

"You first," she said.

"Very well. I love you more than I can properly express. I'm sorry I drove you away, and I want you to come home with me as soon as you feel ready to travel."

Clarity expelled a pent-up breath. "Well!"

"Well, what?" he asked, reaching out to place a hand on Thomas's little swaddled back.

"I did not expect any of that," she confessed.

"Really? Why did you think I came after you?"

She decided to be honest. "Because you were immensely annoyed with me and wanted to tell me off for being such a great disappointment to you as a wife."

"Dear God!" he exclaimed. "Was that truly what you were thinking?"

"Mostly, yes. After what I heard you say to my parents about my needing to grow up. I am probably as grown up as I shall ever be, Alex. You must accept me as I am."

"I do." He sounded sincere. "I didn't know you heard any of that, but I couldn't explain to them my fear of losing you. Somewhat irrational, I believe now. And thus, I made it your fault that I was overly worried."

"I think I'm going to switch the baby now," she said while taking a moment to digest his unexpected words.

When Thomas was comfortably sucking upon her other nipple, she spared Alex another glance to find he was attentively watching everything.

"Besides," he said, "if I was annoyed with you instead of desperately missing you and feeling terribly sorry for how I drove you away, then I could have written that in a letter, kept my distance, and hoped you never returned."

How devastating it would have been to receive such a letter, she thought.

"Do you have anything you wish to say to me?" he asked.

Clarity took a deep breath, then expelled it. "I still want what I've always wanted, which is to make you happy. However, I realized over the past few months that I cannot do it."

His instantly distraught expression squeezed her heart. "What are you saying?" he asked. "Are you finished with being Lady Hollidge?"

Chapter Thirty-Six

"No, never that." Clarity reached over and caressed her husband's cheek, which was slightly rough and in need of a shave.

"I know this might sound as though I am giving up, but I think *you* have to make yourself happy."

Alex expelled a sigh, turned his head, and kissed her palm. When he spoke again, his voice was thick with emotion.

"Mrs. Boswell said something similar, and I believe I understand what you're both trying to tell me. Only I can make myself happy, mostly by being so."

Clarity felt like laughing and crying at the same time. But all she did was nod in agreement.

"Being with you makes me happy," Alex promised. "And at this moment, I know you're doing what comes naturally for a new mother," he continued, "but you look incredibly beautiful, and my body is aching for you in the worst way. I'm happy but frustrated with wanting you."

More unexpected words from her husband had her cheeks heating up again. It had been too long since they'd enjoyed one another, but sadly, it would be longer still before they could quench the flames of desire that even then flickered wickedly through her veins.

"How long?" he asked, seeming to read her thoughts as well as any fortune-teller. "A fortnight?"

"Longer, I'm sorry to say. Mrs. Boswell said I should wait for a month and a week."

Alex groaned. "A lunar month or a calendar month?"

Clarity couldn't help laughing. Just then, the door opened and in came the housemaid with her tea and toast.

"Thank God," she muttered. "I'm decidedly thirsty. And hungry. But mostly thirsty."

"Mrs. Dilbert said you'd want some cool well-water first, my lady."

"She was correct." And Clarity held out her hand for the glass, gulping the first sip with relish.

"Why didn't you tell me?" Alex demanded, getting out of bed, not caring that the maid squealed and fled the room. "Here we were chatting away, and you were parched like a desert camel."

Clarity drank her fill, all the time eyeing her muscular husband as he yanked on his trousers and shrugged into his dressing gown. It would be a long month to wait, indeed. Unless...

"Alex, come here and kiss me," she ordered.

He froze. "What about Thomas?"

"He won't mind, as long as you don't squish him."

Alex was quick to obey, and soon Clarity had his firm lips upon her own.

"*Mm,*" she moaned.

At last, he pulled away and handed her the plate of toast.

"Take a piece," she offered. "Our son will be done soon, and we can go downstairs to a proper breakfast. But do pour the tea, please. I'm parched for it."

He continued to do as she asked.

"You suddenly seem chipper, wife, as if you don't mind the forced cessation of hunt the squirrel."

She burst out laughing at the ridiculous, naughty phrase, spraying toast crumbs onto Thomas's wool-clad shoulder. Alex apologetically wiped up their baby while she had a sip of tea.

"Dearest husband, while we may not be able to play that particular game, when you kissed me, you sent shivers of delight dancing through my body. I realized we can do other things, can we not? Perhaps it will make the wait worthwhile."

A grin spread slowly upon his face this time.

"Lady Hollidge, you are a very clever woman. How did I get so lucky?"

Two weeks later, in the late afternoon, Clarity entered her home on Grosvenor Square, with Alex at her back. She was determined to think of it in that manner, as *her home,* even though before she'd fled, she had felt more like a guest.

"I am going to my study," Alex told her. "I need to take a glance at the correspondence. I'll let you get settled and meet you for dinner."

And then he kissed her in front of his butler and Winnie, who held a sleeping Thomas.

Before he pulled away, her husband sank his teeth gently into her lower lip and tugged, making her knees go weak for him.

Good Lord, but the man knew how to get her sizzling! Another fortnight and they would be able to do much more than the pleasurable stroking they'd engaged in recently while sharing a bed, waiting for the baby to need his nighttime feedings.

"I look forward to it," she said, referring to the end of their abstinence as much as dinner that evening.

He winked, as usual reading her wicked thoughts before heading toward his study.

"Come along, Winnie," Clarity said, taking her baby from the maid's arms. Top on her list was finding a nursemaid, allowing Winnie to return to her regular duties.

At that moment, though, the first thing she wanted to do was settle Thomas into the nursery. Opening the door upstairs, she was thrilled to see it looking as ideal as she recalled.

While laying her son into his crib, she heard steps enter the room and turned to face Lady Aston.

"You're back," his aunt said, neither with enthusiasm nor condemnation.

Clarity had been wondering how best to approach the situation of Alex's formidable aunt.

"Not only am I back," she said, "but I have brought our son."

"I am aware. I received a letter from Alex. Congratulations," she said. And unlike most people, she didn't hurry over to peer into the small bed.

"You may come closer," Clarity encouraged her. "Come see your grandnephew."

Lady Aston flinched, perhaps at the term "grand," which she might perceive as an indication of her age. Regardless, as invited, she came closer and peered down.

"*Hm,*" she intoned. "Young Thomas looks exactly like Alexander did and like his father before him. I recall my brother having the same shaped head and expression. I was five at the time."

That was more than Clarity had expected. Despite all the other slights she'd endured from Alex's aunt, at least the woman didn't think she'd cuckolded her husband.

She glanced at Winnie. "Let me know when he needs me," Clarity told her before looking at Lady Aston. "Shall we go have tea, or do you prefer something stronger?"

Alex's aunt appeared surprised. Clarity didn't wait for a response, partly because she feared the older lady would simply turn her down and leave her standing.

With determination, she led the way to the drawing room, one flight down.

Upon entering, Clarity tugged the bell-pull before taking the winged chair that Lady Aston often commandeered. Immediately, she wished she hadn't. The velvet retained the scent of Alex's aunt's lavender fragrance, not to mention how her confiscation of the favored seat seemed mean-spirited and confrontational.

On the other hand, Lady Aston's perplexed expression indicated Clarity had succeeded in throwing her off-kilter. And that was a good thing.

"Tea or port?" Clarity tried again when Lady Aston took a seat on the sofa.

"Tea," Alex's aunt said quietly, pursing her lips.

The butler entered swiftly, directly addressing Lady Aston.

"Yes, my lady. What do you wish?" he asked.

"We would like tea," Clarity answered before she could speak, drawing Mr. Berard's startled gaze. "And if there is any lemon cake, I fancy a piece. If not, some biscuits will be fine."

The butler gaped, then nodded, but still, he glanced to Lady Aston for confirmation.

Clarity was done with such willful disrespect.

"Mr. Berard, I know you've always looked after the occupants of this house and done so to the utmost of your ability. But I've had a long journey and desire tea. If you are unwilling to fulfill *my* request, please send in a maid who will do it."

It was not the way Clarity wanted to treat her staff, but she was not going to let them behave as if she were a shadow in the corner. Not anymore. Hopefully, she could soon gain their loyalty and then go back to the easygoing way she preferred.

The man's cheeks turned red. "Yes, my lady." He bowed and retreated.

When he reached the door, however, she stopped him.

"If my husband has forgotten to ask, please take him a glass of port and something to nibble on. He is in the study, already working, and I would hate for him to disregard his health."

"At once, my lady."

Clarity sighed. There was more than one dragon to vanquish under this roof, and that one was a baby lizard compared to the one seated opposite her. She might as well start with the bare truth that had been gnawing at her ever since she'd heard Alex say the words months earlier.

"I understand you told my husband he ought never to return to Oak Grove Hall during all these years, nor visit my family in London. You indicated my mother would be uncomfortable since she blames him for her friend's death."

Lady Aston went pale.

"I can assure you that was a mistake on your part," Clarity continued. "My mother would have welcomed her friend's only child. We all missed Alex's presence." She glanced down at her lap and squeezed her hands together for strength before she looked up at Lady Aston again.

"Lady Diamond doesn't blame Alex for his parents' death, not a whit."

She let hang in the air the natural conclusion to her sentence. Clarity's mother blamed Lady Aston instead.

With little hesitation, Alex's aunt nodded. "I am glad to hear your mother holds no ill will against my nephew. I could see that for myself during the ball last July."

"In fact," Clarity added, "it may have done him good to be somewhere warm and friendly with loving people."

"Being with all of you might also have been painful for him when he was younger. Everything would have been the same, except he would no longer have his parents. Thus, everything would also be dreadfully altered."

Clarity paused. She hadn't considered that. Perhaps he would have been hurt and even resentful.

"Do you think the harsh boarding school was a proper environment for a grieving boy?"

His aunt was saved from answering by a tap on the door and the entrance of a housemaid with a tray. Silence reigned while tea was poured and cake was handed out.

Then Clarity stared at Alex's father's older sister and wondered how the woman could have condemned her nephew to such loneliness.

Lady Aston sipped her tea. "He was better off at the school with boys his own age than here." She gestured around the expansive parlor. "For one thing, his parents' absence from this house was like nothing you can imagine."

Lady Aston was correct. Clarity couldn't envision the terrible emptiness.

"Moreover," Alex's aunt continued, "none of the other youngsters of his status remained home. He would have been ostracized as weak, and he wouldn't have made any of the necessary connections among his peers."

Clarity sipped her tea, considering his aunt's words.

"Besides," the older lady said with a stubborn lift of her chin, "he came home on holidays. And then he became a brilliant student at Oxford, where men could give him the guidance his father was no longer here to provide."

"My father would have been happy to assist."

His aunt shrugged. "That's all in the past. I always wanted what was best for my brother's son."

Including Miss Brambury, Clarity nearly blurted. But Emmeline was water under the bridge and an entire pregnancy ago.

They both sipped their tea and simultaneously took a bite of the cake.

"I had no children of my own," Lady Aston remarked out of the blue. "I did my best for an orphan, one who didn't like me much and was at risk of drowning in his own sorrow. A little toughening discipline at school could only help him."

"Not if he was brutalized."

"Nonsense! He was a viscount. They didn't harm him really, or they would have had to answer to me." Lady Aston raised her chin.

"Seeing my little Thomas now," Clarity said, "I cannot imagine ever sending him away."

"You will do whatever is necessary for him to have the best life, I have no doubt," Lady Aston said, "just as I did."

Clarity clamped her lips around any further harsh words. The woman refused to see it any way besides her own. In any case, Clarity was beginning to think there was some merit in what Lady Aston had done, despite not agreeing with all her decisions.

Chapter Thirty-Seven

Alex arrived in the dining room before the females and stood by the table. When they did enter, they were one behind the other. His aunt strode in first, followed by his wife, who was still running a delicate hand over her dark chignon and hurrying her step as if she'd tried to beat Aunt Elizabeth into the room and had barely failed.

Finding himself in a tricky situation, he wanted to pull out the chair for each of them at once. Alex should have asked Berard to be on hand to draw out his aunt's chair, then he could have honored his wife. Making the state of affairs even trickier, at nearly the same instant, both of the ladies went to the empty chair at the end of the table and stood waiting.

Were they going to battle over the seat? It was hardly a good way to begin a meal.

While his aunt's nostrils flared and she continued to look straight ahead, ignoring Clarity, his lovely wife spoke.

"I believe I shall take my place at this end of the table tonight," she said smoothly, "then I can better look at you, dear husband, without constantly craning my neck."

Both of the women in his life were staring at him, one with a determined expression and the other with disbelief. He knew to whom he owed his loyalty.

"Of course," he said. "You ought to have been sitting there from the first night you arrived as Lady Hollidge."

Unfortunately, before he drew out the chair for her, he needed to move his aunt away.

"Allow me, Aunt Elizabeth," he said, pulling out the chair halfway down the long table, opposite where Clarity had been previously seated.

When she hesitated, he wondered if she would say something that would turn this into an embarrassingly awkward moment, even more than it already was.

However, his aunt raised her chin a little higher and strode regally to her new seat, allowing Alex to push it in behind her knees. And then he settled his wife.

Clarity didn't gloat. She said, "Thank you" and gave him a warm smile, which she also bestowed upon his aunt. It was not returned.

At last, he took his own place at the other end, and the meal began. The serving footman, pressed like a sconce against the wall, had witnessed it all, but the server who brought in the next course faltered and stared at the change before continuing service.

They ate in silence, broken only when he remarked on something from his correspondence, which Clarity commented on with interest. Each time, they both looked to his aunt, but she remained silent. Apparently, this was going to be a longer battle than one change of seating.

He couldn't help wondering what would happen at the next meal if Aunt Elizabeth entered first.

At the pudding course, Clarity said something that finally got a reaction out of his aunt.

"I intend to throw a party welcoming Thomas to the family."

"The baby won't know the difference," Aunt Elizabeth quipped.

"That's true, but in my family, we always had a welcoming party. It was for the adults, naturally. It's a lovely way to show everyone how the viscountcy is strong and the Hollidge line continues."

"I like the idea immensely," Alex told her.

His aunt sighed. "I will meet with the staff in the morning to begin preparations. When do you want to have this little party?"

If anyone could offer help in a less enthusiastic way, he would eat his own hat. He hoped Clarity wasn't disappointed by the cool reception.

"Oh, don't be silly, Aunt Elizabeth," Clarity said.

The shock of her calling his aunt by her name was nearly as great as his wife having called Lady Aston "silly." It simply wasn't done.

Before his aunt could respond, Clarity asked the footman to refill her sherry glass. Then she beamed at the older lady.

"I insist on handling absolutely everything. All you need do is show up on the appointed night. I shall tell you when that is as soon as I've picked the date."

Then she stood, not waiting for him to draw out her chair. "I've sat long enough today. I think I am going to take a few turns around the drawing room."

Alex, who had jumped to his feet when she rose, agreed.

"A good idea. I'll join you and have some port."

He stood behind his aunt's chair, but she waved her hand to dismiss him.

"I'm staying here a little longer. You two go on."

"As you wish," Alex said, following his wife to the door while feeling his aunt's gaze like a dagger between his shoulder blades. She had undoubtedly hoped he would stay with her.

Once in the drawing room, after pouring his port, he said, "Perhaps we can begin a new tradition tomorrow night. If it's not raining, we can take a stroll after dinner around the square."

"What about Thomas?" she asked.

"It's warm enough now. He can come, too."

"I think that's a marvelous idea." She squeezed his arm with her free hand. They took a turn around the room, and then another.

"Thank you," she said softly into the comfortable quietness.

"For what?" he asked.

"For not gainsaying me in front of your aunt."

"You said nothing that wasn't perfectly within reason. I am only sorry I didn't force your acceptance as mistress of this household months ago. I see now how it makes a great deal of difference, especially to a new wife."

She offered him a wry smile before setting down her glass and rolling up onto her toes, pressing herself against him.

Flailing, he tried to set his glass of port on the same table and missed before hungrily wrapping his arms around her.

The tinkle of breaking glass did nothing to deter his ardor. But when he was about to claim her mouth, she leaned back in his embrace.

"Remember when we were playing hide-and-seek, and you tried to hide on the bottom shelf in the butler's pantry?"

He was too busy nibbling his way down her exposed neck to answer. Yet he distinctly remembered the glass and crockery shattering when the shelf broke. He also recalled Clarity's large eyes when he grabbed her hand, and they ran to escape punishment. He no longer had to run away.

"I like that," she declared.

He kissed a trail along her collarbone, reveling in the delicate scent of her skin, exuberant when she wrapped her hands behind his back and held on. Drawing her even closer, he crushed her mouth under his and savored its sweet softness. His body hummed with desire.

"How long do we have left?" he murmured against her lips.

"One more week," she answered breathlessly, tilting her hips against his.

"The devil!" he exclaimed, making her laugh.

A tap on the door was followed by Winnie's entrance. They didn't bother to jump apart since his wife's lady's maid had caught them holding one another many times.

"Master Thomas needs you, my lady."

"I knew that," Clarity told him. Stretching up she whispered, "My breasts were tingling already."

"I thought that was because of me," Alex joked.

His wife laughed. And with a wicked wink, she followed the nurse-maid out of the room.

Clarity should have known it would not be as simple as claiming her seat at the head of the table and announcing her intention to handle party arrangements. She was thwarted at every turn. When she tried to meet with the housekeeper, suddenly Mrs. Rigley was called away for some unstated duty she alone could handle. Then she avoided Clarity the rest of the day.

When she entered the kitchen to discuss a dinner menu suitable for the large gathering, Cook dashed out as if her apron strings were on fire. The scullery maid merely shrugged when Clarity asked if Mr. Berard would also prefer to run rather than talk to her.

Finally, she marched upstairs to Lady Aston's private sitting room directly across from Alex's study. Obviously, it ought to be Clarity's domain, a quiet room in which the mistress of the house could retire apart from her bedroom.

Without knocking, Clarity entered to find Lady Aston seated and the housekeeper standing before her appearing distraught.

After a moment of shocked silence at Clarity's rudeness, Alex's aunt found her voice.

"That will be all, Mrs. Rigley."

"Yes, my lady." And with her eyes downcast, the housekeeper tried to skirt Clarity.

"Not quite all," Clarity said. "I wish to speak with you. I told you that earlier."

"I have an errand," the woman mumbled, glancing at Lady Aston, then back at the carpet.

Clarity was ready to tear her own hair out. *She'd had enough!*

"Mrs. Rigley, I shall expect you in—" Clarity paused, again wishing she had her own sitting room or study. "In the downstairs drawing room in twenty minutes."

The woman's glance returned to Alex's aunt before she finally looked at Clarity.

"I am sorry, my lady, but I—"

"It is I who am sorry, Mrs. Rigley, but if you cannot do your job, then I shall have to terminate your employment. You may have until the morning to gather your things and leave. Unfortunately, I shall not be able to give you any references."

Mrs. Rigley went white as a sheet. Moreover, Clarity's heart was pounding hard enough she assumed the other two women could hear it. She'd never given the sack to a member of staff before, and it felt awful. But she would not back down.

Taking a seat that hadn't been offered to her, Clarity waited for something to happen. With her nostrils flaring and her mouth pursed, Lady Aston sent her a harsh stare. She would rather be flayed in the street than argue with the new Lady Hollidge in front of staff. *What would she do?*

And Mrs. Rigley remained fixed in place, wringing her hands, clearly unsure of her status and who had the power over her job.

Finally, Lady Aston spoke. "I urge you not to let Mrs. Rigley go. She was performing a task for me, but I believe she can meet with you in the drawing room shortly. Isn't that correct, Mrs. Rigley?"

"Oh, yes, my lady," the housekeeper said. "Thank you."

"How fortunate it all worked out," Clarity said evenly. "I look forward to speaking with you. You may go," she added.

Relieved, Mrs. Rigley escaped the room where the air seemed decidedly thick.

Clarity stared at Lady Aston again, refusing to blink. When her own eyes were watering, at last the older woman glanced away, and Clarity issued a small sigh.

"I intend to throw this party, Aunt Elizabeth. If I have to give each member of the Hollidge household his or her notice and hire new staff, then I will." She let that sit in the woman's craw for a moment.

"I see," Lady Aston said coolly. "I am sure the staff will cooperate."

"If you tell them to, yes, I am sure they will." Clarity hadn't meant to accuse Alex's aunt of holding the staff hostage nor even insinuate it, but she'd gone and done exactly that.

"I hope you understand I was only trying to help with the party," Lady Aston insisted. "And after the last debacle, the staff is trying to look out for everyone's best interests, including yours. They don't wish you or my nephew to suffer further embarrassment. Believe it or not, nor do I."

"I see." Clarity decided to be frank. "You have advised the staff not to obey me so I would have to turn to you for all decisions. However, that will not be how things are handled any longer."

His aunt gave her a sad smile. "I understand you feel empowered since giving birth to the heir, and I could not be more pleased for Alex. Nevertheless, I think you are in over your head."

"It was not the birth that gave me power," Clarity reminded her. "Marrying Lord Hollidge did. Like it or not. And I am honestly sorry you do not like it because it would be much easier if we could be amicable. Regardless, *I* am the lady of this household. If I make a misstep, it is mine to make."

Alex's aunt rolled her eyes. "I can help prevent that. I can ensure the party is a success."

How could the woman speak of success without blushing?

"You changed my plans for the last dinner party, and it was a disaster," Clarity said.

"Your plans were not well-conceived," Alex's aunt insisted. "I had to step in at the last minute. If I had been in charge from the conception, all would have gone smoothly."

"I disagree. In any case, it would have been your party, and it was supposed to be mine."

They stared hard at one another again, but Clarity would not lose upon this battlefield, or she would lose the entire war. And then she might as well go to her room like a naughty child and stay there.

"For some reason, you have belittled me since I arrived."

"Untrue," Lady Aston protested.

"What would you call it?" Clarity didn't wait for an answer. "If not outright belittling, then you undermined me. You controlled the staff, you second-guessed or stopped everything I did in its tracks. Why, you nearly made Alex think I am barely capable of lacing my own boots, let alone running his household."

Lady Aston crossed her arms over her bosom. "I love my nephew beyond anyone, except maybe my new grandnephew."

"I know," Clarity agreed. "And I believe you did what you did out of love for Alex. You want him to be happy. I want the same thing."

The older lady's expression softened. "You do. I can see that." Then she frowned. "But I fear you are a flighty, frothy thing," she asserted without rancor, as if stating a fact to someone who was too dim to know it. "I don't want you hurting him due to your cavalier, harum-scarum nature. Thus, I've been waiting for you to fill some rather perfect shoes."

"Yours?" Clarity snapped.

"His mother's," Lady Aston returned gravely.

She took that, considering his aunt's words. "You didn't help but hindered."

"I never said I wanted to make it easy," Lady Aston said. "Your sister Purity would have been a better choice to manage a household."

Exasperated, Clarity wondered at this woman's gall and her innate ability to make her wish to scream.

"You base your assumption on the child you knew!"

"I base it on the woman I see. Smiling, laughing, never serious."

Clarity shook her head. "I am happy by nature. That's true. But I have been raised an earl's daughter. Maybe more importantly, I am a countess's eldest. I have watched and learned from my mother since I was old enough to know what was going on around me. Of course I can run a household."

She rose to her feet. "But I will not do so with constant interference, nor with someone going along behind me altering my orders and choices. I am willing to take advice from you, but *I* am Lady Hollidge. I have a husband and a son to look after, and I am in charge of running this house."

She turned at the sound of a cough. Alex was standing by the open door, having witnessed her tirade.

Thinking he would give her a tongue-lashing for her outspokenness, she lifted her chin and waited.

Chapter Thirty-Eight

Alex thought Clarity was bloody marvelous. Even if his aunt's feelings were hurt, he was proud of his wife. She could have continued to let Aunt Elizabeth handle everything. *Lord knew it would have been easier on her!* Instead, she was standing up for herself.

"I came to ask how the party plans are progressing," he said into the tense atmosphere. He hadn't really come for that at all, but it seemed to be the topic of the moment.

To his dismay, his question made Clarity appear crestfallen.

"The plans have not progressed at all," she admitted.

They all knew why. *Did she think he would find fault with her?*

Quite the opposite, although he knew better than to step in or get involved with the two women. Anything he said or did regarding his aunt's interference would make his wife seem weak, as if she needed someone to fight her battles.

And it was obvious she did not.

But he could set Aunt Elizabeth straight about one thing.

"I believe I heard you make mention of my sister-in-law," he said to his aunt. "While Lady Purity has a passing physical resemblance to my wife, that's where the similarities end. She would never have suited me, nor could I have loved her."

Clarity's sweet face lit like sunshine, and he moved to her side.

"My wife brings me the happiness I've lacked for too long, along with the grace and capability to be my perfect hostess and life's mate. And she does it without a whiff of pretension or stuffy propriety. Truly, she is uniquely perfect for me."

He faced her as if his aunt weren't there and took both Clarity's hands in his.

"Have I thanked you for being such utter perfection?"

"Alex," she admonished softly, blushing like an English rose at its peak.

"I mean it, dear wife, and I don't mind if Aunt Elizabeth knows how I feel about you. You are a ray of sunlight in my life, and I thank you."

For some reason, his aunt gasped audibly.

They both turned to her.

"Oddly, I can recall your father saying those very same words to your mother. She was his ray of sunlight," his aunt declared. "How remarkable!"

Alex was speechless. His aunt had never mentioned any of the tender moments between his parents before that moment.

"Thank you for telling me." He could well imagine his father loving his mother as much as he loved Clarity.

"I will leave you two ladies to finish talking." But he didn't really want to release Clarity.

"I believe we had concluded our discussion," his aunt said.

"Had you?" Alex asked his wife.

"I think Aunt Elizabeth and I know where we stand."

They watched the older woman stride out of the room, and Alex hoped they'd put their differences aside.

"Before you go," she began.

"I wasn't going anywhere," he said, holding her more tightly. "I didn't actually come looking for you to discuss the party."

"Why did you?"

"I just read the afternoon paper," he said, barely able to withhold the glee from his tone.

"Tell me," she demanded.

"The parents of Miss Emmeline Brambury are pleased to announce the engagement of their daughter to Lord Murray." He could hardly say it all without laughing.

She frowned. "Why is that tickling your funny bone, husband?"

"Murray is renowned for his interest, nay his *obsession* with fowl. He has a massive fowl-house designed and built by Bedborough and Jenner, the same man who built one for Queen Victoria at Windsor. A Gothic monstrosity, all for his *chickens*," he finished and started to laugh.

"Chickens!" Clarity exclaimed with hilarity, delighted by the story as he knew she would be. They laughed a long moment, picturing Emmeline surrounded by eggs and feathers.

And then his wife said smugly, "I told you Mrs. Boswell had a gift."

"I already knew it," he agreed.

She sighed, relaxing in his embrace again. "While we are both here, there is something I need to discuss. I need a place."

"A place?" Alex repeated. For a sickening second, he imagined she wanted to live separately from him.

"Yes, a place of my own with a sitting area, where I can entertain my close friends as well as my mother and sisters, and room for a writing desk, too."

Whatever she wanted, he would make it a reality in order never to lose her again.

"Do you wish me to remove Aunt Elizabeth from her sitting room? That really should be yours."

Clarity tilted her head, looking up at him. "I thought about it, but no. I would like the bed from my room stored in the attic, and then, if you allow, I shall purchase a new sofa and chairs and desk, turning my bedroom into a sanctuary."

"I love the idea," he said.

"Really? I didn't expect such enthusiasm over my creating a private salon."

"It's not that," he confessed. "But I'm delighted you won't have anywhere else to sleep apart from our bed. Even if we argue, we'll be forced to retire together and work out our differences."

"Even if we argue," she agreed.

He hoped they didn't, but if they did, he wanted her beside him, preferably naked, so he could offer his apology and coax her forgiveness by making love to her.

His loins tightened, and his arousal sprang up at the thought.

"God, I miss tupping you," he told her, watching her pretty mouth turn to an "O" before she smiled.

Then he kissed her, immediately sliding his tongue into her warm, wet mouth, feeling her tremble in his arms.

After a long ravishing kiss, he said, "Let's go look at your room and see how best it can be arranged."

"You mean *before* the bed is taken away?" She knew him well.

"Naturally."

They had become practiced at pleasuring one another to reach a thrashing, shuddering release without him entering her.

Yet instead of complying as he'd hoped, Clarity said, "Tonight."

"Why wait?" he asked, stroking down her back to her pert bottom. She shook her head.

"I believe I have eked out a small victory, and I intend to talk to the staff, each and every one, to complete my conquest of this house."

"You sound combative, like a soldier freshly returned from the Peninsula."

That made her laugh, and he enjoyed the feeling of her full breasts bouncing against him and her round bottom jiggling in his hands.

"I am determined not to let my triumph slip away," she promised, and then she pushed at his chest. "Unhand me, husband."

He did with a sigh. "I will return to my lonely study."

"Don't stare at me with sad eyes, Lord Hollidge. Soon enough, it will be nightfall, and we shall be stretched out upon our soft sheets again."

With that, she took her leave to hunt down her quarry, in the servants' quarters if she had to. He wished the Hollidge staff good luck.

Without the least hiccup or the smallest faux pas, Clarity's party to welcome Thomas, the next Viscount Hollidge, was concluded. Sparkling wine, good food, the musicians she had hired and paid for— all were met with appreciation by the large gathering.

Alex's aunt might not have approved of all her choices, but she had not interfered in the least, except to ask for Major Grover to be added to the roster. Clarity's parents and siblings came as honored guests, and she was exceedingly pleased to see them enjoying the evening.

"You are a fine hostess," her mother declared when they were putting on their mantles and overcoats, the last to leave.

"Thank you," Clarity said, hugging each of her family members before they went out the door. The following day, she would visit with them to find out what Purity and her mother really thought and if anything could be improved upon.

Meanwhile, Alex took her hand and headed for the stairs. They'd waited the optimum amount of time and had decided that night they would finally resume marital relations.

Feeling thrilled by her party's success and full of mischievous energy, halfway up the staircase, she yawned loudly.

"I am exhausted," she declared. "I am certain I shall sleep as soon as my head rests upon my pillow."

She felt Alex falter before finishing their ascent, keeping his light grip upon her hand.

"Then I will tuck you in and cuddle you until the morning," he promised. "Unless Thomas needs you before then."

Saying nothing else, holding in her mirth at her husband's noticeable disappointment yet willingness to sacrifice his pleasure, she led him into their bed chamber. The hearth was warm with glowing coals, the curtains were pulled across the window, and two lamps were lit, casting a cheeriness around the large room.

"Shall I ring for your maid?" Alex asked, looking at her complicated coiffure and reaching for the bell-pull.

"No," she stayed his hand. "I am sure I can manage."

"As you wish." He went into his dressing room where his valet had helped him look his best before the party. As was his wont, he undressed himself. After all, it was far easier to destroy a perfectly tied cravat than to create the effect in the first place.

As quickly as she could, Clarity took off her satin evening gown and her stays before taking a seat at the end of their bed. Feeling positively wicked wearing only her jewelry, her chemise, and stockings, she waited with her pulse beginning to race.

In a minute, he was back, wearing his dressing gown.

"I think all the pins in my hair might be trouble, as you thought. Would you mind assisting me?"

"Not at all," Alex agreed. Climbing onto the bed, he slid a lean, muscled thigh on either side of her and went to work with earnestness.

"Very pretty," he proclaimed after removing half a dozen hairpins, which he was throwing toward his chest of drawers, "and entirely suitable, but I confess to preferring your hair loose."

"That wouldn't suit a married woman, except in the bedroom," Clarity said, stroking her hands along his bare legs.

She heard the hitch in his breath and continued to let her fingers play along his skin.

"Wife," he growled. "Are you sure you're exhausted and ready to sleep?"

"Oh, yes," she said. "I can hardly keep my eyes open. Have you finished with my hair?"

"Nearly."

"Ouch!" she exclaimed when he tugged and got his fingers tangled. It was time to put him out of his misery before she became bald.

"Stop," she said. "Let me try." Quickly, she reached up and felt around for the final pins, tossing them in the same direction as he had before leaning back against his broad chest.

His heart beat a reassuring tattoo through the fine wool dressing gown.

"*Mm,*" she said upon a sigh, running her fingers through her tresses before capturing the single braid that had been coiled around the crown of her head.

"You make a comfortable chair," she teased. "Would you help me remove my chemise?"

"Your chemise?" His voice cracked on the second syllable.

"Why, yes. That is, unless you don't want to."

In answer, he reached around her, brushing his hands across her breasts, causing her nipples to stiffen instantly. Then his capable fingers moved down to her lap before beginning to draw up the finest thin cotton toward her waist.

When he'd exposed her thighs, she rested her head back upon his shoulder.

"There is a single pearl button between my breasts," she told him.

At once, his hands cupped her, kneading her breasts gently before attending to the small button. Once undone, he could open wide her shift and slip it off her shoulders, before his hands returned to palm her breasts.

"If you truly want to sleep now," he said before dropping kisses upon the side of her neck, "then I may need to go into another room for a cold bath and a glass of brandy."

Clarity laughed and slid off the edge of the bed. The chemise fell to her feet. Turning, she stood before him in the sheerest silken stockings, each tied above her knee with a pale blue satin ribbon. It felt oddly sensual to leave them on, along with a single sapphire pendant and her sapphire earbobs.

"My Diamond," he whispered, reaching out to grasp her hand.

With a single tug, he pulled Clarity back onto the bed with him, and she sprawled atop his body, her hair hanging loose around him as he always liked.

Before she knew it, she'd lowered her mouth to his, and they were kissing. When his tongue slipped hotly between her lips, her insides turned to liquid. If Alex didn't slip himself just as hotly between her legs soon, she would lose her mind.

After a moment, she drew back.

"Please, Alex."

"Tell me," he commanded.

"Roll me under you," she beseeched. "Now!"

And he did. In the shake of a lamb's tail, Clarity found herself on her back, looking up at him. She smiled, and he grinned down, and her insides melted.

"Your dressing gown," she reminded him.

He propped himself upon his hands, so she could undo his belt. For a moment, there was a flurry of his sleeves and her hands trying to assist, then his arms until the wretched robe had been hurled across the room.

"That was poor planning on your part," she scolded.

"It was," he agreed, nudging her thighs apart with his knee.

She thought they would get right to the swiving after weeks of fondling and passionate caresses, of sucking and licking. Yet he hovered over her, leaning on one forearm and reaching down to let his fingers glide between her legs.

She gasped. If he did that another time, she might find her relief before he even entered her.

"You are damp already."

"I know," she said, her voice hoarse.

Reaching out, she grasped his manhood. "You are stiff as a tree limb already."

"I know," he echoed her words. Then his glance caught hers. "You are perfection. Are you aware of that?"

"No one is," she said, beyond happy.

"Liar," he bit out. "You are, and you cannot tell me otherwise."

He didn't seem to mind, or perhaps hadn't noticed, the little pale lines on the sides of her stomach. The midwife said they might be permanent, but she rubbed them every day with a beeswax balm her mother had suggested.

"Then I shall not argue, my lord. Let's get on with the tupping, shall we?"

And even though they were both charged with desire and her body was throbbing with need, they laughed.

"I cannot imagine," Alex said, fitting the tip of his shaft to her opening, "that there is another couple in the kingdom who is chortling while desperate for one another."

However, as he penetrated her slowly in case she was still sore from childbirth, they both fell silent.

Clarity closed her eyes, head back, allowing the long-missed sensation of her husband stretching her and filling her to be all that she focused on.

When he was sheathed inside her as far as he could, she opened her eyes and stared into his.

"Yes," she said.

He began a rhythm of thrusting and withdrawing that had her moaning in seconds.

His answering guttural groan told her he, too, was close.

"Touch me," she asked.

Her clever husband knew what she wanted, instantly sliding his hand down between their heated bodies and caressing in a circular fashion around her hardened, aching nubbin.

That was all it took. Gripping his back, she arched away from him, while deep inside her core, she tensed. In seconds, she had shattered and flown apart with the force of her release.

Before she had finished, Alex surged inside her again and climaxed, his entire body shuddering under her touch.

"Blazes!" he said as he collapsed beside her.

"Indeed," she agreed, snuggling against his side. "I wonder if we've created a sibling for Thomas."

He dragged the covers over them both with one hand and then wrapped his arm around her.

"I suppose it would mean we don't have to do *that* again for another year," he said with mock relief.

She giggled. "Still, it might be nice to do it again, perhaps in a few hours."

"Perhaps," he agreed. But when he yawned, a wave of tiredness crested over her, making her yawn, too.

And then she couldn't keep her eyes open another moment.

Epilogue

"**A**t last!" Alex heard his wife exclaim excitedly, causing him to detour into the open door of her former bedroom. Clarity was holding a piece of folded newsprint.

"Isn't writing paper easier to use?" he asked.

"Your aunt was correct. It was a waste. But look, I've done it. Finally!"

Alex stared at the creation resting on her palm and felt a surge of love for her.

"It's a lovely bird, darling. Well done!"

"It's a flower," she informed him.

"Well done!" he repeated less enthusiastically, relieved to see her begin to smile until both her sweet dimples showed.

"You may not be adept at folding paper, but your new sitting room looks as stylish as any of those fashionable parlors in the magazines you're always perusing."

She was preparing to start refreshing and restyling each room in their house, and thus, Clarity was collecting fabrics swatches, paint colors, and wallpaper samples.

He swept her into an embrace, and she let the flower fall to the floor.

"Although you may end up with Aunt Elizabeth's sitting room after all," he told her, "considering the many times Major Grover has visited lately."

"Are they appropriately chaperoned?" Clarity asked, offering him a wry grin.

"Most assuredly. Mr. Berard sits directly between the major and my aunt to make sure Aunt Elizabeth behaves herself."

Clarity burst out laughing, and Alex enjoyed the feel of her warm, soft body bouncing against his own.

"I would have vowed my aunt remarrying was as likely as astronomers discovering a new planet. And then, behold, Neptune appears in their telescope."

She laughed again, a sound he adored hearing as often as possible. It had become his daily mission to make her laugh, and in giving her happiness, his own grew tenfold every day.

"In truth," he confessed, "the major asked my permission in a roundabout way and will be proposing when he stops by on Saturday. I doubt they will have a long engagement."

Clarity tilted her head and studied him. "I think you will truly miss her when she moves out. After all, she has been a constant in your life."

A constant *what*, she didn't say, but Alex could guess what his wife was thinking. He would be grateful always to his aunt for doing the best she could. Her intentions had always been for him to be happy.

"And I think you will be relieved to be the only lady in the house."

By Clarity's small smile, Alex knew he was correct. While the two females had gotten along much better since his wife had spoken her mind, instilled her wishes upon the staff, and thrown a wildly successful party, two willful women under one roof was one too many.

"When Aunt Elizabeth marries the major and moves out," Clarity said, "I could, in fact, use another room. I intend to start offering instruction."

"In what?" he asked.

"Paper folding, of course."

Dear God! Alex felt his stomach churn. *She would become a laughingstock!*

Regardless, to keep her happy, he would support her in the endeavor. Mayhap he could pay each student to declare her a superior teacher.

Trying admirably to keep a straight face, he said, "That's an interesting idea."

"Alex!" She slapped his shoulder. "I was speaking in jest. Would you really go along with such a terrible notion?" She shook her head and gestured to the latest pile of folded paper failures. "I'm going to demonstrate flower arranging to other women who've asked me for advice."

"Thank goodness," he muttered, closing his eyes a moment. He felt her hand upon his cheek and opened them again.

"I've been told I have a good eye and a skilled hand for it," she said.

"You *have* a skilled hand," he agreed, recalling how she'd used it upon him the night before.

Clearly, she read his thoughts. "Incorrigible man," she said, lacing her fingers behind his neck and pulling him down for a kiss. "How I love you just as you are!"

When he claimed her lips, she melted against him, and he would swear he detected an extra fullness to her breasts.

Taking her lovely face between his palms, he pulled her away from him and looked down into her eyes that sparkled like blue diamonds.

"Clarity, darling, is there something you wish to tell me?"

She sighed. "I may not be apt at making paper birds, but I am extremely good at making your babies."

Joy, pure and sweet, drenched him like warm rain, and his laughter burst forth.

"I take it you are happy and not thinking it's too soon for another," Clarity surmised. Then she bit her lower lip, looking as enchanting as ever. "People will think we tup every night."

"We *do* tup every night. We're going to tup right now to celebrate."

"What harm can come from it?" she asked, eliciting laughter from him as only she could.

Sweeping his lovely wife off her feet, Alex carried her into their bedchamber next door. He had learned that happiness could be fleeting and shouldn't be taken for granted. When it came to making love to his wife, he wouldn't put it off even for an instant.

The End

Thank you for reading *Clarity*!

Watch out for *Purity*'s story in book 2, coming this summer!

Lady Purity, known as the "proper Diamond sister," thoroughly enjoys adhering to the rules of society. Mistaken for a light-skirt by a scandalous earl, she vows to turn this unrepentant rake into the nobleman he claims to be without falling for his devastating charm.

DIAMONDS OF THE FIRST WATER SERIES

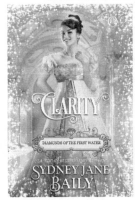

In the meantime, check out other books by Sydney Jane Baily or dive into one of WOLF Publishing's latest releases: The steamy and witty Regency romance by **Tracy Sumner**: The Brazen Bluestocking!

THE DUCHESS SOCIETY SERIES

Also by Sydney Jane Baily

The RAKES ON THE RUN Series

Last Dance in London

Pursued in Paris

Banished to Brighton

Gretna Green by Sunset

The Lady Who Stole Christmas

The RARE CONFECTIONERY Series

The Duchess of Chocolate

The Toffee Heiress

My Lady Marzipan

The Gingerbread Lady

The DEFIANT HEARTS Series

An Improper Situation

An Irresistible Temptation

An Inescapable Attraction

An Inconceivable Deception

An Intriguing Proposition

An Impassioned Redemption

The BEASTLY LORDS Series

Lord Despair

Lord Anguish

Lord Vile

Lord Darkness

Lord Misery

Lord Wrath

Lord Corsair

Eleanor

PRESENTING LADY GUS

A Georgian Era Novella

THE BLACK KNIGHT'S REWARD

Warriors of York

with Marliss Melton

About Sydney Jane Baily

USA Today bestselling author Sydney Jane Baily writes historical romance set in Victorian England, late 19th-century America, the Middle Ages, the Georgian era, and the Regency period. She believes in happy-ever-after stories with engaging characters and attention to period detail.

Born and raised in California, she has traveled the world, spending a lot of exceedingly happy time in the U.K. where her extended family resides, eating fish and chips, drinking shandies, and snacking on Maltesers and Cadbury bars. Sydney currently lives in New England with her family—human, canine, and feline.

At her website, SydneyJaneBaily.com, you can learn more about her books, read her blog, sign up for her newsletter (& get a free book), and contact her. She loves to hear from her readers. To be notified of her new releases, please follow Sydney on BookBub or Amazon. Or you can connect with her on Facebook.

Made in United States
North Haven, CT
17 April 2022